DINNER WITH STALIN
AND OTHER STORIES

Library of Modern Jewish Literature

Dinner with Stalin
and other stories

DAVID SHRAYER-PETROV

Edited by Maxim D. Shrayer

SYRACUSE UNIVERSITY PRESS

First Edition 2014

14 15 16 17 18 19   6 5 4 3 2 1

The translation of this book was made possible in part by a translation grant from the Institute for the Liberal Arts at Boston College. The editor gratefully acknowledges the support of the John Simon Guggenheim Memorial Foundation during the final stages of working on this project. The author and editor thank the Georgian National Museum and Natalia Shegelia for the permission to reproduce "The Feast of Three Princes" by Niko Pirosmani. The author and editor would like to thank their colleagues at Syracuse University Press for their enthusiastic response to this volume, and Maria Hosmer-Briggs for her expert copyediting.

∞ The paper used in this publication meets the minimum requirements of the American National Standard for Information Sciences—Permanence of Paper for Printed Library Materials, ANSI Z39.48-1992.

Syracuse University Press
Syracuse, New York 13244-5290

For a listing of books published and distributed by Syracuse University Press, visit www .SyracuseUniversityPress.syr.edu.

ISBN: 978-0-8156-1033-5 (cloth)   978-0-8156-5278-6 (e-book)

Library of Congress Cataloging-in-Publication Data
Shraer-Petrov, David.
  [Short stories. Selections. English]
  Dinner with Stalin and other stories / David Shrayer-Petrov ; edited by Maxim D. Shrayer.
— First edition.
     pages cm. — (Library of modern Jewish literature)
  Includes bibliographical references.
  ISBN 978-0-8156-1033-5 (cloth : alk. paper) — ISBN 978-0-8156-5278-6 (ebook)
  I. Shrayer, Maxim, 1967– editor.   II. Title.
  PG3549.S537A6 2014
  891.73'44—dc23   2014004917

Manufactured in the United States of America

To Mirusha and Taniusha, with love

David Shrayer-Petrov was born in 1936 in Leningrad (St. Petersburg), and debuted as a poet in the 1950s. After graduating from medical school in 1959, Shrayer-Petrov served as a military physician in Belarus before returning to Leningrad to pursue both literature and medicine. He married the philologist and translator Emilia Shrayer (née Polyak) in 1962 and moved to his wife's native Moscow in 1964. There, he published a collection of poetry, many literary translations, and two books of essays in the 1960s and 1970s. Exploration of Jewish themes put Shrayer-Petrov in conflict with the Soviet authorities, limiting publication of his work and prompting him to emigrate. A Jewish refusenik in 1979–1987, Shrayer-Petrov lived as an outcast in his native country but continued to write despite expulsion from the Union of Soviet Writers and persecution by the KGB. He was finally allowed to emigrate in 1987, settling in Providence, Rhode Island, where he was able to continue his academic work as a cancer researcher on the faculty of the Brown University Medical School. Since emigrating, Shrayer-Petrov has published nine books of poetry, nine novels, five collections of short stories, and three volumes of memoirs. In 1992, Shrayer-Petrov's novel *Herbert and Nelly*, a refusenik saga, was longlisted for the Russian Booker Prize. Syracuse University Press has previously published two volumes of Shrayer-Petrov's fiction, *Jonah and Sarah: Jewish Stories of Russia and America* (2003) and *Autumn in Yalta: A Novel and Three Stories* (2006), both of them edited by his son Maxim D. Shrayer. Shrayer-Petrov's works have been listed for a number of other literary prizes and translated into several foreign languages. Now retired from his research position, Dr. Shrayer-Petrov lives in Brookline, Massachusetts, with his wife of over fifty years, and devotes himself to full-time writing.

Maxim D. Shrayer was born in Moscow in 1967. He left the Soviet Union with his parents in 1987. Shrayer received a PhD at Yale University in 1995 and is Professor of Russian, English, and Jewish Studies at Boston College.

Shrayer has authored and edited fifteen books of criticism, nonfiction, fiction, and poetry, among them *The World of Nabokov's Stories*, *Russian Poet/Soviet Jew*, and *I Saw It*. His memoirs *Leaving Russia* and

Waiting for America, and the collection *Yom Kippur in Amsterdam: Stories*, have been published by Syracuse University Press. Shrayer won a 2007 National Jewish Book Award and was awarded a Guggenheim Fellowship in 2012. He lives in Brookline, Massachusetts, with his wife and two daughters.

Contents

DINNER WITH STALIN
AND OTHER STORIES

Behind the Zoo Fence

B ehind the zoo fence, a hippopotamus bellowed. The hospital was located in the vicinity of the zoo, in downtown Moscow on the Garden Ring. Children and teenagers were treated in this hospital. The windows of the on-call room, in which Dr. Garin was sitting, opened onto the back of the zoo, where there was an open-air enclosure with a pool. That's where the hippopotamus lived. Most likely, an old and fickle one. Usually he bellowed in the mornings and at sunset, demanding carrots and beets from the attendant. But it was the dead of the night, and the hippopotamus was bellowing and bellowing, without letting up. Maybe he was sick? The nighttime bellowing drove Dr. Garin crazy. He couldn't concentrate. Putting aside a patient's chart, Dr. Garin pulled out a pillow and blanket from the closet and lay down on the dilapidated leather couch. Sleep didn't come. He threw off the blanket, which was woven from rough, prickly wool, then fumbled for a pack of smokes and matches. He lit a *papirosa* in the dark. After smoking, Garin covered his head and turned over to face the back of the couch. And all the same, he still couldn't fall asleep. Nor did he have the energy to get up, sit down at the table, and try to peruse and ponder, all over again, Natasha Altman's chart. Dr. Garin

Notes on the individual stories are found in the back of this volume.

1

wasn't finding a solution. This had happened before, although not very often. This had happened before. Just as it happens with every doctor. Illness refused to yield to treatment.

Natasha Altman had been airlifted to Moscow from Anapa by emergency medical service. In Anapa she and her girlfriend had been staying in a youth summer camp. She swam in the Black Sea, played volleyball, and went on dates with students from the Krasnodar Pedagogical University, who were there for the summer field session. Natasha was going into her senior year of high school, and considered herself absolutely grown up. One day, their whole gang of friends went up to the mountains to gather blackthorn fruit. The blackthorn bushes were studded with relentless, horn-like thorns. Most dangerous were the old, withered branches, rolling about in the dust on the rocky ground of the mountain slopes. The tip of a thorn came right under her left heel, piercing the sole of her sneaker. Natasha cried out from the sharp pain, but some-one distracted her, perhaps Boris or Sergei, both of them vying for the attention of the pretty Muscovite girl. She laughed at the joke (from either Boris or Sergei), while realizing that she had stepped on a reddish-brown, withered branch. Seeing that the thorny branch was stuck to the sole of her tennis shoe, she tore it off from her foot, again knitted her brow because her sole burned, and . . . forgot about the puncture. But in three days, her foot started to hurt so much that she couldn't step on it. Her girlfriend took Natasha to see the camp nurse. The nurse put on a bandage. Two days later the pain became unbearable. Natasha developed a fever. The foot became swollen. The terrified nurse drove Natasha to the hospital. She was put in the surgical ward; they made an incision to drain the puss and prescribed antibiotics. The puss trickling out of the incision was yellow-green and foul smelling. For two days the pain subsided. Then it all came back. Her temperature raved, like a beast put in a cage, now flaring up, then falling down on the moist paws of exhausting sweat. Natasha became unconscious. Delirium set in, as can happen with blood poisoning—sepsis. During the rare hours of lucidity, Natasha felt terribly weak. The doctors called Natasha's parents in Moscow. Natasha's father, Professor Altman, the man who had invented the technology for making airplane tires out of domestic oil, flew in for her on a special emergency evac plane. This is how Natasha ended up in the Filatov Children's Hospital, in Dr. Garin's ward.

And now, after seventy-two hours of the most desperate attempts to wrest Natasha from the grip of sepsis, Dr. Garin came to the conclusion that he faced a dead end. And, consequently, the sick girl had almost no chance of surviving. For seventy-two hours, Dr. Garin hadn't left the hospital, while his wife Lara was in the country with the kids, the six-year-old Alik and three-year-old Sonechka. Yesterday was Friday, and Dr. Garin had been planning to take a commuter train and visit his family at the *dacha*. But he ended up staying in the hospital instead of seeing Lara and the kids. For seventy-two hours, IV bags had been flushing antibiotics into Natasha's infected blood. And to no effect. Sepsis was killing Natasha. According to lab tests, the microbes should have responded to the treatment. But they persisted. X-rays showed that the infection had built festering nests in the bones of her left leg. That same leg which the thorn had struck in the heel. Abscesses started to form on the kidneys. If the microbes take over the kidneys, that will be the end, Dr. Garin thought with hopeless surrender, again and again examining the X-ray images, which were speckled with storm clouds like a fretful night sky. But this isn't possible! It's totally and absolutely intolerable. Absurd! Dr. Garin tried to hypnotize himself as he headed, for the umpteenth time, down the dimly lit hospital corridor to Ward 7, Natasha's ward.

After seventy-two hours, night and day became confused. It seemed to Dr. Garin that Natasha had always been in the hospital, and that bandages and treatments formed an endless circle, out of which neither he nor she could break. That is, Dr. Garin, with the clear mind of an experienced doctor, imagined the inexorable denouement; Natasha would die unless he undertook something radical, previously untested in treating this condition. He had already tried all the traditional methods of fighting the infection. Now he only hoped for a miracle.

As Natasha dozed off, she heatedly argued with someone invisible to Dr. Garin. From time to time in her delirium, she sang nursery rhymes, then once again tumbled into a dead sleep. Only the power of his imagination enabled Dr. Garin to picture what Natasha was like before her injury and illness. In the picture, which Natasha's mother (was she feeling desperate?) had delivered to the hospital, he could see a girl taller than average height, grey-eyed, with flying chestnut hair. She was photographed in a short plaid skirt revealing slender bare legs. Dr. Garin just couldn't connect this happy picture with his patient's tortured, withered body covered with grey-yellow skin.

His mind had wandered off as he was standing, yet again, by Natasha's bed in the semidarkness of Ward 7. Then Nurse Korobova stopped by. She started to replace the bag of IV fluids.

"I wish you would go lie down, Boris Erastovich," said Korobova, leaning on him, her chest scarcely contained by the white coat loosely tied across her waist. "You'd lie down, and I'd bring you some tea. Then, Boris Erastovich, you and I would drink a little tea. Eh?" She let her firm breasts roll over his shoulder.

"Thank you, Korobova. Somehow I don't feel like having tea. See how it's all turning out. The poor girl," Dr. Garin said as he moved away from the nurse and started to take Natasha's pulse, shaking his head despondently. "*Delo shvakh*, as my dear grandmother used to say. *Pretty damn hopeless.*"

Nurse Korobova held a vial with a medication between her thumb and index fingers. Gently stroking the round smooth glass, she pressed her young body against Garin's shoulder and eagerly whispered: "Why don't you go lie down, and I will bring you some tea and cheese puffs. Fresh, just baked. Would you like that, Boris Erastovich?"

"Perhaps some other time, Korobova."

It was the hour of the Moscow summer nights when everything stands still. The clatter and wail of trucks flying out of the tunnel onto the Garden Ring aren't heard; the drunken screams and rollicking songs of sleepless revelers don't reach the ears; the steely jangle and whiskered hum of the street cleaning and watering trucks doesn't scrape against one's nerves. In such hours Moscow grows quiet, falling into oblivion, so at 5:00 AM the capital can start another maddening day.

Dr. Garin sat down on the edge of Natasha's bed. She was sleeping. At this moment, outside the hospital windows, behind the fence, in the darkness which, at the border with the zoo, became thick like a cosmic black hole, the hippopotamus resumed his bellowing. As long as the hippopotamus didn't let his voice be heard, Dr. Garin would forget about his existence. But now, in the dark quiet of the night, the hippopotamus's bellowing was the only call of the outside world. The only one without any connection to the hospital, to Dr. Garin, to Natasha and her sepsis. And now Dr. Garin rejoiced in this voice of the night.

"He's calling me," someone said in the semidarkness of the ward. Dr. Garin didn't realize at first that the voice belonged to Natasha. He turned on the night lamp on her bed stand. Dark yellow eyelids concealed the girl's eyes. Her lips were all cracked. And these desiccated lips uttered again: "He's calling me."

Barely waiting until morning, Dr. Garin set off for the zoo. Not as a visitor, however, but with a totally different motive. Yet at such an ungodly hour, no zoos in the world stay open. First they need to feed the beasts, to clean their cages, pens, and enclosures. Dr. Garin had been here a number of times with his kids, Alik and Sonechka. His wife Lara didn't like to go to the zoo. "It reeks like the back staircase!" Lara would say, when it came to be the Sunday set aside in the calendar for the next visit to the zoo. Dr. Garin knew the layout of the zoo, knew that to get to the section where the hippopotamus dwelled, one would have to enter from Malaya Gruzinskaya Street. He headed off in that direction.

The zoo's ticket booths were still closed, the gates locked. He couldn't get inside. Dr. Garin went back to the hospital courtyard and walked along the fence, searching for a secret opening. From the outside, all of this looked odd, to say the least. Not some street hoodlum trying to sneak away from law enforcement, but a respectable, thirty-two-year-old doctor in a decent-looking suit, wearing a shirt and tie and stealing along a tall wooden fence on a path thickly overgrown with nettles, in search of a hole or an opening. But what else was he supposed to do! Dr. Garin firmly believed in miracles. That is, he tried to resort to the most advanced methods of treatment, without neglecting colleagues' opinions or the recommendations of research pharmacologists, but . . . but he didn't close his eyes to those miraculous occasions of recovery, when medicine, alas, turned out to be powerless while the patient seemed practically doomed. To put it another way, Dr. Garin didn't doubt that in exceptional circumstances (if fate so disposed!), different powers of healing, to this day unstudied by science, would intervene. Once in the early days of his career, about eight or nine years ago, at a clinical conference, Dr. Garin was about to expound upon the topic of alternative paths of healing, but he was at once put in his place: "What are you talking about, Boris Erastovich? This is just pure idealist thinking!" After this he didn't ever mention the topic to his colleagues. Yet he didn't stop believing in miracles.

Two boards on the hospital fence, grey from age and covered in spots of lichen, turned out to be broken and missing. Dr. Garin stepped into the grey space of the boundary zone and, to his joy, discovered that two iron rods of the zoo's fence had been parted by someone's unlawful efforts, in such a way that they formed the shape of an amphora, hinting at a woman's silhouette. At that point, rather unexpectedly, he was reminded of the shape of nurse Korobova's body, her brazen forms jutting from and tearing at her white coat. Dr. Garin crawled through the second hole and ended up next to the hippo enclosure.

He instantly recognized this spot. Here he had strolled with Alik and Sonechka exactly three months ago, when it was still the end of May. On that day, Lara took the deposit to the owners of the dacha at Snegiri Junction. Yes, at this very spot he picked up Sonechka in his arms so that she could see how the hippopotamus opened its enormous mouth, which resembled a pair of gigantic galoshes attached to each other, their pink insides facing inward. Later he also raised Sonechka in his arms to show her how the attendant, a burly guy, tossed reddish-brown beets and orange car- rots into the hippo's bottomless jaws. Probably feeling jealous that Dr. Garin lifted up Sonechka and not him, Alik threw a ball over the mesh fence of the hippo enclosure. This was Sonechka's ball, and she started crying very loud. The attendant waved his hand at Sonechka (as if saying, don't cry, kid!) and carried the ball out of the enclosure. And they became acquainted. The attendant, whose name was Nikolai Sorokin, was twenty years old. He was studying to be a veterinarian. In the early mornings, in the evenings, and on weekends, he had a part-time gig taking care of the hippo. Nikolai's dream was to become an animal trainer.

"Then why go to school?" asked Dr. Garin.

"Nowadays, all doors are closed if you don't have a diploma," Nikolai said slowly, gravely. On this note, the conversation ended. Alik still wanted to look at the monkeys. Sonechka started asking to go to the potty.

And now Dr. Garin was here again. On a Saturday morning, when all normal people made up for lost sleep. Or at least stood with a fishing pole on the river bank. There was no one in the concrete pool inside the hippo's enclosure. The hippopotamus, exhausted from the night (Dr. Garin was convinced that the hippopotamus was sick), was sleeping somewhere in the back. What the doctor actually needed was not the hippopotamus, but one of the attendants. Best of all, he wanted it to be that nice student from the vet school, Nikolai Sorokin. He was, after all, a colleague. Dr. Garin walked along the enclosure. No one was there. He even started to doubt whether he was in the right location. Suppose it wasn't the hippo enclosure, but the home of the walruses or polar bears? Such things happened to him on occasion. He would agree to meet someone, and would stand waiting in a different corner of the same square. Or he would end up in front of a building with the correct number, but on a totally different street. Or else he would lose himself in a patient's case and get on some other Metro line. The problem was that he often lost his scraps of paper with addresses. Or stuck them in obscure places. If a trip somewhere or a meeting was related to domestic affairs, his wife Lara would copy down the necessary address twice, just in case. This way he could put one note in his jacket pocket and the other in his pants. But when his meetings were work-related or, like today's, completely unplanned, then anything could happen.

Knowing this weakness in himself, Dr. Garin started looking for the sign which usually hangs on each of the zoo's cages so that visitors would know the scientific name of this beast or that bird. Where he or she is from, what he or she eats, and what scientists can learn from him or her. He found the sign and reassured himself that he was in the right place. The sign stated that the hippo (*Hippopotamus amphibious*) is a very large African animal, that he dwells in water, that he has dark, thick, and almost hairless skin, short legs, and a huge, wide-opening mouth, and finally, that he mainly feeds on plant food. Dr. Garin was indeed in the right place, and without any directing aids from his wife Lara. He even chuckled contentedly.

Everything was coming together in the most successful fashion. It remained to find Nikolai Sorokin and suggest his plan of how together they might cure Natasha Altman's illness. Dr. Garin once again walked along the hippo enclosure, lit up a *papirosa*, and started to wait. He pictured in his head that at the dacha his wife Lara was making breakfast while the children were still asleep. Lara taught math in senior high school, and during the summer holiday she had a lot of time off. If he wasn't on call on Saturday, Dr. Garin usually joined his family in the country on Friday evenings. "You're toiling like a camel," Lara grumbled. "You carry the whole hospital on your back." But he knew that she wasn't angry, she just felt bad for him. On Saturday mornings, when outside the dacha windows the air was filled with that particular summertime tranquility and only now and then was sliced through by the little trills of robins or the whistling calls of the tomtits, Lara would hop out of bed, throw on a thin floral robe, and go to the kitchen to make breakfast. Dr. Garin viewed this through a film of sweet drowsiness. Lara would make breakfast, trying not to wake Alik and Sonechka. Then she would close the door to the room where the children slept, throw off her robe, and dive into bed, hugging him and muttering, "Boba, Bobochka, wake up . . ."

Dr. Garin smoked a *papirosa* and, as he carried the butt to a green iron trashcan, he heard the shuffling of a broom. Someone was sweeping the inside of the enclosure and singing. Dr. Garin molded his hands around his mouth and called loudly, so that the sound would carry over the pool and reach the back room: "Nikolai! Nikolai!" He was sure that the person sweeping was his acquaintance, Nikolai Sorokin. Who else could it be? Especially since it was Saturday. No one came outside. Then Dr. Garin looked around himself and found a pebble. He swung his right arm and threw the pebble across the hippo's fence. He heard the stone fall with a plop somewhere far behind the pool, and then the song stopped suddenly. Dr. Garin heard all this, and then saw Nikolai with a broom, like a Viking with an oar, emerge from the back of the enclosure. The fellow really and truly resembled an ancient

Scandinavian seafarer. Giant stature, a mane of wavy hair the color of ripe wheat, clad in a brown apron and high boots, and still holding a broom, Nikolai looked like a veritable Viking. And given Dr. Garin's nearsightedness, from a distance many objects acquired metaphorical significance. Nikolai threw off the apron, set down the broom and came outside onto the gravel road.

"Doctor, is that you? How did you get in here? The zoo is still closed!" Nikolai asked in bewilderment.

"Please don't ask me, dear Nikolai, how I got here. Better that I tell you *why* I ended up here and *for what purpose* I need you. Or rather, it's not I who needs you, but one of my patients who does."

And Dr. Garin told Nikolai Sorokin about Natasha Altman's illness. Especially how in her sleep she responded to the hippopotamus's bellowing. As if he were calling her.

"That's classic!" admired Nikolai,

"*What* is it that's *classic*?" asked Dr. Garin.

"A classic interaction between the animal and human biofields," explained Nikolai.

"You think they just clicked?" doubted Dr. Garin.

"Probably not 'just' and not 'they,'" Nikolai patiently explained. "First, the hippopotamus's biofield. His voice sent out signals. Then, she responded. Like kindred souls needing mutual support. Gradually he *connected* to your patient."

"Genius!" Dr. Garin exclaimed. "Come with me right away! It's very close by." He waved his hand in the direction of the fence, beyond which stood the hospital building.

"Well, not like this," Nikolai twisted the broom and pointed to his apron. "Plus I'm on duty here. . . ."

"All right, all right!" Dr. Garin hastily acquiesced, afraid that Nikolai would change his mind: "When can you break off . . . hmm . . . these sanitary procedures in the hippo cage?"

"Well, let's say, at about one. I have a lunch break at that time."

"Agreed. I'll wait for you on the other side of the fence," Dr. Garin showed Nikolai the gap through which one could quickly get from the zoo to the hospital campus and back.

They met at the appointed time. Dr. Garin gave Nikolai a white coat and took him to Natasha's ward. She was not awake. Her dry, cracked lips whispered something faintly. Exactly what, couldn't be made out. Nikolai sat next to her on the edge of the bed. He brushed the fingers of his right hand against her open palm. She responded with neither sound nor movement. Then he brought his hand to the girl's chin in such a way that her chin rested on his outstretched palm. Dr. Garin observed everything keenly, watching Nikolai's every motion. At this moment a nurse looked in. Not Korobova, who went off duty in the morning, but a different one. The nurse called out to Dr. Garin:

"Boris Erastovich, you're wanted on the phone, your spouse!"

He explained to Lara, who was calling from the booth at the railway junction, how "alarming" was the condition of "patient Altman," and how it was absolutely impossible for him to leave work and go to the country yesterday. And he couldn't reach her by phone, because in the cottage which they rented in Snegiri—and in all the neighboring dachas—there was no telephone line.

"And what, your wife loses her mind, wondering if something terrible has happened to you—that doesn't alarm you?"

"Lara, calm down," mumbled Dr. Garin, casting side glances at the nurse, who had frozen in her tracks at the entrance to the on-call room.

"You've deliberately removed us to this godforsaken hole where there isn't even a telephone!"

"Lara, my darling . . . ," Dr. Garin repeated, imploring.

"Yes, deliberately, to a dacha without a telephone so that you could freely amuse yourself with your personnel."

"Lara, sweetheart. What are you saying? You yourself found that dacha, and now . . . ," he hopelessly waved his hand, which the nurse understood incorrectly yet very appropriately, slipping out of the on-call room.

"Think at least of the children, if you've forgotten about your wife!" shouted Lara and slammed the telephone receiver down. He heard the whining tones and knew that Lara was no longer hearing him. From frustration and fatigue, and maybe because he was trying to overpower the distance, he shouted into the deaf-mute phone:

"I love you, Lara! I'll come as soon as I'm able!"

He returned to the ward to discover a changed Natasha. It was astonishing. She was quietly talking with Nikolai. Or rather, she nodded her head while saying, "Yes, of course. . . . I feel so bad for him. . . . As soon as I'm back on my feet . . ."

With the tops of his fingers, Nikolai gently touched her chin, cheeks and neck, telling her about his hippo. Where the hippopotamus was born and what he loved to eat before he got sick. Between his unhurried phrases, she caught the pauses and answered in a feeble voice. In a feeble voice, but to the point: "Of course I want to. . . . He must be so cute. . . . The poor old hippo. . . . Just as soon as I'm up and running . . ."

As they parted, Nikolai asked: "Do you want me to bring you a carrot?"

Natasha smiled: "From the hippopotamus?"

Nikolai answered: "From us both."

On the commuter train Dr. Garin read his favorite author, Aleksandr Grin. His stories always helped Dr. Garin restore a spiritual balance. It was Saturday, already past three in the afternoon. He was on his way to Snegiri, to see his wife Lara and the children, Alik and Sonechka. He left Natasha Altman in the care of the on-call attending and the nurses. He was no longer as worried about her as he had been over the past several awful days. Nikolai visited Natasha, and that changed the course of her illness. Dr. Garin imagined the muscular guy coming tomorrow to visit Natasha and bringing her carrots. She would smile and bite off from the orange root, squirting juice, and its fleshy body would be immersed in her mouth. And Nikolai would stroke her chin, cheeks, neck with his open palm. He even stopped reading and slammed Grin shut. But this is that very thing that you didn't even dare to dream about last night. A turning point in the illness, which the old doctors used to call a *fortunate crisis*. Aren't you happy with this? Dr. Garin asked himself, gazing, eyes unfocused, at the flashing utility poles, shrubs, and piles of roadside trash. Of course, he was glad beyond all measure. Of course, he was prepared to stay up for a multitude of sleepless nights and to crawl through all sorts of inconceivable holes, if it would only lead to the recovery of patients as sick as Natasha Altman. But all the same. . . . This excessive stroking of the neck and cheeks, that carrot sent over by the hippopotamus. . . . Something made Dr. Garin uneasy, agitating him. He tried to analyze his condition: hospital, family, the general state of affairs. Yes, perhaps the grating apprehension was related less to the hospital and his patient, but to thoughts about Lara and how she would welcome him. He found this notion reassuring. Dr. Garin looked down at his feet and saw his backpack, stuffed with groceries. Prior to boarding the train at Voykovskaya commuter rail station, he had waited in several lines: at the bakery, at the grocery store, and outside the fruit and vegetable stalls. And he was very lucky, because he bought Lara's favorite Swiss cheese, the Doktorskaya brand bologna his kids loved, a few packs of farmer's cheese, eggs, a plump chicken imported from Hungary, two bottles of the Georgian wine Mukuzani, Ginger Gold apples, Moroccan bananas, and a pound of Little Squirrel candies. So that in the evening they could invite the Gurovs over.

Everything turned out just as he was hoping. At first Lara was a bit sulky, but Dr. Garin so amusingly depicted his adventures in the zoo, so ardently described the extraordinary change of course in Natasha's illness, that his wife immediately forgave him, and the kids quickly demanded to go swimming in the lake. The evening was filled with dinner, family hour with tea and candy, washing the children (one after the other) in a huge enameled green basin, and putting them to bed, happy that *pops came and brought all sorts of things.* Then there was still a get-together with the Gurovs on the veranda over a bottle of heavy red wine, and after that, a long summer night, which Garin and Lara stretched and pulled apart until the very morning. Only at about 3:00 a.m., when they were tired and lay silently, listening to the singing of the cicadas, did Lara suddenly ask: "And your female coworkers, Bobochka, do they make passes at you?"

"Larochka, why, of course not!"

"But what if they did?"

"I love only you," answered Dr. Garin, and for some reason he blushed in the dark.

The next morning was Sunday. Dr. Garin took the landlord's bicycle and raced to the railway junction, where there was a public payphone. The attending physician told him that the night went fine. Boy patient Ts. was admitted with rheumatic heart disease. The hemoglobin level of girl patient P. from Ward 3 had dropped.

"And what about Natasha Altman?" asked Dr. Garin. The on-call attending answered that her temperature was 99.5; her condition had improved, and she had even developed an appetite.

"Did she eat carrots?" asked Dr. Garin.

"What? What?" the on-call attending asked, exasperated, because he was in the middle of writing notes in the patients' charts. "What carrots?"

"It's nothing, never mind what I asked," Dr. Garin hurried to hang up the phone and to have a smoke.

From Monday through Friday of the next week, the days rolled along, like billiard balls—sunny on the green summer field. Nikolai came to see Natasha every day, bringing her carrots and various fruits, telling her about life in the zoo. When he brought a carrot, he would say: "This is from the hippo." When it was a banana, he said: "This is from the chimp." When he brought an apple, he said: "This is from Nikolai Sorokin." Dr. Garin heard their conversations only in snatches, when he dropped by Ward 7 to check on Natasha or the other patients.

One day, Natasha asked: "Kolya, why does your hippopotamus bellow at nights?"

"He's sick and pining," answered Nikolai.

"Pining for whom?"

"For you."

"Strange," said Natasha and grew pensive.

On Friday, Dr. Garin left for the dacha at Snegiri. After returning to Moscow on Monday morning, he stopped by Ward 7 and didn't recognize Natasha. She was sitting on the bed, feet down on the floor, and doing her hair before a little oval mirror with a mother-of-pearl handle. She was combing her thick chestnut hair and singing. The hospital gown had slipped down, and Dr. Garin saw a delicate, opaque shoulder and the low edge of her breasts. Dozens of times he had listened to her chest and examined Natasha, but now he saw her with totally different eyes. She roused herself, hearing his steps, laughed, and covered herself with a blanket.

Dr. Garin greeted Natasha and the other girls in the ward. After examining patients and writing orders, Dr. Garin went to see the radiologist Karpov. They compared Natasha's X-rays and found staggering progress: the abscesses in her bones and around her kidneys had gone away.

"Boris Erastovich," the radiologist Karpov cried out. "This is really ripe for a case report in *The Journal of Pediatrics*!"

"An article, you think?" asked Dr. Garin, but his thoughts were far away.

On the weekdays, he didn't go to the dacha. It just didn't pan out. He worked time and a half and was also section chief. Once a week, usually on Mondays, Dr. Garin would go to the medical library, which was located on Vosstaniya Square. It was really a stone's throw away from the hospital: past the Moscow Planetarium, the consignment store, the café, right around the corner across from the highrise with the big grocery store, movie theater, and ice-cream shop in the lower level. Dr. Garin and his family lived on Chekhov Street. Therefore, it was quite natural for him to stop by the hospital and check on his patients as he walked back home from the library. Dr. Garin read a few articles, which discussed new methods of treating rheumatic heart disease, and headed back home. It was around ten in the evening. Above the Planetarium's roof, rounded like a cathedral dome, the August stars shone brightly. One of them broke off from the sky's black vault and fell into the garden on the hospital grounds.

It was quiet on the department floor. The nurses were drinking tea in the staff lounge. "Is everything okay?" Dr. Garin asked the senior nurse. There were no worrisome cases. One after the other, Dr. Garin peeked inside the wards. The children were sleeping. Suddenly, he heard the hippopotamus bellowing. Dr. Garin hadn't been on night duty for some time, but when he looked in on the patients in the evenings, the hippopotamus had been silent. Maybe he had calmed down or recovered, or finally understood that bellowing at night was pointless. But today, there he was: bellowing again. Two weeks earlier, Dr. Garin had associated the night bellows with a critical period in Natasha Altman's illness. But she was happily recovering, awaiting her discharge from the hospital now any day, and Dr. Garin had gradually stopped thinking about this whole story. And even Nikolai rarely visited Natasha—or at least, Dr. Garin hadn't been running into the veterinary student. Therefore, the vague sense of irritation that Nikolai had provoked in Dr. Garin was lost in the hustle and bustle of hospital routine. But today, standing in Ward 7, Dr. Garin once again heard the hippo's bellowing, which reached his ears from the open window above Natasha's bed. It even seemed to Dr. Garin that the heavy gears inside the hippo's bellows rolled over into the window and crashed into the girl's bed. But Natasha wasn't in the hospital bed. Dr. Garin even ran his hand along the blanket from top to bottom. The bed was empty. He went into the corridor, then walked over to the on-call room. He sat there for about fifteen minutes, reading something from the latest issue of *Medical Gazette*. He returned to Ward 7. Natasha wasn't there. The bellowing suddenly stopped.

A voltaic arc of suspicion flashed through Dr. Garin's brain. He ran out into the hospital yard. In the darkness it was hard to find the gap in the fence, but he found it. It seemed to him that the warm and sweet scent of a girl's body, which had escaped through the opening, was leading him towards his purpose—just as scents used to guide our ancestors, the Neanderthals. Not thinking of directions, he ended up right in front of the hippopotamus enclosure. The big pool with black water was empty. It was dark and quiet all around. The stars watched the doctor with the eyes of a night jungle. Garin walked around the enclosure and saw a wicker gate. He shoved in his hand and undid the latch. In the back, in the winter enclosure, there was another pool, a little smaller. On the concrete platform above the pool stood the hippopotamus. He was gigantic, and his hide looked black and glittery. All of this was like a metaphor of the August night. The hippopotamus stood with his side to the wicker gate, and next to him . . . Nikolai and Natasha. All three of them looked like they were on stage: the hippopotamus with a gaping mouth, Nikolai in coveralls with a shovel, the slender girl with a man's sport coat thrown on top of her hospital gown. She had the profile of the Egyptian queen Nefertiti: a finely delineated nose and slightly protruded, puffy lips. On his shovel, Nikolai held large, fat, triangular carrots, which Natasha took and threw into the snare of the hippo's jaws. Devouring the carrots, the hippopotamus rubbed his nose to the girl's hand, as if saying, give me more! And she indulged him, again and again. He's eating so eagerly, but didn't Nikolai used to complain that the hippopotamus was sick and refused food? thought Dr. Garin. For a moment he lost his concentration, then pulled out a *papirosa*, lit up, and started coughing from nervousness. The alert hippopotamus twisted his ears and slammed his mouth shut. The girl stepped up on her tiptoes, looking into the dark, and Nikolai shouted:

"Who's there?"

Dr. Garin sneaked out of the enclosure and hurried to the clandestine exit.

In his apartment on Chekhov Street, Dr. Garin couldn't fall asleep for a long time. He smoked *papirosa* after *papirosa*, sitting by the window overlooking the hollow well of the courtyard; smoked and listened to New Orleans jazz which was being broadcast on BBC. The trumpet sang: "*Tarararira-tararara-tarara*," getting up on tiptoes and addressing the saxophone on the highest of high notes. And the saxophone, his voice velvety, cajoled the trumpet: "*Tududutu-tududududu-tutu*," while the jealous trombone hooted and moaned in the darkness: "*Taba-paba-paba-paba-paba-paba-babo . . .*"

This sort of thing had never happened to Dr. Garin. Or perhaps all the way back in his prehistoric school years there had been something similar. A forerunner to his current state. A slender, red-haired girl. An evening dance party. Clusters of ashberry outside her front door. An irresistible desire to press himself to this delicate body for all he was worth, and to submit his lips to hers. But that was years ago! He's now a mature person, a family man, a doctor. Immediately I need to put an end to this *delusion*, Dr. Garin ordered himself, put out his *papirosa*, and turned off the radio.

The following Thursday, Dr. Garin was on night duty at the hospital. The third week of August was ending. He had ordered a car for Saturday, to go to Snegiri and bring his family back to Moscow from the dacha. For the entire last week of August, Lara was supposed to be at school: to prepare the math classroom for the new school year and to write lesson plans. Weekly separations from his wife Lara and the children, Alik and Sonechka, had been hard for Dr. Garin, and on top of this, there was also the *delusion* by the name of Natasha Altman. He even stopped visiting Ward 7 and sent a pediatrics fellow to check on the patients. Dr. Garin sincerely desired for his family to return to Moscow, so that their measured life would resume, with dinners on weekdays and breakfasts on weekends, with regular visits to Dr. Garin's parents and Lara's mother. (Lara's father had been killed in the war.) In short, he only had to finish his night call at the hospital and say goodbye to Natasha on Friday, while also contemplating the suggestion by the radiologist Karpov to write up this remarkable case of recovery and submit it to a medical journal.

It was past ten in the evening. The ER called, and Dr. Garin went downstairs. A five-year-old girl had been admitted with an asthma attack. He stayed in the ER for about an hour, until the girl's breathing was no longer labored and she fell asleep, lying on the pillow of her favorite plush teddy bear. "Just like Sonechka," thought Dr. Garin, and knew how badly he wanted to see his kids.

Without going into the wards, he stopped in the procedure room. Nurse Korobova (her night shift, by a strange coincidence, again fell on Dr. Garin's!) was putting medications in envelopes for morning distribution. He nodded to her and went to take a rest in the on-call room. Lying on the sofa, he lit up and lost himself in thought. Everything seemed to have turned out fairly successfully. The summer went by without Alik and Sonechka once getting sick. Not like the previous summer, when Alik fell off his bike and broke his collarbone—a poodle from the neighboring dacha had given him a fright. That same summer Sonechka was savagely stung by bees. They had to keep her on Dimedrole for a whole week. Lara became pregnant at the most inopportune time (there's Soviet family-planning aids for you!), and then she felt sick for a whole month after the gynecological intervention. From all the stress, he developed such a case of shingles that he could neither sit nor lie down, shuffling about the apartment (at home) or the corridor (in the hospital), his gait like that of a petty demon. Comparing the advantages of this summer over the previous, Dr. Garin finally approached the incredible case of Natasha Altman's recovery. This was an unquestionable success! But hardly had he remembered this case when he unintentionally cocked an ear. It was so quiet. He opened both halves of the window. The Garden Ring made a soft hum. The wind blew about the leaves. Then it started raining. These were all normal, expected hums and rustles. Dr. Garin listened again and understood that he was missing one more night sound. The hippopotamus was quiet.

Knowing that he shouldn't be doing this, that the result was predetermined, Dr. Garin got up from the couch and went over to Ward 7. Natasha wasn't there. With the obstreperousness of a maniac who is sure that he is acting in defiance of good sense and yet is unable to stop, he penetrated onto the territory of the zoo, entered the enclosure, and got ready to observe the night-time feeding of the African giant. No one was on the *stage*. He glanced in the direction of the smaller inner pool. The hippopotamus was snoring in his sleep, his legs tucked under him, like a village hog tired of running about for the day. Wisdom suggested that Dr. Garin should return, that he would either not find anything, or see something which would cause him pain, irrevocably undoing the spiritual equilibrium and peace which had ruled his thoughts and heart only an hour ago. He didn't listen to the voice of wisdom.

Groping under the dim light of a dusty light bulb, he found the door. Without wanting to do it, he opened the door just a crack and saw Nikolai's muscular back and Natasha's slender arms gripping this back. There was no doubt it was her, because Dr. Garin saw a bandage on her foot. The bandage on her ankle was really a prop at this point, because the wound had already healed. Her leg was exposed above the ankle and interlaced with Nikolai's thigh. The leg was exposed in such a way that Dr. Garin could see the girl's buttocks pressed upon some kind of sackcloth. No one noticed him. And for another minute or two he observed their movements and listened to their hurried breathing.

Vertical rain beat down upon him. Dr. Garin walked the alleys of the zoo, not knowing where he was going. And he got lost. He walked in circles around the slumbering enclosures and ponds, randomly entered pavilions and gazebos, smoked, then circled round and round. Ultimately, he stumbled onto the fence and shuffled along like a blind person, holding on to the fence until he groped for the hole.

Drenched and spent, he returned to his hospital floor and asked Nurse Korobova for some tea. His teeth were chattering. Korobova brought him tea, sweet and heady, because she had poured in a lot of sugar and added pure medical spirit. Dr. Garin drank the tea and told Nurse Korobova about his children, how they love to go to the zoo. And she told him about her daughter, Alyonka, who goes to overnight daycare five days a week and spends the weekends with grandma and grandpa.

"And your husband?" asked Dr. Garin.

"On a trawler. Fishing for herring," Nurse Korobova answered with a laugh, and untied the belt of her robe, so that it wouldn't feel too tight.

"And my wife's at the dacha," said Dr. Garin.

"That means that we're both single today!" Korobova, who went by Tanya, laughed again and went to turn off the light.

A few years went by. Three. Five. Seven. Most likely, five, because Alik was now in fourth grade, and Sonechka in first. One day, Dr. Garin was walking on the Tsvetnoy Boulevard. There, where the Old Circus neighbors the Central Farmer's Market. It was the end of April. New leaves were unfolding on linden trees lining the bou-levard. He found himself there because he wanted to buy pink car-nations for his wife Lara. The following day was their wedding anniversary. He bought flowers and then saw a circus billboard. Printed on the billboard were the words:

FOR THE FIRST TIME IN THE CIRCUS ARENA!!!
A NEW ATTRACTION:
NATALIA AND NIKOLAI SOROKIN
WITH A GROUP OF TRAINED HIPPOS!!!

There was a picture of Natasha and Nikolai on the billboard. She was dancing on the back of a hippopotamus while he held a huge orange carrot in front of the giant's wide-open jaws.

Dr. Garin went to the circus ticket office. He bought four tick-ets. At the nearest kiosk he purchased an envelope with postage and a greeting card. He addressed the envelope and tossed it into a mailbox, which was blue like the April sky.

1996
Translated from the Russian by Margaret Godwin-Jones

A Russian Liar in Paris

Over ten years have gone by since my wife and I happened to meet this exceptional person. Neither Mila nor I had ever encountered anyone quite like her before. We met her—let's call my protagonist Taisia Ivanovna Basova—at the editorial office of a journal that promoted Russian literature in France. They published French translations of Russian literary works. During that visit to Paris we stayed at the little three-star Hôtel Les Muguets—or Lilies of the Valley Hotel, as long as we're going to dwell on the subject of translation. As it happened, on the way from our Lilies of the Valley to Rue Cardinal Lemoine, where the editorial office was located, we got a bit lost roaming the narrow grubby streets which crisscross the 5th arrondissement like spider veins. Burned by the heat, we even stopped at a wine cellar for a glass of refreshingly cold red wine that had a nose of fermented wild strawberries.

The wine was still humming happily in our heads as we walked up the well-worn steps to the editorial office and knocked. Nobody answered, and we pressed open a squeaky door with rusted hinges and fell into a dimly lit room. Overcrowded with old threadbare furniture from different periods and styles, it resembled a shoddy antique shop. And yet, present in the room was some subtle order in the arrangement of the objects, an order unfamiliar to me but quite apparent. All of this brought to mind a long-forgotten trip to the New England town of Newport, in the early days of our American life. In Newport we had come upon an antique shop cluttered with

23

old pieces of furniture that were put together like pieces of a puzzle. In addition, the shop offered all kinds of household objects from the colonial period: cages for parrots, mirrors, screens, tapestries, unbelievably ugly pictures in gilded ornate frames, and so forth.

Positioned in the depth of the editorial office, Taisia Ivanovna was sitting with her face turned halfway toward the door. Against the backdrop of the heavy tresses of her long grey hair, her prominent Varangian profile made an immediate and powerful impression on the ones gazing. Taisia Ivanovna's aristocratic origins were evident. "What if she's a scion of those same Basovs who owned the village of Otradnoe near Volokolamsk?" I whispered to my wife, seeing that the publisher was so absorbed in her work that she did not perceive us or anything else outside the reality of the page she was reading. Or perhaps she didn't even hear us come in. And so we stood there shifting from one foot to another, our feet heavy from the wine and from roaming the loopy Parisian lanes. We stood awhile and then perched ourselves on a plush couch with a high back. Taisia Ivanovna continued to move her pencil across the manuscript without paying any attention to her visitors. This habit is not uncommon among Russians living abroad and acting like they are above it all: you're there right in front of them, so close they can hear your breathing, but they pretend not to see you. We began whispering louder and louder until we started talking in normal voices. The publisher of the translation review was still engrossed in her work.

Finally, after I noticed a little cupboard with dishes standing near the entrance to the editorial office, it occurred to me to do something daring and rather inappropriate. In the wine cellar where we had earlier refreshed ourselves with wine from a barrel, I had also picked up a decent-looking bottle just in case we should feel thirsty again. Sitting in the cupboard and waiting to come to one's assistance there were glasses and a corkscrew. The bottle emitted first a sweetly whelming noise and then a gurgling sound; this attracted the attention of the hostess, who finally took notice of us.

"Taisia Ivanovna, my name is David so and so, and this is my wife Mila, and we're here to see you. Would you mind it terribly if we all drank to our acquaintance?" I suggested, and poured the wine into three glasses.

"I wouldn't mind it at all!" the publisher fluttered up, hugging us as if we were her good old friends. She raised her glass and drank from it, savoring each sip. My wife and I plunked down on the couch, Taisia Ivanovna sat in an armchair, and the conversation began.

After rummaging through her memory, she recalled reading a story of mine, actually a memoir of a childhood spent in a remote village in the Ural Mountains, and promised to publish it in her journal by the end of the year. She even had a French translator in mind for it, she told me. Then Taisia Ivanovna rerouted the conversation into the stream of what turned out to be her favorite topic: village writers. Fortunately for me, she included many different authors in the category of villagers. Among the authors she mentioned, some weren't at all from the so-called "Vologda school." Long deceased, they wrote prose and poetry that took the Russian readers all over the expanses of their boundless fatherland. The publisher definitely deserved commendation: side by side with poets Koltsov, Klyuev and Radimov, over the years Taisia Ivanovna had featured French translations of works by writers as opposite to each other in spirit as Kazakov and Belov or Nagibin and Astafiev. What united them, regardless of their lineage or literary orientation, was the fact that they chose the Russian countryside as their setting. For as long as the writing was to her liking, she published and promoted it. Our conversation flowed freely with the wine. And then the devil made me ask Taisia Ivanovna to introduce us to the translator who was supposed to work on my memoir. I had just had a new novel come out, and it seemed like a fitting occasion to jump at the opportunity to discuss the novel with the translator. And what if? Even though the new novel had nothing to do with village prose, I hoped, perhaps naively, that the title, *The French*

Cottage, might in turn attract first the translator and then one of the publishing houses in Paris.

I mentioned this to Taisia Ivanovna and then gave her an oral synopsis of the novel. I was shocked by my own audacity. There you have it: *You give them a finger and they'll bite off your hand.* But nothing of the kind! Taisia Ivanovna squinted her eyes for a second and breathed out these words: "Fabulous idea! I can call Natalya Borisovna right now and arrange to meet with her tonight. But . . ."

"But what?" I queried, feeling the futility of my hope to take the Paris publishing world by storm. There's always a *but*!

Seeing my bewilderment, Taisia Ivanovna gave me a patronizing smile and said, "Don't worry, David Petrovich, I will take care of everything. Let me just give Natalya Borisovna a ring."

The publisher of the Russo-French review returned to her antique desk, picked up the phone, and dialed the number. She waited for the lady translator to pick up the phone, then waved her plump hand to us and nodded her head with encouragement. She started a telephone conversation in which she mentioned my visit to Paris, briefly summarized what she had heard about my novel (what a tenacious memory she had!), and suggested that the four of us (the lady translator, Taisia Ivanovna, Mila, and I) meet for supper. I remember that several times in the course of the conversation Taisia Ivanovna repeated the name of the restaurant Le Méridien located in the Montparnasse area. The conversation ended in full accord for us to meet with the translator, Natalya Borisovna, and taste some exquisite French cuisine.

"You're going to love it, you'll see," Taisia Ivanovna said. "This place is not unbearably expensive, but is unique as far as cooking goes. Bunin used to frequent it during his visits to Paris from the Maritime Alps."

Mila and I spent the rest of the day pleasantly idling about, sipping coffee or mineral water and devouring pastries in a series of cafés located at such gorgeous corners of Paris that it would have been silly to interrupt our self-made tour across centuries of European architecture and return to the hotel. We took our sweet time with coffee, had sips of genuine French cognac, and talked indignantly about the way the native-born French people seemed to condone or tolerate all sorts of crazy anti-Jewish behavior by those descending from their former colonies. At the same time (here's the good part), we spoke with admiration about the ubiquitous femininity of French women, who looked as if they came into the world above all to amaze and electrify men. And of course we would now and then be transported in our dreams to a time when the translator would befriend us after being inspired by my novel, a French publisher would offer us a contract, and. . . . Those insatiable dreams of fame and prosperity!

At seven o'clock we met Taisia Ivanovna outside the brasserie La Coupole, famous for having once been frequented by Jean-Paul Sartre and Simone de Beauvoir. We each had a café noisette and then went for a stroll on the boulevard, eyeing the people sitting behind the windows of the countless restaurants.

"I'm taking you to the one with the best food," Taisia Ivanovna declared, pulling at the end of Mila's silk scarf. It was an appropriately cool evening in Paris.

"What about Natalya Borisovna?" I asked.

"She is going to join us later. An urgent commission: translating a new novel by Gromov." In a trusting gesture of complicity with some very important secret, she brought her index finger to her lips and gave me the cunning smile of an aging tart. "We'll start without her. The table's waiting."

We walked for two more blocks. It actually felt that we were gliding on the currents of the Montparnasse crowd. Soon we found ourselves at the entrance to Le Méridien. Taisia Ivanovna said something to the doorman. He said something back and held the doors for us. The maître d'—a dazzling gentleman with a red carnation in the buttonhole and the looks of Yves Montand—showed us to a table set for five and placed a weighty menu and a glossy wine list in front of each of us. We immersed ourselves in the study of menu items, wines, and prices, all of which was turning out to be beyond our efforts because we didn't know the local language. Soon a waiter came up; as if out of spite, he spoke exclusively French. The rest of the communication with the waiter, whose name was Jules, had to be done through Taisia Ivanovna. As a matter of fact, she took charge of selecting both food and wines. So as a result, we had no way of either discussing what we ordered or checking the prices, owing either to the fast pace of Taisia Ivanovna's exchanges with Jules or to some silly embarrassment I personally felt, not unlike what I used to experience as a young man when I took the then-current girl of my dreams out to a restaurant.

"We'll certainly have champagne to start with. Agreed?" Taisia Ivanovna said, and ordered.

We both nodded approvingly, especially since Mila loved champagne more than anything in the world. And here was the real French one from Champagne! Just as the cognac we had at brasserie La Coupole was from the French town of Cognac.

The champagne was excellent. We treated ourselves to pressed caviar. Jules brought a bottle of white wine and we each had a glass. When Mila or I gently inquired after Natalya Borisovna, along the lines of "Is it possible that she got the name of the restaurant mixed up?" Taisia Ivanovna dismissed our questions, cackling and helping herself to lobster salad, foie gras, or jellied sturgeon. How on earth did they get sturgeon in Paris? I thought. Now that's the inviolable Russian-French ties for you! Everything was fantastically delicious and the wine kept flowing: first white, then red, the order going so well along with a joke about the White and the Red Russians in Paris. A funny joke, except one couldn't label as "red" a bunch of former dissidents, most of them Jews, from the former Soviet

Union, could one? True, most of the Jews were baptized, but they were Jews, and not descendants of the White Russians. We were chatting about all sorts of things. But as soon as the conversation touched upon the subject of Jews, Taisia Ivanovna fell silent, concentrating on the next dish. The rabbit ragout . . . I must tell you in all honesty that I had never tasted anything as fine as that. The sauce aroused the appetite, pushing you to eat more and more, and the Burgundy wine which came with the rabbit cleansed the taste buds like water in a fountain cleansing the marble bodies of ancient beauties. At some point I forced myself—like a drug addict tearing himself from a hookah with opium—to stop eating and ask Taisia Ivanovna again about the translator.

"Yes, you're right. Let me call her from the bar," she replied, notes of irritation in her voice. I need to remind the reader that in those days (the early nineties of the previous century), mobile phones were not yet widespread, and calls had to be made from home phones or office phones, payphones, or from such places as bars. Mila and I tried not to exchange glances. We put down forks and knives and waited for the publisher—who was our dinner guest—to return from the bar. Taisia Ivanovna came back looking like a triumphant victor about to address the adoring fellow citizens.

"Let's order coffee and desert—they have the most delicious éclairs here. I have crazy news for you!"

Again we followed her lead. The coffee and deserts were served. Finally Taisia Ivanovna spoke: "Natalya Borisovna was about to call a cab to come and meet us here, when suddenly Gromov telephoned her from Nice and urgently requested her presence. She's supposed to check the proofs of his novel, which Gallimard is publishing. They booked a hotel for her, and she is taking the night train."

"But what about . . . ?" I could no longer restrain myself.

"When are you going back to the States?"

"In a week."

"Well, plenty of time!" Taisia Ivanovna answered matter-of-factly as she peeked into the bill brought by the waiter. I was studying the bill woefully and without much progress, hoping that when I converted the price for our supper (again the problem of translation!) from francs to dollars, it would seem less devastating.

"I must say the prices in respectable Parisian restaurants always remain high," said Taisia Ivanovna.

"High's right," Mila said.

"Yes, high indeed. But the quality of food is always excellent. Even during the occupation, as my late father liked to recall, you could get a nice dinner in Montparnasse."

"So you were in Paris during the German occupation?"

"We had to be. Father was in the Resistance, even though he officially continued to work as a bank president. And my brother and I (being seven and nine years of age at that time) along with our late mother created the illusion of a perfect French family, so the Nazis wouldn't get suspicious. Father helped the Resistance a great deal with both money and counsel. At the beginning, we even sheltered the widow of the poet Korovich, though later she was arrested and deported as a Jew."

Taisia Ivanovna asked for tea and another order of éclairs.

"And so your family continued to live in Paris as if nothing was going on, when the ill-fated widow of poet Korovich was at the threshold of the gas chamber?" Mila asked.

"You don't suppose we had to follow her to the gas chamber when we aren't even Jews!"

The evening, which was botched up by my potential translator's sudden departure for Nice, and all but buried under the gravestone of the huge restaurant bill, nearly ended our association with Taisia Ivanovna, all because of Mila's overzealous desire to get to the bottom of the truth. I looked at my wife with entreaty, patting her hand and coughing purposely, until Mila finally stopped and left Taisia Ivanovna alone. To her credit, the publisher of the journal, where I no longer hoped to get published, pretended that Mila's venomous questions weren't directed at her. After the restaurant, we took a cab and dropped Taisia Ivanovna off at her apartment, halfway between Le Méridien and our hotel.

Some vague suspicions forced me to start buzzing with the literary and paraliterary bees that swarmed around the émigré newspaper *La Pénsee Russe* and the literary magazine *Stethoscope*. In this way I was hoping to get the message across to Natalya Borisovna, the translator: I was in Paris and would like to meet with her. Strange though it was, she called me at the hotel and we agreed to meet at the very same café La Coupole, which Jean-Paul Sartre and his girlfriend Simone de Beauvoir had once frequented.

Natalya Borisovna turned out to be an attractive woman with chestnut hair, of that beautiful and perilous age when a woman can still balance on the verge between the lingering summer and the premature autumn of her life. She immediately put me at ease by saying good things about my memoir of a village childhood. She confirmed her readiness to translate it.

"So how is the weather in Nice?" Mila asked her with caution.

I thought Natalya Borisovna was a bit surprised by the question, but she answered politely: "I believe it's warm and lovely, as it always is in the spring. Though I could be wrong. It does rain there occasionally."

I mustered all my diplomatic courage and said, "I hope the rain didn't upset your visit?"

Now I definitely sensed that Natalya Borisovna was puzzled by my question.

"Actually, I was last in Nice two or three years ago, and in September, not in May—so my impressions are hardly reliable."

Now our vague suspicion, that Taisia Ivanovna had simply duped us like provincial simpletons, was fully confirmed: she was just a professional liar, who had taken us for an expensive dinner ride.

"Tell me, did you happen to meet with Taisia Ivanovna a few days ago?" asked Natalya Borisovna, lively sparks dancing on her hazel irises.

"Yes, we went with her to Le Méridien and spent the whole evening waiting for you until it turned out you were taking a night train to Nice," I said.

"Now I see. Taisia Ivanovna's usual ruse. Newcomers get caught in her snares like pigeons."

We left the trip to Nice alone, especially since Natalya Borisovna suddenly shared with us that her son, a medical student, had been attacked and beaten on a commuter train.

"We live in the country, about forty kilometers outside Paris. As it turned out, those guys were children of Algerian immigrants. They took my son for a Jew."

"And aren't you?" asked Mila and stopped herself short.

"Absolutely not! The thing is: we're always taken for Jews. Always. It was particularly hard during the occupation. Swarthy skin and dark eyes run in our family, as they do in many Russian families. We've had them since the Tartar-Mongol yoke, and yet my poor father and grandfather were having to explain this to the *boches*. And now these Arabs!"

"Yes, no doubt it's terrible when you get taken for someone else," I said, realizing once again how difficult it is to break away from the cursed Jewish question without cutting yourself on the barbed wire of lies.

2009
Translated from the Russian by Emilia Shrayer

White Sheep on a
Green Mountain Slope

This happened a very long time ago, the year my son was born. It was a particularly happy year for me: I had a son, and my first poetry collection came out. I suddenly became a father and a writer. Before that, I had only been a young husband and a young poet.

The third piece of luck was my business trip to Azerbaijan. An editor at Knowledge Publishing House, where another book of mine—about the intersections between poetry and science—was due to appear, said to me, "Daniil, how would you like to go on a creative work trip to Azerbaijan?"

"Why Azerbaijan, of all places?" I asked.

"Well, you've recently been translating Azeri poets, haven't you?"

"Yes I have," I replied.

"Why not go, then? You'll get a chance to visit the republic. You'll see the Caspian oil fields, talk to Azeri poets. How bad does that sound?"

"It sounds good," I said. "Actually, great."

"Consider it done!" The editor slapped my shoulder. "You leave in two days. You'll meet the rest of the group on the plane. See my secretary Marya Ivanovna tomorrow about your ticket and per diem. Any questions?"

"None," said I and rushed home to pack for the road.

We landed in Baku and were put up in the city's premiere hotel. They showed us the promenade along the Caspian Sea, where decorous elders of the Caucasus strolled unhurriedly under multistoried plane trees. They took us to teahouses where, for hours on end, decorous elders played backgammon, pulling aromatic tea from pear-shaped glasses: a tea that beckoned one to Persia, India, China. After being wound into the coiled seashell of an old fortress, we stood in ancient streets so narrow that a man could hardly pass between the stone walls of its dwellings. And there were many other sites which they took us to see, various people to whom they introduced us, and countless meals to which they treated us. For visitors from Russia, the Caucasus is the stone gate of the Orient, its outpost. A place where one can never escape the festive meals replete with toasts, toasts solemn like the mountains and endless like the desert.

Finally, on a December afternoon, warm like in September back home, our entire delegation of writers was taken by minibus to the north of Azerbaijan, up near the border with Dagestan. I will not recount the stops, of which there were quite a few, each in the courtyard of a little local restaurant and each with an abundant spread. Toward evening we arrived at Friendship Sovkhoz, a large state-owned farm which was slated to host an evening of Russian letters on the following day. At the event, two poets (including yours truly), two prose writers (a humorist and a novelist), and one playwright were supposed to give the multiethnic workers of the farm an apposite introduction to what was new and exciting in Russian Soviet literature. They gave us accommodations in the farm's own guest house, which, I must say, was quite decent. Granted, they allotted only two rooms for our entire group, but back in those days, that would have been quite common. Soviet society had yet to become sensitized to matters of hetero- and homosexuality.

After checking us into the guest house, they took us directly to a celebratory dinner. We drove for awhile up into the mountains. That is to say, we climbed pretty high up a mountain road before we reached our destination. There, like a lone castle hovering over the sea, stood the house to which we were invited for dinner. I lingered on the stone porch before going in. The night was dry, clear, and still. The kind of a night when the thermometer might promise frost, the sky looks summery, and your heart is happy. You can breathe freely because over your head is the star-filled sky, within your arm's reach are the dark silhouettes of the mountains, and behind your back there is a big stone house with golden light shining through the windows and the master of the house waiting on the porch to embrace and welcome his guests like family.

The host's name was Suleiman. If I'm not mistaken, his last name was Avshalumov. He was editor of the district newspaper and chairman of the local chapter of the Knowledge Association. Suleiman invited us in. His wife (I can't remember if he ever introduced us to her) brought out tea and began to serve it. Such is the custom in the Caucasus: as soon as the guest has entered your house, you serve tea with preserves, dried fruits, and nuts, and start a pleasant conversation. While the guests drink their tea, a feast is prepared. For a guest's visit is always a cause for celebration, and what is a celebration without a feast! There were five of us, visitors from Moscow, and also an accompanying functionary from the Baku branch of the Union of Writers. Esteemed honorary guests!

They served tea in the traditional potbellied (pear-shaped) glasses, just like the ones in the Baku teahouses on the Caspian Sea embankment. I sipped my tea. The tea was aromatic like a garden in full bloom. It was easy to drink because it didn't scald one's lips. The reason for that was the pear shape of the vessels in which it was served. The glass widened toward the top and increased the surface of the cooling area. This kept the level of the hot tea well below the glass edges, away from the zone dangerous for your lips. You didn't even need to blow on the tea to cool it. Or to wait for the tea to cool, as it happens when you use the Russian straight glasses: the tea glass holders protect the fingers but not the lips.

Over tea with cornelian cherry preserves, our conversation flowed smoothly as we discussed the year's notable books and memorable theater productions, and also politics and sports. We kept our conversation well within the bounds of permissible topics, with everyone understanding everything but nobody saying anything forbidden. Although from time to time, one of us would brush against a *dangerous zone*. For instance, the conversation turned to a meeting with collective farmers scheduled for the next day. Suleiman said, "People of different nationalities live and work here alongside the Azeris. Lezgins, Tats, Avars, even Circassians."

On hearing this, the humorist remarked, "Quite a few Circassians live in Israel! Even though they're Muslims, they distinguished themselves with their bravery during the recent war."

He was talking about Israel's victory over Egypt in the summer of 1967—only six months before our trip to Azerbaijan. The functionary who accompanied us was obligated to respond in some fashion. "There are all kinds of Muslims," he said, evading controversy. "Here, in Azerbaijan, we have long since solved national and religious questions."

The hostess was bustling about somewhere outside the living room. Suleiman eventually excused himself to cook *shashlyk* from the meat of a freshly slaughtered turkey. That's what he said. We were relaxing over tea, chatting. Back then, the situation in the country was still relatively tolerable. Khrushchev's fast-tracked, tragicomic personality cult had given way to the first, temperate years of Brezhnev's rule. The Red Empire commanded the boundless expanses of Siberia, the amber Baltic shores, the cotton fields of Central Asia, and the blue mountaintops of the Caucasus, while also resting its claws on China, India, Indochina, Mesopotamia,

Ceylon, and Egypt. Even in arts and letters, the official pressure had yet to exceed the mark established by Khrushchev's debacle at the Manezh public exhibition of 1962. The political climate was relatively temperate, which might have been why my poetry collection was allowed to come out. So there we were, having a pleasant conversation. We (the visitors from Moscow) expressed admiration for Azeri folk culture, music, cuisine. We complimented the writings of the Ibragimbekov brothers, Rustam and Magsud. We hummed along to a recording of Rashid Behbudov performing popular songs in several languages. In turn, the Azeris effusively praised the famous Moscow attractions (the Kremlin Armory, the Bolshoy, the Luzhniki Stadium, Moscow State University on the Lenin Hills, and so on).

Finally, Suleiman's wife and her younger sister made an appearance. They both wore dark headscarves that left exposed only their eyes, noses, and top halves of their mouths. We had seen similar headscarves in Baku and other towns we had visited in Azerbaijan, so we weren't surprised. We did, however, feel a lingering sense of awkwardness, especially since there was a woman in our midst, the wife of a famous baritone, who was also his piano accompanist (they had arrived separately from the rest of the group). Sitting at the table with us, the pianist was wearing a perfectly European dress with a deep décolleté that revealed her beautiful breasts to men's gazes. The pianist's dress was emerald green. I recalled the mountain slopes that we had passed during that day's journey: emerald green with white summits. Capped with snow or dotted with clouds. The pianist was a blonde, of the type that abounds in Russia's Northwest. Her husband was an Armenian from Moscow, a renowned performer of Russian classical love songs.

The tea sets and the little saucers for preserves were cleared. Brought out and placed, towering over the middle of the table, was a serving platter with mouthwatering, crimson-brown chunks of steaming turkey meat amid heaps of fresh herbs. The main dish was accompanied by a cornucopia of pickled vegetables, among them shoots of both homegrown garlic and wild garlic (ramson). There was also pickled purple cabbage and fire-hot pickled peppers. Azeri pilaf was the crowning number in this raging feast of the Caucasus. A cast-iron pot was ceremoniously carried in, and its contents were arranged on an oval earthen plate that took up half of the table. Slow-cooked with orange sprigs of saffron, the pilaf was fragrant like a springtime orchard. The orange pilaf was topped with chunks of coal-roasted turkey meat, and the meal began.

Suleiman's wife and her younger sister never joined us at the table, but were constantly attending to the guests. When I voiced a concern, or, rather, a carefully worded wish to see them seated at the table with us, Suleiman casually dismissed it: "Esteemed Daniil, whose job is it to feed us, if not the women's?"

A case of Azeri cognac was brought up from the cellar. The first bottle was uncorked. The toasts followed one after the other, starting, of course, with the traditional opening toast to all the guests, then to each of us individually, in the order in which we were seated at the table, then to the friendship of our nations (Russians and Azeris), then to the friendship of all of the Soviet nations, and so on and so forth. It was in some ways a typical dinner conversation, mainly about stage and screen actors and actresses. During the Soviet years, this topic was both attractive and safe. In fact, stars of the silver screen, along with sports and science news and problems of child-rearing ("family-and-school"!) constituted the honed and acceptable programs for dinnertime conversations. People avoided discussing politics (foreign—and with few exceptions, domestic—entirely), except when giving laudatory podium speeches. The truth was dangerous, but people were still embarrassed to lie. In general, in those years, if new acquaintances gathered at the table, the conversation plodded along like a tightrope walker balancing below the circus dome. Say, someone would mention Vladimir Lugovsky's poem "The Cadet's Hungarian Dance," and immediately cut himself off for fear of evoking an association with the Hungarian Uprising of 1956. The Great Wall of China could likewise conjure up the shadow of the Berlin Wall. Or, God forbid, someone mentioned the Armenian "Ararat" brand cognac among the Azeris! Wouldn't that sound like you were aggravating the problem of Mt. Ararat, the Armenian national symbol annexed by Turkey? People had to juggle words for balance, like on a tightrope. Which is why it was easier to talk about screen or stage actors and actresses. We were doing some heavy drinking. The pianist, she the wife of the Muscovite baritone, kept up with us.

At some point the conversation flagged. It felt like we had already exhausted the permissible topics before the feast had reached its peak, when the hosts usually serve desert and then show the guests to their rooms, where cool beds await them. I should explain that at the very beginning of the dinner Suleiman had told us we didn't need to hurry: all the guests were spending the night at his house. So nobody hurried to leave. Two questions disrupted the lull. The blonde pianist, taking notice of the household noises made audible by the halt in our conversation, asked, "Who's that, playing?" Behind the wall, a piano was softly singing. Suleiman chuckled. His stern, elongated, dark brow unfurled for a moment (the whole evening it had stayed alert and guarded), and he replied, "That's my wife's sister, Soraya. She's a student at the Baku Music Conservatory. Soraya just won first place at a competition in Moscow. Visiting here for the weekend."

"Fascinating!" exclaimed the Russian pianist. "What's her last name?"

"Ilizarova. Soraya Ilizarova," said Suleiman, growing dour again.

"Wait! Is your sister-in-law related to the surgeon Ilizarov?"

That was the second question. My question. This time it was not a lull but a heavy pause that hung over the table, like a thunder cloud. The Moscow baritone's sly black eyes kept shifting between

Suleiman and me. One of my colleagues, the poet-songwriter, excused himself and went outside to smoke, and the novelist, the humorist, and the playwright all joined him.

The pianist rose from the table, saying, "Let me go find your laureate."

Her husband the baritone followed her. The host and I remained alone at the table.

"Is your sister-in-law related to the surgeon Ilizarov?" I repeated my ill-fated question.

"No, she's not," Suleiman sliced. "We are Azeri, and that Ilizarov is a Tat, a Mountain Jew."

He said this very loudly. So loudly that if anyone had been eavesdropping or unintentionally listening in, Suleiman's response to my question would have been unequivocal: "We are Azeri!" As proof, there were the headscarves covering half the faces of his wife and his sister-in-law.

Someone was playing the piano behind the wall. I followed its sounds to one of the adjoining rooms. Soraya was sitting behind a piano. Next to her stood the Russian pianist. Neither one of them could see me. Soraya was playing, pausing intermittently to say something to the other woman. I could only hear fragments of her phrases: " . . . collected in Northern Azerbaijan and Dagestan. . . . Jewish melodies. . . . composition class. . . ." Unnoticed, I quietly walked out and returned to the living room.

The dinner feast was almost over. Once again, we were served tea with preserves, cookies, and other sweets. We raised our glasses to the master and mistress of the house, thanked them for their hospitality, and started to get up from the table. Suleiman showed the guests to their rooms. First, the pianist and the singer. Then my literary colleagues, one by one. I wanted to follow them, but Suleiman signaled with his eyes that I should stay behind in the living room. I waited for him, not a little irritated. Why was I the last one to be accommodated, when I was totally exhausted and when all I wanted was to rest my head on a pillow, pull a blanket over my head, and surrender to the oblivion of sleep? At long last, Suleiman returned and asked that I follow him. We made our way down the hallway, passing by the bedrooms from which (to my deep envy!) I could hear the peaceable breathing of sleeping people. Or, perhaps, I simply imagined hearing it. At the end of the corridor there was a door, which Suleiman unlocked with a key that he pulled by a string out of the pocket of his pants. He turned on a flashlight. The door opened onto a spiral staircase descending into the basement. We went down two spiral flights. There, Suleiman unlocked another door, using a key that he kept in the side pocket of his jacket. We made our way down a small passage to yet another locked door. The third key came out of the inner breast pocket of his jacket. Suleiman let me in and turned on the light. It was an oval-shaped, windowless room. A room in the depths of the cellar. In the system of using floors to measure a building's levels, the oval room would have been on the minus second floor. I looked around, while Suleiman hurriedly locked the deadbolt from the inside. He was silent that entire time. It was as if he were playing the silent game. Was he following the rules of a sect of hermits who gave the vow of silence so as not to distort the truth with words, since any word (except the word of God) was but a lie? Or perhaps there were other reasons for Suleiman's silence?

On the side of the oval room opposite the door stood a small pedestal draped in a white silk cover, which was adorned along the edges with dark stripes and silk tassels, like those on a *tales*. Resting on the cover was a thick opened leather-bound tome with silver clasps. Behind the Book there stood a silver menorah with blown-out candles. I came closer. The pages of the Book were strewn with Hebrew characters that resembled unearthly notes recording the music of Divine words. Suleiman leaned over, pressing his index finger against his lips, "My family comes from the Mountain Jews that were forced into Islam back in the day. But we still remained Jews."

I woke up early, just before dawn. Suleiman's stone house was steeped in the stillness of the pre-morning hours. I put on my clothes and quietly exited to the back porch. Right outside the fence enclosing the garden there was the road, and beyond it, mountain slopes. The young grass, nurtured by the autumn rains that had followed the summer draughts, had colored the slopes green. Blankets of snow lay atop the mountains. Or were those clouds, taking a rest on the snow-covered stone berths? Green slopes; mountain tops covered with snow and clouds. I saw a white cloud inching its way from the road onto the green of the mountain slope. A cloud? I peered closer. It was a herd of white sheep ascending the mountains. White sheep on a green mountain slope. A shepherd in a long *burka* and a shaggy fur hat followed the herd. It was a biblical picture, of a world I had never known. Mountain slopes. Green grass. White sheep. A shepherd.

"Just like in ancient times, back in Abraham's day, right?"

I turned around and saw Soraya standing in the doorway. She looked European: a charcoal-gray short skirt, a white blouse, black hair draped over the collar of her raincoat, and lips touched up with gloss.

"Yes, this biblical feeling. Music of the mountains and deserts in which our ancestors wandered," I responded.

"How delightful that you, too, can hear *this*. I've been trying to compose music that. . . ."

Before I had a chance to ask her, "What music? May I hear it? Where?" a Volga sedan pulled over. Soraya ducked into the car. As it sped off like a temperamental young stallion, she managing to roll the window down and yell out something that I didn't quite make out, catching only the words " . . . in the fortress. . . ."

In a few days, our group returned to Baku, where we still had two or three events on the docket. And then, back to Moscow. I missed my wife and my son who had just turned six months old. I moped. I called home. Aimlessly I roamed the streets of the city, alone or sometimes with another member of the group. On our last day in Baku, three of us were having breakfast: the Moscow baritone, his wife the accompanist, and I. Our flight to Moscow was leaving the next morning at dawn. Out of the blue, the baritone stared talking about his trip to Israel. He belonged to that category of easygoing people who speak about things present or past with compelling transparency. Another person in his place would have thought twice about telling someone he didn't know well about a trip to Israel, a state that my ex-homeland didn't exactly favor. Or is it that by "another person" I mean a typical Soviet philistine? I guess that's it! Be that as it may, Avetik (the baritone) and his wife Valya were talkative and easy-going people. Avetik was telling me about Jerusalem's Old City surrounded by fortress walls, about the Arab, Jewish, and Armenian quarters.

"You know, this fortress in Baku is like a replica of the Old City. Everything is so much like it, but on a smaller scale. It especially reminds me of the Arab Quarter."

"Avetik, do you know that I haven't actually been inside the fortress? You went there, but I couldn't join you that time. I was occupied."

"Well, Valyusha, how about we go right now? And you, Daniil?"

"Let's go!" I eagerly acquiesced, hoping for a miracle.

We entered the fortress through one of the gates. A narrow street wound between dilapidated stone structures of one or two, occasionally three, stories, the kinds of structures that could hardly be called houses, although referring to them as shacks or huts would strike a false tone. They had served and still continued to serve as people's dwellings. Who knows how many centuries ago these houses were built out of mountain rocks and clay bricks. In the past, this must have been an affluent neighborhood, or at least one that was home to prosperous artisans. Then came the Revolution

and the Civil War, chasing the native inhabitants of the fortress
from their family nests, dividing the stone buildings into individual
rooms and communal apartments, and sometimes leaving to the
original owners—like hope for a better future—a separate apartment with two or three rooms. Desolation reigned inside the fortress. And yet, people lived there; children ran in the street, kicking
a soccer ball or jumping rope. Young men and women in modern
dress—probably students—walked by us. They laughed loudly, rev-
eling in their youth.

We were walking down Asaf Zeynally Street; there once was
a composer by that name. Winding, the streets took us deeper
into the fortress, which was crowned with a tower. "That's Maiden
Tower," remarked a passerby, a man with a beard and a shaved
head, who was holding a shopping bag in his right hand and a pack
of Kazbek *papirosy* in the left. In the Caucasus, smoking Kazbeks
was considered fashionable. "Beyond it is the minaret. But the
mosque itself was demolished by the Whites," added the bearded
man with the shaved head. We weren't sure how to respond, so we
just thanked him and kept going. Then we heard the sounds of a
piano coming from the open window of a two-story house. Something made us stop. I'm sure we each had our reasons. How often
different reasons motivate different people to do the same exact
thing! We came up to the open window, which was at eye level. It
was noon. The winter sun (yes, it was winter in Baku) rolled off the
roof of the house directly across, sliding into the window whence
the music came and pouring light into the room. Soraya was sitting at a grand piano, half-turned to the window. She was playing
and then writing down the musical phrases she had just played.
Then she would repeat the section again, make changes by writing or erasing something in a big musical notebook, and continue
up the spiraling street of her emerging music. I heard the bells of
caravan camels, the creaking of desert sand, the tinkling of a brook

and the dying bleat of the white sheep that our forefather Abraham sacrificed to the Almighty so that one day He would reconcile Abraham's two sons, Ishmael and Isaac.

2003

Translated from the Russian by Margarit T. Ordukhanyan

Round-the-Globe Happiness

I was standing in St. Peter's Square. The cathedral's golden dome glowed like St. Isaac's. I felt for a moment that I was back in Leningrad. But I was in Rome. The huge crowd was waiting for the Pope to emerge from the Vatican gates. I got there late, when there was barely any room left in the back rows. Standing room only. Finally, a white lacquered carriagemobile outfitted in bulletproof glass appeared in the Vatican gates, crawled past the masquerade of Swiss Guards, and rolled into the square. The crowd rejoiced. The Pope began to say the Mass. I found all of this fascinating as a materialization of something incredible, and yet real, that had happened to my wife, my son, and me. We had emigrated from Russia and found ourselves in the heart of Western civilization, in Rome. Something incredible had happened not only to us but also to the hero of the crowd's celebration. A shunned Polish priest-poet had become the leader of the Catholic Church. His Italian, it turned out, was so perfect that the crowd of Romans heeded his sermon as if he was the voice of the Almighty speaking to them in their native tongue. That was when I felt, for the first time, that there were no limits to human daring, and in vain was the earth cut up and molested with borders, barbed wire, posts, passports, and other markers of tyranny, which meant absolutely nothing to the free spirit. There's the whole globe, and any inhabitant of our planet is free to walk, drive, or sail around it as he or she pleases.

At this Mass I, a Russian Jew, for the first time felt like a citizen of the world.

On top of this, a chance encounter reinforced my conclusion that absolute personal freedom is an inalienable part of one's happiness. I stood behind the last row of the listening and praying crowd. My wife and my son had stayed back in Ladispoli, a little resort on the Tyrrhenian coast. Refugees from Russia, we spent the whole summer there, waiting to get our entry visas to the United States. I was standing behind the listening and praying Romans and pilgrims from other cities and countries.

A man pushing a cart packed with bags, satchels, packages, and some other belongings parked himself next to me. I took my neighbor for a hobo, a homeless person, a drifter of the sort that abounds in Europe. However, the face of the hobo with the cart grabbed my attention. It was the face of a composed intellectual who knew exactly what he wanted. A tall brow, tidily combed chestnut hair, a prominent bald spot, graying temples. He sported a fresh shave and neatly trimmed nails. And yet, he had a hobo's cart with the typical itinerant's belongings in it! Back then I didn't know yet that there are all sorts of freedom searchers in the world. Many years later, in San Francisco, I saw a hobo who had nestled down for the night in the entryway of a jewelry store. He lay with his head on an inflatable pillow, reading a thick tome by the light of a portable lamp. Lying next to the pillow there was another book. I made out the title and the author's name: it was *Theatre* by W. Somerset Maugham. My Roman hobo must have belonged to the ranks of the road-roving intelligentsia. He saw that I was eyeing him with curiosity. "With curiosity" was an understatement! I ogled him, composing a biography for my new protagonist. Taking note of my stares, the stranger addressed me in English. I managed to respond in the nominally English argot of a new Russian émigré, in which words are strung together without prepositions, and all action unfolds in the infantile language of simple verbs.

"You're Russian, then?" rejoiced the stranger, switching to the language native to us both. "I knew you were Russian right away but couldn't bring myself to strike up a conversation."

How is it that upon hearing a single word, people can tell one's country of origin if that country happens to be their homeland? And what about ants in the grass? Birds in the skies? Fish? All descendants from Russia express themselves similarly. The stranger and I introduced ourselves. He (Alexander Borisovich Lurie), just like me, belonged to an ethnic group rather widespread in Russia: he was a Russian Jew. In 1918 his grandfather and grandmother had fled from the proletarian revolution. His grandfather was among the not-so-many Russian émigrés who had managed to move their capital to British banks ahead of time. In London, he opened a luxury fashion business with stunning Russian models. His son, the father of my new acquaintance, went into the movie industry. The young Alexander Lurie attended medical school at St. Mary's Hospital in London, the same place where his namesake and senior colleague Alexander Fleming had discovered lysozyme and penicillin. Talent, more so than money, passes from generation to generation. Alexander Lurie was a talented physician, an ophthalmologist. Patients waited for months to have him operate on their eyes. He was a successful doctor, a happy husband, and a doting father. In fact, he still loved his ex-wife Katherine, his daughter Lily, and his son Peter. His mansion near Regent's Park was a landmark of Neo-Baroque architecture. His garden, encased in the ornate patterns of a cast-iron fence, blossomed with roses from every habitable land. . . .

And yet, one day Alexander Lurie woke up determined to leave all of this behind. Incognito, he wanted to get away from his family, colleagues, and patients, and travel to the farthest ends of oceans, islands, and routes. To see the places from which hailed his garden's exotic roses. He had been traveling for almost two years. He had started off in Australia. He had visited Borneo and the Philippines.

He had sailed across the seas to the Japanese island of Hokkaido, and from there, to Sakhalin. He had hitchhiked across Siberia, crossed over the Ural Mountains, visited the Volga Basin and Central Russia, been to Moscow and Leningrad, gotten to know Europe from north to south. His current plan was to journey down to the toe of the Italian boot, visit the island of Sicily, and then return home to England.

"But what about visas?" I asked him. "Costs of travel? Unforeseen expenditures? What about the family you haven't seen for two years?"

He laughed as if my questions were those of a naive child or a peasant from a remote hamlet. He wasn't very far off. We, Soviet émigrés, were as naively ignorant about the lives of Western Europeans and Americans as a peasant from the backwoods of Russia is about the daily lives of big city dwellers. He (Alexander Lurie) chuckled, "Listen, Daniil! I've inherited enough money from my grandfather and father to provide for my ex-wife (she sent the divorce papers to Sydney, and I signed them with an easy heart) and for my children. My son and daughter both have received a stellar education. And visas? Believe me, my résumé is spotless. My lawyer in London takes care of entry and exit visas that I need for countries like Russia, where the idea of the freedom of movement diverges from the norms accepted in the West."

I took leave of the hobo-doctor, Alexander Borisovich Lurie. As I thought, forever.

It was the end of January on the island of Antigua in the Caribbean, where Mira and I were vacationing. We were staying in a cottage wedged between the shore and the marina. So ingeniously was the marina built that it created the illusion that the water was surrounded not by light wooden shacks but by boats anchored in the middle of the sea. It evoked dreams of distant voyages and coral reefs, of palm trees nimble like the long-limbed dark island women, their lithe arm-branches inviting the traveler to dock and stay with them forever. Yachts came to the island and unloaded seafarers. They amused themselves on the shore, dined at the little oceanfront restaurant, went into town for a little while, and then sailed off again in search of happiness. Mira and I lazed around in the chaise lounges with a book or a magazine, swam in the sea, roamed the beach by the edge of the water, and watched as the boats sailed off, heading God only knows where.

That day after lunch we went into town, the island's capital. The cab driver unloaded us in the middle of a street where Antiguan artists moored their canvasses. Here, as at most art fairs of this sort, eclectic styles went hand in hand with crude craft and imitation. A local Shishkin was selling pictures of simian families roaming around a palm grove under rays of the morning sun. A local David painted the death of a hero of the island's slave rebellion. A local Repin took a dozen dark-skinned, muscular men, naked down to their waists, and harnessed them to drag a heavy schooner onto the shore. A local Gauguin glorified the gentle grace of the dark-brown Antiguan beauties bathing in the evening ocean tide. A local Pollack captured the frightening splendor of an Antiguan thunderstorm in yellow, blue, red, and black zigzags. A local Kandinsky, a local Chemiakin, a local Tselkov. . . . We bought a marine landscape with a schooner sailing away into the open sea. It was Mira's choice. The uncomplicated art of the local craftsman beckoned us to some remote place, away from suitcases and from plane tickets with a set return date to Providence.

Either the same one or another smiley and gregarious cab driver quickly delivered us to our temporary abode by the ocean. Bonfires burned on the shore; the breeze carried appetizing smells of grilled meat laced with tantalizing scents of beer, wine, the fun and games that go hand in hand with picnics, carnivals, and other gatherings of unencumbered revelers who have temporarily escaped from the bourgeois civilization and its daily routine. Indeed, our side of the island was sparsely populated and well suited for such revelries. Three huge yachts gently rocked in the roadstead, and small boats ferried between them and the shore, transporting passengers. Drawn by curiosity, we sauntered past the bonfires, checking out the island visitors and listening to the sounds of their carefree voices. Despite the late hour and the nearing supper, the boaters were, to put it mildly, underdressed. Most of the men wore only swimming trunks; the women, rather revealing bathing suits. They paid no attention to Mira and me, or to any of the other cottage renters, as if it weren't they who had just set ashore here in Antigua but we who had appeared out of nowhere and were loutishly staring at their feast. They were truly partying without restraint: drinking tons of beer and wine, avidly biting into large pieces of grilled meat, chomping on juicy corn cobs, exultantly hatcheting the scarlet faces of watermelons. Feasting with abandon, they looked like people celebrating their liberation after spending long years in captivity.

Their bonfires cut through the darkness of the southern night. It was time for us to go back to our cottage, have our evening tea, and read or watch the news, but we couldn't pry ourselves away, as if something drew us to the crazy revelry of the visitors from the yachts that had arrived that afternoon. Near one of the bonfires, I noticed an old man in shorts. He was puffing on a cigar. The red glow of his cigar grew stronger, then receded, following the rhythm of the smoker's cheeks. Whether it was the cigar's bursting light or a momentary turn of his head toward the bonfire, I managed to make out his face. It was none other than my chance acquaintance from St. Peter's Square in Rome!

"Alexander Borisovich?" I addressed the old man in Russian—in a manner both quizzical and friendly. Baffled, he looked at me and then, as if wiping clean the mirror of distant memory, gave me a bewildered smile, "Oh, yes. I remember. In Rome, five or six years ago. . . . You were relocating from Russia to the United States. Forgive me, but your name escapes me."

I told him my name and introduced him to Mira.

"And this is Martha," Lurie pointed at a young, strongly built woman in a tiny bikini, who was rapturously singing along with a boombox that blared heavy metal across the beach.

Martha acknowledged us, gulped down half a bottle of beer and ran off to one of the other bonfires.

"So you're still on the road, Alexander Borisovich?" I asked the old man, careful not to appear too curious. Even though I asked this largely to make small talk, I was keen to find out where destiny had taken him, especially now that Martha, a young and assertive epicurean, had entered the picture.

"Well, if you recall our meeting in Rome . . . I was wrapping up my voyage and preparing to return home to London. My business affairs were in order. My accountant reported that the capital my father and grandfather had invested in stocks and other financial instruments was yielding good returns. As to eye surgery, this profession requires both a jeweler's eye and a mathematician's precision; during my absence it had advanced enough for me not to try playing catch-up, especially since I was nearing retirement age. My ex-wife, Katherine, had married one of my former friends who had become a widower. Peter, my son, followed in my footsteps: he completed his training and is now a practicing ophthalmologist. Lily, my daughter, is studying film criticism at Oxford."

He paused, taking a long drag off his cigar and looking at my wife intently.

"Don't ever let your husband go on journeys round the globe! It's like alcohol or heroin. At first it seems like happiness, but then it sucks you in forever."

"He couldn't, even if he wanted to," Mira said but corrected herself. "Even if we wanted to! We can barely scrape enough together to go to the Caribbean once a year."

"I understand. Limited funds, huh? Well, it's probably just as well," he said with a melancholy smile. "Look at us. We've been traveling on large yachts for over a year. This is a fun crowd. Navigators have mapped our route with great precision, so that we stay clear of any seasonal storms and hurricanes. And my Martha is such a happy person that I wake up every morning grateful that she's with me and fall asleep anxious to see her again in the morning." He said this, driving away the shadow of doubt or sadness that momentarily flashed over his face. Then he waived us goodbye and stepped inside the circle of half-naked bodies overlaid with streaks of fire.

In the morning, the shore was empty. The yachts were gone. The sequel to the story of the hobo I had met in Rome seemed like nothing but a dream brought ashore by the ocean waves.

"What do you make of him?" asked Mira as she poured coffee into locally made, curvy ceramic mugs. The mugs must have been modeled after the luscious bodies of the island women.

"Of whom?" I asked, still in the grips of what seemed like a dream.

"Of the seafarer we ran into last night," my wife made explicitly clear, slamming a plate of toast with melted cheese on the table. I had no choice but to a) acknowledge yesterday's encounter as real, and b) try to figure out Alexander Lurie's motives for gallivanting round the globe, or at least to identify his most compelling reason. But could Mira and I ever be his impartial judges? By nature, Mira and I were both *domosedy*—"homebodies," as they say it in English. Back in Russia, I would get homesick the minute I left on a work-related trip—to Siberia, the Caucasus or the Baltics—and would count the days until I would return to Moscow, where my wife and my son were waiting. Mira, in turn, barely made it through a two-month business trip to Japan. Once we moved to America, we always traveled together: to California, to the Midwest, to Louisiana. And we always journeyed to Europe together. We never wanted to be apart, even though things between us weren't always as smooth as the gleaming surface of the island coffee mugs. Had we, too, sometimes come close to crossing the line beyond which a man was capable of leaving his home and going off to the edge of the world, either alone or with a chance fellow traveler?

A few more years passed. Something mysterious and tragic occurred with one of our American friends. His fiancée, Linda, a journalist who worked for a New York based Jewish magazine, traveled to Jamaica to research the dissemination of Judaism among the descendants of slaves that were brought there from West Africa. Linda was due to return within a month or a month and a half, at the most. Two months later, she still wasn't back! Nor did she call home a single time. Which was completely unlike her, a child of punctual German Jews. Harry—that was our friend's name—and Linda's parents got first the local police and then the FBI involved, but to no avail. There was no trace of Linda, alive or dead. Harry traveled to Jamaica and spent an entire month in Kingston. He became quite chummy with the local police prefect, organized search parties to the remote parts of the island, and networked with Jamaican Jews. Nothing helped, however. He was a persnickety kind of fellow, and it's not just that he liked to see everything carefully through, but also that by the end, everyone was usually sick of his zeal.

"Do you remember how exasperated Linda felt by Harry's efforts to pick the most fashionable wedding dress, the trendiest jazz band, and the fanciest restaurant, with Jewish cuisine, no less, for their wedding?" Mira reminded me.

"Of course I do. So what are you saying?"

"Can't you guess?"

"Suppose you're right. . . . Then what?"

"I don't know. . . ."

"I'll tell you what, why don't we just go to Jamaica? January's around the corner, and it's been more than half a year since we've taken a vacation."

The room in the little hotel, which we hastily booked over the phone, was on the oceanfront just a couple of miles outside the town of Port Antonio. It was a dilapidated two-story barn, its upper floor converted into guest rooms. Two or three centuries ago it must have been a storehouse for sugar cane from the local plantations. On the first floor of the hotel and in an adjoining open veranda, there was a bar that, in addition to alcohol, served coffee, sandwiches, and a few hot entrees, which enabled the owners to call this dive a restaurant.

Now, the owners of this establishment—they were a colorful couple: a decrepit old man in a worn cowboy hat and faded canvas shorts with the ragged edges of years of wear, and his wife, a sprightly, thirty-year-old vixen dressed in a silk skirt barely long enough to conceal the folds of her groin, and something like a tanktop, from the lacy foam of which her untamed breasts gushed out like streaming beer. With a Parkinsonian jerky gait, the old man circled the dining room, bussing plates and glasses. His wife either stood behind the bar or joined large groups of revelers at their tables. The walls of the bar—which we should probably call a saloon—were decorated with paintings of pirate skirmishes: hijacked ships, cannonballs flying at schooners, brigands taking as hostages or murdering the crew and passengers of a captured vessel. Some of the tableaux were especially vile: a slave auction on Kingston's main block, or scenes of slave labor on sugar cane plantations. This hit us all at once when the old man gave us our room key. The hotel's front desk was also located in the same bar. We immediately recognized each other: Alexander Lurie, us, and we, him.

"So we meet again," the old man said by way of a greeting, and yelled out to the barmaid, "Martha! Martha! Drinks for my Russian friends!"

Martha brought us two bottles of Jamaican beer, on the house. It was late afternoon. The bar was getting crowded. The owner didn't have time to wax sentimental about past encounters. And what was there to reminisce about? Two chance meetings from the past—and now this one. Plus, we were tired from the road and couldn't wait to take a dip and stroll along the ocean that lay outside the windows of the bar like a cobalt platter.

Our room had a view of the boundless ocean and the sky merging into eternity. We hurriedly unpacked, pulled on our bathing suits, and rushed to the beach. Vacationers were ambling along the shore, past the vendors of Jamaican curios who had laid out their merchandize on the ground. This makeshift fair featured wooden masks of dark-faced African chiefs; black, varnished-wood carvings of animals, most frequently pigs; necklaces made of seashells or polished wooden beads; strings of shark teeth; and unprepossessing fruit grown by heedless farmers. . . . Plumes of marijuana smoke floated above the evening beach. The sun vanished. It was getting a bit chilly. Or was I imagining it? We had a quick bite at the bar, resolving to pick a more civilized spot for our future dinners. But do our intentions always become realized? We were tired and went to bed early, although at first the loud music and guttural voices of holidaymakers from Central Europe kept us up. In the middle of the night, I woke up with a headache and fever. I was coming down with something, probably a virus I had picked up on the plane from a neighbor who sneezed, blew his nose, and coughed the entire flight.

The most unforeseen happened: I came down with the flu. My fever felt like it was about 102, but how were we to measure it? Whoever takes a body thermometer to the south seas? We were lucky enough that they sold fever-reducing pills at a large hotel, to which Mira had to walk for forty minutes along the beach. I spent my days lounging in bed, besieged by a headache, cough, aching joints, and terrible weakness. When the drugs kicked in, my fever subsided; covered with sweat and listless, I would lie prostrate under the sheets. In brief moments of relative reprieve, I managed to read a couple of paragraphs from the memoirs of a venerable screenwriter in a recent issue of the *New Yorker.* Or else I would stick my head out the window and breathe. Through a gap between mango trees surrounding the hotel, I could see the ocean, a chunk of the beach with a dock, and the bar's veranda. Speedboats, catamarans, and yachts with multicolored sails furrowed the ocean. Young athletic black men took the tourists for rides on huge inflatable yellow bananas. Once in a while, I got a glimpse of a parachute's swaying cupola; a tiny, tireless motorboat dragged it by a silk cable. Or the parachutist would sail by, perched on a child seat and dangling his legs. I caught snapshots of island fun and then tumbled back into my bed to await, as an inextricable extension of myself, the next round of violent chills, weakness, and headache. And again: anti-fever medication, torrential sweating, and unquenchable thirst coupled with complete aversion to food, followed by a brief interval of relief.

Sometimes I would go downstairs. The same raucous group of Central Europeans partied in the hotel bar from morning until late at night. They were powerfully-built men, all between the ages of thirty and thirty-five. They must have been engineers working for the same firm or bank employees from Frankfurt, Vienna, or Nuremberg—work buddies who had decided to spend their vacation as bachelors on the tropical island of Jamaica. They wolfed down big plates of hotdogs and pasta, chugged coffee and beer from the identical huge mugs, threw the money down on the table with a thud, and (whoever was within reach) zestfully slapped Martha on her zestful backside, clad in little skirts or shorts. In retrospect, it's difficult for me to draw a line between what I really observed and what I conjured up in my state of high fever or the maddening weakness that usually followed suit. But the guttural voices, the neighing laughter, and the sound of hands slapping on the table boards—those all were real! From time to time, old Lurie limped across the veranda. For the most part, though, it was Martha who bustled around the bar, serving food and drinks to the hotel guests and to bar visitors who stopped in on the way someplace. Which is why, in the intermissions between the bouts of my illness, I saw plenty of not-very-discreet expressions of physical attention with which the bar visitors showered Martha. Among the group of Central Europeans, one young gentleman stood out for his habit of hanging out on the veranda dressed in nothing but black swimming trunks. He paraded his body, that of an anatomically evolved male. And he had plenty to show: globes of chest muscles, bulges on arms and legs, millstones around his neck. He was a body-building metaphor incarnate: from the compressed forehead over his laughing cheeks, the hirsute torso, and the long narrow whiskers down to the muscle strategically stretching out his skimpy black trunks. I dubbed him "Adik." He was a partier and a generous chap. I observed his hand draw an imaginary line around their whole group, after which Martha would rush to bring over half a dozen mugs of beer, foaming like the ocean tide. Only now, many years later, do I realize how much of the hotel's daily life I was able to take stock of, even though I was ill and not in good form and only observed things in snatches.

Mira would run out for a morning dip in the sea. Then she would come back with breakfast: coffee, juice, mineral water, bread, butter, and cheese. I would force myself to eat something, wash it down with some water, and go back to bed. Then Mira went back to the beach, popping in once in awhile to check up on me. I napped, read, or watched the ocean, the sky, and the veranda of the bar, without paying much heed to my wife's comings and goings. Sometimes Mira ordered in from the bar and had the food sent up with Martha or else a morose local woman dressed in an invariably black robe. At the hotel, this woman combined the roles of maid, dishwasher, and back-up waitress. But even this aboriginal room service did not stir up my desire to eat, no matter how hard Martha tried to awaken my appetite, suppressed as it was by the malicious virus. Acting like a long-time acquaintance, she would put the tray down on my bed and coax me to eat *this* or drink *that*. She would peel a ripe mango oozing its sweet golden flesh, and bend over, feeding me like a child. As she leaned over to feed me chunks of mango, her ripe breasts all but erupted from her lacy top. A few times, the old Lurie himself paid me a visit, bringing me, of his own accord, hot tea, mineral water, or orange juice. But either because of the sickly revulsion I had developed toward everything, or because of my headache, or else because of some unconscious fear of touching filth, our conversations didn't go very far.

We entered the second half of the vacation week. On Saturday we were due to return to Providence. The episodes of chill and fever recurred daily. Our vacation was completely ruined. I prayed to God to let me get home without further complications. Mira tried to feign optimism. She recounted various beach incidents to me: someone was stung by a jellyfish or stepped on a shard of glass or had to be taken to the local hospital and treated for extreme sunburn. Sometimes, with a faint sigh, she spoke of excursions into the heart of the island or boat trips to see the coral reefs. An excursion into the jungle came off the table as soon as I reminded her of Linda, our friend's vanished fiancée. Yes, the uncertainty still weighed heavily on both of us. Because of my illness, we had failed to find out anything about the missing journalist.

"You know what, sweetie? Why don't you go see the coral reefs tomorrow? At least one of us will have something exotic to remember," I said to my wife.

"And what about you?"

"I'm a little better. I'll just take it easy, wait for you, and even drag myself out onto the beach if I don't have a fever."

"You mean it?" she asked, hope in her voice.

"Absolutely! If you're having fun, perhaps I'll catch the vibe as well."

The night went well. For the first time since our arrival, I even had the energy to go to the beach in the morning, to splash my face with the gently lapping greenish-blue water of the awakening ocean, and to stretch my limbs. Then, Mira and I had breakfast on the veranda of the bar. I overcame my aversion to food and downed a cup of coffee with cream and two soft-boiled eggs. Next to us, the rowdy group of Central Europeans was taking its morning meal. They were going on the same excursion as my Mira, to some remote coral reefs. The yacht was supposed to pick them up at the nearest dock. Suddenly, as if by a superior's command, the rowdy group left the veranda.

"Time for you to go," I said to my wife.

"In a minute," she nodded but didn't leave, placing the palm of her hand on my wrist.

"You're going to be late!"

"So what! I don't really feel like going," she responded, as if waiting for me to agree with her that she should stay.

The boat was due back around four o'clock in the afternoon. It was already well past lunchtime, and I was feeling okay. I even walked up and down the beach a few times. I didn't feel like eating in the hotel bar, so I kept making up various excuses to stay in my room. It was as if I was reluctant to go back to the spot where Mira and I had sat together for the last time before the boat sailed off to the coral reefs. I killed a little more time. I tried reading the short story I had started before our vacation, but couldn't concentrate. I was gripped with an anxiety that I wouldn't necessarily describe as baseless. It was like a cobweb that had not completely shackled one's body but had already given one an outline of the impending disaster. I could no longer bear being by myself.

In the bar, at the table beneath the picture of brigands murdering the crew of a highjacked ship and taking its passengers hostage, sat an elderly couple from Detroit whom we had casually met on our arrival day. I nodded to them, but they didn't recognize me. I must have changed a lot during my illness. Perhaps the expression on my face was so unlike the countenance of a smiling, relaxed gentleman, which I bore on the arrival day, that they took me for a person they had never seen before. I nodded to the elderly couple, who didn't acknowledge me, and sat at a table by the edge of the veranda, which gave me a good view of the water and the dock. Martha was tending the bar. Lurie limped over with a tattered menu in hand. I really didn't need to consult the menu—I had long since committed to memory our restaurant's paltry offerings. I didn't feel like having anything, but, for fear of offending the old doctor, I ordered a bowl of sliced-up mangoes and oranges, coffee, and a cognac.

"How about a drink with me, Alexander Borisovich?" I asked.

"With pleasure," he answered, and staggered over to Martha to put in the order. In the meantime, the sun rolled closer to a flock of clouds hovering over the horizon. The excursion boat should have been back from the reefs a long time ago.

Old Lurie brought cognac and coffee for both of us, and fruit salad for me. What I really wanted was to down the cognac—which I didn't expect to be any good, just like everything else in this rundown establishment—drink up my coffee, and go back to the room. But as I raised my glass to make a trifle of a polite toast, my old acquaintance stopped me with a motion of his tremorous hand.

"Here's to the happy return of your devoted wife!" said Lurie.

We drank up. I wanted a drink, and I was the one who had proposed that we have a cognac together, so I didn't want to hurt the old man's feelings. His toast, much like the cognac he had served, stunned me for a moment, yet offered no relief. Why did he propose such an odd toast? I wondered. Why did he emphasize the words *your devoted wife*? Intelligent people, and especially those whose smarts run in their bloodlines, can squander their wealth, become drunks or addicts, and lose their moral integrity, but they never deplete their intelligence. And intelligence is comprised of the power of observation, sagacity, and the ability to read the interlocutor's thoughts—perhaps not even just thoughts, but the uncontrollable swarm of unconscious revelations forming the kaleidoscopic pattern of premonition. Lurie had detected the pattern.

"Listen, there's no reason to worry," he said. "This happens with our boat trips. The picnic on a coral reef may have taken longer than expected. Or the passengers decided, on the spot, to pay extra and stay a bit longer to enjoy the views of the setting sun off the boat. And here's the most common case scenario: the passengers get hungry and convince the captain to make a stop at the Marriott's dock; the restaurant there serves incredible oysters. Don't worry, Daniil."

"I'm not worried, it's just that . . . ," I mumbled and reached for my wallet to pay the bill.

"Wait, what's the hurry! Let's wait together for the return of your yacht. And to bide the time, I'll tell you a puzzling story," old Lurie held me back. Reluctantly, I stayed.

"Two years or so ago," Lurie began, "of course it's easy to lose track of time in these latitudes, a young American woman checked into our hotel. I believe she was a journalist."

"Linda?" I interrupted him.

"I can't remember her name," Lurie took a small sip of coffee, looked over his shoulder and noticed the couple from Detroit motioning for their check. He got up and limped over to them. What if it turns out that Harry's fiancée had stayed at this hotel? The thought dashed across my inflamed imagination.

"Anyway, as I was saying, some American woman checked into the hotel," old Lurie returned to my table. "She would go off for a day or two and then come back. Had some business with the Jamaican Jewish communities or something like that. We don't ask our guests where they spend their time. Especially if they're paying cash. Once, just as the American lady returned from a trip inland, boats with travelers sailing around the world stopped at our shore. Remember, just like Martha and I, when you ran into us in Antigua?"

"Of course, I remember!"

"So the boats docked here. The revelry began. Bonfires. Grilled meat. Beer. Wine. Some of our hotel guests joined in the picnic and festivities. In short, everything went as it usually does when people lose themselves in reckless and interminable merriment . . ."

"Unending?" I couldn't contain myself.

"The whole thing continued for two days. That is, the party in which the American lady took such a very active part went on for two days. On the third day at dawn the yachts sailed off. The maid, when she was cleaning the American lady's room, found a note and money on the table. Our guest had left more than what she owed us for her stay, and vanished along with her travel bag."

"Do you think she . . . ?"

"—I never let myself get curious about my guests' itineraries," old Lurie cut me short and stood up. I left the money on the table and went to the dock.

Like a black curtain, night fell over the flat surface of the invisible ocean. The water rolled over the shore and crawled back, hissing like snakes that crawl out of their nests into the grass and prepare for a new attack. Foolish thoughts troubled me, teeming in my head and shoving one another to the side. Was Linda that young American woman? Had the yacht carrying Mira crashed into a coral reef? What was my wife up to?

For how long did I wait in the darkness near the dock? Ten minutes? Half an hour? An hour? At last, amid the blackness of the ocean I made out flickering golden stars that grew bigger and bigger. I heard the sound of an engine. Then I made out the lights that ran from the deck to the top of the main mast. I heard voices, laughter, and the kind of noisy big-band music that almost unfailingly accompanies sea excursions. The yacht approached the landing, illuminating the shore with its deck and mast lights. A sailor hopped onto the dock from the boat. Someone tossed him the cable. He tied down the yacht. The passengers, animated after a day at sea, poured onto the shore. Finally, Mira came off the boat. She was leaning on the arm of the indefatigable bodybuilder with the narrow black whiskers of swimming trunks, the one whom I had dubbed "Adik." Mira was in that tameless, gleeful state of mind that children experience when they have broken free of wearisome supervision and want to demonstrate with their entire being that they have no intention of returning to the state of legalized servitude forced upon them by family ties. Mira's undone black hair was scattered over her bare shoulders. Her huge Gypsy eyes looked at me teasingly and fearlessly, bringing to mind Pushkin's Zemfira. I even felt that she was enveloped by something like a campfire's bitter smoke or a prickly cloudlet of champagne fumes.

"Danya!" she cried, giving me a peck on the cheek. "I thought for sure you'd be asleep by now! How do you feel?"

I mustered a pseudo-cheery *okay*, which Mira, I thought, barely registered before she immediately started telling me about the *amazing day* she had spent on the coral reefs and about the *incredibly gorgeous* fish and *exceptionally delicious* oysters.

We were heading back to the hotel along with the other boaters when we heard Adik's gratingly guttural voice:

"And now we're all going to the bar to celebrate our safe return!"

"Are you going?" I asked.

"And you? You must be really tired," Mira brushed her hand against my back. "Why don't you go to bed. I'll be up soon."

I woke up at dawn. Mira was sleeping in her bed, hugging the pillow. I looked out the window and saw the edge of the cobalt ocean platter upon the shore's yellow table. The excursion yacht was gently rocking near the dock.

2003
Translated from the Russian by Margarit T. Ordukhanyan

A Storefront Window of Miracles

For Maxim

L eft over in our town from the good old days is only one repair shop for cameras, binoculars, typewriters, and computers. In general, no one brings typewriters in for repair. For that matter, are there still typewriters left in our town? Nowadays even cameras aren't brought in for repair, because it's cheaper to buy a new one. Computers fare a bit better, although this, too, requires some reckoning: is it better to economize or to buy a brand new one? Therefore, a typewriter, placed in the storefront window to advertise the services, was in and of itself among our town's oddities. Not to mention the proprietor and sole repairman, the one who kept this extraordinary shop. He was in all respects a peculiar, unusual, unique person. His name was Mark. A good half of the working day he spent directly in the storefront window, behind a thick glass, framed in such a way that part of the window could easily be transformed into a glass door, through which clients would come in and place their orders. In the storefront window Mark had a little table with two Remington typewriters: one with Latin, the other with Russian keys.

Sometimes Mark would retreat into the back of his shop, where he kept an extensive collection of tools used to repair photo equipment, typewriters, and computers. Also in the back there was a studio apartment where Mark lived: a couch, stove, shower, sink, refrigerator. . . .

The shop's main source of income was the composition of lyrical messages for various occasions, for a fairly moderate fee. Mark wrote these poems in English or Russian. As a matter of fact, he had come from Russia and ended up in our town about thirty years or so ago, still quite a young man. His parents died when he was in technical college, where young men and women are trained to become skilled workers: electricians, plumbers, mechanics, photographers, cooks, and so forth. Thus the foundation of his knowledge was installed at the nearby technical school, which was called, grandiloquently, Technical Academy. All the above refers to his ability to repair photo equipment, typewriters, and computers. But then from where, or from whom, did he learn to compose lyrical messages, executed in perfect verse form (which never fell below the standards of Russian or English classical poetry)? Very simple! Mark, if he wasn't working, would read poetry. He knew, verse by verse, all of the English-language classics, starting with Shakespeare and ending with Larkin. As for Russian poets, he could quote each of them from memory: Trediakovsky, Derzhavin, Pushkin, Nekrasov, Blok, or Brodsky. From each of them, Mark borrowed a particularly distinctive device marking a poet of genius. He never seriously thought of himself as a poet, content as he was with the craft of a versifier.

Mark ate breakfast and supper in his studio apartment. And at noon he usually went for a bite at The Seven Little Kids Café across the street from his shop. This café was one of our town's most extraordinary and remarkable spots. You couldn't find another place with such delicious brioches and croissants. No other bakery-café made such airy and fluffy Napoleon cakes or such ravishing apricot pastries. It should also be said that it was none other than Mark who had come up with the name for this bakery-café. Besides poems and typewriters, he also loved fairy tales. And "The Wolf and the Seven Little Kids" was by far his favorite fairy tale. However, the café owner Victor Maurois, a Swiss émigré, requested that the wolf be sent back to the forest. This way, only the goat kids remained on the café sign. But they were so adorable! On its baby horns one of the goat kids was balancing a tray with a steaming cup of coffee. Another kid carried a basket with pastries. The third hurried to deliver a long French bread to hungry customers—a baguette filled with Swiss cheese, Italian salami, and New England tomatoes. The fourth . . . fifth . . . sixth . . . seventh! All of the goat kids were occupied with the most important task of their existence: to deliver pleasure to the residents of our town. Children especially loved The Seven Little Kids Café. They literally pulled their moms and dads in the direction of this most delicious and happy café in the world. Of course, they got to go there after promising that their school reports would not look like beehives. Only As and A-minuses!

In the evenings, the crowd in the café would change. In the summer, spring, or early autumn, the garden surrounding The Seven Little Kids Café became its liveliest spot. Light jazz music was playing. Behind each little table there sat couples in love, drinking coffee with cream, nibbling on pastries, and leaning into the shade of lilac bushes to steal kisses. There were always many more couples in the spring. At exactly this time, the bushes of Persian lilacs, white and violet, bloomed so impetuously, casting off such a thick shadow from the light of the antique lanterns in the cast-iron ornate mountings, that it was simply impossible to refuse a kiss. This was the only time that Mark's shop didn't operate, and he felt bouts of loneliness. He would close the shop, lower the heavy metallic blinds, cross the street, and enter the café. After ordering a cup of coffee with cream, he usually walked out into the garden and looked over the tables. More often than not they would all be taken, a pair of lovers sitting at each one. Mark couldn't very well ask permission to join one of the couples; this would disturb their amorous chatter. Then Mark would find a table inside the café and sit there in total solitude, flipping through the town's daily newspaper and sipping his slightly bitter, aromatic beverage. Sometimes the owner of The Seven Little Kids Café, Victor Maurois, would join him to start a fascinating conversation about Switzerland, how for a number of centuries already the Swiss have been successful at resolving the nationalities question. To which Mark would respond gently but quite firmly that America, too, has dealt rather well with this difficult issue.

"Look for instance at our town, Victor. What harmony, and there's much more diversity here than in Switzerland!"

To this, Viktor would only issue an ironic *"Mais non!"* and wave his hand, waiting for Mark to finish his first coffee. After which he brought Mark a new cup of coffee with cream "on the house."

Sometimes Mark was lucky: he would find a free table in the garden adjoining The Seven Little Kids Café. He would settle and listen to music. If the lyrics were in English, Mark would immediately devise a Russian text to go along, always trying to follow the meter and rhyme. In this way, he would while away the evening. Despite being something of a celebrity in our town, Mark was in essence very lonely. His school friends had dispersed all across the country. He didn't have any living relatives, and casual acquaintances with young women didn't last longer than one or two dates. His whole being was so deeply focused on poetry that he only wanted to—or could—talk about this one subject. And who's interested in talking about one and the same thing all the time, even something as important as literature?

But even so, a miracle occurred. They say that a determined gold prospector, if he is sure that he has found a true gold vein, should keep washing and washing the sand until a gold nugget sparkles. Something similar happened with our hero. One day at the end of May, he was sitting at a table in the garden. Through the open doors of The Seven Little Kids Café and from the speakers, concealed by the blooming lilac branches, sounds of jazz were wafting into the air. Louis Armstrong, Ella Fitzgerald, or Glen Miller's band. Mark sipped his coffee and sang along in Russian so ably that it sounded like he had composed the lyrics of the songs. Which was, in fact, true, since he could improvise faithful Russian translations of any song he liked. This time he got a bit carried away and was humming rather loudly.

"You sing wonderfully. And the lyrics are so pretty!" someone's voice said just above his ear.

Mark turned around and set his cup, which served as his imaginary microphone, on the table. The voice belonged to a young lady standing before his table. She was, without a doubt, lovely, or at any rate had a lovely voice. Mark couldn't get a complete view of the girl's face because a lilac shrub threw a shadow on it.

"Thank you," answered Mark. "Would you care to join me?"

"I'm not disturbing you, am I?"

"Of course not! I'm just passing time: drinking coffee and humming along with the songs."

"But you do it so well! And the Russian words lie with the American music so naturally, as if it were the original lyrics. Are you sure I'm not disturbing you?"

"Not at all!

"Well, thank you!" She sat down next to him.

He liked that she sat on the chair next to him. Otherwise her face would have remained in the shadows. But now she was sitting, illuminated by the light of a lantern, and Mark could get a good look at her face. Life experience had taught him to scrutinize: lenses, springs, keys on keyboards, parts which fill various modern electronic gadgets. In a similar way, he scrutinized verses of his favorite poets. Assonances, rhythms, rhymes, and tropes meant for poetry what different parts meant for electronic equipment, just as for the reader they served as different sources of emotional energy.

"You know, you're beautiful," Mark said to the girl.

"Do you mean it?"

"Of course I do. You have huge blue eyes, light golden hair and a beautiful figure."

"Well, my figure, it's quite ordinary, really. Especially when . . . ," and she straightened the opening of her low-cut blouse. "As a matter of fact, I've been looking for you. . . . Hmm, yes, I came to see you on business. I want to commission a poem."

"Excuse me, young lady! If it's business, I'll deal with it tomorrow morning. Right now my shop is closed. I'm relaxing. Allow me to treat you to a cup of coffee and an apricot pastry?"

"Thank you so much! I did get a little hungry on the way here. I live in a different city, but even there, your café, The Seven Little Kids, is famous for its great coffee and extraordinary pastries. Unfortunately, I missed the train and arrived here too late; your shop was already closed. And I'm under a lot of time pressure."

She didn't even notice that the chair next to her was empty. Mark had actually gone inside to get coffee and an apricot pastry. When he returned with a little tray, the young lady was hurriedly writing something in a yellow notebook, ruled with dark blue lines.

"Here . . . this . . . is . . . for you," said Mark, making pauses after each word and slanting the tray toward her.

She guessed why he talked this way. He didn't know her name. Perhaps you haven't noticed that we need names to fill the empty spaces between words? When there's absolutely nothing to say, or when words begin to spill over the rim, we insert the names of our interlocutors, and the pace of the conversation gets restored.

"My name is Tanya," said the girl, after guessing about Mark's pauses. "And this coffee is amazing!"

"I'll bring you more."

"Thank you! Maybe later. Please, hear me out."

"Fine," said Mark. "But so we're clear, if it's about an order, then you'd better come to the shop tomorrow morning."

"It's a plea for help," said Tanya.

"Well that's a different story. I'm listening."

"Tomorrow is my wedding day."

"Your wedding? Tomorrow?"

"Yes, exactly, tomorrow. And I want to give my future husband a beautiful poem."

"That's a common thing. Many people order poems for their brides or grooms," answered Mark in a voice feigning indifference. At the same time he felt the opposite of indifference. Sadness gripped his heart—the kind of sadness he hadn't known in all of his *professional* life.

"You're certainly correct, in general," Tanya continued. "People read poems at weddings. But my Alexander, he's utterly deaf to poetry. How many times have I read poetry to him, but it never once grabbed him. This is why I came to you, so that you could write a poem that would grab him, make him fall in love with poetry. Otherwise . . ."

" . . . Tanya," Mark interrupted her. "My shop is now closed. Come by tomorrow at 9:00 and we can talk."

"Oh Mark, please understand, the wedding is set for noon tomorrow. I must catch the first train back tomorrow morning. And I'll need some time to get ready and put on my white lacy wedding dress."

She was on the verge of tears as she beseeched him to write a poem for her fiancé. The unfinished coffee gleamed in her cup like the eye of a night bird. And the pastry remained untouched. A big band played and sang about a cold December which, under the effects of love, turned into the warm month of lovers, May. Tanya's eyes implored. For the first time in his life Mark decided to depart from the rules.

"Okay, I'll give it a shot."

She told Mark about her Alexander: what he's like, his appearance, what he does for living, what he's interested in, what he believes in and what he's skeptical about, and so on and so forth. Finally she gave him the yellow notebook with dark blue lines, where she had listed principal facts and dates in her fiancé's life. It was time to leave, because the café was closing and all the little tables in the garden had grown empty. The owner, Victor Maurois, had already come up to them a couple of times to ask if they would like more coffee or pastries, tactfully coughing into his cupped hand.

They got up and exited onto the street. The thick tires of the last bus rustled past them. The bus winked at them from the rear with the brakes' bloodshot eyes, and disappeared beyond University Hill.

"Okay, Tanya, I'll try. Come back tomorrow at 7:00 AM."

"Thanks," said Tanya. "Thanks very much."

"I'll do my best," he repeated.

"I'm sure you can do it. A true master like you." And she headed up the street.

"Well actually, where are you off to now?" Mark's words caught up with her.

"I don't know," she turned around. "Maybe I'll spend the night at the train station. Or stumble across some hotel."

"You can't just go like that! It's late. Why don't you stay at my place."

"Are you sure you don't mind?"

"Of course not! You can have my couch," answered Mark. "And I will settle at my typewriter and try to compose a poem for your fiancé, he whose name is Alexander."

They crossed the street and stopped in front of his shop. Mark led Tanya through the yard to the back door. They entered his place. He made a bed for her on the couch, showed her where everything was, and wished her a good night. Without raising the blinds, he sat down at the typewriter in the storefront window and turned on the desk lamp. For the first time in his life, Mark began to compose a commissioned poem not during the working day but at night. It's well known that our feelings and thoughts become sharper at night, behaving so unusually that it seems we're on the verge of fantasy, fairy tale, or the so-called telepathic experience. Perhaps this is why Mark continued to talk with Tanya, who was fast asleep on the couch in the back of his shop. He asked her about her childhood, her parents, the city from which she arrived by train and to which she was going to return to her fiancé. He even told her about himself, that he had never met a girl he liked as much as her. From their imaginary conversation, verses were born. But this wasn't the poem she was expecting from him. Tanya had arrived in our town to commission verses for her Alexander. Congratulatory verses for their wedding.

Morning came. Tanya woke up, washed, and looked into the storefront window, where Mark was bent over the typewriter.

"Good morning," said Tanya. "I need to rush in order to catch the morning train. Did you finish the poem?"

"I think so. Although I'm not sure you'll like it. Here it is."

From Mark's hands Tanya took a sheet of paper, rolled in a tube like an ancient scroll and tied up with a red silk ribbon. He always gave his clients the poems copied out in longhand on fine paper, rolled into a tube and tied with a silk ribbon.

"How much do I owe you?"

"Don't worry about it!" said Mark. "It's a gift. Would you like some coffee for the road?"

"No thank you. So long! I don't want to miss my train. I'll get coffee at Dunkin' Donuts—if I have time. All the best to you!"

On the train, Tanya untied the silk ribbon, unrolled the tube of the manuscript, and read the poem. There wasn't a single word said about her fiancé Alexander, nor about their approaching wedding. This was a poem about first love, blooming lilacs, and a golden-haired girl with blue eyes and a beautiful figure. At first she was simply surprised, but then she reread the poem and finally realized that she had raced, all for nothing, from one place to another, only to spend the night on a hard, uncomfortable couch and return to her fiancé empty-handed. Surprise turned into disappointment, disappointment into resentment, and resentment into fury. She ripped up the sheet with the poem into tiny scraps, lowered the train car's window, and tossed out the ripped-up manuscript. Scraps of paper with disparate characters dashed off, like a flock of frightened birds. Falling behind the train on which Tanya was riding, they flew back in the direction of our town.

In the meantime, Mark pulled up the blinds and sat at his little desk in the storefront window, waiting for customers. But he kept looking out onto the street: What if Tanya would come back? It seemed to him for some reason that she would definitely come back. She would read his poem, get off the train, and jump on the next one going in the other direction—back to our town. But Tanya didn't return.

An old lady came in and asked Mark to write a poem for her newly-born twin grandkids. He promised to carry out the commission by evening time, and set out to work. But things weren't quite gelling that morning. Something wasn't working. The rhythm stuttered like a broken grandfather clock, and the rhymes turned out colorless, like withered flowers. He struggled with the old lady's order until noon, then headed over to The Seven Little Kids Café for a bite. It was, as always, full of children. They were drinking their hot chocolates or cold milks, taking bites of sandwiches, rolls, and cakes, and talking to each other about the toys they wanted for their birthdays. Birthdays were obligatory for every boy and girl, thought Mark, and on birthdays, kids were supposed to get presents.

As always, the atmosphere was noisy and cheerful both inside the café and in the garden outdoors. Mark was lucky to get the last free table. He had started to eat his baguette with Swiss cheese and Italian salami, when a flock of small birds settled down on a neighboring lilac bush. These were some unusual birds: white with black spots scattered over their little wings. He got up from his chair to take a closer look at the wondrous birds. He was a little shortsighted and was accustomed to examining objects from a close distance.

Imagine Mark's astonishment when he saw that these weren't birds of any kind, but scraps of paper on which Cyrillic characters, written in his own hand, showed black. He carefully shook the odd scraps from the lilac branches into the palm of his hand and carried them back to his shop. There, with the help of tweezers, the kind which repairmen of fine equipment and stamp collectors like to use, he arranged the scraps on a sheet of paper. The result was the poem Mark had composed for Tanya.

Since that day, Mark has not taken any orders for composing poems. Nor does he sit in his storefront window of miracles. He's become an ordinary repairman of photo equipment and computers. He took his typewriters into the back of the shop. Sometimes, only if he's in the mood, he writes poetry. Of course, not as a commission, but just on the off chance that a girl with golden hair and blue eyes would turn up in our town and bring in a broken camera.

2009
Translated from the Russian by Margaret Godwin-Jones

Mimicry

I was invited to lunch at Professor Viktor Turkin's. The professor and his wife, Rita, live in Little Compton, Rhode Island. Turkin teaches comparative entomology at Brown University. Rita directs a student marionette theater. Their house is full of puppet marionettes. In fact, their collection of marionettes and butterflies is so remarkable that it alone justifies a visit to the Turkins. One can come and wander around their house, looking at the toy folks. Or admire the butterflies that resemble wondrous flowers, leaves, or something else so extraordinary that you've never encountered it before. Could it be that they look like objects from another world? "In essence," Turkin likes to say, "the function of butterflies is to remind us of beauty. Beauty on this earth but also in the entire Universe." And Rita always adds, "My marionettes are like butterflies with human faces. Above all else, they remind us of things humorous." Her marionette theater is called "Mimicry." The art of imitation.

Women with gorgeous legs do not need to imitate anyone. They flaunt. I brought one such carrier of gorgeous legs with me to the Turkins. Her name was Astrid. She had come from Armenia to do some digging in the archives of the university's Oriental Library. She was interested in Jewish-Armenian connections in the pre-Christian era. At the time, I was also scouring the archives in search of materials about a certain French epidemiologist who had worked to eliminate cholera and the plague in India, Asia Minor, and the Caucasus. At the Oriental Library I saw Astrid. First, her gorgeous legs, and then the rest of her. We started chatting. I had emigrated from Moscow. She had come from Yerevan. Over coffee at the Greek restaurant Cyprus, we talked about a centrifugal force that scatters Armenians and Jews all over the world. The topic infused mutual trust into our encounter, which was already growing warmer by the minute. We drank a bottle of wine over dinner, and then I suggested going back to my place for some cognac. "Ararat, I hope?" laughed Astrid. "Same barrel, different label," I joked. She had gorgeous legs and beautifully shaped hips. Her swarthy breasts with chocolate nipples, and the delicate line of hair that ran from her navel to her loin, could drive anyone mad. Besides, as a consequence of my transitory state and of language barriers, I hadn't had much success dating American women. My involuntary abstinence had become somewhat protracted. In short, Astrid spent the night at my place. Over mugs of morning coffee, we discussed Astrid's prospects for getting a position at the university and for bringing her husband and son from Yerevan to Providence.

It was then I remembered about the Turkins' invitation. "Why didn't I think of it sooner! I'll introduce you to Rita. First of all, she's a great gal. Second, her husband, Viktor, is Russian. So you won't have to worry about your English. And third, back to Rita, she herself embodies a model of the Jewish-Armenian connections. Her father hails from Turkish Armenia, and her mother is a Polish Jew."

And there we were, visiting the Turkins.

"Way to go, old man! That's quite a nymph you've ensnared!" Turkin pronounced with admiration the minute we took our whiskeys out into the garden, leaving Rita and Astrid behind. "The legs alone! And what a pair of knockers! No mimicry there!"

Nymphs (*Nymphalidae*) are Turkin's favorite butterflies. Likening anything to them is his highest form of praise. When conjoined with marble columns, the metaphor of beauty becomes a symbol of the insuperable.

"Anyway, we just met, and there's really not much of a chance, since she has a husband and a child," I tried to put on a mask of decorousness. Victor didn't really buy my *evasion tactics*. Still, he nodded with compassion: "Yes, I understand. The circumstances are above us but they hit us right below the belt."

We returned to the living room. There was someone at the door, and Turkin went to greet the newly arrived guests. As the door chime sang its plaintive melody, Astrid said with elation: "I'm blown away by these marionettes. Especially the Turk. He looks so real. And the scimitar!" The Turk wielding a curved sword (the scimitar) and sporting a bloodthirsty smile was a character from a Balkan fairy tale that Rita had staged with her student marionette theater.

The two new guests were Professor Michael Kaminsky and Dr. Stephen Ahmet. Kaminsky, like Turkin, was an expert in mimicry, although he studied not butterflies, but reptiles. Especially chameleons, which have the ability to adapt to their environment by changing skin color. Turkin was a devout morphologist, for whom the likeness of butterflies to leaves, flowers, or other insects was, perhaps, nature's whimsy but certainly not a form of natural selection. Kaminsky's views were far more flexible. He did not refute the possibility that different species could spontaneously develop identical features. However, he firmly believed that once a particular structure manifested itself, it would be silly of nature not to take advantage of it. "Say, a woman is endowed with a certain rudiment of masculine prowess. It would be both stupid and crude for a gentleman not to know its function and not to allow his female partner more pleasure." This was Kaminsky's favorite argument.

Dr. Ahmet, a neurosurgeon, was at the Turkins' for the first time. Judging by his thick head of hair, half of which had been silvered by the years, he was about fifty. As it turned out, all the men at the gathering were in the same age group. The host himself was about five or six years older than his wife. Astrid alone belonged to the generation that came twenty years after ours. Which is why she instantly became the object of rivalry among Kaminsky, Ahmet, and myself.

This wasn't my first time at the Turkins', and Kaminsky was a regular at their house. The tour of the house was given for the benefit of Astrid and Dr. Ahmet. Of course, the rest of us tagged along. Rita paused in front of every marionette and told its story— not only the story as such (the fairy tale) in which the marionette was a character, but also the story of that marionette's creation. She remembered every marionette maker who crafted marionettes for the theater. As it turned out, Rita had each of them made in the country where the particular fairy tale came from. Rita showed us Cipollino, Mowgli, the Princess-Frog, the four musicians of Bremen, Thumbelina, Sholem Aleichem's Motl and An-sky's Dibbuk, and many other heroes from tales both familiar and unknown to us, until we got to the Turk with the bloodthirsty smirk and scimitar. The Turk resided in the farthest room, the workshop, where Astrid had already been with Rita.

Everything might have turned out fine. That is to say, it would have gone unnoticed, had it not been for Astrid. She (out of a natural desire to say something flattering to the hostess) exclaimed, "He looks so amazingly real! I'm struck by how precisely you've captured his essence!"

We all . . . I mean, as soon as Astrid mentioned the Turk, we all. . . . It wasn't that we were afraid—there was nothing and nobody to be afraid of, or at least it didn't occur to any of us—but we all froze in our tracks, stifled by embarrassment and holding our breath. When Astrid saw our petrified faces, she realized the awkwardness of what she just said and added, "You know, this composite image of a bloodthirsty Turk with a scimitar is very popular with us, the Armenians."

That only made the situation worse.

I didn't know where to turn my gaze, all because of Dr. Ahmet, who was cheerfully staring at Astrid. Who knows, perhaps he wasn't even thinking of her but contemplating a new type of neuropathy.

In an attempt to clear the air, Rita said, "There's more to see. A Haidamak with a whip is hiding in the pantry. He's also from a Slavic fairy tale. Now this one is a real brute, doesn't get much worse!"

To this, Turkin added, flashing the blue icicles of his eyes, "Well, there can also be such a thing as false mimicry, you know."

Everyone laughed. Kaminsky remarked, in passing, "Just because I'm Polish doesn't mean I should get annoyed by a toy Haidamak!"

Our whole group returned to the living room. The sun was pounding on a skylight, reflecting off the yellow faience plates the hostess had handed out along with knives, forks, and cups also made of faience and also awash with sunlight. For lunch, we were served blintzes with cottage cheese, blintzes with blueberry jam, and apple compote. Rita ladled the compote out of a red enamel pot. All of this was so Russian that I couldn't contain myself: "Rita, dear, this so reminds me of my late mother's Saturday midday meals!"

"What about you?" Astrid turned to Kaminsky. She was sitting with a plate on her lap. Her chair was next to the armchair of the renowned chameleon expert.

"Oh, I haven't been in the Slavic milieu for so long that I couldn't tell you! You know, they took me from Poland when I was five."

"Poor baby!" laughed Astrid. It was obvious she was flirting with Kaminsky. She must not have ranked very highly my masculine rigor from the other night.

"In the evening we'll make *shashlyk*," Rita announced.

"Is that to balance off the Turkish marionette?" asked Dr. Ahmet, but with such a benign smile that it was clear he hadn't taken offense.

"The *shashlyk* dinner will be our metaphor of the *Caucasian Chalk Circle* (as in Brecht) or of Noah's Ark (from the Bible). To each sort, two chunks of juicy meat hot off the coals!" said Turkin.

"No doubt about it, *shashlyk*—or shish kebab—for the people of the Caucasus or, say, blintzes for the Slavs, are material symbols of different cultures. But someone must have *disseminated* these blintzes from country to country?" Dr. Ahmet queried. "Who could have been the blintzes *carrier?*"

"It's easiest to assume that it was the Jews, who spread from Germany to Poland and Lithuania, and further on—to Ukraine, Belorussia, and Russia," said Turkin, slicing open a blintz's purple belly.

"Come on, Viktor. Must we really perceive Jewish domination in every form of progress?" Kaminsky objected, irritation in his voice.

"That's very much in vogue these days, especially in today's Russia," Astrid said. "Thank God, we don't have this problem. Granted, thousands of Jews migrated to Armenia during the rule of Tigranes the Great. But they were fully assimilated, becoming 100 percent Armenian."

"Is that why your country is overrun by hunger and devastation?" asked Dr. Ahmet.

"Because the Jews migrated to Armenia, or because they were fully assimilated?" I needled him.

For the next few minutes, everyone cut, chewed, and drank in silence.

"You know, sometimes things just get to the level of the absurd," Kaminsky reactivated the discussion. (His own curly hair, its thick clusters interspersed among bald spots on his elongated skull, left no doubts regarding the dominance of Semitic-Hamitic genes). "Not long ago, I was flipping through a book titled *Shakespeare and the Jews* at our local bookstore. In the author's opinion, not only the notorious Shylock but also many of the playwright's other characters are endowed with one Jewish trait or another. This is some kind of mass *Judeomania!*"

"It's retaliation for mass Judeophobia," Turkin put a word in sideways.

I turned to Kaminsky, "By the way, Michael, did you actually read the book?"

"Well, I read a very long review in the *New Yorker*!" the chameleon expert dismissed my question.

Lunch was dragging. The sun had already exited the skylight's frame, swimming westward.

"How about going for a dip?" Rita suggested. She felt uneasy, upset by the direction our conversation had taken—a direction which was bound to hurt my feelings, and hers as well.

But at this point, Astrid reentered the dialogue. Perhaps she realized that her words might have been offensive to me or to Rita. After all, the night before, Astrid had been making love with a Jew. Plus the hostess had an Armenian father and a Jewish mother. Or perhaps Astrid herself had been holding a grudge against Dr. Ahmet for his remark about hunger and devastation. And what was I thinking, adding fuel to the fire with my ill-timed wit! In any case, still seated in her chair that was pressed against Kaminsky's armchair, Astrid tossed words in the air, "Yes, we may well have hunger and devastation today. But our tragedy began when Turks slaughtered thousands and thousands of Armenians. They forced the rest to flee or to become Turkified, and they annexed the fertile lands of Western Armenia."

"Allow me to note," said Dr. Ahmet, still smiling, although not as sweetly as before, but bitterly. "Allow me to note that speaking through you is, first and foremost, the feeling of *unrealized revenge*. If they only had had a chance, the Armenians would have slaughtered every Turk, young and old. Besides, the Turks were not alone. The genocidal urge, delusional as it is, has numerous historical precedents (recall Moses bringing the plague upon the Egyptians), and it resulted in the annihilation of six million Jews by the Germans."

"Why only the Germans?" Turkin asked the whole gathering. Nobody responded, and he continued: "The Balts, the Ukrainians, and the Poles also murdered Jews with eagerness."

"Oh, enough with the Poles already!" protested Kaminsky. "We ourselves suffered at the hand of the Germans."

"By the way, apropos of that *New Yorker* review," I pounced on Kaminsky's remark, "its author recounts how he once encountered a Spaniard who wore a shirt with what looked like *tzitzit*-fringes on the edges. The Spaniard insisted that he was a scion of an old aristocratic family, but also recalled that in his family, such fringes had been worn from generation to generation by the eldest sons. And yet he vehemently denied descending from Marranos—those who became outwardly Christians but remained crypto-Jews. What is this, origins erased from memory or a case of artificial—artful—mimicry?"

To this, our host replied, "My last name is Turkin. Does that mean I descend from the Turks?"

"It's not beyond the realm of possibility. However, what does it matter if you are phenotypically Russian, come from a Russian family, and nobody around doubts your Russian origin?" I said, casting a deliberate look at Kaminsky. He was about to say something, but Rita got ahead of him:

"I think this means that we must immediately end this discussion, and head to the beach and let the passions cool off!"

Yes, the situation was quite tense. Nobody said anything to Rita's proposition, and she demonstratively began to clear the dishes from the table. Astrid offered to help her, but just then, Kaminsky leaned over to my nymph. He must have whispered some inappropriately frivolous things. Astrid retorted tersely, "He's *most definitely* a Jew. And he did not disappoint me. With you, though, everything's kind of vague."

"No, it's all very clear. I'm a cosmopolitan."

Rita slammed down the plates, and Turkin said, "Cosmopolitanism is a form of entropic mimicry."

"My sister, Anahid, teaches in the Oriental Studies department," Dr. Ahmet said, a sweet smile having returned to his face.

"One of her research projects is called *The Cosmopolitanism of the Peoples of Asia Minor in Antiquity.*"

"Your blood sister?" Astrid cried out.

The beach at Little Compton was semi-wild. To clarify, the beach itself was quite civilized, with bathrooms and showers, but the spirit of wilderness and of boundless space dominated the scenery. Moreover, there was a big cliff about twenty yards from the shore. The cliff was so sharp-edged that for some reason it made me think of the toothy steel-and-concrete fortifications of the Mannerheim Line, which girded the Karelian Isthmus back in the days of my postwar childhood in Leningrad. Even at low tide, swimming over to the cliff and climbing onto its ledges would have been a challenging proposition, and especially so on the windswept afternoon of our visit with the Turkins. The tidal water had covered half the beach. Those who were sunbathing, or, rather, hiding under their beach blankets with shirts and sweaters pulled on, had moved up to where the beach met the dominion of whitish coarse sedge soaked with the ocean's bitter salt. We had all been heated up by the drinks the Turkins had been serving with the usual generosity—and the number of the consumed drinks had been growing proportionately with the amount of time we had spent sitting around the Turkins' table. We had all been warmed up by the drinks and by arguments. Nobody took heed of the waves that rolled onto the shore with such speed and force that it threatened to throw back anyone who attempted to swim out to the cliff.

Men are capable of losing their heads over women with gorgeous legs. Women with gorgeous legs don't have to dominate in philosophical discussions. But they always win en plein air. Outside, in the sack, in the sand dunes. Briefly: Astrid proposed a contest to the three of us (Kaminsky, Dr. Ahmet, and me). You swim over to the cliff, climb onto a ledge, dive back in, make a circle around the cliff and return to shore. The winner gets a prize.

"What's the prize?" Dr. Ahmet inquired.

"*Amerikanka!*" Astrid answered in Russian, not doubting for a second that everyone could understand the value of this prize: the fulfillment by her, Astrid, of the winner's wish, any wish.

The Turkins were splashing near the shore, having had enough of our company.

We set out. Each of us swam his own course but kept turning around to check on his rivals' progress. Swimming toward the cliff was just as easy as in calm weather. The cliff itself protected us from the wind. We reached it and stopped to rest, holding on to the rocks. There the water was still relatively calm. We climbed onto the ledge. Astrid ardently waved from the shore.

"Well, gentlemen, let's dive in and keep swimming," proposed Kaminsky. I nodded in agreement, but Dr. Ahmet said, with a contrite smile, "I think I'm out. I'm afraid I can't handle the cliff. The winds are strong, and I'm a lousy swimmer."

Dr. Ahmet got down from the ledge and swam for the shore. It was now just Kaminsky and me, which was all for the better. Destiny itself had arranged for Kaminsky to become my sole rival. I forgot all about Dr. Ahmet. I hated Kaminsky and was thirsting for revenge, because only revenge can cure the suffering caused by hatred. Kaminsky had made me suffer from the moment he arrived at the Turkins'. His revolting way of masking his own, so unmistakably apparent, Jewishness with cheap talk about cosmopolitanism, the vapidness of his soul mimicking as wit, and even his field, the study of chameleons (what a fateful overlap of personality and occupation!)—all of this provoked my irritation, bitterness, and revulsion. Everything about him made me suffer, hate, and desire revenge. Believe me, I didn't feel a drop of jealousy. In fact, I didn't feel jealous toward Dr. Ahmet, whose return to shore— and to Astrid—was obviously a subterfuge. And the woman herself couldn't possibly stir up my jealousy, because I wasn't even in love with her. The evening prior to our visit to the Turkins', something short-lived had been ignited: a beautiful woman, a shared language of home, an imitation of a long-forgotten romantic behavior. But after taking a closer look—and listen—at the Turkins' home, I became deeply disappointed in her, although I continued to play the part of a man in the throes of passion. That was why I had agreed to take part in the stupid swimming competition. I acted the part and played along with the others. I had consented precisely because I didn't want the chameleonologist to get Astrid. I hated Kaminsky and I didn't want him to get this pliant woman with gorgeous legs and swarthy supple breasts.

I was eleven or twelve when I first realized that I was capable of suffering from hatred and of thirsting for revenge. It happened onboard tram No. 18, which I usually took to get from my house on Leningrad's Vyborg Side to my grandmother's. She lived on the Petrograd Side. During the war, my father had left mother and me for another woman. My paternal grandmother was that power line that connected my fatherlessness with the normal daily living of a Jewish family. I was standing amid other passengers in the back of the train car, my right hand clutching a metal handle mounted on a wooden seat. A happy-looking family occupied the seat: a father, a mother, and a boy my age. The father was wearing a colonel's uniform. The Military Academy of Signal Corps was not far from my house, and the colonel must have been employed there. I had no doubt that, like myself, those people were Jews. But the father's greatcoat and colonel's astrakhan hat, which poked at my chin, the boy's fluffy rabbit fur hat, and the woman's fox coat—these were attributes of prosperity, and they separated me from them. Those three were no less foreign to me than were all the rest of the passengers on the train. They were foreign in their own fashion. To them, I was like a fallen leaf, a Jewish kid from an outlying working-class area of Leningrad. A Jewish kid without a father, dressed in a poor, patched-up coat.

Just another stranger on the train. A stranger to them and to the others. Alone in the world. And those three pretended not to notice me, as if they were ashamed of our connection. For this alone I already hated them, and then the boy in the rabbit fur hat whispered to his father, and quite loudly, "Papa, look, the patch on his coat [that is, on my coat] looks like a military ribbon!" He said this, flung a snide look at me, and giggled. The boy was sitting between his father and his mother. The way I was standing, I had to throw a left hook. And I did. But my hateful and avenging hand was intercepted by the hand of the military man. He saw my face and my tears of anguish and hatred. He understood everything, and let me go.

Dr. Ahmet headed back to shore, and the two of us, for lack of other options, dove off the cliff and swam on. It was difficult to swim. We stayed neck-and-neck. In my heart of hearts, I cursed myself for getting dragged into this foolish game. When we were cutting around the cliff on the ocean side, a heavy wave hit with such force that it threw Kaminsky onto a rocky edge hidden under the water. I saw him go limp. I swam up to him. Blood was gushing from a wound on the back of his head. "Hold on to me!" I yelled, and we swam together. He held on to my shoulders while pushing the layers of water off with his feet. God only knows how I managed to get back to shore with all the extra weight. Strange, the moment I saw him helpless and bleeding, my hatred vanished all at once. The hatred vanished and nothing came to replace it; all that was left was an immense urge to get Kaminsky to shore. I completely forgot about Astrid, about our contest, and about all our arguments at lunch. Everything was wiped out by those wild waves that could easily destroy a person. I have no idea how long it took us, but by the time I dragged Kaminsky onto the beach, nobody else was there. Our clothes lay on the sand. But there was nobody around. The beachgoers had left because of the wind. And

the rest of our group? There was no time to dilly-dally. The blood
from the wound kept oozing.

"Take my shirt. Rip it along the seam. And please don't worry.
Nothing terrible will happen to me. Certainly no more terrible than
. . . ," Kaminsky didn't finish his sentence, and I could sense he was
anxious, but not about the wound. I bandaged his head.

"Let's get back to the Turkins' and decide which of the nearby
hospitals to take you to," I said.

"Thank you for everything. And forgive my cynicism. It's probably just my way of keeping the mask on—someone else's mask.
I'm, you know, one of those few whom they didn't manage to kill
in gas chambers. I was five at the time."

I didn't know what to say.

At that point Astrid and Dr. Ahmet had caught up with us. "It
was cold, so we decided to go for a quick jog along the beach. The
Turkins have gone home to get the grill going. To make *shashlyk*,"
said Astrid.

Dr. Ahmet noticed Kaminsky's pallor and the bandage, and
asked what had happened.

We briskly walked back to the Turkins' house. It was the latter half of August. Along the sides of the road, beach plums still
showed pink blossoms, through which the ripening cupolas of the
fruit blustered like blood. Kaminsky kept trying to crack jokes, as if
to convince us that he wasn't worried about his wound, while the
rest of us walked on in silence. How ridiculous our earlier conversations must have seemed to us, how artificial in comparison to reality: the waves, the strike, the gushing wound. Astrid was probably
feeling worse than any one of us—after all, she was the one who
had gotten us embroiled in this game.

When we got back to the Turkins', Dr. Ahmet drove Kaminsky
to the nearest hospital, and Astrid asked me to take her back to
Providence.

"What about the *shashlyk*?" Rita protested.

"Maybe some other time, if you'll have me back," Astrid replied.

"Next time we might not have such a flamboyant group," Turkin said, joking.

I kept silent because I was inclined to leave immediately and take Astrid with me. If it hadn't been for her, I would have had a lovely day, without getting involved in unresolvable ethnic and ethical debates. I mean, Astrid had served as the catalyst of the arguments that had ended so badly for Kaminsky. If it hadn't been for her. . . . But here I caught myself thinking that if it hadn't been for Astrid, I would never have known the taste of those swarthy breasts draped in the silky shawl of her luxuriant hair, or heard the guttural moans and tender repetitions of her fading entreaty: "Pyotr jan, jan, jan. . . ." So it wasn't about her, after all. Or at least she wasn't to blame. She was a woman and lived her life guided by the feminine stimuli that I could never fathom, especially since every woman has her own unique set of rules and answers for every twist of fortune.

Turkin had gone off to check on the grill. The smoke lazily crawled into the veranda where Astrid and I were standing. Was it the smoke, like a genie escaped from a bottle of oblivion, that whispered into my ear how to translate my primitive revenge into a symbol, a metaphor? Or had the answer been there all along, undergoing a series of metamorphoses over the years: from the straightforward revolt of an insulted youth, through the bared teeth of my truth-seeking writings, and finally, to the fortuitous discovery (". . . the more fortuitous, the more genuine . . .") of a phantom of revenge, a version of the Japanese scarecrows created in order to quell people's wrath? Like substitution therapy? Like mimicry of a real crime? Like Rita's marionettes? The bloodthirsty Turk from the Balkan fairy tale! That was the key that had wound up the spring of the whole imbroglio.

Rita went back to the kitchen. Astrid and I were alone on the veranda. In the living room, a CD of Utyosov's old album was playing on the sound system: "'Tis hard to live, my friend, without a friend in this small world. . . ." It was hard for me to live alone. Without a girlfriend, among American women who didn't get me. I didn't get them, either. And while I knew that the night I got to spend with Astrid was a matter of chance, a stroke of heaven-sent luck, without that single night, thousands of other nights of my masculine aloneness would have been too hopeless. "'Tis hard to live, my friend, without a friend in this small world. . . ." I put my arm around Astrid's shoulders and said, "Darling, trust me, it's not your fault at all. Not even a little bit. We were joking around, talking, and having a good time. Everything happened by accident. A concurrence of circumstances. Let's stay just a little longer, at least until Kaminsky and Dr. Ahmet get back."

I went to the kitchen and brought back some vodka for both us. We drank it up.

"And you, aren't you mad at me?" she asked.

"I like you a lot," I replied and kissed her on the neck.

Turkin was still fussing over the fire. It had rained the day before, and the coals were damp; they smoked, yet refused to smolder. The grilling of *shashlyk* was still a long way off. Rita and Astrid were setting the table in the living room. I pretended I was going to the bathroom, but instead slipped into Rita's workshop. Darkness was falling outside. I didn't want to turn on the light. And I didn't need to. A black fire burned in the Turk's awesome eyes. Threatening and warning me, the Turk (nobody was pulling at his strings) waved his scimitar over my ear. I barely evaded the blow. He gave me a bloodthirsty smirk. I took the Turk off the hook, shoved him under my shirt, and went outside.

The grill was now smoking with might and main. The coals were burning. Headlights pierced the darkness and a car rolled up to the house. I heard Kaminsky and Ahmet enter the house. They were talking about a hospital and about bandages. Their voices were assertive, excited, and happy. It was obvious that everything had turned out fine. I had to hurry. I approached the grill, removed the top grate, and put the Turk onto the coals. I heard somebody's steps on the porch. Crazy rodents of fire ran up the marionette's strings. The Turk in a death shroud was floating on the waves of the flame. I couldn't tear my eyes off him. Someone ran down the porch, and came up to the grill and embraced me. "Take me back to your place right now, Pyotr jan." I slammed the grate back over the fire. We walked onto the road, where my car was parked on the side. We drove, headlights off, to the first turnoff. I stopped the car in a dark alley going down to the beach, and we started kissing madly.

1996
Translated from the Russian by Margarit T. Ordukhanyan

Where Are You, Zoya?

For Charlie and Natalie

Zamkin called and invited us to stay at his summer house. His dacha on Cape Cod. The Zamkins are American Jews whose ancestors hailed from Russia. Zamkin's grandfather arrived in New York on the same steamer with Sholem Aleichem. There was no way of telling where the Zamkins got their family name. Was it from the Russian word *za*mok, meaning "castle," za*mok*, meaning "lock," or from the name of an ancestor who was known in their shtetl as "Zyamka"? Zamkin and his wife, Dorothy, like to offer patronage to Russian expatriates. Especially former refuseniks like ourselves. Every summer the Zamkins invite me, my wife, and my son to stay for a week at their summer house. The house stands on top of a hill, surrounded by a pristine pine forest. Just a little further on, the forest parts. Once, this land belonged to a golf club. But now it's just ungroomed mounds overgrown with tall grass; little ponds with throaty frogs. Deserted slopes where slippery jacks and yellow mossy mushrooms grow in plenty under the tall pines.

As a rule, Zamkin greets us at the foot of the hillock on which his house stands; he walks in front of our car, directing my ascent up the winding asphalted path. On the second day I get accustomed to this serpentine road and no longer drive over the Gerbera daisies and nasturtiums planted on both sides of the asphalt and buzzing with bees. I relearn to go swiftly down without knocking over a single one of the pegs with the red reflectors. But on the first day, Zamkin directs me.

We park our truly little Fordik beside the garage, so that Zamkin can freely maneuver his big Cadillac. We park our Fordik, take out our bags, and carefully carry a box with a wrapped vase into the house. This is a gift for the Zamkins from the three of us.

Berta Yakovlevna lugs her own present. Her other things we have already taken in from the car. Berta Yakovlevna is our indispensable companion in vacationing at the Zamkins'. Not that she gets imposed on us. Not in the least. We have grown attached to Berta Yakovlevna, and back in Worcester, after a few weeks, we even miss her if we don't speak on the phone. But then again, telephone friendship isn't the same as in person: "How's your health? You wouldn't happen to need help?" Of course, vacationing with one's own family is much more comfortable. However, we immigrants can't be too choosy. And in this case, there's no other choice. The Zamkins love to lump their guests together.

On the first day, without fail, we discuss literary subjects. Berta Yakovlevna, naturally, is the center of attention. A prima donna of such literary conversations. She is the widow of the celebrated Jewish poet Gankin, who wrote in Yiddish. This is the exact reason why the Zamkins are so fascinated with her. Yiddish literature is their passion. After a day or two, the Zamkins usually go back to their main residence in central Massachusetts and leave the four of us at the Cape house. Berta Yakovlevna cannot be alone in a house surrounded by woods. Who knows, maybe it's because of her that we get invited. So it is possible that it's we who are her dacha companions, and not the other way around.

"So, what's new?" asks Zamkin, while his wife Dorothy bustles about in the kitchen. She's making a traditional *shabes* lunch. The Zamkins are very comfortably off, but they still cook and do the housecleaning themselves. We always arrive on Saturday around eleven or noon, and leave the following Saturday, after having breakfast and tidying up the house. "So, what's new?" Zamkin asks all of us, but we know that his question is first and foremost directed to Berta Yakovlevna.

"Surely you've discovered something new and wonderful!" confidently adds Dorothy, sliding the noodle kugel into the oven.

Dorothy loves the word "wonderful." *Wonderful poems, wonderful flowers, wonderful sprats, wonderful people.* Wonderful! It goes without saying that the conversation between us and our hosts is conducted in English. When we become tired or don't understand our hosts, or when they have reached a deadlock, courtesy of our barbaric pronunciation and limited vocabulary, help comes in the form of Slavik, who is fifteen. We've been living in America for eight years. For him, English is a second native language. Ira, my wife, is a programmer. Her English is fairly good, although other languages are much more important to her: COBOL, Fortran, C+. . . . My English is acceptable only in applied math. In my own work, I devise models to describe the rate of development of tumorous cells. Both in normal conditions and with chemotherapy. But communications are especially difficult for Berta Yakovlevna. For her, we're both her *translators* and her *transporters* across the shores of the English language. Without us, she would be silent and still. This is another reason for our companion visits to the Zamkins' dacha.

Sometimes the Zamkins' questions seem not quite tactful from our Russian point of view. American mentality is different from ours. The Americans either stun us by their self-restraint, or they are too uninhibited, too naturalistic. But we're friends, and the Zamkins are not embarrassed to ask. Every year they (and we too, whether we want it or not) learn something new about the late husband of Berta Yakovlevna.

Berta Yakovlevna's husband was famous even before the war. Many of his poems, after being translated from Yiddish into Russian, became lyrics of popular Soviet songs. And his poems for children were so popular that no one even thought about their authorship and original language. It seemed as though these poems had been around forever. But without a legend, even a very talented poet cannot become truly famous. One needs a literary legend. Not to say that a poet should sculpt himself into a legend. Of course this happens, too, but such mannequins quickly crumble. A genuine legend finds the poet and makes him truly famous. That's exactly what happened with Berta Yakovlevna's husband, the poet Gankin. He was a wartime correspondent for an army newspaper. Naturally, he wrote for this paper in Russian. In August of 1944, Soviet troops came upon a site of mass executions of Jews outside Kovno (Kaunas), in Lithuania. Gankin conducted an investigation. It turned out that Jews were murdered by *polizei* recruited from the local population. Gankin wrote a long poem which was instantly published in Russian translation and read by the whole country. Then came the year 1949, and state security remembered this long poem, arresting Gankin on charges of Zionism and of inciting hostility among the peoples of the USSR. The poet was sent to the Gulag. He died just a few months shy of 1956, when they started releasing political prisoners. The site of his grave was unknown. The whole time, he wrote poetry and prose. He composed in Yiddish, translated his own work, and passed his texts to fellow camp inmates. "So that something may survive," he said. And indeed from time to time his manuscripts would emerge from the abyss of time. These were scraps of newspaper, on which Gankin wrote down his poems, or bits of wallpaper, or even layers of birch bark on which he scratched out his texts. Berta Yakovlevna corresponded with literary scholars who studied her husband's works, and she was on top of the latest findings.

Every summer it's as if we have arrived for a screening of a new episode in the film about the poet Gankin, narrated by Berta Yakovlevna.

"So what new and extraordinary things have you learned this year?" asks Dorothy Zamkin. And Berta Yakovlevna shares with us that she received a letter from Nizhneangarsk, a fishing town on the shore of Lake Baikal. Or rather, a letter first came to one of the literary scholars, who then forwarded a copy to Berta Yakovlevna in America. The letter was from a nurse who cared for Berta Yakovlevna's husband as he lay dying in the camp infirmary. The nurse had long since retired from practice and was a pensioner. In addition to the letter, the envelope contained an unknown poem by Gankin. The poem was about a wondrous bird, who arrives to return the lyrical hero to freedom and love. The name of the old nurse was Zoya.

Berta Yakovlevna finishes the new installment, reads the poem, drinks up her cup of coffee, and wipes her lips, waiting for our reaction. And we just sit in silence, because we're afraid of destroying some tender fabric, a song ringing in the distance, the lilac blossoms of marsh tea over Lake Baikal—everything that has entered the poem. The Zamkins wait patiently while Slavik translates the letter and the poem for them, line by line. Then this part of the program ends. Zamkin brushes away a stray tear. "Wonderful!" Dorothy exclaims. My wife hugs Berta Yakovlevna. And I put on a show, pretending to be staring at a blueberry shrub beyond the French doors which open onto a little clearing separating the house and the woods. It turns out that older men can also be sentimental.

Americans are very proactive. They can shed a tear, feel bad for you, show empathy, but after all this, without fail, they will want to do something.

"What are you planning to do, my dear Berta?" asks Zamkin.

"I wrote a letter to Zoya, the retired nurse in Nizhneangarsk. I want to go there to meet with this woman and to find my husband's grave."

"Wonderful idea!" exclaims Dorothy.

The three of us are astounded by the news. And also a little perplexed. How will Berta Yakovlevna, at her age, travel to Lake Baikal in Eastern Siberia? Alone, without support, practically without funds. Even getting to Cape Cod is an annual super-objective for her. But we don't say anything. From the Americans we have adopted self-restraint, having learned not to breach another's heart with superficial and unsolicited advice.

We're getting ready to disperse to our rooms, in order to unpack, take a quick rest, and get ready for the long-awaited walk up and down the hillocks, when suddenly something quite extraordinary occurs. A miracle of coincidence takes place not in a dream, but right there before our eyes. Mystical parallel lines of fate have intersected across time and space. A big bird lands in the clearing outside the Zamkins' dacha. It's just a little smaller than a heron. The bird, more than anything, resembles an ostrich, but is a little shorter. About the size of a large wood grouse. The bird's plumage is colored in chocolate hues. The coloring of her long tail is lighter than the wings: brown stripes striating white squares. On her breast, the bird sports a coquettish white curl. Around her neck is what looks like a red scarf. Her head seems to be studded with red rubies, and above her prominent yellow-grey beak there's a bright red growth in the shape of a rudder. We rapturously stare at the miracle-bird while Berta Yakovlevna, bedazzled, whispers: "This is Zoya. Zoya has flown here to see us!" Each of us utters something ecstatic along the lines of Dorothy's stock phrase "wonderful," and Zamkin runs for the camera.

The bird Zoya. Right away we start calling her "Zoya." Slavik, who's into ornithology, immediately identifies Zoya as an Eastern Wild Turkey, truly an American bird, miraculously surviving here since the time when Native Americans were the only local residents. Slavik quietly slides open the French doors and throws Zoya some bread crumbs. And we observe with trepidation how she picks up bread from the ground, now and then casting hesitant glances at Slavik. In turn, each of us gives her something to try. Berta Yakovlevna is the last to come out to the clearing with a handful of oat flakes, and she's the only one Zoya allows to get closer. The bird fearlessly trusts her alone. Zoya displays various signs of disposition toward Berta Yakovlevna; emitting tender calls, she stands on one leg just for her, stretches her neck, spreads out her tail shaped like a wigwam, opens her glossy wings like a gorgeous fan.

The next day the Zamkins depart, leaving us with supplies of various grains and flakes in colorful cardboard boxes: oats, wheat, and rice. In the morning we eat these cereals with milk and offer Zoya various treats. We stroll through the hillocks, picking mushrooms and berries. We relish those days on Cape Cod.

From then on, Zoya began to visit to us often. Sometimes two or three times a day. She became especially attached to Berta Yakovlevna. And Berta Yakovlevna, too, felt an inexplicable bond with our guest from the woods. She now stayed behind at the dacha when we went walking in the woods or drove to the beach.

Berta Yakovlevna would wait for the bird, then she fed Zoya practically out of her hands. But we also knew that walking for hours along the hilly fringes of the pine forest in search of mushrooms and berries was getting to be harder and harder for her.

It's Friday, the eve of our return to Worcester, and we set out for another walk without Berta Yakovlevna. She stays behind at the dacha.

"I'm going to feed Zoya. And I want to bake a farewell desert—blueberry pie," says Berta Yakovlevna. She's an extraordinary master of baking pies. And we've picked a ton of blueberries during this stay at the Zamkins' dacha.

The three of us exit the dacha: Ira, Slavik, and I. In my hands I hold a bag for mushrooms, and Ira and Slavik each carry a jar for the berries. Along the path, which was cleared between heather shrubs, we make our way to where the edge of the woods yields to the abandoned golf course—mounds girded by cart paths overgrown with tall grass. Here and there one can still see pegs with peeling paint and also barely discernable holes. From time to time one of us finds a small, hard, white plastic ball. This time Slavik raises a ball with red stripes and shouts: "Papa-Mama! This is for good luck!"

Just the three of us. No one can interfere with our happiness. In another three or four years Slavik will leave for a faraway university, and we will remember these walks as the best days of our lives.

"But Berta Yakovlevna is all alone," says Ira. "We should probably have her over for dinner when we return to the city."

"Definitely we should," I agree and kiss her on the neck.

Here at the cottage Slavik is with us all the time. He sleeps in an adjacent room. I've missed being with Ira. We climb down to a little pond which looks like an orb of mystery in the woods. The little pond is set in a border of green arrows and brown maces of reeds. All at once the frogs tear from the bank into the water, as if in a swimming competition. And there is our first mushroom. It's a slippery jack. It has a tiny lacquered beret shining in the sun and a playfully curved stalk. Then we come across a purple *syroezhka*— a Russula mushroom, which, according to its Russian name, may be "eaten raw." More and more slippery jacks, mossy mushrooms, little bushes of silvery blueberries and thickets of dark-purple black-berries. We rejoice like children. We eat berries and stack mushrooms in the bag. For a time, we don't think of Berta Yakovlevna.

"What cavemen we are!" Ira finally says. "We're pigging out, and she's all alone at the house."

The birds call out to each other. Grasshoppers chirp. A dragon-fly hangs frozen in flight. Each voice can be heard clearly, because it's so extraordinarily quiet in these woods.

Then, suddenly, the roar of an engine reaches us from below the nearby hillock that the abandoned golf course stretches onto, and we see a yellow monster on steel tracks moving in our direction. The yellow excavator brings to mind a dinosaur. About fifty yards from us the excavator stops, extends its neck, aims for the rock bed, and sinks its voracious teeth into the side of the hillock.

"This is the end," says Ira.

"All the mushrooms will be ruined," says Slavik.

"This will scare away the birds," I say.

We hear a response—the flapping of wings. And we see a big brown bird, flying out of a pine tree growing on the hillock which has just been pierced by the excavator's scoop.

"That's our Zoya," says Ira.

"She'll be scared and fly away forever," says Slavik.

"Berta Yakovlevna will be terribly upset," I add.

We don't want to distress Berta Yakovlevna, especially since tomorrow morning we'll be leaving, saying our farewells to the Zamkins' house in the woods—and to Cape Cod—until next summer. Maybe things will turn out okay after all?

We see that Berta Yakovlevna is distressed. A premonition? Or perhaps we're imagining things? There she is, baking a pie, but she's doing it as if by rote, without her usual enthusiasm. In the previous years, the farewell blueberry pie has been her religious rite, a special ritual, a tradition of our small community. Serving us another piece of pie on a plate, Berta Yakovlevna would repeat: "To make a pie or poem without getting tired, you need, my dear friends, to feel inspired!" But today . . . Berta Yakovlevna puts the pie on the table, waits for us to finish drinking tea, and wishes us good night. We trip over one another to praise the pie and say how wonderful it will be to see her once again in the summers to come. But she's barely listening, anxious or distressed about something. We don't ask her anything, because we don't want to tell her anything about the yellow excavator, the one that frightened Zoya. Upon reaching the middle of the stairs, which go up from the hallway to the second floor where the bedrooms are, Berta Yakovlevna stops and says in a soft voice: "Right before you came back from your walk, Zoya stopped by. I wanted to feed her, but she didn't take anything. A bad sign." And Berta Yakovlevna retires to her room.

The next morning we head back home to Worcester. In the car Berta Yakovlevna is once again her usual self. In earnest she's talking about the trip to Siberia.

"You know, Zoya from Nizhneangarsk saw my husband in the last days of his life. She knows where he is buried," says Berta Yakovlevna.

"We will help you get ready," suggests Ira.

"I have a map of Siberia," remembers Slavik.

"I'll take you to Logan airport and guide you through boarding," I say.

"Thank you, my darlings," answers Berta Yakovlevna, and shines her amiable, intelligent smile at us.

Upon her return, Berta Yakovlevna sent a letter to Nizhneangarsk by airmail, to the retired nurse Zoya. The letter stated that she (Berta Yakovlevna Gankina) would be flying to Nizhneangarsk in a month to meet the person who saw off her late husband, the poet Gankin, on his final journey. If possible, the letter requested, write back and confirm that you are ready to meet and assist (Zoya, that is, to meet and assist Berta Yakovlevna).

Days flew by in the preparations. Ira helped out as much as possible. Presents were purchased for nurse Zoya and her family. "No doubt Zoya has a husband," Berta Yakovlevna mused. "And a daughter. Or son. And they have husbands or wives. And of course Zoya has grandchildren."

She never received a reply from Nizhneangarsk. Berta Yakovlevna waited until the beginning of October. Then she called the local hospital in Nizhneangarsk. They told her that the retired nurse Zoya Nikolaevna Bikalyova had passed away in the middle of August. That is, just when we were staying on the Cape with the Zamkins. We did our best to comfort Berta Yakovlevna. We visited her, invited her over to our place, and even called the Zamkins, our very good friends. What if they could think of anything to distract Berta Yakovlevna from her bitter thoughts? But the Zamkins had left for a guided trip to Spain. Berta Yakovlevna was inconsolable. One day (and to this day we blame ourselves for not attaching significance to this) Berta Yakovlevna said to Ira over the phone: "I told you that it was a bad omen that the bird Zoya was so distraught. She was warning me about this misfortune."

Another week went by. Maybe more. Who counts the autumn weeks! Ira was occupied at work, and so was I. Slavik had school. I do remember exactly that about ten days before Thanksgiving, Ira called Berta Yakovlevna to invite her to our place for a holiday dinner. Berta Yakovlevna wasn't home. Ira called the next day, and then began calling morning, noon, and night. Was it conceivable that Berta Yakovlevna could have gone away, or flown to Siberia without notifying us, her only local friends? The next Saturday, Ira and I drove over to her place. The door was locked. Her neighbors said that they hadn't seen Berta Yakovlevna in several days.

"You know, and what if? God forbid, of course, but these things happen. Let's drive down to the Cape, to the Zamkins' dacha," Ira suggests. She's the shrewd one. Sometimes it amazes me how my Ira can foresee a potential problem. Or has a premonition of something.

We drive in silence. We don't even turn on the radio. The roadside woods are madly painted in ochre and vermilion. How empty is Bourne Bridge, connecting the mainland to Cape Cod! How dead the canal and its banks! A solitary barge edges across the bluish waves. Even the seagulls have gone into hiding. There's the road to the Zamkins' dacha. Now we're at the paved circle with a flower bed in the middle. From here the torturous little paths go up the hill to the cottages.

We leave our Fordik in the circle below. We climb the path to the Zamkins' dacha. It's locked up. We walk around. No one's there.

"It was silly of us to drive down here," I say.

"I sure hope I made a mistake," Ira replies.

"Mama-Papa, let's check out the golf course," Slavik proposes.

We walk along the overgrown paths and abandoned grounds. We look about every shrub, every hollow, every hillock. We circle the pond, but we see nothing suspicious. In the end we find ourselves at the hillock, there where an excavator rumbled last summer, where we saw a big bird scared by the roar of the yellow monster. Beneath our feet is a deep foundation pit. There is someone lying at the bottom of the pit. We're scared to look and we don't want to believe it. Slavik wants to climb down, but we stop him. We know that in this country, for every situation there are rules and regulations one needs to follow. We run back to the car. We dash off to the nearest bar, where there is a phone. We call the police.

Unfortunately, it is our Berta Yakovlevna. She probably fell over into the foundation pit, couldn't crawl out, and died. Next to her lies a box of oat flakes, which our Zoya loved so much.

1996

Translated from the Russian by Margaret Godwin-Jones

Alfredick

He just won't leave me alone. Won't get out of my head. Lanky. Bony. Back in the day we used to call the likes of him "carcasses." There's so much I could tell him! So much I could pin up to his egg-shaped memory. . . . It would surely give him pause! He would be sitting there in the personnel cafeteria of Moscow's Sheremetyevo International Airport, digesting my words over a cup of coffee with a sweet roll. Stirring his coffee and biting on a sweet coffee roll dusted with powdered sugar, like a winter hat sprinkled with mothball flakes. Mulling over my words and spreading them on the roll. For me it would be a duel. For him, an interpretation of paragraph X or Y in the *emergency manual*, a paragraph whereby the jurisdiction of the customs police yields to the jurisdiction of the secret police.

Lanky . . . Bony . . . No, perhaps not so. A particular type in mind, I've misspoken . . . mistyped. We tend to think that elongated or lanky creatures with narrow bone structure must be *bony*. Not at all! First of all, as far as anatomy units are concerned, we all have the same number of bones. Second of all, a lamprey is fatty and entirely boneless. And an eel? And how about worms? No, he was long and gristly. Bald like a sand shark. A bald sand shark grinning piously after it accidentally gets caught on a fisherman's hook. His whole body, clad in a gray uniform jacket and gray officer's trousers with piping, would wriggle around the simple joints and hinge on the compound and complex joints. His ears worked faster than radar intercept devices. His nose poked around the suitcases, pecking out of them anything of value to the country I was finally leaving: a tiny elephant made of African tusk, a towel colored with apoplectic roosters, a little note scribbled on the back of a cherished photo. I can't imagine I was the only one to think of his resemblance to eels or lampreys.

You stand for a long time with your cart in line at customs. You wait for your suitcases—packed for your future life as an émigré—to be inspected. For all my sins, surely I wasn't the only one standing in the long customs line to think that his long, gristly, meandering form constituted this type's innermost quality. And isn't form in itself nature's device of molding the contents of the genetic code into the living art of an individual? A device of inimitability. And on top of all the above, the first name of this customs police captain was "Alfred." Not exactly a common name for our swampy latitudes. His parents must have been fond of Verdi's *La Traviata*, where the young lover is called Alfredo.

Alfredo-Alfred-Alfredick-Dick.

"Alfred Andreevich . . . ," his fellow customs officers respectfully addressed the captain. He was the shift supervisor on the day when my luggage was searched. My memory should have responded right away! But at the spur of the moment, as I was called out to be screened with X-rays, mine detectors, or Lord knows what else—for I honestly don't know what equipment they used or what they were screening me for—as my name was called out, Dick's story had completely slipped my mind.

I kept repeating the same thing over and over again to myself: Just please let this be over soon! I have to go through it, to bear my dear motherland's farewell kiss. This wasn't fear, even though all comprising elements of fear were present: obedience, doom, lack of willpower, dejection, unresponsiveness, dulled senses. Dominos pieced together in haste. It wasn't fear, because a man losing the land of his birth has nothing to fear. Nothing to be afraid of. No, this was not fear. And yet, I tried to be polite and cooperative, and also did my best not to stick out, so as to avoid recognition. I tried to dodge an exchange with Dick, even though we would have had plenty to remember. Now in retrospect, I could easily come up with an analytical case history. Something along the lines of a discharge note about the patient by the name of "Dick-Alfredick". . . .

About ten years before I emigrated, I was living a normal life as a citizen of an abnormal country. One day I was invited to dinner at my neighbors' apartment. The invitation was made casually, on the same day, rather than with a month's notice, as is customary in the land where I've since found refuge. My neighbors lived on the eighth floor, just two flights of stairs up from me. I was invited over by the Sculptor. This is what I'm going to call him, the Sculptor. The Sculptor's wife came from a distinguished literary family. They both—the Sculptor and his pedigreed wife—took a certain interest in me. It was a kind of affinity, albeit camouflaged by their cultured and cosmopolitan behavior. An affinity they felt for the man with whom they shared Jewish ancestors in Ukraine, Belarus, Poland, Lithuania, Germany—and before that, in the Holy Land.

I came to dinner a little late, because at first I couldn't talk my lady friend of the day into joining me. Eventually, she gave in. We arrived when the bottles had already been unsealed and uncorked. Also unsealed was a bowl of lettuce leaves rolled and stuffed with strands of whitish-pink crabmeat. And just as we came in, the contents of another salad dish were rolling into the plates on tomato chunks (like a bullock cart) and cucumber slices (like a push bike). Dinner conversation was just starting.

"Sit down, fill your glasses and your bodies," the Sculptor joked. "And please feel at home."

"They actually are at home," the Sculptor's wife observed. "This is Kirsch, our dear neighbor, an ethnographer by trade. And this is his friend Sonya. Sonya is a professor of Gothic and Lithuanian."

"Gothic and Lithuanian? Did I hear it right?" asked one of my neighbors' guests, a man wearing a red wig.

"Yes, and she also translates from Gothic into Lithuanian and back," our hostess tried to make a joke. And she immediately received a friendly rebuke from Sonya: "Into Lithuanian, that's true, but not into Gothic—this sort of thing hasn't been done for many centuries. One way tickets, only, from Gothic."

We were all having a ball. Then it was time to tell jokes about the bushy-browed Lyonka (Brezhnev), whose plane had by mistake landed in China on the way to Birobidzhan. And how he got off the plane and said to the Chinese, whom he took for the Jews: "Come on, Yids, stop squinting!" The guest in the red wig, whose name was Fred, did a fabulous impression of the senile Soviet leader. With his forefingers he stretched the skin around the slits of his smallish eyes and bellowed with a Ukrainian accent, imitating Brezhnev's voice. We were all having a ball. The other guests joined Fred in telling jokes: "Lyonka rides to the airport wearing a black shoe and a brown shoe. . . . Chapayev, Pet'ka, and Anka the machine-gunner go to Paris . . ." and so forth. One joke after the other.

Fred the red-wigged guest turned out to be a professional man of letters. He wrote detective stories and novelettes and published them in weeklies and anthologies. And he, no doubt about it, was a master of dinner table jokes and stories. Not everybody can simultaneously excel in different areas. I, for instance, am completely monovalent. I can more or less understand the daily lives of ancient Germanic tribes. I write scholarly articles on the subject. I even managed to write a play. But table talk . . . God help me!

Meanwhile, Fred began telling a story: "There was this young lady living in the writers' apartment building . . ."

"Sorry to interrupt, Fred, I just want to make one clarification, and then you can go on," said the Sculptor's wife. "We're talking about a young female who ended up as a grass widow after the death of her husband, the playwright Krotov."

"Thank you, comrade!" Fred said with a mocking intonation, and continued his story. "First she was his literary assistant. They were quite far apart in years. Krotov was eighty-five, she about thirty at that time. But after awhile, as they say, you like it when you get used to it. She became his lawful wife. However, in the writers' apartment house on Chernyakhovsky Street they said behind her back that she was lucky, very lucky to have bewitched and fooled a living literary classic. Two years later the writer Krotov died with state honors and glory, leaving to his young widow a three-bedroom apartment, which had been all paid for. And heaps of money in his will. Plus the copyrights to all his works."

"Wait, wait, isn't that the same Krotov who had started out so famously with a play about the old King of the Goths? The King who gave up his throne for a roving Gypsy girl?" asked my friend Sonya.

"Yes, in the 1920s Krotov did write something along these lines for the Romantic Theater," Fred's girlfriend Alya confirmed. "Back in the day, there used to be a theater by this name . . ."

"Alya knows all about theater. She works in the editorial office of *Stage* magazine," Fred snatched up the thread of the conversation and didn't let go of it again. "Let me tell you what happened next, but first let's have some more *vodochka*." He poured vodka for everybody from a potbellied bottle with a crown of red and gold on the label. Fred raised his glass: "To you, Kirsch, and to your wife . . ."

" . . . who's actually my friend: Sonya," I corrected him. He noticed that I was ogling Alya. She was indeed a looker. Tall, sprightly, blue-eyed. Her hair, the color of red cedar, was tied up in a knot. A lovely forehead, a solicitous face. Blue-eyed and smiley. Fred saw me ogling her and tried to put me in my place. And not for nothing. He knew it wasn't for nothing. And everybody else saw it, too: Alya, Sonya, the Sculptor, and the Sculptor's wife, the one who came from a literary clan. It was she who cleared the air, "So, what happened next with the author's widow?"

"Next happened the most zesty thing," Fred continued. "Six months after playwright Krotov's death, his widow gave birth to twins. Two boys. And so, because all the dates were at least theoretically possible, the two boys—Petya and Pavlik are their names—were registered as the children of the deceased literary classic."

We were now listening without interrupting him with questions. It was clear this wasn't the end of the story. Fred would not have just *planted* all this information without a reason! Curving his arm like a gooseneck, the storyteller managed to remove the potbellied bottle of Smirnoff vodka, adorned with the crown of red and gold, from the table's honor guard of bottles. Fred refilled our glasses and proposed another toast, "To Elmira!"

"Strange though it is," Alya said, "the Gypsy girl from that ancient play of Krotov's was also called 'Elmira.'"

"There are such people, you know, who think they can pull everything together," Fred said. "These people are trouble. Around them, one had better hold one's tongue."

"Is this about me?" Alya asked, daring in her voice.

"Maybe it's about you," Fred replied. "Or maybe about someone else who might get it into his head to write a sequel to Krotov's old play."

"You're being a bit paranoid, Fred! Let him write, what's it to you?" Alya pressed on. "Can't you throw some details Kirsch's way! And you, Kirsch, you'll dedicate the play to Fred, won't you, Kirsch?"

"And Alya will publish this play in *Stage* magazine?" Sonya caught on.

Everybody was quite amused by this prospect. We started joking about the old king (he being the late playwright Krotov) and Elmira, and Elmira's reincarnation from being a Gypsy girl, first

into the king's secretary (i.e. literary assistant to playwright Krotov), and then, later, into his wife. And so on and so forth. With all
this great fun we easily emptied a second bottle of Smirnoff vodka.
The Sculptor and his wife lived quite comfortably and knew how to
throw a good party.

During a short intermission, my friend Sonya asked, or rather
suggested, "But seriously, Alya, wouldn't you be interested and
willing—I mean seriously in the sense of an absolutely real possibility—to read a play Kirsch has already written?"

I was floored. Honestly, I was furious with Sonya. She must
have had too much to drink. Who asked her to speak on my behalf?
It's the author's own business whether to pass his plays around or
keep them in the desk drawer. This was much too much on Sonya's
part, I was thinking, and at this rate we could soon end up saying
our vows. Sonya must have also understood that she had gone too
far. But then again, she didn't do it for her own sake. Well, depend-
ing how you look at it! If you regard the whole situation in terms of
possible and desirable (for Sonya) prospects of marriage to me, then
she didn't go too far at all, but just put in a good word for me at an
opportune moment.

"So you have a play ready to be considered, Kirsch?" Alya asked
me tenderly.

What was I supposed to do? Deny it? It would have been ridiculous! Say that the play had been ready for a long time and was just
waiting for the right director? Then I would have had to summarize
it. And also to reveal the play's dramatic spring, with which I was
especially pleased?

"Let's just say: the play is finished. But it needs a good editor. A
sensitive, friendly, and intelligent editor," I said, and looked Alya in
the eye. She understood. It would have been silly not to.

The Sculptor's wife, a socialite to the bone, rushed to rescue
the situation:

"Kirsch darling, this is all so very exciting. But first things first. Let Fred finish his story about the Gypsy Elmira . . ."

"In *my* story, if you would only let me finish, Elmira was at first a literary assistant, then a wife, and by the end, a widow. Also she was not a Gypsy but a Jewess," Fred explained.

"For each part of the story, a new bottle of Smirnoff," the Sculptor laughed raucously. He was a self-made man whose talent had once been singled out in a crowd of young artists by a young lady from a literary dynasty. She singled out the Sculptor and introduced him to the top generals of Soviet art, launching his career.

We all supported the Sculptor's proposition, and Fred continued: "We left it off where Elmira, the young widow of the deceased playwright Krotov, gave birth to twins six months after his death. Two boys. And so, because the dates were at least theoretically possible, the two boys—Petya and Pavlik are their names—were registered as the children of the deceased literary classic. But, as we all know, 'a holy place is never empty.' People began noticing things. And in the writers' apartment house life is such that while concierges and housekeepers have it in their job description to keep a vigilant eye on the traffic of visitors, the residents themselves work at home—and so involuntarily, they watch out for everything and everybody. So it became known that a certain individual had been paying regular visits to Krotov's young widow, now the young mother of twin boys. Collectively, the residents recalled that this individual had been stopping by even before Elmira gave birth, except previously this information had not been of consequence. Now, retrospectively, they began to recollect, reconstruct, connect the dots, make educated guesses, and so on."

Fred paused to a have a drink. We all joined him for another round.

"And then?" my friend Sonya asked. "What's the point of the story?"

"The point of the story—and you, my dear Sonya, are quite right to press me on that—the point of the story is that after three years (this must have been the term necessary to take full legal possession of her husband's estate and also to dismiss all sorts of suspicions that she had connived her way into an unequal marriage in order to profit from it), Elmira's paramour (she called him 'Dick') demanded that the children be registered under his name. He made her a marriage proposal and demanded that the children be registered under his name. She flatly refused—either to marry him or to declare him the children's father. Moreover, she showed him the door. The reason? Unknown. But she refused to see him. Dick initiated litigation. It went as far as a court trial and legal paternity testing. He claimed to be the father of the twins. What was in it for him, when there was nothing left but hostility between Elmira and him? Certainly no hope of family happiness."

"But there must be other motives besides profit and greed!" said the Sculptor.

"You're quite right, there are other motives. Although sometimes everything is caused by profit and greed," Fred replied.

"I'm going to make some coffee," the Sculptor's wife got up from the table.

"Some bigwigs got involved," Fred continued. "Both literary bosses and those above them. The case was closed. Dick was denied his claim of paternity. He disappeared."

"And so what happened next?" asked Sonya.

"A few months following these stormy developments, Elmira applied for an exit visa to emigrate to Israel."

Silence now reigned over the table. The conversation came to a dead end. Not the conversation topic itself, but emigration did. Our dinner conversation came to a dead end because in those days the subject of Jewish emigration was outside the boundaries of table talk. We had coffee with almond tarts. Then the guests started to get up and thank the hosts for a delicious dinner. Fred and Alya were the first to leave. I followed them to the hallway.

"I'll be waiting for your play about ancient Germans, dear Kirsch," Alya said to me. "Do you know the address of my editorial office?"

I knew it.

"Send it to my attention. I'll read and call you."

"Thank you, Alya, I will."

I never sent my play to *Stage* magazine. I could have done it, of course, but I didn't. Not because of the play, even though I figured its chances of being accepted for publication were zero. Alya, too, was very tempting. A real looker. Tall, sprightly, blue-eyed. But in truth Alya wasn't at all on my radar screen. Nothing else was, except that very *real* story. The memoir with a sequel. The widow of the famous playwright Krotov with young children applied for an exit visa to Israel. How will things turn out for her? How do such stories turn out for people? I abandoned my research projects. I stopped calling Sonya. Possessed by my thoughts, for several nights in a row I had trouble falling asleep until the break of dawn. At the Lenin State Library I asked for an old directory of the Union of Soviet Writers and looked up the telephone number and address of the late playwright Krotov. This directory had been published five or six years ago, when Krotov was still a living literary classic.

I dialed the number. A woman's voice answered the phone. I introduced myself as an ethnographer-Germanist. She asked what was the reason *behind* my call? I answered that I had read an early play by her late husband and was interested in consulting his personal copy of the first edition.

"Leave me your telephone number. I will call if I find it. It's not easy. My house is turned upside down."

I didn't say anything.

"I will call you anyway, even if I don't find it," she added.

She called a week or so later, when I had lost all hope.

I actually hadn't hoped for anything or wanted anything. The first edition of Krotov's early play was just a pretext for meeting Elmira. Was it all because of Dick, her rejected lover? I suppose not. I had never met him. He was of no interest to me. Because of Alya? Perhaps yes, because of Alya, whom I never mailed the play to or called, even though I could have easily cuckolded this repulsive Fred. But what did Elmira or her Dick have to do with any of this, if I only wanted to teach Fred a lesson for ogling my (still mine at that time) friend Sonya during that dinner at the Sculptor's? Yes, yes, and yes! The key to everything was Fred with his garrulous account of the intimate life of one Elmira Krotov, the playwright's widow. This Fred, with all the gastronomic looks he cast at Sonya. Fred who had such a knack for imitating Dick that it felt like he was his double. Doggedly wild guesses took hold of my mind.

Elmira called to ask when would be a good time for me to stop by. She had located the book.

"Whenever you let me," I said.

Her reply was, "Oh, I'm home all day."

"Perhaps some time tomorrow night?" I suggested.

"Very good, Kirsch. At ten. I'll put the boys to bed and then I'll be free. Do you know the address?"

I entered her apartment house with a cake and flowers in hand. A concierge stuck her head out of a glass booth and asked:

"Whom are you here to see?"

I gave her Elmira Krotova's name.

"Is she expecting you?"

I nodded.

"Do you know the apartment number and floor?"

I answered that I knew both.

"Go up one flight of stairs. The elevator is to the right."

I went up and rang the doorbell.

"Well now, why all this, Kirsch! The cake, the flowers. . . ."

I spread my hands in a gesture acknowledging both the genuine truth of her comment and the complete pointlessness of changing anything. Certainly I couldn't toss the flowers out the window and throw the cake in the garbage, could I?

"I guess I'll have to give you tea."

She put the kettle on the stove and placed the flowers in a gallon jar that had originally housed Hungarian pickled cucumbers and tomatoes.

"By the way, the cake is from Budapest. Café Budapest," I made a clumsy joke.

She laughed. Was it at my joke? My clumsiness? Most probably she laughed because she was tired of bad times. She had tasted enough misery and wanted only good things from life. That was already clear to me, based on what Fred had divulged at the Sculptor's dinner party.

"Would it be okay if we had tea in the kitchen?" she asked. "The living room is a total mess, and in the other room there is also a big mess. Plus the kids are sleeping."

"Sure! Of course! There couldn't be a better place!"

"All right then. I'll go get your book. And meanwhile, do you mind cutting the cake?" And she stepped out.

Did I mind? I would have agreed to anything she asked for. Elmira was so beautiful! So enchantingly beautiful. I was smitten by her beauty, the way this sort of thing had happened back in the prehistoric days of my studenthood. The smile never left her face. Her soft hazel eyes gazed at her company (*at me!*) with joy. There was no doubt she liked me, enjoyed my presence, was happy to see me. Although, let truth be told, I don't have the most romantic physique: short legs, weak eyes, a broad chest. And Elmira was a queen from a Judean dynasty. Her raven-black hair, thick and long, fell down to her shoulder blades. She turned her back to me when she went to fetch her late husband's book, and I saw waves of her hair lapping at the oars of her shoulder blades. Elmira was wearing a yellow dress made of a fabric so light that I could all at once see the lapping of her hair, the amphora of her torso, the swaying of her heavenly hips. All this resembled a sea, a boat, rushes.

She brought back the book. The binding, its color a light beige, had tiny cracks, like wrinkles on old women's faces. The publisher's name was printed in proud Latin: ACADEMIA. The title: *THE KING AND THE GYPSY*. And the name of the author: KRO-TOV, who was then a young novelist and playwright, member of the legendary literary group The Serapion Brothers.

"You can borrow it," Elmira suggested. "Browse it at your leisure and then bring it back."

"Don't you have any qualms about letting me borrow it? Aren't you worried that I might 'lose' it?"

"No qualms, and no worries, either. My home is ruined. Books have been given away or sold to book dealers at fire sale prices. I'm not afraid of parting with anything anymore," she said, and started laughing. That was the first time I saw how with laughter she unburdened her heart. With laughter she was breaking the back of some big sadness unbeknownst to me. With the milky quartz of her teeth she bit off the tether anchoring her to that big sadness. She had already repeated a few times that her home was "ruined." Actually, still back at the Sculptor's dinner I had heard of the lawsuit involving Elmira and someone by the name of Dick. But this knowledge was only a background—or else a pretext—for my acquaintance with the woman to whom I had become so inexplicably drawn. This mysterious attraction had predated meeting Elmira in person. It was all like a system of cosmic mirrors, when the light from one star (the heroine of Krotov's play) reached another star (the real Elmira) and was reflected by it at such an angle that it would be bounced by the celestial bodies it met in its path before it would reach the Earth (my imagination). Thus the light from a cosmic Elmira would reach the real me.

I returned the book one week later. I was tempted to do it the next day. Not so much to return the book but to see Elmira again. I came back to return the book in a week, and then I started visiting every day. Directly after work. And on research days, on the way back from the Lenin State Library. Petya and Pavlik got used to me. When I stayed over, Elmira trusted me to give the children breakfast and walk them to day care.

Eventually Elmira told me the story of her marriage to the playwright Krotov. And about meeting a littérateur by the name of Alfred. Alfred-Alfredick-Dick.

"He wanted me to call him Dick. At first I was taken with him. I had been living a lonely life. But one day I learned some things about Dick—things that made any kind of further involvement with him *impossible*."

"What will happen with the children?" I asked.

"I'm taking them away. They will forget Dick. They've almost forgotten him already."

And that was the last time she ever mentioned Alfred who liked to be called by the diminutive name Dick.

It was springtime. The middle of May. Elmira called my office at the Research Institute of Ethnography. "Can you come right now, Kirsch, please!"

"Did you get a visa?"

"Yes."

"Congratulations!"

"Come, please," her voice quivered.

I was helping Elmira pack for the long journey. She had an aunt in Tel Aviv, her late father's sister. Only one day remained before her departure, and my heart was heavy.

I said to Elmira: "I need to get some air. I've got a splitting headache." Actually, I walked over to a store and bought a bottle of cognac. I could have gone there by bus or Metro. But I decided to take a long walk. To Sokol and back. The big store near the Sokol Metro station had a decent liquor department.

When I came back, I saw Fred in the living room, which was crowded with boxes and things. Fred, whom I had met at the Sculptor's dinner party. He wasn't wearing a wig, which confirmed my initial suspicions about his penchant for practical jokes and dress-up. Fred was playing with Petya and Pavlik. Thrilled by their presents, they were driving little remote control cars around the living room.

Elmira said, "Kirsch, this is Dick. Or Alfred Andreevich. He came to say goodbye to the children."

We nodded to each other, pretending we had never met before. A uniform jacket was hanging on the chair, a uniform with the insignia of some special troops unfamiliar to me. A brimmed uniform cap lay on the table. Masquerade again, I thought, confirming my hypothesis.

Several years passed. Not exactly a short time, especially when a man counts each day of his loneliness. Elmira was living in Jerusalem and working for a Russian-language publication. In Israel Petya and Pavlik had started kindergarten, then went to elementary school. Hebrew became their native language, and Israel, their native land. I received a letter of invitation from Israel and submitted an application, but my request was denied. I became a refusenik. The story of Alfred-Alfredick-Dick-Fred had retreated far into the depths of memory. I was in love with Elmira and only wanted to be reunited with her.

Then, finally, I got my exit visa. I packed my books and things, gave away everything I didn't want or need, returned the ownership of my studio apartment to the city of Moscow, and bought a plane ticket from Moscow to Vienna. I went to the Sheremetyevo Airport.

For a long time I stood in line with my luggage cart, waiting to have my suitcases inspected. The luggage contained what I was taking with me to a new life. I was waiting in line when I saw a certain captain of the customs police, a gristly, bald, and slithering type, whom his co-workers respectfully addressed as "Alfred Andreevich."

1987–2003
Translated from the Russian by Emilia Shrayer

Dinner with Stalin

I once read this account by a nineteenth-century Russian memoirist. On the balcony of an opera house, at the end of the 1890s, the memoirist saw Pushkin, as an old man. The memoirist was so struck by this that during the intermission he ran to Pushkin's box to assure the great poet that he had never accepted his death after the duel as real. Pushkin's presence was felt this strongly every minute of every Russian's life. Just before the memoirist reached the box, someone whispered to him that Pushkin's son Aleksandr, already an old man, was present in the theater.

At the beginning of the 1980s I came across another example of such a striking effect brought on by the resemblance of an individual not well known to society—actually, a resemblance to his famous relative. Not long before that, I was expelled from the Union of Soviet Writers and the Literary Fund for having submitted an application to the OVIR—the Visa Office—to emigrate to Israel. I didn't have a paying job. I could have been convicted of parasitism and sent out of Moscow "to the hundred-and-first kilometer"—as people commonly referred to this government action. I had to find a solution. That is, I started to look for some work, not literary work, of course. But I just couldn't find any legal and honorable employment. I turned to a couple of my fellow literati from among those who had not rejected me, had not become frightened of being in contact with a "traitor to the Motherland." Shereshevsky, a colleague whom I had known from translating Lithuanian poetry, suggested a certain writer, whose name I have to change here to a fictitious one, let's say, Krasikov. Even today I see his name mentioned, not often, but I do see it now and again, on the satire and humor page of the *Literary Gazette*. Shereshevsky mentioned Krasikov, and I remembered that there was a time when I used to "send his way" some poetry translation work, if time was of the essence and a particular commission was more than I could handle. To make a long story short, I called Krasikov, we met, and he, if truth be told, without particular enthusiasm but out of a sense of duty, nevertheless did agree to help me become a member of the Moscow writers' local union. This Krasikov was a very important figure in the local writers' union. Considering the times, Krasikov's action (hesitancy aside) was a heroic deed on the part of this writer loyal to the powers that be.

From time to time I was invited to attend a poetry panel at the local writers' union. While the union was the lowest rung of the literary ladder, the verses of my new colleagues were no worse and no better than those read in the poetry section of the Union of Soviet Writers. Since I missed the literary world, I didn't refuse such invitations, but I myself did not read, knowing that my poetry would immediately and totally expose me. An inveterate billiard player, Mitasov, with whom I used to play at the Central House of Writers, read his poetry at one of these events. I had known Mitasov through the poet Shklyarevsky. Mitasov's poetry was saturated with the Voronezh regional dialect; there were many good poems, almost a whole collection. He read vigorously. He did everything vigorously: played billiards, sang Gypsy romances (himself looking quite the Gypsy), and read poetry. There were about twenty people in the room. All of us were listening enthusiastically. Listening to or reading good poetry is like skiing down a mountain slope: you fly by, taking no notice of the mountains or trees that you leave behind on the sides of the trail. So I kept flying down the mountain without immediately noticing that other listeners had come to a halt. I also braked to a stop and noticed that Mitasov was looking somewhere over my head, and the rest of the people sitting in front of me were looking back. Not at me, of course, but looking somewhere over my shoulders. I also turned around. Looming behind the last row of chairs, like the legendary cop Uncle Styopa sprung from the pages of children's verses, was the tall figure of the chief poet of the Soviet land, Sergei Mikhalkov, author of the lyrics to the Soviet national anthem. What was he doing here among the semi-destitute brotherhood of third-rate literati? Could he really have come to hear Mitasov read? Hurray for Mitasov! Mikhalkov stood there for a while and left without saying a word. Mitasov resumed his reading and somehow made it to the end of the trail. Someone, as was the fashion in those harsh years, made some comments about the form and content of the poetry that had just been read. Some praised it, others criticized it.

I left the building together with the distressed Mitasov. "Forget it, don't take it to heart!" I consoled him. "Don't let that Mikhalkov get to you!"

"That's the whole point—it's not *that one*!"

"What do you mean not *that one*? Which one, then?"

"That was the older brother of the *real* Mikhalkov. He's also a member of our local writers' union. They look alike, like twins. Nature graced the Mikhalkov look-alike with the same appearance as his famous brother, but not so with talent. Probably for his own gratification he occasionally appears at some literary events, produces a deafening effect, and departs. Satisfied, like a silent extra on stage made up to look like a celebrity."

I asked Mitasov, "What do you think, do the wax figures in Madame Tussaud's Museum enjoy their fame, if only as the result of one of the visitors' momentary confusion?"

Together Mitasov and I went to the Central House of Army Officers, where he was employed as a billiards coach, and we drank zealously to the success of his next book.

Many years went by. The story I want to tell deposited itself onto the previous ones, like layers of soil, one on top of the other. Push-kin and Balzac liked to create multilayered narratives. Many years went by. My wife, son, and I emigrated and settled in Providence, capital of the smallest US state, Rhode Island. Providence can be compared to Monte Carlo, and Rhode Island to the principality of Monaco. But no matter where one lives, in a village or in a city, in Monte Carlo or in Providence, one is drawn to one's own country-men. Immigrants from Russia and its former colonies are no excep-tion. Over the years a group of us had gravitated to each other. One after another. There was a married couple from Yerevan, both psy-chologists. Another husband and wife, atomic energy experts, were refugees from Nagorno-Karabakh. Then there was a sculptor and his wife, she a painter, both from Moscow. And all the others were also from Moscow: a pair of mathematicians, a historian and his wife the horticulturalist, and finally, myself, an author, and my wife, a transla-tor from Russian to English and vice versa. As members of our circle joked nostalgically, "There and back, there and back again."

We would take turns getting together at each other's homes. More often than not at the apartment of the energy experts from Karabakh, Grisha and his lovely wife Galya. Grisha and Galya's hos-pitality was charged with such volcanic force that it would constantly erupt through the planned, round-robin schedule of the get-togeth-ers in other homes. Without discussing it with us, the members of our circle, Grisha would call us up (and to tell the truth, we would always be happy to hear from him) and announce: "This Friday (or Saturday) a special get-together will take place at my house. The occasion is very deserving. My best friend and schoolmate from Baku (Moscow, St. Pete, Yerevan, Tashkent, Nizhny Novgorod, Tbilisi etc.) is coming to visit. On his way from New York." How could anyone say no to Grisha?

I must admit that the events which unfolded during one such special, sumptuous dinner at Grisha's were provoked by two

amusing incidents, both of them resulting from a similarity of out-
ward appearance. Only a couple of weeks before that special dinner,
during a party at the home of Alyosha the historian and his wife
Tosya, I had just been telling my friends about these two incidents.
It was then that I remembered about the memoirist who mistook
Pushkin's aging son for the great poet himself, as though Pushkin
had survived the duel. And during that very same evening (whatever made me do it!) I also mentioned the incredible resemblance
of the two Mikhalkov brothers and the almost hypnotic effect of
believing in the presence of a famous personage.

To make a long story short, Grisha tucked this idea away and
prepared quite a spectacle. This time he justified the extraordinary
get-together by the arrival of a "People's National Meritorious
Actor" from Tbilisi, Georgia. Without putting any particular pressure on us, but with the confidence in the power of the fact itself,
Grisha explained: "My friend is a leading actor at the Marjanishvili
Drama Theater in Tbilisi. He knows many interesting details about
the lives of famous people!" Even if one had something very pressing to do, it was impossible to resist the double temptation: to find
oneself yet again in the hospitable home of Grisha and Galya, and,
on top of that, to spend time at the same table with a leading actor
from the renowned Marjanishvili Theater.

Grisha and Galya lived in a small apartment on the first floor
of a typical American double-decker, the kind they build to rent
to those who have not acquired taste or have not saved enough
money to buy property. Our friends had neither acquired nor saved.
It seemed as though everything that they could have put away from
their earnings went to the monthly gastronomical festivals. There
was a television set in the living room, and the table was set for dinner. On the desk in the other corner of the room there was a com-
puter. Photographs of their grandson and granddaughter hung on
the walls. A very strange picture of the operatic abduction of Pushkin's Ludmila by the grey-bearded dwarf, the sorcerer Chernomor,

strutted above the person who would be seated at the head of the table. A hunting rifle hung on the opposite wall above the television set. Hunting was the only form of amusement that Grisha allowed himself. All of us came on time, as was the Russian custom (snobs call it provincialism). Dinner is at five, but the guests all arrive by 4:45. That was the established way. And should one of us be half an hour late, Grisha would keep running outside every ten minutes, constantly calling the guilty person's cell phone.

And this time also everybody had arrived at the appointed hour; some were drinking beer, some whiskey, and others wine. Grisha went to pick up the guest of honor at the local airport. We were all drinking a little, discussing the latest political events and sports news from both *here* and *there*, and we all kept looking at the door and at the clock: when will Grisha bring the guest? Flights are late sometimes. Grisha's wife Galya suggested we come to the table. We did not object. The *zakuski* were excellent: smoked salmon, caviar, salads, and various pickled vegetables! And all this was accompanied by the best wines and vodkas. Just the Grey Goose alone cost a fortune! In fact, we were starting to forget the main reason why we had all gathered together. The honored guest from Tbilisi swam in our collective imagination somewhere outside of the realm of that wonderful meal. Had it not been for the fact that we missed Grisha's toasts, we could have done perfectly well without the expected Georgian "People's National Meritorious Actor."

Our resident humorist, Sanya the sculptor, had just finished telling his vintage joke about some fools jumping into a pool where there was no water, when the front door slammed, and, walking with quick steps, Stalin entered the room where we were feasting. Mincing his steps, our hospitable host Grisha (a man of gigantic height with a bull's unbending neck and head) followed Stalin. And what a sight it was! Bristling, Grisha seemed to have shrunk in height. His steps were tiny, and his head was bent down. In the meantime, Stalin pushed the empty chair back and sat at the head of the table, under the picture of Chernomor and Ludmila. He burrowed in the pocket of his military jacket and pulled out a pipe and a tobacco pouch. I was sitting nearby, and I reached for his pipe in order to pack it with tobacco, but Stalin grabbed the pouch. "No need! I pack it myself!" Alyosha the historian passed Grisha a box of matches that were earmarked for the Sabbath candles they had bought especially for Mira and me. I thought that Stalin looked askance at the candles that had just been lit, but he kept silent. Alyosha caught the leader's unkind or disapproving glance. As though making a joke, he said that it was getting too hot and moved the candles away onto the sideboard. Strangely enough, Mira and I pretended not to notice this manipulation involving the Sabbath candles. Even now, I don't understand why we did it. Tosya, Alyosha's wife and pure soul that she is, spoke her mind, "What do you mean it's too hot! For ten years it hasn't been hot, and suddenly we're sweating from candles!" Alyosha chuckled ambiguously and swallowed a half a glass of Black Label scotch.

Stalin slowly finished smoking his pipe, knocked out the leftover tobacco and ashes onto an empty saucer, and finally allowed Grisha to pour him a full glass of Alazani Valley, a famous Georgian red wine.

"Thank you, esteemed Grigory, for remembering the leader's favorite wine!" And then he repeated, "You didn't forget Alazani Valley. The leader's favorite wine. Yes indeed, one can often find fault with both the wine and the one drinking it."

"We never forgot you, Iosif Vissarionovich!" said Grisha and folded into himself even more. It seemed to me that his wife Galya was about to explode but then held herself back, the way sincere and well-mannered women can burn from embarrassment or from shame. She was ready to explode, but kept her silence. The funniest thing (or whatever else you may want to call it) was that even to me everything was beginning to seem both real and grotesque. Like in Ray Bradbury's short story "Darling Adolf." Bradbury's actor took to his role as Hitler enthusiastically; and what about here?

In the meantime Stalin finished his wine, chased it down with a few cilantro leaves that he pinched off the stems, one after another, with his yellow, widely spaced teeth, and again looked over the table. I thought his glance stopped at the mathematicians Zhora and Ella. What attracted the leader's attention: Zhora's mane of grey rumpled hair or Ella's face, overly enhanced with theatrical make-up? I wouldn't venture to guess. Stalin picked up his dark brown curved pipe from the table, grabbed the mouthpiece with his lips as if he were about to smoke again, then returned the pipe to the table, and asked Zhora:

"If I'm not mistaken, we met in my Kremlin office at the end of 1950? At a meeting about thermonuclear energy. Right?"

Zhora was silent. Stalin continued, "I could not be mistaken. I have a photographic memory!" With his strong accent, he enunciated "fah-tah-grah-fik."

"It was probably my father. They say we really look alike, Iosif Vissarionovich," Zhora answered.

"Your last name?" Stalin asked.

"Zelman," Zhora answered.

"Time flies so quickly, but memory attempts to slow it down!" Stalin said and downed a big shot glass of Grey Goose vodka that Grisha had poured for him.

I should add that Grisha never did manage to sit down, all the while standing behind or next to our guest's chair in order to keep refilling his wine glass and shot glass. Stalin was fastidiously following some private algorithm of alternating Alazani Valley and Grey Goose. The guest from Tbilisi was eating very little: some vegetables, one chunk of the lamb *shashlyk*, a small scoop of the pilaf. His face was not cleanly shaven, or it seemed that way owing to his uneven, pockmarked skin, the result of having had bad acne or even smallpox. But his mustache! The Leader's classic mustache.

Children of Stalin's time still remember Stalin's portrait in a military jacket or overcoat, a Marshal's brimmed cap, and a pipe with his mustache pressed against its mouthpiece. The beloved Stalin's mustache. I was staring at this mustache as though hypnotized, and couldn't tear my eyes away.

"What's wrong with you? I have asked you to pass me the shrimp three times already!" Mira pinched me to bring me back to reality.

"Sorry, I was just thinking!" I muttered, thankful for her timely gesture of spousal concern.

Thank God, Stalin was paying no attention to me. I forgot to mention that at the very beginning Grisha wanted to introduce all of us one by one to the guest from Tbilisi, but the guest waved him off: "We'll become acquainted (*aak-vain-teed*) as the evening progresses!" Actually, by that point in the evening the host had had a chance to mention my name. The guest of honor nodded coldly, and I thought of an anti-Stalinist long poem I had written in 1956. I remembered it and then pulled myself together. "No, he couldn't have read it, he died in 1953!"

I have already mentioned that there was a couple from Yerevan in our group of friends, a husband and wife, Vlad and Asya. They always initiated heated discussions about psychology. That is, they would analyze any occurrence or event from the point of view of modern psychology based on Freud's or Jung's thought, although not without a distinctive Soviet seasoning being detectable in their arguments. So during discussions, as needed, they would also invoke Sechenov and Pavlov, the Russian patriarchs of the physiology of the nervous system.

This time, as well, Vlad was first to venture to ask Stalin a professional question, "Iosif Vissarionovich, and how would you solve the present-day problems of Karabakh, using psychology?"

Stalin took a sip of wine from his glass. He continued to alternate Alazani Valley with Grey Goose. He drank some wine, picked up his pipe from the table, turned it over so that it looked like an ancient pistol, aimed it at Vlad's chest, and answered, "I wouldn't even bother with psychology. I'd just shoot the instigators on the Azeri side as well as on the Armenian side. Both groups are bourgeois nationalists undermining the friendship of brotherly nations of the Caucasus!"

For a while everyone fell silent, concentrating on their plates and glasses. But a natural *tamada*, a feast's appointed toastmaster, does not tolerate silence at the table. Particularly if this *tamada* is also a welcoming host. By this time, Grisha had allowed himself the right to sit down, albeit near the guest from Tbilisi. In any case, it was better than standing like a butler behind Stalin's back. Grisha took a seat, poured himself a full glass of vodka, a tall glass meant for Borzhomi mineral water. He drank this powerful dose of Grey Goose to the friendship of nations. All of us did. Stalin took a sip and retreated into himself, as if he were pondering how and where he would direct the rest of the evening. By this time the gigantic glass of vodka began to buzz in Grisha's head; he got up from his chair, returning to his powerful height, haughty bearing, and orator's talent.

"I must sincerely apologize, Iosif Vissarionovich, but what should my wife and I have done? We're both from Karabakh. I'm Azeri, and she's Armenian!"

Stalin turned his head to him, "I already said: first of all (*forced-off-all*) the instigators should be shot, secondly (*say-kand-lee*) reinstate the friendship of nations at the government level and at the level of the family! That's what Marx and Lenin taught us. The family is the primary unit of the state!"

Stalin said this and cast a glance over the hushed guests at the table. We were all silent. Suddenly the leader turned to Sanya and his wife Sonya. They were accomplished masters of mixed media installations combining sculpture and painting. They had started working together a long time ago, when they were still at the university. And even today no one in Russia could compete with them in this genre. Since their commissions came both from Russia and from America, they would spend half a year in Moscow and half a year in Providence. Suddenly Stalin turned to "our artists," as we affectionately called Sanya and Sonya.

"Listen, my dear friends, did we not meet in the old days?" he asked.

"We did, Comrade Stalin!" Sanya answered, and shook his angled bangs that flew above his large Varangian nose.

"And I also remember it," Sonya added, gently smiling at the leader.

"Can you be more specific?" Stalin asked.

"A few students from the Surikov Art Institute were chosen, and Sanya and I were among them. They brought us to the Kremlin. You, Iosif Vissarionovich, were standing there, next to a Persian lilac bush. Sanya and I drew sketches. You, Iosif Vissarionovich, personally approved our work."

"Where is this work now?"

"We don't know, Iosif Vissarionovich," Sanya the sculptor answered this time.

"You don't know! Enemies and traitors destroyed my portraits and my statues to demean the honor of our socialist Motherland! And you didn't even try to defend and protect a work of art. Am I not right?"

Sanya, a talker and a witty man, was silent, looking down and not shaking his bangs as he usually did when he felt confident. And Sonya was almost reduced to tears, afraid to raise her eyes and anger the leader even more.

Luckily, Grisha found an answer. He poured everyone wine and vodka. Filling his own glass again with Grey Goose, he raised a toast to the eternal youth of art and literature and "to Comrade Stalin's youthful verses as a clear example of everlasting poetry!" I watched the leader's facial expressions. He frowned but remained silent, puffing on his pipe. I'm not sure how this came to be, but as the need arose, I would pack his pipe and give him a light. Stalin no longer objected.

"Now I will read a wonderful lyrical poem, 'Morning,' written by Comrade Stalin in his youth," Grisha announced, and took a sip from his glass. We all waited, amazed by the way our *tamada* managed to anticipate everything. Grisha began to recite,

> The rosebud has opened up,
> It's leaning towards the violet,
> While waking up in the gentle breeze
> The bluebells bow over the grass.
>
> And in the morning blue, the lark
> Is flying higher than the clouds,
> And the sweet-sounding nightingale
> From treetops sings the children a song:
>
> "Bloom, o my Georgia! Let peace
> Reign always in my native land!
> And you, my friends, through studies praise,
> And glorify our Motherland!"

We all applauded. Grisha wiped the sweat off his brow. Stalin was morosely silent. I was praying to God that our guest from Tbilisi would not remember my profession as a man of letters. I'm sure that he didn't forget about it even for a minute. But out of some unwithering sadism he turned not to me, but to Mira. I had seen how incensed she became while listening to these verses. She was the only one who did not applaud. Without addressing her by her name and patronymic, or at least by her first name, Stalin asked my Mira, "You, a professional translator. What do you think of the poem that was just recited?"

"One would have to compare it to the original . . . ," Mira replied, evading the question. "It's hard to expect a great deal from the poems of a young person—and in translation, on top of that!"

Suddenly Stalin became agitated, his eyes lit up, and he said, "Listen to this poem in Georgian." He pushed his chair back, raised himself to his full, not very tall, stature, and waving his pipe around, began to read sonorous verses in a language we couldn't understand. We applauded again. But this time with complete sincerity.

It seemed that a certain balance was established when the haze of imagination, mystification, or hypnosis began to scatter, and each of us wanted the visiting actor to liberate us at last from this terrible fairytale that harkened back to an even more horrible time of our real past. But at this point, as they say in Russia, the devil pushed Ella, a song-loving boozer, to remember her accordion. She slid off her chair, darted into the hallway and returned with her accordion, almost half the size of the musician herself. Ella stretched out the bellows, which sighed thankfully, like the hero of Russian epic songs, Ilya Muromets, after waking up from a long slumber. Stuttering slightly from excitement and all the wine she had consumed, Ella announced, "And now together we will all sing an inspirational popular song from the time of the Great Patriotic War, 'March of the Artillerymen.'" She gave her raucous instrument a rhythm, and we picked up the song: "Artillerymen, Stalin ordered you! Artillerymen, our country calls to battle! From many thousands of guns we shall avenge our mothers' tears, for our Motherland: Fire! Fire on!" Ella remembered all the lyrics. We followed her and her accordion and sang the entire song to the end. Stalin sang along with us, and when the song ended, he said, "Comrades, let's drink to the Motherland! To Stalin!"

Everyone drank with the exception of my Mira and the historian Alyosha.

"And you, do you two need a special invitation?" asked our guest from Tbilisi, stretching forth his hand, which had emerged from the sleeve of his army-green jacket like a vulture out of its nest, and pointing his old man's, tremorous finger first at Mira, who was sitting to his left, and then at Alyosha.

"We've had enough of this masquerade!" Mira's words sliced the air. "But if you really want to know, I will drink under one condition: if you, the genius leader and teacher, explain to us why it is that in order to have peace on earth and humanity's progress it was necessary to fabricate the Kremlin doctors' plot. Why was it necessary to break the joints of my uncle's arms and legs, he a famous surgeon who spent the entire four years saving lives at the war front? For the sake of what lofty ideal was it necessary to design mass deportations of Jews, as had been done earlier to the Volga Germans, the Crimean Tatars, and the Chechens? For what, if not to complete the genocide of Jews Hitler had started?"

Stalin was deeply pensive. Mira covered her face with a napkin. Her shoulders were heaving from sobbing. Finally the leader said, "We wanted to save the Soviet Jewry, poisoned by Zionist propaganda, from the justified anger of the Russian people. It was for this reason that workers' settlements with modern housing were built in distant regions of Siberia—for example, Birobidzhan—and factories, plants, and collective farms established nearby. Let my words be confirmed by another doubter. In those years *his* father was in charge of the Ministry of Construction." This time the predatory bird of Stalin's hand stretched toward Alyosha.

"That's not true!" Alyosha intoned. "Actually, the construction of housing for future deportees was handed over to Lavrenty Beria. And he made sure that the barracks were built with boards that had spaces the size of a finger between them. My father reported that to the Politburo. He stated that it would be a crime to settle Jewish families in such inhumane conditions. For this, he was immediately arrested by state security police!"

"Don't turn your father into a starving little orphan! As soon as they let him out, he immediately exacted revenge for his own arrest by executing Beria, without a trial or an investigation."

"And what did you want, a new bloody terror?" Alyosha asked.

"By that time I couldn't want anything because, thanks to your father's unbridled and inflammatory speech at the Politburo, an artery exploded in my brain, which led to my final demise. Your father, although he had always danced to my tune in the literal and figurative sense, was the first to spit into my grave. He even threw my corpse out of the Mausoleum!"

"But unfortunately you're alive now! You have returned from the other side, and you continue to emit a foul odor."

Alyosha had had a lot to drink. He had emptied an entire bottle of Black Label scotch. We knew that he was uncontrollable in heated arguments, and we had learned to avoid confrontation. In everyday life Alyosha was a most civilized and pleasant person. But now! We had never seen him in such a state. His cheeks flushed red, his eyes were darting around the room, as if looking for something. He knew exactly what he wanted. Alyosha jumped from his chair, and before we realized it, he snatched Grisha's hunting rifle off the wall.

"Stop! You've lost your mind!" the guest from Tbilisi shouted and ripped off his glued-on mustache.

But it was too late: a shot rang out. Everyone froze. When the smoke had settled, we saw a man in a military jacket lying face down on the table and covering his head with his hands. Above him, the picture of Chernomor and Ludmila was rocking back and forth, riddled with large pellets.

2008
Translated from the Russian by Aleksandra Fleszar and
Arna Bronstein

The Valley Of Hinnom

Leah, Homer, Esau—these are the main characters of my story. And although the names are fictitious, the personages are quite real. Everything I recount in this story happened before my eyes. In other words, I describe only what I personally observed. I have no need for imaginary scenes I couldn't have observed. They, undoubtedly, were even more stirring than what I saw. One can imagine the raging passions of my heroes, to whom I've deliberately given exaggerated names. It often happens this way with Russian Jews. In everyday life they could be: Borya, Misha, Ira. But in one's imagination: Sasha, D'Anthès, Natasha. In everyday life: Borya, Sasha, Lida. Or else: Petya, Tolya, Natasha. But in the imagination: Osya, Marina, Dima. There's really no end to the combinations that arise even from the most common Russian names. My story is not common, but extraordinary. In the spirit of Biblical narratives or ancient Greek tragedies. Therefore name-symbols have been adopted: Leah, Esau, Homer.

The story that I'm about to tell started in the 1980s in the milieu of Jewish refuseniks. There were many of us. They say that in Moscow alone there were about fifty thousand refuseniks. And even though we lived in different districts of Moscow, on different streets, we were in effect a large community of Jews who had set their minds on escaping from the Soviets. On escaping anywhere: to Israel, America, Canada, or Australia. We didn't want to live where Jews were disenfranchised. We didn't want our children to grow up, marry, and have children in a country like that. We believed that Jews had the right to another destiny.

With one of the fellow refusenik families we became quite close. His name was Esau, and hers, Leah. They had a four-year-old boy by the name of Sid. Before submitting an application to the OVIR for an exit visa, Esau worked as an engineer at a machinery factory. One of its shops produced periscopes for submarines. Esau was denied the exit visa because of the classified information that he allegedly possessed. This is how he and Leah became refuseniks. And with them, little Sid. I had originally met Leah's brother, Aram. He actually ran an underground Jewish theater. They invited me to play in the klezmer ensemble that accompanied the performances. Prior to that I had lost my position as second violin in the orchestra of the Moscow Variety Theater. I was getting by with giving music lessons and working night shifts as a parking lot attendant. When I had a few free hours, I would rush to a rehearsal of our underground Jewish theater. I actually got the parking lot gig through Esau, who had many connections. Such was our crazy life at the time: odd jobs, waiting in a reception line at the OVIR, endless get-togethers at one refusenik apartment or another, and discussions, discussions, discussions of how to get out of the Soviet paradise—how to secure an exit visa. Our rehearsals took place at different apartments and had a rather haphazard quality because the troupe never could gather in full. On account of this problem, a system of replacements had been devised. For example, my wife or my son usually came with me. They were ardent admirers of the Jewish underground theater. Sometimes one of them replaced me. My wife played the piano; my son, the guitar. This way, in apartments where we rehearsed there would always be understudies and enthusiasts. Homer became one of the enthusiasts of our theater after someone gave him the telephone number of Aram, Leah's brother.

This is the story of Aram. He was about to graduate from the State Theater Institute as a director. But at the last minute they wouldn't let him complete the final graduation requirement. Aram wanted to restore a production of Mikhail Lermontov's *The Spaniards*. To restore this production—the way it was done at the Moscow State Jewish Theater under the great director and actor Mikhoels. The administration of the State Theater Institute vetoed Aram's idea. He didn't want to stage anything else. The administration wouldn't budge. Aram refused to compromise, didn't get his diploma, and submitted an application to emigrate to Israel. He applied at the same time as his sister Leah, her husband Esau, and little Sid. And they all became refuseniks. And that's when Aram had the idea to organize an underground Jewish theater. Aram was its director and the principal actor. He was made for the stage. Tall, with glowing eyes, a mighty voice, a head of Gypsy curls, and a curly beard, Aram was born to play the Jewish heroes—Judah Maccabee or Bar Kochba. And Leah was just perfect playing opposite him: slender, long-legged, with the delicate, elongated face of an Egyptian princess, tense, slightly protruded lips, a shapely chest, and provocative hips. She liked to wear floral silk dresses with plunging necklines.

Then Homer appeared in the orbit of our underground theatre. He was a professional translator from the Greek. More often than not he translated articles on art or politics. But Homer had also tried his hand at literary texts. For example, he translated *David and Goliath*, a play by the contemporary Greek playwright Petropoulos, and started offering it to various theaters. First in Moscow and Leningrad. Then in Arkhangelsk and Novosibirsk. Then in Tula, Kalinin, Omsk, and Barnaul. It was uniformly rejected. Even the Birobidzhan Theater rejected it. Homer spent several honoraria, which he had earned by translating for an academic journal, on postage and telephone calls to literary directors at different theaters.

They all politely said "no" without giving an explanation. There was nothing to explain. What Soviet censor could allow the production of a play in which the Jewish shepherd David prevails over the Palestinian giant Goliath? Homer was given this advice: "Give us a play, Greek or Turkish, no matter, but with a contemporary and progressive plot." Among the good plays, none fit this description. However, Homer discovered for himself the wonderful Greek poet Cavafy. He was simply intoxicated with Cavafy's verse, constantly mumbling something along the lines of:

> The body remembers not only how passionately it was loved,
> Not only the bed of love,
> Not only the naked thirst of love,
> Which trails every glance
> Of the lovers and each note of the cries of love. . . .

And so forth, many other verses translated from Cavafy's Greek into Russian. This time, however, Homer drew a lucky number. His translations were published in *Foreign Literature* magazine. He was also contracted to publish a book of translations from Cavafy's Greek. And not just by any publishing house, but Raduga Publishers. He made a name for himself. But he still hadn't abandoned his old dream of seeing *David and Goliath* on stage. That's how Homer came to our underground Jewish theater.

I distinctly remember the day and the hour, and even the minute, it seems, when Homer came to meet Aram. It was the end of a cold April day in the early eighties. Red as a dahlia flower, the sun was falling behind the bell tower of the Elokhov Church. We were rehearsing in the Ilyins' apartment. Their daughter Nadya, red-haired and sweet as Jamaican rum, played Dvoyra, Benya Krik's sister whose marriage was being arranged. Aram was directing a production based on Isaac Babel's Odessa stories. He played the gangster, Benya Krik, and Leah played the pretty Russian wench, Katyusha.

We were rehearsing when Homer rang at the door. Because of all the noise (we played as a full klezmer quintet—violin, accordion, guitar, percussion, and trumpet), nobody heard the doorbell. Then someone entered and, smiling gently, observed our rehearsal. It was Homer. He was wearing a fine black wool overcoat with a white silk scarf thrown over the shoulders. His hair, the color of autumn oak, was combed, pomaded, and divided by a white parting. I would have expected to see a white carnation in the buttonhole of his lapel. A slender, refined-looking aristocrat with a mysterious smile. We were rehearsing in our host's library, which doubled as his study. The actors were in the middle of the room. Musicians sat on the chairs with their backs against the bookshelves. Spectators and understudies occupied a leather sofa of a very respectable age. I suspect that the sofa dated to "the time of Ochakov and the conquest of the Crimea," so wrinkled was its whitish elephant skin. Red as a dahlia flower, the sun was falling behind the bell tower of the Elokhov Church. Homer listened while staring at Leah. She stopped. That is, she had been kicking and throwing out her bare legs, all the while singing a jolly tramp's song: "Gop-and-smyk," made up from a mixture of Yiddish, Russian, and Ukrainian criminal jargon. While singing her jolly song, Katyusha flirted with Benya (Aram) as she swung her hips and hiked up her skirt higher and higher. Finally she stopped, and the other actors also interrupted their performance; the klezmer band stopped playing. Homer came up to Leah, took her hand, and recited a love poem:

> The body remembers not only how passionately it was loved,
> Not only the bed of love,
> Not only the naked thirst of love,
> Which trails every glance
> Of the lovers and each note of the cries of love. . . .

He recited it while staring at Leah, whose face was lit up by the dahlia-red sun sailing over the bell tower. He recited the poem while holding Leah's hand, and then he kissed her long fingers, with red grapes for fingernails. She said: "Thank you." And she kissed Homer on the cheek.

Leah's husband, Esau, never stayed long at our rehearsals. Even though he was also an ardent admirer of our theater. And, of course, he believed in the stage genius of his wife, Leah. Unfortunately, he was always pressed for time. Forever in a hurry. He dropped by a rehearsal in a hurry, disappeared in a hurry, ate, drank, and slept in a hurry. Probably kissed his wife in a hurry, too. But who else could, at a moment's notice, dart off the devil knows where in order to find a large piece of cardboard needed for the set or to procure a missing stage light. A stage light with yellow-blue-green-red filters or something like this. Or a wig made after some incredible fashion. In other words, he could locate any prop that our genius director, Aram, needed at a given moment in order to realize his newest stage idea. Esau would heed the request, call someone, rush somewhere, procure all that was necessary, and instantly disappear to take care of what he needed to do to put food on his family's table. At night he usually picked up Leah and little Sid in his upscale model, a Zhiguli 6, of which he was very proud (he also used it as an illegal cab). And along with his wife and son, he would usually give a lift to me or one of my family members, or even all of us together. We were just one Metro stop before Esau, Leah, and little Sid. We lived at Aeroport, and they at Sokol. Esau was dark-haired, stocky and sturdy. He burned with excess energy. In the dead of the winter, he flew about Moscow with no hat and with his shirt collar unbuttoned. Hair pushed out of his shirt like smoke out of a roaster oven. Esau adored his Leah and his little Sid.

Aram and Leah were twins. Both of them vibrant and gorgeous, full of verve and passion. Like thoroughbred Arabian horses waiting for the signal to take off and run—before a roaring crowd—all the way to victory. Thoroughbred people-horses, centaurs, having found themselves captives. Locked in a paddock along with other refuseniks, fellow captives of the preposterous Soviet laws. . . .

We were all so enthralled by our theater, so busy with our paltry, low paying day jobs, and also so absorbed in the incessant, unrelenting struggle for exit visas, that at first we didn't notice that Homer and Leah were in love. Of course, we saw that Homer visited our rehearsals more and more frequently. He was becoming one of ours. With Aram he would discuss the stage play, which Aram had parsed from Babel's stories. He was a generous fellow, this translator from Greek. Once, on a frosty day, he brought over a large bag filled with hot *pirozhki* "straight out of the oven," which he had snatched up outside the Metro station; another time, in the heat of July, he delivered an armful of Eskimo Pie bars for the whole troupe; yet another time, he gave each actress a bunch of lilies of the valley. Only gradually did we begin to notice how Homer and Leah would be standing in one corner or another of our "rehearsal area," standing there and talking-talking-talking about something, no doubt something fine and romantic, because they would look at each other and smile the whole time, and would sometimes bring their fingers to each other's shoulders, cheeks, or hands. It's all floating up to the surface of memory now, when the story has come to an absolute end. How obvious is the outcome of a thunderstorm: darkening, gathering, sparking, thundering, pouring out, quieting down. Or: darkening, gathering, lightning across the sky, house burning down. But could we see it back then? Our lives as refuseniks were too hard to be paying attention to someone else's passing attraction. That's assuming anyone had even noticed anything.

They probably talked of exalted love. But they also talked of real life.

"Leah, you were remarkable today."

"How about about yesterday?"

"Yesterday also."

"And the day before yesterday?"

"Every day."

"If I play the same part every day, you'll get tired of watching."

"I will never get tired of watching you."

"How do you mean, never?"

"Leah, do you love Esau?"

"He is my husband and Sid's father."

"I will be your husband and Sid's father."

"It will kill Esau."

"But this is killing us both."

"What will happen to Sid?"

"I will adopt him."

"But for this I need to divorce Esau."

"Of course! Leah, my love! You'll get a divorce. We'll get married and I'll adopt Sid."

"Esau won't agree to that!"

"To a divorce?"

"Either to a divorce or to you adopting Sid. Also, this will mean withdrawing the visa application from the OVIR. Both mine and Esau's. And then resubmitting the papers all over again. Do you love me, Homer?"

"Very much!"

"Then we can do it. I'll divorce Esau. We'll get married. We'll get a new invitation from Israel and apply, the three of us—you, me, and Sid."

"I love you, Leah."

"And I love you, Homer."

"Let Esau leave—and we'll stay here."

"You don't want to go with us?"

"I don't want to leave at all. I want to live in Russia, translate from Greek into Russian, and love you. That's all I want, Leah."

Such conversations probably occurred between them often. The conversations ran their own course, and love, its own.

The production based on Isaac Babel's stories opened in September 1982. I believe that's when it was. After that came our final refusenik years, even more hopeless than before. Yes, I do believe our theater helped refuseniks to survive. We performed in various apartments, lugging all of our stuff up and down Moscow. Did the authorities know? I have no doubt they did. Why did they pretend not to notice? Those were complicated times: the Soviet troops jammed in the inglorious war in Afghanistan; chronically poor crops that forced the government to ask America and Canada for grain; some deep disagreements inside the ranks of their devilish organizations, the Politburo and the KGB. In other words, the authorities herded us into the refusenik ghetto while waiting for a fitting opportunity either to send us to Siberia or to sell us for some unheard-of profit. In the meantime, our underground theater continued to exist. Aram turned to his next production. He was putting on Petropoulos's play *David and Goliath*, translated from the Greek by Homer. As to be expected, Aram played David, and Leah, his beloved Abigail, the wife of the rich and harsh Nabal, he whom the Lord punished by death. Punished by death and gave Nabal's wife Abigail to David, the one who had vanquished the mean Goliath. Our troupe rehearsed this mythological plot, which partially coincided with reality. Only Esau was nice and not harsh or mean. On top of it, he loved Leah and Sid so much that he kept overcoming his own jealousy. Since Homer wasn't going to leave and Leah was determined to emigrate, it made no sense to initiate a divorce.

I recount only what I saw with my own eyes. Esau no longer picked up Leah and Sid. Homer took them home by taxi. Things were going well for Homer. The Drama and Comedy Theater was doing *The Clouds* by the ancient Greek playwright Aristophanes, in Homer's new translation, while a Leningrad-based publisher was putting out Homer's translation of a historical novel by a contemporary Greek author. Everyone knew about the adulterous affair. In the beginning, some accused and others exonerated; some even

stopped talking to Leah and others to Esau (because of his supposed "lack of principles"). But five years is a long time. Practically
a jail sentence. So all the talk had petered out, and Leah and Homer's new love and intimacy had turned into routine. We would run
into the lovers not only at our theater but elsewhere. Their passion
did not abate, but, it seemed, only grew stronger. Everyone could
see this at rehearsals, performances, and "in public." Being in public for us meant attending parties hosted by American diplomats,
where new films were screened and plenty of food and alcohol was
served. Leah came to the screenings with Homer. Usually these
parties were given by the American cultural attaché or members
of his staff.

Then came the final year of our life as refuseniks. Of course,
we didn't know it at the time, but we felt the approaching political
changes and hoped that we would soon get permission to leave the
country. This became especially clear after Chernobyl. Anxiously
anticipating a change of fortune, Leah still hoped that Homer
would reconsider at the last minute. That he would get an invitation from Israel and apply to the OVIR for an exit visa.

On one particular occasion in March my wife and I got invited by
the charming American diplomat Duane MacRoy and his wife Isabelle to watch the musical *Fiddler on the Roof.* It was already springtime, but the weather was still gloomy and unsettled. Change was
beginning to sweep the country. Nonetheless, every visit to a diplomat's home was risky business. We had no choice. American diplomats were our only lifeline, sustaining our struggle to leave the
country.

The MacRoys lived in a Stalin-era apartment building on the
Kutuzovsky Prospect. Right across from the massive, pyramid-
shaped Hotel Ukraine. A stone wall separated the diplomatic
building from the Kutuzovsky Prospect; armed policemen, playing

the role of border patrol, were stationed at a gate. We had to wait patiently outside until the diplomat who invited us came out and walked us through the guarded gate. My wife and I had come early and stood there, waiting, talking about some insignificant things just to bide the boggy time. A whitewashed sun, like a bat, swept its wing over the guard's booth and fell behind the Triumphal Gate at the west end of the Kutuzovsky Prospect. Soon Leah and Homer joined us at the usual waiting spot. I thought Leah's eyes looked red and swollen, as if she had been crying. Homer was unusually reserved. Finally, out of the gate came Duane MacRoy, tall, handsome, with gleaming white teeth. It seemed that the radiant smile on his broad, dark-skinned face chased the clouds away. We walked past the guards, entered the building, and took the elevator. Once inside the MacRoys' apartment, we felt warm, comfortable, and safe. I might say that we never felt so relaxed as we did in the apartments of our friends from the American Embassy. Even though this, too, was an illusion. As was to be expected, our every word was picked up and recorded by the Soviet security services. By then, we had learned to choose our words carefully or to replace certain words with gestures. Or to use self-erasing notepads. In the hallway, an iceberg of a refrigerator dispensed chilled beer. Plates of cold cuts, cheese, fresh vegetables, and sweets crowded the table in the TV room. A bottle of California Shiraz had been uncorked by our genial hosts. The coffeemaker exuded exotic scents of the tropics. We drank, ate, relaxed, and watched *Fiddler on the Roof.*

We were finishing our wines and coffees. The film was over, but the main musical theme—of love and longing—lingered in the air. The conversation turned to the correspondence between love and sacrifice.

Isabelle, the diplomat's wife, said: "When you are truly in love, the very act of sacrificing for the one you love gives a person pleasure!"

The diplomat and his wife were African Americans. They were passionate, warm, candid. Every one of Isabelle's words came from the heart.

My wife asked: "Isabelle, dear, is this a general statement or are your words based in a personal experience?"

All eyes turned to the hostess: what will she say? And then Leah asked, as if looking for help: "Please tell us about yourself. You must've lived through something like this . . . ?"

Leah didn't say what that something was, but we all understood. Isabelle looked at her husband. He filled our glasses with Shiraz and smiled at his wife. Isabelle began her story:

"I was born in rural Alabama, not far from Selma. My father was a farmer of moderate means. His dream was that at least one of his five children would graduate from college. And then, if possible, go to medical school. That was my late father's dream. I was a good student, and his choice fell on me. Learning came easily to me. I went to the University of Alabama at Birmingham, and the year after I graduated I was accepted into the medical school there. A year later, at a friend's party, I met a brilliant young officer from the State Department. He was visiting his mother in Birmingham. We started writing to each other. He called almost every week. Then he came for another visit. And invited me to Washington, DC. Museums, theaters, night clubs. At the fountain in front of the Capitol building, he proposed to me. I came home with a little diamond ring on my finger. We decided to get married the following summer. I was going to stay in Birmingham and finish medical school, and then I was going to join him permanently in Washington. But life disposed otherwise. My fiancé was unexpectedly given an assignment to work for several years in one of the Latin American countries. He got on the next plane to Birmingham, to see me. I had to marry him right away, quit medical school, and go with him, 'or else.' I chose Duane."

Leah hugged and kissed the hostess. "Thank you Isabelle, thank you, darling. Homer, we should probably go."

After they left we sat in silence. Everyone knew how difficult it was for Leah and Homer to make the right choice.

In May 1987 we finally got permission to leave the country. Things started to move. Refusenik friends kept calling: "Such and such person received a visa." More and more each day. We immersed ourselves in the minutiae of preparing for departure. We had to comply with a thousand formalities, one of which consisted of obtaining the imprimatur of the Lenin State Library to take books abroad. We all had special books, dear to our hearts, with which we had spent our lives and which, like close friends, we couldn't leave behind: Pushkin, Sholem Aleichem, Esenin, Ehrenburg, Akhmatova. . . . And also some reference books on engineering, medicine, history, literature, music. . . . My son and I stuffed two duffle bags with books and set off for the Lenin Library. The office that inspected books was somewhere in the bowels of the library, its entrance located in an alleyway off the Kalinin Prospect. Some of our books were good to go, taxes were levied on others, and many were "prohibited from being taken out of the country." Such was the bureaucratic wording that a colorless lady squeezed out of her mouth after searching the authors' first and last names and the book titles in a prison register stamped many times over. My son and I left this "selection" office feeling low. All the more refreshing, then, was our chance meeting with a smiling, spirited Esau who hauled on his back a hiking backpack filled with books, like the hold of a cargo boat with merchandise. With Esau was Sid, a quick-eyed preteen with another, smaller backpack towering over his back. We stopped to talk. Briskly, as always without a shadow of a doubt or wavering, Esau said: "I got us tickets to Vienna. First class! My dear Leah won't have it otherwise. So much to do! But we'll get everything done in time. The main thing is that we got our visas!" I agreed that this was, of course, the main thing. We wished them a safe flight. They wished us the same. Dark smoldering hair curled up on Esau's head and burst from under his shirt like jet engine fumes.

We caught glimpses of the three of them (Esau, Leah, and Sid) on Vienna's boulevards, where in the evening musicians in parti-colored Baroque costumes and plumed hats played Mozart, Salieri, and Strauss. Through the windows of dollhouse cafés we saw well-to-do denizens of Vienna take unhurried bites of pastries and incredibly appetizing Viennese sweet rolls. They enjoyed their pastries and slowly sipped Viennese coffee from dollhouse Viennese china cups, while gently swaying in Viennese chairs shaped like monograms. Yes, exactly! Sometimes (or did it only seem so?) we saw Esau, Leah, and Sid through café windows. From Vienna we were being transported to Rome under the protection of guards with machine guns (the first time the threat of terrorism entered our lives), and early in the morning (for some reason, I couldn't sleep), early in the morning I saw, in the train corridor, Esau's face illuminated by sparks of sunlight breaking out of the blackness of tunnels. Sparks of sunlight like flashes of gunfire.

Then we saw the "holy family" in Rome. They were standing near the gaping eye sockets of the Colosseum's skeleton. Sid was feeding bits of sausage to long-legged stray cats, whose ancestors had gorged on table scraps from the feasts of Nero or Vespasian. Sid was feeding the cats, and Esau and Leah silently watched him, oblivious to anyone around them. We saw them among the crowds on St. Peter's Square, in the Vatican museums, at Villa Borghese. They stopped in front of the marble beauties of the ancient world, but the eyes of Esau only looked at Leah. We tried not to bump into them, afraid as we were to touch an open wound. And it was hard to make small talk. In general, we didn't want to return to our pasts. But in the end, we had to.

From Rome, they moved us to the coast of the Tyrrhenian Sea, to the town of Ladispoli. There, under the aegis of Jewish charities, former refuseniks had to stay for about two months while waiting, yet again, for their visas. This time, for entry visas to come to America. Besides the American charities, a local representative of the Lubavitcher Rebbe offered his patronage. A kind fellow, this rabbi whirled around Ladispoli on a motorcycle, causing moral suffering among the Russian Orthodox old ladies who had left Russia along with their Russian daughters and Jewish sons-in-law. The old ladies didn't know what to do: to cross themselves seeking protection against the motorized infidel or to cross themselves asking the Lord to keep him from breaking his neck. Our rabbi was such a sweet man. He always treated old ladies, Jewish and Christian alike, to candies and peaches.

The local Chabad House had a library and also a playground. So when I went there to borrow books, I often spotted Sid playing with other kids and Leah reading in the shadow of a plane tree. We exchanged superficial greetings. In the evenings, when the July-August heat subsided and a heavenly sea breeze descended upon the earth, we went for walks along the waterfront promenade, stopping at the fountain to talk to our Moscow friends, or else we sauntered in a crowd of native Ladispolians up and down the main street, Via Garibaldi, if memory serves. Or maybe Via Vittoria. Sometimes Esau caught up with us. He was swarthy like an Arab. Striated with dark stains of sweat, his shirt resembled a map of the world. Smoke of his dark hair and steam of his speeding body engulfed Esau. He would catch up with us, slow down for a minute, and ask if we had seen Leah and Sid. "Our landlord got me a job at his brother's farm," he would yell back, already walking ahead of us in the crowd. "Picking and loading watermelons. Working in the fields with the Poles. They are waiting for Canadian visas. Not too bad, huh? (Poles or watermelons?) We stuff our faces and bring some home!" A chunky watermelon rolled over in his backpack like a chopped-off head.

Once we ran into their whole family by the fountain. It was on a Sunday. "A day off at the farm, or have you picked all the watermelons?" I remember asking. We talked about some trifles. Sid circled around us on a bicycle. ("From a junk pile. Fixed and cleaned. Good as new!" Esau said about the bicycle.) My son saw a group of young Italians he had befriended and was off with them. We stood near the fountain among the other Soviet refugees and made small talk.

Esau couldn't stay put. "Back in a minute," he said and dashed off.

"Leah, how are you?" my wife asked.

Leah looked at us, wells of sadness in those eyes we had known to be dancing with joy. "I'd like to come over in the next few days. May I?"

Esau came rushing back with a bouquet of colorful ice cream cones. The words "Gelato! Gelato!" were streaming over in the crowd of sauntering Italians. For us, refugees, even ice cream was an incredible luxury. And there was an armful of huge gelato servings. Esau showed off his generosity like a young hussar!

We were having supper in the kitchen. Wafting into the apartment from the open balcony were children's voices, music from cafés, evening sounds of a seaside Italian town. Just as I reached for a large green jug of Chianti, someone rang the doorbell. It was Leah. Her face was swollen from crying, her hair fell in disarray over her forehead, shoulders, and neck. She was hysterical. Unable to speak, she only sobbed, uttering the same words: "I can't go on like this, I can't, I can't. . . ." We tried to comfort her. We spoke to her about her son, her duty, about something else and something else after that—all things very important to us and useless to her in her present state of mind, the things which normal people with normal families philosophize about when they come across the actions that destroy their very idea of normalcy. All, even these though so-called "normal family people," could tomorrow find themselves—or have previously found themselves—in similarly abnormal family circum-stances. We did our best to calm Leah down (of course, calming her down only outwardly). We gave her supper, poured her some wine. And we began to reminisce about our refusenik theater, the actors, the musicians. And of course we talked about Aram, our director, Leah's brother, who had already emigrated to Israel.

"Maybe I should've gone to Israel? Maybe I should've stayed in Moscow? But what about Sid? In a few years, he would be drafted into the army!" She started sobbing again. At last, Esau came over and took Leah home.

We ended up on the East Coast, in Boston. They, on the West Coast, in San Francisco. For a year or so we exchanged holiday greetings. Then the connection lapsed. The same, fateful inverse square law also applied to connections among human souls. It took a few years to get acclimated, find work, make new friends—in other words, all that can be summed up by one word: immigra-tion. The greeting cards we mailed to Leah and her family were returned. Their cards to us, probably, also couldn't reach us, their addressees; in the beginning, we moved around a lot.

About ten years after immigrating to America, we finally decided to visit Israel. Times were turbulent. But we couldn't keep post-poning the trip. Besides, will things ever quiet down over there? We had family and friends in Jerusalem and Tel-Aviv. A magnet, Eretz had originally inspired us to contemplate another life, and eventually tore us away from Russia. At last my wife and I were going to Israel. In Jerusalem we had arranged to stay at Mishkenot Sha'ananim, a center for artists, writers, and musicians. Founded in the mid-nineteenth century by Sir Moses Montefiore, a British aristocrat of Jewish origin, Mishkenot Sha'ananim had been origi-nally conceived as an almshouse and became the first Jewish settle-ment outside the walls of Jerusalem's Old City. The building, with studios resembling monastic cells, one of which was assigned to me and my wife, stood at the foot of an old windmill bearing the name of Montefiore.

The walls of our cell-studio were built of large slabs of granite. A stone hedge separated us from what was once the moat surrounding the Old City. Now a gully, the former moat was traversed by footpaths coming down steeply to a stone road. Trodden over and packed by the steps of the millennia, the road was barely visible from above. We could stand for hours and look at the Old City, soaring above the world like a heavenly sphere. To enter the Old City, one had to descend to the bottom of the moat by one of the footpaths, then go over the stone-packed road and climb up a path ascending to one of the gates above. To the right of the moat ran a narrow, menacing ravine or corridor, overgrown with weeds and wild shrubbery, above which stood the remnants of a gate. This was Gehenna, the Valley of Hinnom where dwelt the souls of sinners. The Messiah had to pass through this gate, cross the Valley of Hinnom, save the poor tormented souls, go up and enter the main gate of Jerusalem, then reach the Wailing Wall and restore the Temple.

A young pomegranate tree grew outside the entrance to our studio-cell, its trunk only about two inches thick. There were only a few branches at the top and a side branch with a single fruit, reddish-brown in color. A crack came down the north pole of the fruit, like a gorge. The pomegranate was ready to explode with its engorged seeds.

If you walk to the right along the stone hedge, in about a quarter of a mile you will come to the steps of a little restaurant, its verandah hanging over the Valley of Hinnom. Sometimes we ate breakfast or lunch in this restaurant. That time, too, we leisurely strolled there along the hedge, stopping every now and then to enjoy yet another vista of the Old City. It was a crystal sphere under the blue skies. And inside this sphere there shined the domes of the temples: golden, blue, green. It made us think of eternal happiness, eternal life, endless love.

"And how is our Leah?" my wife suddenly asked.

"Why did you think of her?" as a genuine Jew, I answered with a question.

"I forgot to tell you: right before we left, Ostrovsky telephoned. Remember him, he played Goliath?"

"Of course I remember!"

"So, Ostrovsky said that Esau had moved from San Francisco to Jerusalem."

"What about Leah? And Sid?" I asked.

"They must've moved with him," answered my wife. "Actually, who knows?"

That was the conversation my wife and I had that morning, on our way to breakfast at the little restaurant overlooking the Valley of Hinnom.

We sat down at a table near the edge of the veranda. We ordered coffee, omelets, and rolls, and started peering closely at the Old City surrounded by ancient walls. At a distance from the Valley of Hinnom, an olive grove climbed up the slope of the Mount of Olives. The same olive grove where Roman legionnaires arrested Yehoshua of Nazareth. I sat with my back to the entrance to the veranda. All of a sudden, my wife screamed: "Look, it's Leah! And with whom? This is unbelievable!" I turned around. In the doorway stood Leah with a white and blue baby carriage. With her was Homer. We didn't know what to do, what to say. Astounded? Bewildered? Shaken?

Riddled with contradictory feelings and seditious thoughts, and overcome with superstitions, more or less appropriate for the occasion, and also with other logically-nihilistically-metaphysical gibberish, we didn't know how to conduct ourselves. With what words should we approach this newfound trio? Should we feel happy for them? Or feel sad for Esau, all over again? I think that ninety percent of the doubts were mine, and only ten belonged to my wife, who knows few doubts. My wife jumped up from her chair to hug Leah and Homer. I followed, full of contradictory thoughts. A baby boy lay in the white and blue carriage. He wasn't even a year old. He shuffled colorful plastic balls threaded across the carriage and cooed happily in the language of babies, birds, and angels.

"This is David," said Leah. "Remember Homer's play?"

"We were just remembering that!" my wife said. "That—and our refusenik years."

But what difference did any of it make, now that little David lay in the carriage talking to people, angels, and birds, and rattling blue, red, yellow, and green plastic balls. They joined us at the table, and Leah told us about what happened:

"You remember how Sid, Esau, and I settled in San Francisco. Esau took some classes and got a job as a programmer. We rented a nice apartment. Sid started school. I was looking for a job. Homer and I decided, even before I left Russia, to end our relationship forever. He promised not to look for me. I swore I would write to him only after ten years. After ten years, when our passions would have completely subsided. I tried not think of Homer. I was taking English classes. I even tried not to write or call our old friends, just to keep the door onto the past permanently shut. Even when I talked with Aram, my beloved brother, when I called him in Jerusalem, we avoided the subject of Homer. Only a few times did I break down."

"Once you called us from San Francisco. But you couldn't even talk. Just started crying and hung up," my wife remembered.

"Yes, one time. So, this torment lasted about two years. Esau suffered just as much. Maybe even more. Finally, he couldn't take it any longer. We talked. Imagine what it took for us to have that talk. 'You must call Homer,' Esau said. 'Who knows, it's been two years.' But I knew. Homer was waiting for me. Esau sent him an invitation. Homer flew to America to visit us. I decided to go back to Moscow with Homer. Esau and I divorced. We had to determine who was to get Sid. Neither I nor Esau pressured him. He was a big boy, almost a bar mitzvah. He had to decide for himself. He chose his father. Esau and I agreed that Sid would visit me during school breaks. Can you imagine? After all we had lived through as refuseniks, to end up living in Moscow again! Of course, I missed Sid terribly. But I was happy. We couldn't live without one another! Right, Homer? (Homer smiled and kissed Leah's neck.) At first it was tough. Literary work didn't pay at all. Homer went to work at a car wash. I learned to do manicures. My clients were rich ladies from among the 'new Russians.' Gradually literary life went back to normal. A new normal. Homer tried his hand at science fiction. It worked. His first novel, about transmitting human genes to a chimp, sold out instantly. And things only got better. Now he's a famous science fiction writer. Like Pelevin or the brothers Strugatsky."

"Oh sure, we've read your novels, Homer," I inserted a comment. "Fun stuff, no doubt about it. But we had no idea that the prima of our old underground theater is now your personal muse!"

Leah continued her story:

"Esau and Sid moved to Israel. First they lived in Jerusalem with my brother Aram. Sid finished high school. Served in the army. Now he's at university. Esau is still living with Sid. He never remarried. We actually flew in from Moscow just yesterday. And we made plans to meet Esau and Sid in this café. It's all such a coincidence that you ended up here!"

"So they're coming here?" asked my wife.

"Exactly, any minute now," Leah said. "They haven't seen David yet."

My wife and I hurried to leave. This would have been much too much for the first meeting. Or do people actually have a sixth sense?

We said goodbye. I wrote down their addresses and phone numbers; they, ours. I lowered my gaze. Down the slope from the olive grove a lone human silhouette was descending toward the

Valley of Hinnom. Already at the door, we yelled for them to give our address to Esau and Sid, in case they decided to visit the East Coast. The sun was blazing in full force. It was the start of a very hot day in Jerusalem. We went back to our cell, grabbed a backpack, a bottle of water, and a map; it was time to leave for a sightseeing excursion to the Dead Sea. As I was locking the cast-iron gate I heard an explosion on the right, exactly where we had come from. We ran back to the restaurant where we had just bumped into Homer and Leah. Where only half an hour earlier little David was playing with multicolored plastic balls threaded over his white and blue stroller. Playing and cooing in the language of babies, angels, and birds. Flames of fire had swept up to the roof of the restaurant. Sirens howled. The police had sealed off the area. Medics carried the victims to the ambulances.

On the following day, the newspapers reported: "A young Palestinian woman, a mother of a three-year-old girl and a one-year-old boy, blew herself up with a bomb, killing eight and wounding eleven patrons and employees of a restaurant. Among the dead was a mother with an infant. The terrorist left a note recorded on a videotape: 'It has been my long-cherished dream to turn my body into deadly shrapnel aimed at Zionists and to knock at the gates of Paradise with the split skulls of our sworn enemies.'"

2004
Translated from the Russian by Leon Kogan

Mimosa Flowers
for Grandmother's Grave

That morning, Solomon worked in animal care. It wasn't even noon, but three hundred white mice had been infected with TB bacilli and put back in their cages. Solomon was at a turning point in his animal experiments. If successful, the new method of treating TB could enter clinical trials. There was cause for hope. For a minute, Solomon allowed himself to be distracted from the sweetly pungent atmosphere of the animal care facility. He was no longer irritated by a tremulous ray of sunlight, peeking in, like an orphan, through a bottle-glass window. Solomon pretended not to notice Kat'ka, the orderly, who reeked of undiluted alcohol. He was daydreaming. Thank God, the money he had saved up would be enough to buy a dozen stray dogs. He would get the dogs from street drunks who were ready to sell their own soul. Solomon needed the dogs in order to conduct the last experiment before the new method could go to clinical trials.

You may wonder about the connection between Solomon's dreams, the saved-up money, and the planned experiments on dogs. There was a very specific one. In Leningrad's Institute of Tuberculosis, where Solomon was working on his PhD, they didn't use dogs for experiments or normally keep them in animal care, and no funding was available for this. Which is why it would have taken Solomon at least a couple of years to overcome various administrative hurdles—and delayed his dissertation defense by several years.

"Solomon! Hey, Solomon. You deaf or something?" Kat'ka the orderly had ripped him away from his reveries. "You're wanted urgently on the phone."

Solomon removed his rubber gloves, untied the checkered brown apron, shed his white coat and surgical cap. In the receiver he heard Aunt Betya's sobbing voice. His Auntie Betya, his father's unmarried older sister, lived with her mother. Solomon's grandmother.

"Solomon, come quickly! Mama's not doing well," Aunt Betya said.

Something happened to grandmother, grandmother's not well, not well, not well, faster, faster, faster, the chain gear of terrifying words turned in Solomon's mind as he rushed out of the Institute's gates on Ligovsky Prospect and grabbed a taxi, as he swallowed with salt tears all the cars, buildings, public gardens, and bridges flashing by in the taxi windows. . . .

Finally the taxi left behind the little park at the corner of Zelenin Street and Chkalovsky Prospect. On warmer days she would sit here on a bench, flanked by lady friends of many years who regarded her as their elder. Indeed, Solomon's grandmother had no equals in terms of her wisdom and composure—and the truthfulness of her heart. But she's not there anymore, and the park itself, overcome by vernal anticipation of change, has lost its snowy pureness.

Instead of the snowdrifts, tall fluffed-up pillows. And on the pillows, grandmother's large face, furrowed and cinnamon-hued, with a beautiful straight nose, solidly shaped eyebrows, a high forehead encased with snowy hair. Except that grandmother's eyes, always engaging, shining with a special light of caring about the person she was speaking with—because this person was a living, dear and inimitable human being—except that these velvety-brown eyes set in a mosaic of wrinkles were now closed.

Solomon leaned over to kiss his grandmother's cooling cheek and the corner of her eye from which the tiny rays of kindness emerged.

"Grandmother, what's wrong? Can you hear me?"

But grandmother probably could no longer hear him. Her soul, having exited her body of almost ninety years, had not yet left the room and was saying goodbye to the people and objects she so loved: Aunt Betya, sons and grandchildren, her husband's portrait, the family album, the Book in a gilded binding, the TV set and the armchair; everybody and everything.

Even though Solomon had always lived in a different apartment on the Vyborg Side of Leningrad, since his early school years he had been accustomed to visiting grandmother two or three times a week at her apartment on the city's Petrograd Side. It's hard to say which was the dominant factor in their friendship. Was it the pity she felt for her grandson, who grew up with a living father yet without one? Unlike the other children who were growing up in functional families, Solomon grew up in the street, amid gang members, and was always getting in trouble. Or did fear for her grandson trump pity? Or could it also be that all of these things paled in comparison with the unceasing likeness of character between her grandson Solomon and her elder son, Isaac? Her Izya, whom she hadn't seen in over forty years. Her elder son was also a daring seeker after the truth, who suffered from injustice and lack of freedom, and experienced the same burning hatred and unconditional love. He—her Izya—was the best horseback rider among the boys of Kamenets-Podolsk, where their family hailed from, and he also scored the best goals and was the most devoted friend. It was he, her elder son, Isaac, who came home one spring day and said:

"Farewell, mama. Papa, farewell. Farewell, sister Betya and you, my brothers. Be happy. I'm leaving for Palestine to build a new life."

He was only sixteen at the time when he said farewell to his beloved family. He mounted a horse and later, in Odessa, boarded a ship and disappeared beyond the Bosporus.

Isaac knew how much grandmother loved mimosas—the flowers of spring. Middlemen used to buy them in bulk in the south and bring them up north. Like a last kiss, he sent her a bunch of warm yellow flowers from Odessa on the eve of his departure.

That faraway spring had long passed. And the summer after it had fired away. Then autumn and winter followed suit. Then spring came again, but no one in the house—neither grandfather, nor Aunt Betya, nor their brothers—had the heart to remove Izya's wilted mimosa twigs from the room. This is what Solomon's kin began to call them: Izya's flowers.

Isaac's letters began to arrive from the Mandate of Palestine. He grubbed up tree stumps, dried out swamps, irrigated deserts. Izya would send them letters and photographs. A *halutz*, he was bringing that ancient land back to life. In some pictures he stood among the Bedouins, proud witnesses to the land's past declines and victories. Dozens of letters over a decade. Isaac had become a grown man, but his eyes, the same as grandmother's, still shone with youth.

Then came the trying prewar years and the terrible war. It was nearly impossible to maintain contacts with her elder son. Everywhere she went—in Leningrad, where her husband had moved the family in the 1930s, in the closet of a room that grandfather and grandmother rented during the wartime evacuation to a remote village in the Urals, and back in Leningrad following the victory and grandfather's death—everywhere, at her bedside, in a tall silver goblet she kept the desiccated twigs of Isaac's farewell mimosa flowers.

Grandmother was lying in her spacious bed, head resting on a white pillow. Behind the pillow, the backdrop of a dark brown headboard framed the view, as though this was no longer his dear living grandmother but her frozen, sorrowful portrait. Aunt Betya brought in a tea tray and all of them, the family members who were already there, had some tea at the round dining room table. Grandmother lay beside them, so that one could make oneself believe this was not forever, not for eternity, but just temporary. It was as though grandmother was just tired and had fallen asleep, and the family members didn't wait for her to wake and were having some tea.

Then Solomon's father arrived, and his father's younger brother a little later. In half-whispers they talked, mostly about the way grandmother was in life. Solomon found this all bewildering, since each word was simultaneously truth and understatement, some rough assemblage of grandmother's image through their joint efforts. He knew for a fact that grandmother was and would always remain exactly what she had meant to him. Only his heart and her heart conjured up this double vision: nobody in the world understood him as she did, and therefore he didn't love anybody in the world the way he loved her. They were frank with each other like two inseparable friends who did not know competition or envy. Nothing could stand between them: separation by distance, difference in age, intrigues of the jealous others. Nobody could undermine their friendship, and the age difference shielded and protected their bond from quotidian jabs and blows.

Grandmother lay beneath grandfather's framed photograph.

Aunt Betya kept offering tea to those just arriving or getting ready to leave. She had always been thin, unprepossessing, unimposing, although behind her beige exterior and willingness to stay in the shadow of her brothers and parents there lived a moral depth and impeccable purity of character. It was she, Aunt Betya, who had volunteered in 1941, trading her beloved pediatrics for the cruel craft of military field surgery. During the war, grandmother and grandfather would get triangular letters from Aunt Betya. With her field hospital she traversed half of Europe, from Karelia all the way to Vienna. She came back adorned with the epaulets of captain of the medical corps, an order of the Red Star, and other decorations. She came back home, once again to treat young kids and to remain in the shadows of her unquiet family, its members dispersed around the world. And somewhere in an open field, her *only one* had found eternal rest, he to whom Aunt Betya was the most comely of all, the beloved. After the war, Aunt Betya always shared a home with Solomon's grandfather and grandmother, genuinely regarding her nieces and nephews as her own children. Not everyone in the family cared for Aunt Betya's gentle bluntness. Not only Solomon himself, but also his father, who was constantly preoccupied with his marriages and families, or his father's younger brother, an associate professor who was comforted by his success and position, would have elected to hear grandmother's wrathful tirade instead of enduring Aunt Betya's soft-spoken words of scorn, which went straight to the heart.

And now Aunt Betya, slumping her chin onto her fists, waving off stray tears and dipping pieces of cookies in her tea, started telling them about grandmother's last night. In the evening, Solomon had been to see them. Usually grandmother liked to play a game or two of dominos. She would get unaffectedly disappointed when she didn't have the right chips to add on to the black zigzag traversing the table. Grandmother pursed her lips, lowered her eyes for a split second, and then, like a swimmer before leaping into the pool, took an unknown black chip from the *bazar*. She picked it up with two fingers, as if this wasn't a domino chip but the neck of a live crawfish, the only spot at which one could grab the unclean creature. She would swiftly pick it up, bring it to her eyes, and proudly add to the lineup. Or, if she didn't get the right one, she slammed the useless chip on the table. On her last night, Solomon, as always, had offered to play dominos with grandmother. She had agreed, but played with some reluctance, without excitement; this time both winning and losing left her indifferent. And when Solomon told her and Aunt Betya some amusing anecdotes about Kat'ka the orderly, grandmother only frowned: "Ah . . . a *shikseh*."

An oppressive premonition wouldn't let grandmother be. Suddenly she remembered that March 5 was nearing—the day of *Yossele's* death. She called Joseph Stalin this. "Yossele and I are the same age, you know."

Around nine in the evening, Solomon had said goodbye to grandmother and Aunt Betya. On the way home, he still had to pick up his young wife, a philology student at Leningrad University's evening college.

Grandmother had a fretful night of sleep. At three o'clock she woke up, asked for water, and then dozed off. Delirious, she spoke in her sleep, something she had never done before. At first Aunt Betya couldn't make out her words, but grandmother's speech grew clearer and more articulate. Words arranged themselves into sentences, and sentences were conjoined into a meaningful conversation. Grandmother talked to somebody, called for somebody, seemed anxious about something. Aunt Betya heard the name of her father, Solomon's grandfather.

Solomon's grandfather had been in the milling business. The family liked to reminisce about those antediluvian times. On Fridays, grandfather would return home from the mill. His *brichka* usually raised such dust that a mile away from their house a small milky cloud would ascend to the pristine sky over the steppe. The yard guard dog, Polkan, would tear off at the approaching *brickha*, and the children were ready for stories about the never-ending gyration of the gears set in motion by the water falling from the dam. Sometimes things got out of hand and grandfather wouldn't come home for several weeks. During floods it sometimes happened that the dam would be plucked away by a fierce stream possessed by a daughter's desire to return to mother ocean and merge with her primordial element. They had to put up a new dam. And time and again the water would triumph. To give up the family business? This would have been a sin. One had to feed his family and return the grind to the peasants who brought to the mill the grain grown by their unending labor.

After addressing her husband, in her sleep grandmother spoke to her children. First to Solomon's father, whom she lovingly pitied the most but also scolded more often than she did the others, for his convoluted family life. Then she thanked Aunt Betya. She chided her youngest son for talking her into severing the correspondence with Isaac, who was living in Israel—the year was 1950 and one couldn't be cautious enough. Then her eldest son Isaac entered her night visions; those may also have been her moments of clairvoyance. She didn't part with her firstborn son until her last breath. Grandmother thanked Isaac for those farewell mimosa flowers smelling sweetly of tears soaked with sea, spring, and separation. She thanked him and begged his forgiveness for not having replied to his letters, for having been the one to cut the fine thread that had kept her connected with her eldest son. Grandmother spoke with Isaac as if she had finally been reunited with him and was now confessing her heart to him, who for almost twenty years now had had little news of his mother, father, and siblings in Russia.

Gradually her visions lost their architectonics. Unhindered by anything but a link to the mystique of life and death, her eternal consciousness had surrendered itself to chaos. Once again Solomon's grandmother began to recall the story of the mimosas, almost as though she wanted Isaac to see how dried-up and scrawny the twigs had become after those forty years. But something prevented her from locating her talisman, and so grandmother summoned Solomon and asked him to help her find Isaac's mimosas. As she passed on, two dearest names, Isaac's and Solomon's, were merged in a moment of farewell clarity. Aunt Betya, the pure soul, repeated the same account without concealing or embellishing anything.

Then came the day of the funeral. Solomon hadn't slept all night. He kept mulling over Aunt Betya's account of his grandmother's last night. Finally, he had made a decision. He was going to try and carry out grandmother's wish.

The day before, he had gone to see his boss and ask for the day off.

"Of course, do what you need to do. Goes without saying! I'm so very sorry for your family," the professor said. And then, so as to cheer up his graduate student, he added: "You know, dear colleague, the administration has finally given its consent to keeping the dogs for your experiments in the old stables. That's half the challenge!"

"I appreciate it," was all Solomon could muster in response.

On the morning of the funeral, Solomon hired a cab and drove to the farmer's markets he knew well: Nekrasovsky, Sytnyi, and Sennoy. There in flower stalls he bought up all the mimosas—yellow, downy twigs giving out a sweet scent of south and sea. He packed the trunk and back seat with mimosa flowers. Tears flooded Solomon's eyes; he felt unbearably sorry for grandmother, and in his chest he also felt a pinch of anxiety that his long-awaited experiment had to be delayed.

When Solomon arrived at the Jewish cemetery and entered the old sanctuary, the service had just started. He placed the flowers on a bench close to the rear wall. The rabbi, who stood at the *bimah*, all clad in black garb, was solemnly speaking the words of the funeral rite. Solemnly and sorrowfully. Solomon didn't understand the ancient prayer, yet he felt benevolence falling upon him and bringing relief. He stood beside his father, Aunt Betya, and his younger uncle, staring at the grandmother's casket. The service ended. The rabbi motioned at the staff, and the roof of grandmother's final dwelling was nailed in forever. It was all over.

Not conscious of where he was going and whence the flowers in his arms, Solomon followed the casket. From the Neva, a gust of piercing wind carried streams of wet, cold air. A silent small crowd walked after the casket. Men ahead, and women a bit behind, helping Aunt Betya.

Suddenly, from behind the turquoise dome a bright sun slipped out, setting alight the stone crypts surrounding the synagogue. Grandmother's pine-yellow casket and the yellow mimosa flowers in Solomon's arms, and also the yellow sun of those days approaching Passover—everything had merged into a single graceful chant. Up on a birch tree, wrapped in a white prayer shawl striated with black phylacteries, a tomtit twittered like a carefree balalaika. Everybody walking behind the casket felt relief after the chill and semidarkness of the sanctuary. Solomon thought that it wasn't the casket that was preparing to transport his grandmother to another world, but a sparkling gold chariot was getting ready to soar to the sky. This was only for one shining moment.

The casket was carried between the black fences crowding their sight. Behind one of the fences stood a tall marble pyramid—grandfather's gravestone. Next to the gravestone, on top of the dark, tramped-down March snow, there lay fresh clumps of soil—sand and clayish loam mixed in with dry stems of last year's flowers. And past the verge of the freshly dug soil, a bottomless cold opening showed black. Solomon stood, leaning on his grandfather's gravestone and hugging the heap of yellow mimosa flowers. For the first time now he had irrevocably understood that this bottomless pit and the sand and loam piled over the dark March snow were the last trappings of his grandmother's earthly existence. Now for the second time since that terrible shock when Solomon had first laid his eyes on the dead grandmother, he screamed like a wounded beast, toppling onto the casket and kissing the wooden lid. Tears started pouring from his eyes. He didn't try to take himself in hand, only lifting up his glasses and shaking off the tears. And again and again the impossible and finally recognized woe wrested from Solomon new sobs and inconsolable tears. They recited the Kaddish. The casket was lowered into the ground. The grave was filled. Solomon's father carefully removed the heap from his son's embrace and began to cover the sandy and clayish ground with the gold of mimosas.

Solomon didn't see any of this. Hugging him, his father removed his son's glasses, then helped him to the car.

And then came the morning of the next day. Solomon opened both sides of the window. The unmuddled sky struck Solomon with its saturated blue radiance. Everything was illuminated, yet nothing sparkled the way objects sparkle under bright sunlight. Trees amazed Solomon with their unusual shapes and the locally unseen, foreign lushness of their verdure. What's more, the inner courtyard of Solomon's building, where he had grown up and where every little stone, every stoop had been fused in his memory with some special event or adventure, was now an alien, unfamiliar courtyard. Even the yardkeeper, Uncle Vanya Klyuchnikov, wasn't standing under the overhang of the communal laundry room. He was nowhere to be seen. In fact this wasn't his native yard, not a yard but some tidy space, framed by wondrous trees and flooded with a never-ending, otherworldly blue radiance. Solomon felt so fine and peaceful—felt he didn't even desire anything, as if his whole life he had been striving to wake up on this soothed and soothing morning all colored over in cobalt blue.

Suddenly, in the middle of the plane the earth started bubbling up. He saw green saplings. Then branches, a trunk. Finally, a whole tree had been born in the center of this dark blue expanse. The tree gently swayed its branches, like fingers playing with strings. And indeed Solomon heard an unearthly music. It was Mozart. His Symphony No. 40 in G minor.

"I will never forget you, darling. . . . Please remember me, my love. . . ."

Whence these words, which Mozart didn't choose but which were perfect because to Solomon they unlocked the melody's secret meaning?

"I will never forget you, darling. . . . Please remember me, my love. . . ."

The tree rhythmically swayed its branches as they were filled with golden warm flowers. It was a mimosa tree. The tree with grandmother's beloved flowers.

Just ahead, a tall and stately woman stood under the tree. Her eyes were gorgeous and sorrowful, and they peered into Solomon's heart. The woman resembled his grandmother, but she was much younger—Solomon had only seen her this way in the family portraits from before the Revolution.

"I will never forget you, darling. . . . Please remember me, my love. . . ."

A man on horseback approached the tree. He dismounted and came up to her, she who resembled grandmother back in the days of her youth. He was a youth who looked to Solomon like both himself before he went into the military and his Uncle Isaac who had disappeared beyond the Bosporus. The woman broke off a blossoming mimosa twig, embraced the rider and gave it to him. Now in one hand the young rider held the reigns, and in the other, leashes to which bright-orange fluffy dogs were attached. A whole pack of blazing dogs. The rider mounted and urged his horse on.

"Wait for me, Uncle Isaac," Solomon called out, but his voice couldn't catch up with the spirited horse.

A pack of dogs, all golden like mimosa flowers, dashed across the morning's saturated blue, and the rider disappeared. And the woman, who looked like his young grandmother, gazed with sadness into Solomon's eyes as she sang:

"I will never forget you, darling. . . . Please remember me, my love. . . ."

1984
Translated from the Russian by Maxim D. Shrayer

The House Of Edgar Allan Poe

Eduard Polyakov, a Russian émigré of the "third wave," was walking down the hill from the Rockefeller Library of Brown University toward Benefit Street. Polyakov had come to Providence, the capital of the diminutive state of Rhode Island, to collect materials for a future biography of Edgar Allan Poe. The book had been commissioned by one of the largest Moscow publishers. He had come for two months from the Californian city of San Diego, where he was a professor at the Department of Slavic Languages and Literatures. Polyakov dropped off his carry-on bag and suitcase at the university guesthouse and immediately headed out in search of the house of Edgar Allan Poe. His future book had received its original impulse from the poet Valery Bryusov, one of the first Russians to translate Poe's works. It was none other than Bryusov, who had been Polyakov's object of study for about a decade, that eventually steered him to Poe, but not until Sashenka Tverskaya became fascinated with the American writer. At the time, she was Professor Polyakov's graduate student at San Diego. For a year now, Sashenka had been working as a junior faculty member in the Department of Comparative Literature at Brown University. From Providence, Sashenka sent Polyakov pigeon flocks of electronic messages, in which the frequency of the words *waiting* and *love* exceeded the incidence of all other words. Sashenka was supposed to be coauthoring the future book with Polyakov.

169

Polyakov was a little over forty. He was just slightly taller than average height, with a resolute chin, grey eyes, and a mane of light brown, grizzled hair. Sashenka, by contrast, had managed to stay this side of the thirty-year barrier, although, in the unanimous opinion of her friends and colleagues, she had no apparent reason to slow down the natural passage of time. She was a long-legged and blue-eyed Russian beauty of Muscovite vintage, equally good at making friends and becoming infatuated. For five years now, she had been infatuated with both Edgar Allan Poe and Edik Polyakov. Their love affair had been going on for almost as many years as it had taken Sashenka to complete her graduate coursework and her doctoral thesis. To be absolutely precise, for four of the five years Sashenka had spent as a doctoral student and dissertator, she and Polyakov had been enmeshed in a tumultuous affair, which they had to conceal from everyone. It seemed that, given their love and passion, there would have been no reason for them to separate almost a year ago, and for Sashenka to migrate from the West Coast back East. There seemed to be no reason for their love affair not to become a family affair. No reason? Of course there were reasons! Or at least there was one reason, the most important one for all Americans: there was no teaching position for Sashenka at San Diego, whereas a junior faculty appointment had opened up at Brown. She applied for the Brown job and got it. She and Polyakov couldn't fathom living apart for more than a year. Which is why each had silently decided they would spend two summer months together in Providence—and if no miracle occurred, they would give each other freedom to choose new partners. It seems that even love stories have to reckon with their job openings and faculty searches.

Immediately upon arrival, Polyakov rushed down to Benefit Street because he couldn't wait to see the house where Edgar Allan Poe's beloved once lived, the woman whom the great fantasy writer saw on visits from Boston. She was actually one of his two great loves, and he gave preference to neither one of them until his dying day. Some incomprehensible force led Polyakov to the mysterious house of Edgar Allan Poe, as if the researcher from California sensed the approach of an entirely new era in his life. He also had another reason for going there. Polyakov was very much in love with Sashenka, and his desire to see her all the time, at least in the course of the two months allotted to them by destiny—to talk with her about their research or about nothing in particular, to kiss her laughing eyes and her giggling, playful lips, and to possess her to the full measure of the ardor that a young beautiful woman and a passionate mature man are capable of—this was the main purpose of his research trip. And it was precisely what he could not allow himself to do, either in the small room of the university guesthouse or in the apartment that Sashenka shared with two other junior faculty members from different departments. Therefore, his expedition to Benefit Street served two interlinked goals: to see Sashenka, and to find the house of Edgar Allan Poe. To find it, and, to the extent possible, to obtain the owner's permission to have a look at the rooms, cellar, attic, and garden or orchard, if any of this had survived from the mid-nineteenth century, when the enamored Poe came here to visit the object of his passion. Part of Polyakov's task was to open a membership at the esteemed old private library, the Athenaeum, located in very same Benefit Street, and to look for any additional materials related to the love triangle in which the great American fantasy writer had occupied such a prominent vortex.

It was a hot midsummer morning in New England. The whole town was deserted, especially the section of Providence dominated by Brown University. The students had left for summer break. Many of the professors weren't around, either. Only those doing basic science research kept plugging away in their laboratories, fishing particles of experimental facts out of the ocean of nature. Polyakov came down College Hill. On Benefit Street, lined with young linden trees that had already shed their yellowish-green fuzzy flowers, Polyakov passed the palatial edifice of the Providence Athenaeum and soon found himself near a white clapboard house next to the corner of a little side street that rolled down to the river and toward downtown; a white, modest-looking Protestant church adorned the side street. The white clapboard house was marked with the number "88" and had a plaque mentioning Edgar Allan Poe. Polyakov knew that in this house Poe had visited his beloved Sarah Helen Whitman. Polyakov examined the exterior of the house and also looked at the back from around the corner of the side street which, as he discovered, was called "Church Street." There wasn't a soul around. Polyakov decided to come back later that day, and until then to roam about looking for a studio apartment where he and Sashenka Tverskaya could have their trysts. The expected proximity of the Athenaeum, of the house that Polyakov dubbed *the house of Edgar Allan Poe*, and of an apartment for secret trysts promised precisely the kind of perfect combination of utility and pleasure that Eduard Polyakov had championed his whole adult life. Besides, the appearance of Sashenka on Benefit Street in the company of Professor Polyakov (and the likelihood of that would be high, indeed, in the closely knit community of the Brown professors and graduate students) could always be explained by their joint research visits to the house of Edgar Allan Poe or the Athenaeum.

The side of the street on which Polyakov was walking was dotted with wood frame houses, many of which, according to their plaques, had historical significance—this, however, being true of most New England buildings erected over two hundred years ago. Polyakov approached the far end of Benefit Street. There was no sense in continuing. Even if there were a place for rent available past that point, it would be too far from the Poe house and the two libraries. Something had to be done, however. After all, he couldn't furtively climb through the fire escape into the second-floor room of the communal apartment that Sashenka was renting. And what were they supposed to do, blast the radio when Sashenka visited him at the university guesthouse?

He stopped, unsure of where to go next. There was no sense in aimlessly walking on. Just a few blocks ahead there was a squalid neighborhood adjoining the interstate, the river, and bridges half-eaten by rust. Returning empty-handed was silly and a little disappointing. After all, he hadn't arranged this entire research trip to limit himself to brief encounters with Sashenka during which everything had to be done *hush-hush*! He looked around. On the corner, on his side of the street, there was a decrepit red brick house with an unkempt garden. A dwarf with a large head covered in thin curly hair stood on the bottom step of the stoop. His arms and legs were short and stubby. The dwarf amiably waved to Polyakov with his farmer's hand and pointed right below his feet. Polyakov looked closer. The ground near the toe of the dwarf's right shoe was bulging and rippling, as if there was something fumbling in it. The dwarf bent down and pulled out of the ground a large bluish beetle, of the kind commonly known in Russian as *zhuzhelitsa*, or ground beetle. The beetle had thick, protuberant eyes that periodically retracted into its ocular burrows and then popped pretty far out while also emitting a golden glow, like a pair of spotlights.

"Do you want to buy the beetle for a buck?" asked the dwarf. "It can show the way. Like a real navigator."

"I don't know . . . It's not the price, really," Polyakov hesitated. "Won't it run away?"

"I'll tie a leash to its collar. Trust me, it won't escape, but it will show you the way!"

And indeed, when the dwarf picked up the beetle and handed the creature to Polyakov, the researcher made out a tiny collar around the beetle's neck, with characters that were illegible without a magnifying glass. The dwarf took Polyakov's dollar and fastened a leash to the collar with a small snap swivel, the kind they use in freshwater fishing. In fact, the leash was a piece of a fishing line with two little loops: one for the snap swivel and one for Polyakov's index finger.

The beetle trotted on the sidewalk in the direction of the house of Edgar Allan Poe, back to where Polyakov had been only recently. From time to time, the beetle paused to make sure that its new owner was keeping up. Each time the beetle turned to Polyakov, the creature's eyes glowed like golden headlights. His index finger threaded through the loop of the leash, Polyakov could barely keep up with the sprinting beetle. Near house number "88," the beetle stopped for a moment, as if in contemplation, then turned the corner onto Church Street and started climbing onto the back porch. Polyakov stopped and lit a cigarette. He was happy to linger there, smoking a Camel, which he lit by striking a match against the brown rough side of the matchbox; preferring matches to a lighter was one of his lingering Russian habits. Polyakov liked to collect various miniature boxes, cases, caboodles, and cages, thinking of them as models of mysterious abodes, repositories, treasure chests, or something of this nature. While he smoked, the beetle with the golden eyes climbed up the steps and started crawling up the wall toward the button of the doorbell. By pressing its head to the button, the creature indicated to the owner that he should ring it. "Smart creature," Polyakov chuckled and pressed the button. There was no answer, and our researcher picked up the beetle by the back with his thumb and his index finger and was about to put it away into the matchbox when the door flung open and a wheelchair rolled out onto the porch. Riding in the wheelchair was a young beauty of Sashenka Tverskaya's age and—this was the most amazing part—a carbon copy of Sashenka herself: blue-eyed, smiley, with closely cropped chestnut hair, bright lips, and a dimpled chin. She probably had long legs as well, but they were covered with a lightweight blanket and thus hidden from plain view.

"You did the right thing by not shoving the beetle back into the box cage. This extraordinary beetle has belonged to my house for over two hundred years. It lives here, like any other pet: a cat, a dog, or a guinea pig. So let it go, please. Sometimes it roams the streets of our town, and if somebody happens to find it, people always release it once they have read the inscription on its collar. And the beetle returns home. Sometimes it gets resold, just for kicks," said the young woman in the wheelchair, and smiled solicitously.

"That's exactly what happened to me!" Polyakov said loudly. "This dwarf sold your beetle to me!"

"You have it all wrong! Karl, the kindly dwarf, simply drew your attention to the significance of what's happening. People very often attribute no importance to gifts, and value only what they purchase for money!" said the wheelchair-bound young woman. "But let's get acquainted, shall we? It's not for nothing that my golden-eyed beetle has brought you here. My name is Helen Whitman, Lena in Russian. I was born in Russia, although I have been living in America for a long time, so long that I've even managed to become a widow. My late husband was the owner of the Newport Line Shipping Company. The company's origin dates back at least three centuries. In a word, I'm the owner of the shipping company and the mistress of this historic house. And you?"

"I'm also Russian. A Russian Jew. Although in America everyone born in Russia is called 'Russian.' Well, actually it's not very important."

"Of course, important—and of course, unimportant! It's important for me to get to know you better and it's unimportant that you are a Russian with a cute little Jewish tail."

"Yes-yes! Indeed, with a little tail! How very witty of you!" said our hero. "My name is Eduard Polyakov. I come from San Diego, where I try to teach students about Russian literature, and, in particular, about the influence of Edgar Allan Poe on Russian fantasy writers."

"Then what were you doing near the house of Karl the dwarf?"

"I was looking to rent an apartment for two months."

"Stay at my place," offered Lena Whitman out of the blue. "I'm going to Boston for precisely that time period. The surgeons in the

Massachusetts General Hospital are going to operate on my spinal marrow. The surgery is supposed to restore the nerve regulation and blood circulation in my legs, which will then regain their ability to walk."

"Oh, how wonderful!" exclaimed Polyakov. "That's just incredible!"

In his head, he immediately pictured two Sashenka Tverskayas hopping on the paths and green fields of the Brown campus, or two Lenochka Whitmans running out to the porch of the house of Edgar Allan Poe.

"You actually caught me just as I got a phone call that my limo will be here any minute. Here are the house keys. Take any of the guest rooms on the second floor. The bathrooms have been cleaned and sanitized. There are fresh linens in the closet. The housekeeper and the cook will take care of you. I'll call you when I'm about to leave the hospital, if I don't forget," said Lena Whitman, just as a chocolate-brown giant of a driver in a blue uniform cap with gold piping, a black tux with a big white bowtie, and a white chrysanthemum in his lapel stepped out of a limousine and carried Lena to the back seat.

Five minutes later, Polyakov was already calling his beloved Sashenka Tverskaya from the cordless phone that he found on the coffee table in his two-room guest "suite" (he couldn't think of a better word for it!) on the second floor of the house of Edgar Allan Poe. They agreed to meet at seven o'clock on Thayer Street by the entrance to Café Paragon, which, in Sashenka's opinion, was both hip and inexpensive.

"Remember, Edik, I've always spared your dignity and your wallet," Sashenka was not only an uncommon beauty but also quite a wit.

The day was already drawing toward the evening, and our guest from California was feeling peckish. Truth to tell, he wanted to see Sashenka very badly, yet he was anxious about their meeting.

It was easy to understand why he longed to see her. She was so beautiful that Eduard Polyakov sometimes wondered: how was it that Sashenka had become so attached to him? It was impossible to explain their mutual attraction with anything but the simple word "love."

Polyakov was feeling rundown after the apartment hunt. He still needed to shower and change. Only then did it occur to him that his clean clothes were in his suitcase, and the toiletries in his carry-on bag. Both were back at the university guesthouse. Polyakov immediately thought of the golden-eyed beetle. As if obeying a telepathically conveyed command, the trained beetle darted from under the dresser and directed its golden eyes at Polyakov.

"Oh, it's you, good friend! To be honest, I'm not even sure whether to pick a male or a female name for you. How about Beata?" said Polyakov, half-jokingly and half-seriously.

The most charming thing was that Beata ran up our professor's pants and leapt over to the sleeve of his blazer, giving his wrist an approving tickle, as if to confirm the appropriateness of the name choice. Polyakov petted the back of the golden-eyed Beata, indicating that he was ready to follow her signals. She jumped onto the writing desk, from there onto the sofa, and ran to the closet. Polyakov opened the closet doors and discovered everything he needed: summer suits, including a few linen ones, underwear, undershirts, shirts, socks, and even summer shoes and sandals. The most incredible part was that the clothes matched Polyakov's height and girth as if every item had been made or bought especially for him, using his precise measurements. He gave Beata another gentle tap on the back. She flashed the headlights of her eyes at him, as if winking. More pleasant surprises awaited him in the bathroom, but he was no longer as amazed as before: fine towels of various sizes, sealed dental care products, and an electric shaver. In the mirror cabinet, he also located an old-fashioned straight razor with a sharp elongated blade and a strop.

All over the house, clocks chimed bim-bom, reminding the guest that it was already half past and that he had to hurry to the rendezvous with Sashenka. We should note that the intelligent beetle dove into the right hand pocket of his blazer where the matchbox was. Guessing correctly what she wanted, Polyakov dumped most of the matches onto a tray next to a jug with flowers and placed Beata into the vacated miniature cage, which he shoved back into his pocket.

As it turned out, Café Paragon wasn't far at all. Polyakov walked there leisurely, as if trying to defer seeing Sashenka. He forced himself to think about his former graduate student, his beloved and the trusted witness to his research aspirations, but instead of imagining the impending rendezvous and the night that would follow, he kept seeing Lena Whitman, whom the giant black man was lifting from the wheelchair and carrying in his arms to the back seat of the glossy white limousine.

Sashenka was waiting for him on the corner of Angel and Thayer Streets, right outside Café Paragon, while across the street, a flower girl stood proffering roses, tulips, and lilies to the promenading residents. Polyakov dashed over, pulled a bunch of scarlet roses out of the bucket, thrust a twenty into the flower vendor's hands, and then pretended that he had only just noticed Sashenka. Through the thickets of the bouquet she made her way to his lips and started kissing him so fervently that he had immediately forgotten all the women in the world except Sashenka.

A leggy hostess in a black dress, cut provocatively to accentuate her breasts and back, showed Polyakov and Sashenka to a table by the window, overlooking Thayer Street, the main drag of the university section of town. Our couple, however, was indifferent to the evening street crowd or anything else. Their legs and hands kept touching like lovers reunited after a long separation. They ordered, drank, ate, and drank something again, but all of that seemed insignificant, and only their future together was important. It is usually the case, when people lack a firm foundation for achieving a certain goal, that they cling on to an intermediate plan, which, like a shifty pontoon at a river crossing, has the capacity to get those seeking new ground to the other shore, but at any moment it threatens to topple over and drown the unfortunate ones. The plan Professor Eduard Polyakov proposed to his beloved was this: they would gather materials for the future book about Edgar Allan Poe, which they would co-author. They would turn the draft of the book manuscript over to the king of the Moscow publishers. Then, without procrastination, they would compose and submit a grant application, its successful outcome meant to provide added support for their future family life—a grant, along with Polyakov's professorial salary. Armed with a grant, Sashenka would find an adjunct position in the San Diego area, perhaps for three or even five years, but that seemed like a long time for those who cannot live without each other.

They left Café Paragon in excellent spirits. A new crescent moon shone over Providence. Beata was peacefully asleep in the matchbox. At least, no sound came from the pocket of the blazer. It was all so odd: while savoring their batter-fried shrimp appetizers with Sam Adams, the famous New England beer, which was served in iced pint glasses; while biting the juicy meat off the fire-roasted lamb ribs; and later while perking themselves up with sips of espresso, the two of them thought of one thing only. To get back to the empty house of Edgar Allan Poe, which was left to them for two months after such a miraculous turn of events. And the most peculiar thing was that Polyakov, who told Sashenka about his lucky meeting with Karl the dwarf, the golden-eyed beetle Beata, and the generous mistress of the house, Lena Whitman, said nothing about her astonishing resemblance to Sashenka Tverskaya. He kept it from Sashenka in order to be able to explore a few possible explanations behind this mystifying situation: she knew nothing about Lena Whitman (his first hypothesis); she knew about the existence of a twin sister but destiny had separated them so long ago that both the story of Lena's American marriage and her last name, Whitman, were unknown to Sashenka; and (his third hypothesis), there was no sisterly connection whatsoever between Lena and Sashenka, their resemblance owing itself to the law of big numbers. The combined population of Russia and America totaled about 500 million, Polyakov reasoned. How could there be no doubles among them?

They called a cab, stopped at the university guesthouse to collect his suitcase and carry-on bag, and rushed over to the house of Edgar Allan Poe. A small glitch occurred on the house porch. An awful rattling came from Polyakov's pocket, as if a folk ensemble of one the most musical African tribes, comprised of ratchets, tambourines, and tam-tams, was staging a mass protest. What could it be? wondered Polyakov. Well, of course, it's all because of the incredible likeness between Sashenka and Lena, our hero answered his own question. The golden-eyed beetle was rattling and thrashing against the walls of the matchbox. Naturally she had grasped the essence of what was going on. Now the last thing Polyakov needed was for Karl the dwarf to trek over here from the other side of the street to protest the substitution of the double (Sashenka) for the mistress of the house (Lena). Polyakov opened the box and let Beata out. She slipped in through a crack under the back door and disappeared into the house. It should be noted that in Providence, like elsewhere in America, people have what, to a Russian émigré, seems like a frustrating habit of using the back door on a day-to-day basis and opening the front door exclusively for special occasions and parties.

Polyakov and Sashenka stayed at the house of Edgar Allan Poe for almost two months. They collected all the materials they could ever need for the book. Such a wealth of valuable manuscripts, letters, journals, and photographs had been accumulated and preserved since the death of the genius of fantasy writing, there was enough there for a number of monographs and dozens of research grant proposals. After they added up all the discoveries they had made at the Rockefeller and John Hay libraries and at the Athenaeum, they became convinced it was time to wrap up the research and get down to writing. It was decided that Professor Polyakov would write his part of the book draft and of the grant proposal after he got back to San Diego, and Sashenka would do her part in Providence. They would collate and parse the sections, and send the manuscript to the Moscow publisher and the grant proposal to several American foundations.

While they had buried themselves in collecting materials, Polyakov kept driving away thoughts about Lena Whitman. How did her surgery go? Would she be returning soon or would she stay in Boston for post-op treatment? Would there be a sequel to their brief encounter? He still hadn't told Sashenka about the stirring resemblance between her and the mistress of the house. Why? Sashenka and Lena must have been separated in a childhood that was so distant and removed from their lives in America that neither one of them had remembered the time when they were still together or could make sense of it. Then Polyakov recalled that Sashenka had told him about growing up in an orphanage in Russia; owing to her natural intelligence and tenacity, she put herself through university in Russia and was later accepted to graduate school in America. As for Lena Whitman's story, aside from the fact that she was a widow of a millionaire shipowner, she was for him an absolute terra incognita, as Polyakov metaphorically envisioned the complete obscurity of her background. Ideally, he wanted to leave Providence as quickly as possible, and to take Sashenka away from this town, without further delay and as soon as financial circumstances would permit it. The thought of even a chance encounter between the two young women did not thrill him one bit.

In order to develop a close bond with the golden-eyed beetle, Polyakov adopted for himself the notion of Beata as a very rare pet.

After all, there are pet iguanas, pet parrots, pet skunks. Even bees living in garden hives can justly be considered pet insects because both the garden and the house are parts of the owner's estate. In this case why not Beata, with all her intelligence and training? This is why first Polyakov and later Sashenka began to feed Beata various treats. They even purchased a toy tea set that they arranged on a small tray by the kitchen stove, where it was always warmer. They poured water or milk into the little cups. Onto the small plates they put finely chopped hard-boiled eggs. Or tiny slices of fruit. Or pieces of chocolate. Once, Sashenka noticed how Karl the dwarf, who had walked over from the other end of Benefit Street, tried to entice Beata with chocolate. But the loyal insect wouldn't go to him. After all, the dwarf could have snapped on the leash and then tried to sell the golden-eyed beetle once again. Sometimes Sashenka marveled at how tender Beata was with her and how she ran to Sashenka's every call. Polyakov guessed why, but kept his secret.

The time came for their parting dinner. Polyakov was leaving for California the following day. Sashenka was going back to her shared rental apartment. At first, they thought of having a blowout feast in one of the restaurants on Atwells Avenue, in the Italian section of Providence. Then they changed their minds; they wanted to stay for as long as possible in the miraculous house of Edgar Allan Poe. They bought wine and lots of different *zakuski*; they lit candles. In the window dusk of the unshuttered August evening, the silver candlesticks and the waxy, braided candles glistened, like pillars of a toy temple. As is the habit with many Russians, they dined in the kitchen and then moved over to the living room for coffee. Beata followed them there and even seated herself on an embroidered couch pillow, although she kept looking over her shoulder and flickering her legs.

"So we've seen everything in the house and committed to memory all the books, paintings, and photographs here, yet for some reason I have the feeling there's something else. And Beata is trying to say something to us," Polyakov observed thoughtfully.

"Why don't you put her leash on? Perhaps there is something Beata would like to show us," suggested Sashenka.

With the snap swivel, Polyakov fastened the leash on to the collar of the golden-eyed beetle; she immediately hopped off the couch cushion onto the floor, as if she had been waiting for that moment. Beata ran out of the living room into the hallway, and from there, down the staircase leading to the cellar.

"We've never been here!" exclaimed Polyakov.

"It's as if the staircase door was so cleverly hidden that it looked like part of the wall," said Sashenka.

The beetle tugged on the leash like a hound, illuminating the way down to the cellar with the golden spotlights of her eyes. Polyakov was the first to take a step down the cold, musty stairs. Sashenka hesitantly followed him. All of a sudden, a black hole opened to their eyes; leading further down, the hole swallowed the beetle and then Polyakov. Soft choral music wafted in from the hole, penetrating Sashenka's timorous heart and making her feel less afraid. Beata, Polyakov, and Sashenka crossed deeper into the dungeon. The golden-eyed beetle stopped on top of a stone plate, indicating to Polyakov that he needed to lift it. Under the plate there was a chest. They opened it. It was filled with gold coins: guldens, doubloons, ducats, Louis d'ors, crowns, condors, florins, écus, and many others, including Russian gold rubles. Under another stone plate, to which Beata also pointed with her golden spotlights, there stood amphoras full of Indian pearls, rough-cut diamonds, rubies, sapphires, and emeralds. Whatever spot the golden-eyed beetle moved to, our researchers discovered stone plates concealing jewelry chests, various richly encrusted luxury objects, and weapons unrivaled both in the quality of their steel and the splendor of their decoration.

They were still standing in the middle of the cellar, bewildered and rapturous, when the buzzing of the doorbell, muffled by its remoteness and the spiraled trajectory of the sound, reached them. The beetle leapt up with joy, tugged on her leash, and raced up the stairs back to the hallway and from there to the door opening onto the back porch. Parked outside was the white behemoth of a limousine, the same one that had taken Lena Whitman to the hospital for her surgery two months earlier. It was definitely the same one, because Eduard Polyakov had remembered the gold piping of the black driver's uniform cap. Only this time, Lena jumped out of the limousine and ran up the stone steps porch on her light feet. From the porch she motioned to the driver that he was free to return to the garage. Then she quickly bent down and offered the golden-eyed beetle an open palm, onto which the creature eagerly climbed.

"You smart girl!" laughed Lena Whitman and petted the beetle on the back.

Polyakov froze in bewilderment. Sashenka Tverskaya stared at Lena Whitman as though into a mirror. The mistress of the house, however, did not seem surprised at all.

"Hello, sister mine," she addressed Sashenka. "Here we are, finally. We were little when they separated us at an orphanage somewhere outside the city of Tula, I think near Yasnaya Polyana. Way back, Leo Tolstoy had made arrangements for the future orphans. I was taken from the orphanage by wealthy Americans—the ship-owner Whitman and his wife, but she died soon after that. The moment I turned eighteen, Whitman married me and then left me huge amounts of wealth—in stocks, gold, and treasures—that had accumulated in his family over the three centuries that the New-port Line Shipping Company had been in existence. In theory, I now own all of it, but in reality, I've only seen the bank statements and the annual reports from my estate manager. There are treasures which I still haven't managed to locate."

"But they are here, the treasures!" exclaimed Sashenka as she tried to pull Beata's leash out of Lena's hands. But the beetle would have none of it. The mistress of the house of Edgar Allan Poe wasn't letting go of the leash, either. Polyakov had no idea what to say, especially since it was not in his plans to share the discovered riches with anyone at all, including Sashenka Tverskaya or the mistress of the house of Edgar Allan Poe. He chose to keep silent, observing the two whom he now presumed to be twin sisters. For her part, Sashenka Tverskaya was prepared to make do with only a fraction of the treasures she and Polyakov had discovered in the cellar. To this end, she readily offered Lena Whitman a short version of her own life story that boiled down to the following: after crying bitterly over having to part with her dearly beloved sister Lenochka, she finally acquiesced, eventually earned a degree from Moscow University, and was accepted to graduate school at San Diego. We're already familiar with the story of her graduate work under the tutelage of Eduard Polyakov. . . .

"You aren't planning to sue them, are you?" obnoxiously asked Karl the dwarf, who had materialized from the cellar and was able to read Eduard Polyakov's brazen thoughts.

"Naturally, we won't let things get to trial," retorted Polyakov, "especially since I'm engaged to one—or, arguably, both—of them."

Sashenka didn't say anything, and Lena Whitman looked sincerely surprised.

"Simple as day," Polyakov came back, "if one assumes that you're identical twins, embryologically speaking, one and the same organism split by subsequent genetic commands . . ."

"—Professor, you don't think your hypothesis goes a little too far?" Lena Whitman asked.

"What would you suggest?" Polyakov feverishly asked.

"You take as many treasures from the cellar as you can fit in your briefcase and leave Providence at once. Karl, please help the professor and see him to the airport, just to be sure!" Lena ordered the dwarf.

Polyakov and Karl the dwarf dove into the cellar.

"You, my darling sister, you will stay here in my house. I have my sights set on a young writer from the Creative Writing Program. With him, you'll forget your Eduard Polyakov for good."

Finally, Lena Whitman turned to the golden-eyed Beata: "And you, my beautiful girl, as soon as Polyakov leaves, you go and close the cellar door until another time. And shut it so tight that even a mosquito wouldn't be able to get its nose in."

2009
Translated from the Russian by Margarit T. Ordukhanyan

Trubetskoy, Raevsky, Masha Malevich, and the Death of Mayakovsky

Then, suddenly, I didn't have any work. Neither academic, nor literary. This happened because we (my wife and I and our son) had applied for an exit visa to emigrate to Israel. We were fired from our academic jobs, and I was also expelled from the Union of Writers. For a year we had been waiting for the permission to leave. Then the war in Afghanistan began. The authorities turned down—refused—our request for an exit visa. We became refuseniks. One had to go on living: put food on the table, pay for the apartment, fill the tank with gasoline, mail letters, buy wine when we were going to a party or expected company. There's always something to pay for! I had to find some paying work.

I had an old pal by the name of Zhen'ka Fyodorov. Our connection spanned across many years of my scientific career, when I was a researcher at the Moscow Institute of Microbiology. As a graduate student, Zhen'ka took pains to complete his dissertation in our division of infectious pathology. We all helped him, myself included. I suppose I might have helped him a bit more than did others. Zhen'ka studied anaphylactic shock caused by infections of the bloodstream. I helped him inoculate rabbits. Eventually he completed his dissertation and found an academic administrative position at the Academy of Medical Sciences located downtown on Solyanka Street. Our acquaintance continued, following a pattern of mutually-attracting opposites. I was a research microbiologist and a writer. He was a microbiologist (in a manner of speaking) and a musician—in the evening Zhen'ka played in a jazz band at the Metropol Restaurant. I was a Jew, he a Jew on his mother's side. On the whole, Zhen'ka Fyodorov was one of those trusty people who, even if they don't end up helping you, would at least not go telling the whole world that such-and-such a person is on the verge of disaster and from this low verge has crawled to them begging for help. Even if he couldn't help with action, he gave sound practical advice.

It was the end of June. Four-fifths of the twentieth century had flown by, but the good old Soviet tractor, squeaking and releasing exhaust fumes, still furrowed the hilly expanses of our fabulous homeland and all its Asiatic and European environs. I, having left behind first the bronze monument to the first Cheka leader Dzherzhinsky, passed the headquarters of the central committee of the Bolshevik party, the standing remnants of Moscow's medieval walls, and the Choral Synagogue. Eventually I found myself on Solyanka Street. I located a barely legal parking space for my old Zhiguli on one of the side streets, and entered the building of the Academy of Medical Sciences. My pal Zhen'ka Fyodorov (round-faced, chestnut-eyed, clean-shaven, with pomaded dark wavy hair) was sitting in his office, its half-open door adorned with the sign "E. M. Fyodorov, Academic Administrator, Microbiology." I knocked, he opened the door to let me in, I entered, he insisted that I sit in an armchair, I apologized for my invasion, he waved my apology away with both his hands, I revealed the purpose of my visit, he grew pensive, I continued to sit, he continued to think, I wasn't leaving, he made some tea, I took a sip from a glass, he hardly touched his tea, I kept gulping with impatience, he slowly stirred his with a spoon, I . . . he . . . I . . . he . . . I . . . he. . . .

Finally Zhen'ka came through: "Your situation blows, good pal."

"I know it does."

"How will you make a living?"

"I'll find something."

"First you'll find something, and then they'll find out you're a refusenik and kick you out."

"So what can I do, Zhen'ka?"

"Seek reliable connections."

"And?"

"In a side street catty-corner across the road, toward Pokrovsky Boulevard, there's a medical college. It's part of our Academy system. So they're looking for somebody to teach microbiology. You'll go see the dean of the college. Her name is Nina Mikhailovna Kapustina. Tell her I suggested it. And be sure to mention that you're also an author. Having trouble getting commissions. Isn't it true?"

"Of course it's true," I answered.

"That's what I said. Tell her how hard it is to get your work published. Which is also true, isn't it?"

"100 percent accurate. They have stopped publishing me."

"Yeah, and tell her you must hold on to your medical profession. And then flash some sort of a membership card? From the Union of Writers? Or perhaps the Literary Foundation?"

"They took away both."

"Don't you have some document attesting to your literary qualifications?"

"I still have the writers' local union."

"That will do the trick! Go, my good man, go now, otherwise someone could stand in your path," Zhenka instructed me as he saw me out of his office.

In September I started teaching a microbiology course for future laboratory technicians. There were about twenty-five students in my class. For the most part, they were young people who had graduated from high school yet didn't get into university to study medicine. There were a few more girls than boys. I lectured on theory and also conducted the labs. The lab manuals were kept in the microbiology office. A man by the name of Minkin was in charge of microbiology instruction. Not surprisingly, he had immediately figured out my story, but for a period of time he kept up appearances. Especially since I had been recommended to him by the college dean N. M. Kapustina. As it happened, I believe the dean had also seen through my not very intricate explanations that wove together the absence of book contracts and publishing opportunities with a sudden urge to return to medicine. (I hadn't said anything about my career as a research microbiologist or about the academic position from which I had been fired.) It wasn't hard to put two and two together. But the dean also kept up appearances. And it turned out that she had been looking the other way for reasons quite contrary to Minkin's. Once, catching up with me in the hallway, N. M. Kapustina let slip this remark:

"By the way, Daniil Aleksandrovich, did you know that one of the first deans of our college was Yelena Bonner?"

"Very interesting," I responded, not sure whether to take her words as a sign of trust or a police detective's trick.

For a whole academic year, I continued to teach microbiology without any troubles. The spring semester exams were nearing. In the meantime, a storm gripped our medical college. Human storms brew exactly the way ocean storms gather strength. Everything seems calm and quiet for a while, while in fact numerous poles of tension are accumulated within the same quadrant of human society (in this case, the college). Then we see flashes of lightening, hear loud thunder, then scandals erupt, which in turn result in panic and bring out in people the unnatural desire to finish off the ones who have already been stricken. Due to a strange confluence of destinies (or was everything simply slapped together by the one on high?) my class had, along with some ordinary boys and girls, several students with rather extraordinary, downright famous last names: Misha Trubetskoy, Sasha Raevsky, and Masha Malevich. It was difficult (however much I wanted it) to believe that Sasha and Misha were related to the famous Decembrist insurrectionists, and Masha to Kazimir Malevich, the great suprematist painter. As much as I wanted this all to be true, I immediately failed in my speculations. Misha Trubetskoy (brown-haired, tall, a hockey player) descended not from the Russian aristocracy but from a working class family residing at Krasnaya Presnya, while Sasha Raevsky (hair black and curly, lips pouty) was a Jewish boy originally from Poltava in Ukraine, whose parents had moved to Moscow ten years earlier. Only Masha Malevich (a red-haired, freckle-faced girl with an invisible hula hoop constantly spinning around her whirly hips) gave back some hope of being able to transcend fantasy into reality.

"Yes, it's true," Masha admitted. "I'm actually Kazimir Malevich's grand-niece. But despite the close kinship, I don't understand the meaning of his 'Black Square' painting."

When this all happened I was trying to tell my students about the most significant discoveries in the field of microbiology. About the discoveries which were made parallel with the century's great scientific discoveries and the great advances in the arts. Say, Malevich's "Black Square" and Einstein's theory of relativity. Or microbial viruses—bacteriophages—discovered by d'Herelle around the same time when Rutherford predicted the planetary model of the atom. In this connection, I told my students the story of the "French cottage." I told them about the brilliant observation made by the great French-Canadian microbiologist Félix d'Herelle, that some viruses are capable of killing microbes that cause cholera, plague, diphtheria, and other dangerous infections. How d'Herelle befriended Giorgi Eliava, the talented Georgian microbiologist, and how together they decided to found the Institute of Bacteriophage in Tbilisi, the capital of Georgia. Then Eliava was executed by the order of Beria, and d'Herelle, who had managed to return to Paris not long before World War II, was kept under house arrest for refusing to collaborate with the Germans. And later, in the 1970s, I had gone to Tbilisi to learn about this from those former colleagues of d'Herelle and Eliava who had survived. I located the building (the "French cottage") where d'Herelle and Eliava were supposed to have been living with their families. But things had turned out differently and the cottage had been taken from the Institute of Bacteriophage and transferred over to some secret agency overseen by Beria himself. . . .

I must have gone too far in my recollections, and (as a consequence of my excessive openness) on the next day this resulted in four unexpected conversations.

No sooner had I parked my Zhiguli right outside the college than the head of microbiology instruction, Minkin (a corpulent, unctuous shorty whose bald head rolled from under a well-worn corduroy fedora like an ostrich egg out of an overturned nest), bolted out of his tanklike swampy-green Pobeda and stood in my path:

"Hey, Geyer. Speak of the devil!" Minkin saluted me. "Just thinking of you, and there you are . . ."

"How can I be of help?"

"How's the old horse?"

"Still running, but the oats are pricy these days," I tried to joke it off.

"I know exactly what you mean. After what you were used to. . . ."

"—Give me a break, Minkin!"

"We can talk salaries later. But first, about oats—that is, gasoline. Do you know how much my Pobeda used to burn? You'll never guess: half my salary. Well, most definitely a quarter of what I earned."

"I feel for you, Minkin."

"Too late for that, Geyer."

"Eh?"

"Too late to feel sorry for me. You should feel sorry for yourself."

"All these ambiguities. Could you speak a bit more clearly, Minkin."

"More clearly, okay: convert to diesel. Truck drivers will sell you a tankful for a buck or two and will thank you for it."

"But my engine isn't a diesel one."

"Now we're getting to the point. The point is that I had the original engine replaced with a diesel one."

"I'm not capable of such radical change."

"Don't be so modest, Geyer. I'm well aware of your grand plan, now temporarily on hold. I myself was one foot in the Visa Office when the whole thing happened."

"What happened, Minkin?"

"Oh, don't pretend, Geyer. You know Ilya Minkin."

"I met him a couple of times at the House of Writers."

"He's my first cousin," Minkin said. "He got five years of labor camp for writing *chernukha*. . . ."

I would have never guessed such radically different people could be related. I've already introduced my teaching colleague: a corpulent, unctuous shorty with a bald head jutting from under the well-worn fedora's corduroy nest. And very pushy, I remember thinking. But what if I had made an error of judgment, taking the physical attributes of the head of microbiology instruction to represent his character? Hadn't I met enough impeccably honest people with beer bellies and bald heads? I even felt pangs of remorse. The man's close relative, one my literary brethren, ended up in the Gulag for composing anti-Soviet satirical poems, and I. . . .

"Forgive me, Minkin. I hadn't made the connection. What happened to your cousin is terrible. Please accept my sympathy."

"What can we do, Geyer. We must keep on going. And not repeat the same mistakes. By pure chance I learned about the lecture you delivered yesterday. You chose an amazing topic: science and art. And the story of the 'French cottage' and Beria! Remarkable stuff. You're a brave man. But be careful, Geyer. There are informants in every class."

"I can see that, Minkin. How else would you have known?"

He pretended not to have heard my last words and melted away in the halls of the college.

I hadn't even finished putting up tables and drawings of various microorganisms and placing glass slides with stained bacteria under the students' microscopes, when the dean's secretary entered the classroom and asked me to come with her. Nina Mikhailovna Kapustina greeted me with a smile, but her smile showed both sympathy and a measure of rebuke directed not so much at me but at herself, as she had ended up—was this due to my actions?—in a rather precarious position. That's why her smile was fleeting, and only for a moment did it smooth the wrinkles and furrows on her kindly face, that of a sixty-something Russian village teacher.

"Daniil Alexandrovich, I heard about your outstanding lecture. I sincerely regret (she was speaking slowly), sincerely regret that I didn't know about it and therefore couldn't be there."

"Thank you, Nina Mikhailovna," I replied.

"But Golyakova, our associate dean for education, she also wasn't there, yet seems very alarmed."

"Alarmed by what?"

"By the general direction of your ideas and the way it stirs up the minds of our students."

"But isn't the goal of education to stir up the minds of students?"

"This is what you and I think, Daniil Aleksandrovich. But associate dean Golyakova has a very different view of the matter."

"But . . . well," I attempted to mount a response.

"Think about it, Daniil Aleksandrovich. Especially since I'm retiring, and starting with the coming academic year Golyakova will assume the position of dean."

I gave a rather uninspiring class. And I should have been more animated, especially because this was one of the last classes of the academic year. Ahead lay the final exams and the summer break. Based on the semester's results (or so I believed), the administration would decide whether or not to renew my contract for the next year. I was, after all, only a part-time instructor.

I was moving the tables and microscopes from the classroom back to the microbiology office when a gentle voice with but a trace of a Georgian accent called my name.

"Daniil, do you have five minutes to chat?"

This was Tamara Ordzhonikidze, the mathematics instructor and the only person in the college who called me by first name and without patronymic. And naturally I also called her Tamara, without patronymic. I felt a strong attachment to Georgia going back to my childhood, when I had read Anna Antonovskaya's multivolume novel *The Great Mouravi*, about the life and exploits of Giorgi Saakadze. And much later, in the 1970s, I spent time in Tbilisi trying to investigate the story of d'Herelle and the "French cottage." Thus everything Georgian was of interest to me.

Tamara Ordzhonikidze was standing by the open window and smoking a Kazbek brand *papirosa*. Her attractive face, framed by long black hair with silver strands, was half-turned to the midday sun bursting through the green branches of poplars that grew all around the perimeter of the college. This made the dark chenille of her eyes even thicker and warmer. We called each other by first name, as was the custom of her homeland. How could I possibly say no to Tamara?

"This isn't about my lecture from yesterday, is it?"

"Yes indeed. The college is all abuzz with your lecture, my dear Daniil. This research and your findings around the "French cottage," have they been published?"

"Not yet. The manuscript of the book is under consideration by the publishing house Merani in Tbilisi. The editorial director is

Karlo Kaladze. I had translated some of his poems into Russian. So we'll see what happens."

"Daniil, in your lecture you mentioned Beria. You know, I remember him well from Tbilisi. Our families lived in the same building. In 1937 my parents were executed by his order. Sergo Ordzhonikidze was my father's brother, my uncle. My brother and I used to play outside with Beria's children. They say this is why he spared us."

I shook her hand and headed out. Outside, right near the front entrance, there stood Vanya Bogolyubov, one of my students, and next to him, a middle-aged man. The man was dressed unseasonably: a grey suit of heavy wool, a thick shirt buttoned all the way up, a derby hat. In his right hand he held an umbrella, and in the left, a battered briefcase. Vanya introduced the man:

"This is my father, Vasily Pavlovich Bogolyubov."

"Very nice to meet you," I said. "What can I do for you?"

"It was heartening to hear my son's accounts of your teaching. I thank you from the bottom of my heart," said Bogolyubov senior.

"Thank you. I do my best to instill . . . values and the like . . . ," I replied, sensing that Bogolyubov senior didn't come to talk about my teaching philosophy.

Bogolyubov senior saw that I was waiting for the subject of the conversation to take shape, but he wavered, coughing into his hand and wiping first his lips and hands, then his perspiring brow, with a paper hanky which he removed from a pack he kept in his briefcase. Then he finally said:

"Vital circumstances having to do with my son Ivan have brought me here. I would like to have a word. But not here. If you could give us half an hour or perhaps an hour of your time. . . ."

"Okay. What would you like me to do?"

"We would like you to go with us to the Baptist church to which we belong, and to talk with our pastor about Ivan's situation. It isn't far from here. Chistoprudny Boulevard."

Truth to tell, I was more than surprised. More. And not just surprised. What's the secrecy? Couldn't we talk right there in the street? Or go back inside and find a vacant classroom? We could have comfortably talked in the microbiology office—Minkin had just driven off in his diesel-gulping Pobeda.

"But couldn't we . . . ? I would be happy to wait. . . . Telephone your pastor and tell him to come here. . . . I would gladly . . . ," I tried to stay on neutral territory. But was there such a thing as "neutral territory"?

"Not possible, Daniil Aleksandrovich. The pastor's appearance in the college would ruin everything," Bogolyubov senior explained.

So I had to agree. We got in my car and rode off to see the pastor. The Baptist church was located in a lane off Chistoprudny Boulevard. We entered the church. I looked around. It was a hall with a high ceiling, rows of benches, and a pulpit. I counted about thirty or forty yellow benches, of the sort that one saw in rural activity halls or in peasant houses. From a dark door behind the pulpit, a man of uncertain age came out to greet us. He was dressed in a black suit and a buttoned-up white shirt with a high collar. The clean-shaven face of the man in the black suit expressed sorrow and empathy. He extended his hand, its whitish skin having probably forgotten about sunlight or fresh air.

"Pastor Gribov," said the man in the black suit.

"Geyer," I said. We traded handshakes.

"Ivan Bogolyubov has told me what an unusual teacher you are, citizen . . . Mister . . . Comrade Geyer."

"Daniil Aleksandrovich," I prompted.

"Yes, exactly, a very unusual teacher. Isn't it so, Ivan?"

Ivan nodded in embarrassment.

I patted him on the shoulder: "Thanks, Vanya."

"This means, Daniil Aleksandrovich, that you carry the Lord's word in your heart. And to us, Evangelical Christian Baptists, this is paramount, since we believe in one's personal answerability before the Lord. Which is why we've turned to you, with a plea to help our brother Ivan Bogolyubov. We turn to you, Daniil Aleksandrovich, even though you're not of the Baptist faith but of the Jewish faith. (I nodded, confirming that I was not of the Baptist but of the Jewish faith and also that they did the right thing by turning to me.) Yes, of the Jewish faith, which is especially meaningful to us, since the Baptist teaching considers ancient Palestine to be the place of its origin."

"And what would my help consist of?"

"Ivan's being drafted to the military. He already received a summons from the military commissariat. And in accordance with our beliefs, an Evangelical Christian Baptist may not bear weapons of murdering another human being. Thus, a situation is about to ensue where for refusing to bear arms Ivan will be imprisoned," said Pastor Gribov and looked in the direction of Bogolyubov senior. The latter bowed his head and hunched over as though burdened by the weight of a coffin.

"Can something really be done?" I queried, weighed down as I was by the oppressive predicament in which my family and the families of the other refuseniks found themselves. The same machinery of the secret police, like the medieval Inquisition, wrenched out the arms and broke the lives of Christian Baptists and Jewish refuseniks. "How can I help Ivan?"

"If you, Daniil Aleksandrovich, would agree to write a letter to the chief of the district military commissariat, requesting that Ivan be given a deferral for a year until he has finished his diploma, this could save him. Perhaps he could get into medical school, and then he wouldn't be drafted. But even if he doesn't get in, in a year Ivan would receive his laboratory technician's diploma, and with it he would serve in the medical corps, and not as a regular soldier. Here's the address of the military commissariat."

I went home, wrote the letter, and sent it to the chief of the district military commissariat by certified mail. Several days passed.

There was an old tradition at the college. On the eve of the finals, the college hosted a tea party and a lecture for the teachers. Usually the invited speaker would lecture about theater, cinema, music, or politics. They would set up a long table with deserts in the main lecture hall upstairs, bring up teacups from the cafeteria, and brew some tea in a pot; the teachers would fortify themselves on pastries, arrange the chairs, and sit down for the presentation. Very often slides would accompany the talk. Unlike the required meetings of the teaching council, these cultural and educational activities were optional, and the teachers attended them with enthusiasm. This time, the invited speaker was a researcher from the Literary Museum, a skinny, nervous, sloppily dressed woman. Probably because her own fate (as compared to the collective fate of Russian literature) was of little interest to the researcher, because of this self-indifference or self-despondency, or else because she knew so desperately that in her hands was a terrible secret, the lecturer spoke, showed evidence, and delivered arguments with great passion.

She spoke of the death of Vladimir Mayakovsky. She showed X-rays of the skull and neck vertebrae of a burly man. And she offered proof that those were the images of Mayakovsky's skull and skeleton, that he was in fact shot in the back. She showed and argued that the great poet's "suicide" was scam and camouflage, tricks of those who had murdered him. But even if this was a suicide, the death of the great poet was nevertheless on "their" conscience. The lecture left us with a sense of dejection and complete hopelessness. Nobody even asked questions. Before leaving, the lecturer took a gulp of the tea and asked the leader of the teachers' local union to sign the paperwork for her speaking fee. My gaze met the gaze of Tamara Ordzhonikidzhe, but she uttered a hasty goodbye and was gone. I went down to retrieve my briefcase from the microbiology teaching office. Minkin followed me there.

"They bring the man to the brink of disaster, and then—he's all alone. Either they will shoot you from around the corner or they will push you to suicide," he said, wrathfully ogling me and wiping his forehead, which was dotted with beads of sweat from drinking too much hot tea.

Or was it the sweat of fear for the fate of Russian literature? "What a great lecture!" Minkin added.

"Yes, a fascinating hypothesis," I replied.

"Hypothesis? This is much more than a hypothesis. We must, as they say, look the facts in the face."

"Or in the nape of the neck," I clarified. "They shot in the back. But the bullet must have gone right through. If we can trust the speaker."

"Geyer, we must trust people. We must! People are pleading for help, and we refuse to trust them until it's too late, until tragedy has already occurred. Take Ivan Bogolyubov. I worry that we'll miss the boat in his case. I hope we don't act too late, Geyer. But then again, you aren't the type that. . . ."

Driving home at the wheel of my trusty Zhiguli, I kept going over the conversation with Minkin. On the one hand, he had a cousin in a labor camp, but on the other. . . . Something about him didn't make sense to me. Although, I suppose, physiognomy isn't my forte. I go in for superficial details. Something in a person's face rubs me the wrong way and I grow weary. This way, because of my suspiciousness, I probably miss out on many good folks.

The day before the microbiology final I held a review session for my students. They asked questions. I answered them, although I tried to involve the whole group in finding the best approach to the problem. Students were still confused about differentiating between types of food poisoning. We kept going over the biochemical and immunological properties of intestinal bacteria. The review session was chugging along, but I could see that the students were worked up about something. Not worked up about the upcoming exam but rather alarmed by something else. Even the seating arrangement suggested something was the matter. Misha Trubetskoy, Sasha Raevsky, Masha Malevich, and Vanya Bogolyubov all shared the same long table. Bogolyubov sat between Raevsky and Malevich. They looked like a chain of climbers intent on storming a high mountain.

Masha Malevich raised her hand and asked:

"Daniil Aleksandrovich, you told us how Beria's associates arrested d'Herelle's colleague, Professor Eliava, and then shot him. In your view, how would d'Herelle himself have acted, had he been not in Paris but in Tbilisi at the time?"

"I think, I'm almost certain, that d'Herelle would have protested. . . ."

"Well, we also wish to protest that Vanya Bogolyubov is being drafted into the army," Sasha Raevsky said, and all three of them (Trubetskoy, Raevsky and Masha Malevich) stood up, as if shielding Vanya Bogolyubov with their bodies.

At that moment the associate dean Golyakova entered the classroom. She was a bleached-blonde in her forties, clad in a navy "official" suit of the sort that female party activists frequently wore. With her was a junior law enforcement officer, a fellow with broad shoulders and the little charcoals of his eyes sparkling on his massive square face. In his hands the officer held a green piece of paper.

"Sit down," Golyakova said to the standing students. "And you, yes you, Ivan Bogolyubov, stand up and approach the officer from the precinct."

Misha Trubetskoy sat down. Sasha Raevsky and Masha Malevich remained standing. Associate dean Golyakova pretended not to notice this. With hunger in her eyes, she observed Vanya Bogolyubov as he climbed from behind the table and walked toward the officer.

"Sign here, citizen Bogolyubov," the officer gestured to the green notice of summons. "If tomorrow you don't appear at the military commissariat, you'll be arrested and tried."

"Excuse me," I addressed both the officer and Golyakova. "You're disrupting my review session. The exam is tomorrow, so please. . . ."

" . . . it isn't your place, Daniil Aleksandrovich, to tell the dean and the representative of law enforcement what we should and what we should not be doing," Golyakova stopped me short. "Although one could expect worse things from you."

In the meantime, Vanya Bogolyubov signed the summons. The officer and Golyakova left the classroom.

The next day, driving to the exam, I was anxious. And my students, too, were distressed by yesterday's invasion. One of the few privileges that the Soviet regime hadn't taken from the students was the freedom of taking the oral exam in the order of their own choosing. This is why up to a point I hadn't been paying attention to the absence of Vanya Bogolyubov. But now half the students had taken the exam and left. I tested and released more students. Now only Trubetskoy, Raevsky, and Masha Malevich remained outside the door. They must have been waiting for Bogolyubov. Then they, too, came in, drew their pieces of paper with questions (the "tickets"), gathered their thoughts, and, one by one, passed the exam. It was over. Vanya Bogolyubov never showed up. I decided to wait a little while longer. I sat in the classroom and leafed through the paper. I was having trouble concentrating. Anxious thoughts wouldn't leave me. Finally, as I prepared to leave, I was called to the telephone. It was Bogolyubov senior.

"Very sorry to bother you, Daniil Aleksandrovich. Ivan is still at the military commissariat. He was hoping to make it to the exam. But it's not working out today. Could he possibly take it tomorrow?"

Of course I agreed to conduct Ivan's exam on the following day.

But Bogolyubov didn't show up for the exam. In the evening, his parents came home from work to find him dead. He took his life. The next day or perhaps the one after that, Vanya Bogolyubov's father telephoned to tell me that the funeral service would be held at the Baptist church. I bought flowers and drove to Chistoprudny Boulevard. A law enforcement officer stood on duty outside the entrance. I thought it was the same fellow who had delivered the summons during my review session (broad shoulders, little charcoals of eyes sparkling on his massive square face). The casket stood in front of the pulpit. I laid down the flowers and looked around. Sasha Raevsky and Masha Malevich sat in the second row. Misha Trubetskoy wasn't there. I joined my students. The pastor ascended the pulpit and gave a eulogy, then said a prayer. The congregation repeated after the pastor: "Forever and ever, amen . . . amen . . . amen. . . ."

After the cemetery I gave the students a ride home, dropping off first Masha Malevich, then Sasha Raevsky.

My wife greeted me with alarming news: "You got a call from the college. You're urgently wanted by the associate dean. She's expecting you tomorrow at 10 a.m."

The next day I knocked at the door with the sign "Associate dean for education, C. M. Sc. [candidate of medical sciences] Galina Stepanovna Golyakova."

"Enter!" said a voice from behind the door.

Golyakova was sitting at her desk. "Sit!" she ordered.

I sat down.

"Read!" said Golyakova and handed me a sheet of paper, filled with lines hopping up and down the page. I read: "I consider it my civic duty to warn the administration of our college that the microbiology instructor D. A. Geyer has applied for an exit visa to Israel." There was no signature, but I immediately recognized Minkin's penmanship. There was something revoltingly toadish in his handwriting. Toadish, as when a repulsive swamp creature covered with warts hops heavily from mound to mound. From mound to mound. From mound to mound. . . .

"Tell me, Geyer, is it true that you want to leave the Soviet Union?"

"Yes, it's true."

"And with that you weren't embarrassed to join the faculty of our medical college?"

"What's to be embarrassed about, Galina Stepanovna?"

"What? I'll tell you what there is to be embarrassed about, citizen . . . yes, you're still a citizen, although I would immediately strip the likes of you of citizenship! . . . You, citizen Geyer, should be embarrassed about the fact that you betrayed your motherland, who has raised you, fed and clothed you, and given you an education. And also, judging by your CV, has taught you to compose literary works. Although I have trouble believing your works could be worth anything, citizen Geyer."

"I didn't betray Russia, but actually, what's the point . . ."

"—Don't wave off my words, unless you want me to tell you what I know to be the truth about Ivan Bogolyubov's tragic death."

"What do you know to be the truth?"

"Why did you stick your nose into the affairs of the Baptist sect? Why did you promise their pastor to write a letter to the military commissariat? And why did you write it and send it via certified mail? You planted needless illusions in the soul of a youth intoxicated by the opium of religion, a youth who was supposed to carry out the sacred duty of defending his motherland. Ah, what would be the point of discussing sacred values with you! You didn't even spare your students. Why did you talk them into attending the funeral service at the Baptist church? You ought to be banned from getting anywhere near the students! Very soon they will be taking children from the kikes of you, I mean the *likes* of you, taking them away and placing them in orphanages, where they will educate them as worthy citizens."

"Is that why you called me in?" I asked.

"Yes that's why! And also to inform you that starting with the next academic year you will no longer be employed as an instructor at our college."

I descended to the microbiology office in order to collect my books and notebooks. Outside the main door, flowers in hands, Sasha Raevsky and Masha Malevich were waiting for me. We said goodbye, and I hugged them both. In the inner courtyard of the college, boys from adjacent buildings were kicking a soccer ball. Uncle Vasya, the college custodian and caretaker, kept chasing them away by dousing them with water from a hose. But the boys just laughed and went on with their game of soccer, running back and forth through the water's radiant rainbow.

2004

Translated from the Russian by Maxim D. Shrayer

The Bicycle Race

I've been writing this story my whole life. From the time when I first started to mix the paint of words. When I began to combine the pieces of life, those which occurred in reality, with imaginary circumstances (plot twists, phrases, movement, arrivals of characters in a story). I didn't invent the courtyard of my old house on the corner of Novosiltsevskaya Street and Engels Prospect. The courtyard was there. And also the communal laundry in the back of the courtyard. And the black trunk of a bird cherry tree. And the gamboling of lilac leaves. And the TB clinic nearby. And the little garden on the site of a church which was razed to its very foundation during the Revolution. Just as the song goes: ". . . forthwith the old foundation, and then. . . ." And there were a couple of other two-story stone buildings, faced with yellow stucco. The same architecture and color as my old building, the laundry, and the TB clinic. And most likely, the church demolished by the proletarians was in the same style as the other buildings. Then, to the desperate accompaniment of "The Internationale," the church was razed to its foundation. All these buildings had been part of an almshouse before the Revolution. Where did all the old men and women disappear to? I don't know. How did we all end up living in our house? I couldn't say. Our courtyard was full of legends and lore. But my story has little to do with either the church or "The Internationale." Perhaps there's a slight connection to the yellow color of the age-old stucco covering the walls of our house and the TB clinic. Yellow, the color of unfaithful love. The color of infidelity. Red, the color of true love. All-incinerating.

Novosiltsevskaya Street flew past our house like a black arrow. Or it seemed to us that it flew past us, because during the bicycle races the street was suffused with lightning-fast movement, speed, racing cyclists, all of the things that aroused our imagination, recreating the visual metaphor of a hero, fortune's favorite, Hercules. No trams, buses, or trolleys ran on Novosiltsevskaya Street. On the left side of our street there was a vast park on the grounds of the Forestry Technical University. On the right, a procession of wooden frame cottages. It was an ideal place for a bike race. The walking patients from the TB clinic were bored out of their minds. On long summer days they roamed about the park under the centuries-old oak trees like lost souls, or even strayed into our courtyard to watch us play bat or skittles. In the yard there was some talk that the patients were contagious, that they spread Koch's bacilli and one could get infected. But we didn't chase away the sick ones.

Our hero was the famous cyclist Shvarts. Or Cherny ("Black"), as frenzied fans chanted his name, literally translated from a Jewish one into a Russian one. Everyone was a fan of Shvarts. He was the idol of the postwar crowd. He was about thirty, swarthy, lean, swift. When he raced to the finish line, his likeness to a black arrow was especially apparent due to a graphic correspondence: his helmet, resting above the line of a pedigreed Jewish nose, gave him a slant of surplus speed that always hit the target. The target was victory. Shvarts won every time. The finish line happened to run in front of our building. Shvarts would fly across, slow down, and roll to the very end of the cast-iron, spiked fence of the Forestry Technical University. There he would turn around, undo the pedal straps, jump off the bike, and walk up to us, smiling jubilantly. I've never since seen anyone with such a radiant smile. The smile of an ancient conqueror-hero. Hercules, David, Jason.

The bike races happened every summer. Several times throughout the short Leningrad summer. Maybe every month. Or even
every week. On Sundays. In the postwar years, the only day off was
Sunday. All of Leningrad, or at least, everyone from the Vyborg
Side of Leningrad where I lived, would congregate along the sides
of Novosiltsevskaya Street, from where it starts near the Kushelevka
railway station all the way to the intersection with Engels Prospect.
Fans would convey these words to each other: "There! There they
are! Go Shvarts! Shvarts! Shvarts! Come on, Black! Come on, go!"
And the name, like a black arrow, propelled itself to the finish ribbon line. It was impossible to defeat Shvarts.

The residents of our building enjoyed a privileged position.
The finish ribbon was attached just in front of the driveway leading to our courtyard. We would stand in a dense cluster: my friend
Bor'ka Smorodin and I, Yurka Dmitriev, his father, Uncle Fedya
the Boozer, the yard keeper Uncle Vanya, Lyuska the sales clerk,
my mother, the Pole Yodko who worked as a guard at the Forestry
Technical University, and still a few more of the residents, including the hoodlum Mishka Shushpanov, if he wasn't in juvie, and also
a few girls from our building. Among them was Natasha. She was
astoundingly beautiful: dusky skin, black eyes, long legs. Through
her duskiness pulsed a hot wave of Circassian blood, the way the
summer sun shows through clouds above the sea. That and a sail of
jet-black hair, covering her high chest. Bor'ka and I were between
thirteen and fourteen, Natasha, almost seventeen. When Shvarts led
his bicycle past us, Natasha would become incredibly agitated, and a
blazing blush would spread over her cheeks, like a forest fire at night.

This was a long time ago, a very long time ago. Over sixty years
ago. I was in love with a girl with a chocolate name, Natasha. The
girl was four years my senior. She lived on the first floor of our
building in a long communal apartment. Two other communal
apartments were on the second floor. I lived in one, Bor'ka in the
other.

I was in love with the girl Natasha, and I dreamed of becoming a famous racing cyclist. Like Shvarts. Natasha's mother was Circassian. Natasha's father had brought his wife from an *aoul*—a mountainous village in the North Caucusus—where he was stationed as a commanding military officer in the early thirties. He was transferred to service in Leningrad and was given a room in our house. In this room Natasha was born. During the war, some of us were evacuated—for instance, my mother and I, or Natasha with her Circassian mother. Others—Bor'ka, for instance—remained in the besieged Leningrad. By the time residents returned to our house, the war was over. However, not everyone returned or stayed alive. Slavik from Bor'ka's apartment died of starvation, and Natasha's father was killed in battle.

I remember for a fact that I fell in love with Natasha during a bicycle race. It was the middle of May. Sunday. The bicycle race had started, and our street was full of people. We stood in a dense pack at the near end of our courtyard. Right there, where it bordered Novosiltsevskaya Street. To the right there was a lawn surrounding three centenarian oaks, their bark wrinkled yet relaxed, like a philosopher's forehead. To the left of us there were firewood sheds, and beyond them the garden of Yodko, the guard. The residents were a little afraid of Yodko. On that Sunday there was a bicycle race for the title of the Champion of Leningrad. A wave of voices rolling from the far end of Novosiltsevskaya Street got nearer as the racers approached the finish. From a distance we tried to identify the leaders and the losers in a cluster of cyclists flying on the wind of speed, in turn connecting and breaking up into separate figures. Although we couldn't see the faces, the fan's voices, the particular incline of the helmeted head and the joyous thump of our hearts told us the same thing: "Shvarts! Shvarts! Shvarts!"

He was first once again. And when Shvarts, after breaking through the finish ribbon, walked back guiding his machine by the saddle (he must have been a picture of erotic allure!), Natasha separated from our courtyard gang, took a step toward Shvarts and kissed him on the lips. Exactly then I understood that I was in love with Natasha. But this boyish love was intertwined with a rapturous admiration of Shvarts. Some special type of adoration; an infatuation with a hero. A cult of personality which was not imposed but which I embraced voluntarily. Because Shvarts was a real personality. Perhaps the first remarkable personality in my life. But isn't love between a man and woman a cult of personality established mutually by the people in love? Her cult in his eyes, his cult in the eyes of a woman who loves him. I suppose my love for Natasha and, simultaneously, my adoration of Shvarts, arose from multiple intersections and reflections of glances, movements, and words within our extraordinary love triangle. I knew that at Natasha's first call I would throw myself into fulfilling any of her desires, would happily indulge her every whim, defend her from any danger. And simultaneously, should Shvarts order me to do something, anything, I would carry out his order (request) without hesitation. I aimed my thoughts both to the imaginary wishes of Natasha and to Shvarts's potential orders. Even the most passionate love cannot survive without imagining the future of this love. The beautiful and the awful. A youth sprouting within me, I couldn't resist picturing Natasha and myself in erotic situations, however approximately drawn. It was a totally different thing to imagine in my head (what would it look like?) how the great Shvarts might test my devotion to him, and my adoration. I imagined that Shvarts would entrust his bicycle to me, and I would speed off, like the black arrow, along Novosiltsevskaya Street under the rapturous cries of fans. And they, those who were once devoted to Shvarts, would be calling out my name, and not his. I imagined that I would slow down at the end of Novosiltsevskaya Street, jump off the champion bike and lead it, holding its firm black saddle with the same erotic nonchalance as Shvarts did. I would walk up to Natasha and ardently kiss her on the lips.

It was the end of May. Sunday. Past noon. Our adult residents crowded in the space between the laundry and the house, debating whether to start a game of skittles or dominos. The kids were trying to decide whether to play bat or knife throw. On that Sunday there was no bike race. Natasha opened both sides of her window and stood gazing out at the yard. At the time Russian girls and young ladies had a renowned habit of standing at an opened window and looking out. We had no TV at that time. The world of the court-yard displayed all of life's highly complex motions. Natasha loved to stand by the window for hours. She watched us play skittles or bat. And in the summer, when the residents of our house would bring out a gramophone and dance, she watched the dancing. Natasha never danced in the courtyard. Maybe she was forbidden to dance by her Circassian mother, who was eternally working at a "Beer-Water" stall and was never home. Or did Natasha intuitively know the price of her own beauty? In any case, Natasha never mixed with others. She was like a portrait in the frame of the window. She and two geranium plants, which stood in the corners of the window, their flowers a blaze of red. Like Natasha's cheeks. Sometimes she would call me over to talk with her. Say, about books. Reading tired her out, but she loved it when I described to her all the things I read. Especially novels about love. I was a voracious reader. I read every-thing that I managed to get ahold of at different libraries: school, local public, or my friends' homes. By strange coincidence, that day I was retelling for Natasha *The Lady of the Camellias* by Dumas, *fils*.

"Danya, would you marry me if I were sick with consumption, like Violetta?" Natasha asked me. I didn't know what to answer. I definitely didn't feel like getting married. It was exactly my being in love that proscribed such a boring predicament as marriage, one that brought people a multitude of hardships—which is how mar-riage looked to me at that time. Actually, still now it sometimes does. Even the very terms which accompanied this whole process (Office of Recording Civil Acts, ceremony, matrimony, alimony) didn't have anything to do with chivalrous, romantic love, with adoration of the Beautiful Lady, rivalry, duels. . . .

"No Natasha, what use would that be for us?! Better if I would be your knight, and you my Beautiful Lady. Remember, I was just telling you about . . ."

"—yes, but if you, Danya, don't marry me, my mother won't allow me to live with you at your place. And I'm so sick of my squalid little room on the first floor. And I'm sick to death of mother with all her endless prohibitions."

I didn't know what to say, so very vividly did I picture in my head how upon hearing my description of the conversation with Natasha, my mother's face would assume a teasing expression, little rays of irony sparking in her light blue eyes. And, really, I could understand that even though I was already a bar mitzvah, meaning I had reached the full legal age of a man according to Jewish law, it was still a bit too early to get married, even to such a beauty as Natasha. I first needed to finish school, then go to university. Which university and to study what, I still hadn't decided. Sometimes I had thoughts about applying to the Naval Academy.

I didn't reply at all, because I didn't want to lie; I stood in silence, not wanting to offend her and ruin our friendship. Natasha got very upset with me. Of course she did! Although she asked it as a joke, all the same she asked me to marry her, and I dawdled with the answer and ruined her play. All she was asking of me was to play at her game of imaginary marriage.

"You're so boring, Danya," Natasha said crossly and was about to slam the window shut, when she suddenly first froze, then opened her eyes wide and laughed happily.

I turned around. Behind my back stood Shvarts. With his left hand he held the saddle of a racing bicycle, and with his right, a box of chocolates, "La Traviata," which he extended over my shoulder toward Natasha's window. In those years, the Mikoyan Candy Factory, named for one of Stalin's close associates, produced a series of boxed chocolate sets with operatic brand names: "The Queen of Spades," "La Traviata," "Ruslan and Ludmila," "The Snow Maiden". . . .

"Thank you, thank you, Shvarts. I love chocolates so very much," said Natasha. "But we haven't properly met. My name is Natasha."

"Beautiful name!" said Shvarts.

"And this is my friend Daniil—Danya," said Natasha.

"Shvarts," said Shvarts, and offered his hand in handshake. The hand was sinewy, tanned, swift. All of him was like an arrow. "Shvarts," Shvarts said one more time.

"I know you're Shvarts. Everyone knows that you're called 'Shvarts.'"

"Actually, Shvarts is my last name. My first name is Vladimir. Vladimir Shvarts. But everyone's gotten used to 'Shvarts.' Since when I was in the navy."

"You were a sailor?"

"I served in the navy."

"How exciting!" Natasha cried out. "Our Danya is also joining. Right, Danya?"

"Well, if they take me with my eyesight," I answered.

"Surely they'll take you!" Shvarts said resolutely. "I have friends in the navy. So, Danya, don't you worry about it, everything will work out just fine with the navy! I give you my honest word as a champion!"

"That's great!" I said.

"So don't even worry about it!" Shvarts repeated.

"There, see!" said Natasha. "You'll also be a sailor, like Shvarts."

"And a champion," said Shvarts. "In the navy they respect champions. Well, if not champions, then at least good athletes. Do you like sports, Danya?"

"You bet I do!" I said. "Soccer, hockey, and especially bicycle races."

"Bicycle races!" Shvarts took up the topic. "Yes that's the most important thing for a navy man—to love bicycle races. The sea is like a great big track. And the waves keep overtaking one another. Just like in a bicycle race."

"You tell stories so beautifully, Shvarts," smiled Natasha. She had some kind of special smile. I just wanted to stare, without turning my gaze away. An enchanting smile.

"So you like how I tell stories, Natasha? May I address you informally, with *ty*?" asked Shvarts.

"Of course you can, Shvarts! Only I'll still address you formally."

"Whatever you feel comfortable to start off with," answered Shvarts and he turned to me: "So you and I were talking about bicycle races. About cycling, which is essential if you want to become a navy man. Do you have a bicycle?"

"Sure, a prewar one. My father's. With a Swedish hub on the back wheel!" I answered and then hushed up. What was I going to tell Shvarts about my father, who was also a navy man during the war? About my father, who left me and my mother for another woman. "Sure I have a bike!" I said.

"And would you, Danya, like to try a racing bike?"

"Who wouldn't!"

"So why don't you take it for a turn. If you like, take it for a whole hour!" said Shvarts, and, lifting his hand off from the bicycle saddle, he shifted my hand from Natasha's windowsill onto the supple black skin of his champion bicycle. "Don't rush! I mean, don't rush to come back!"

I rode around for a whole hour, or maybe longer. I didn't have a watch. Back then, none of my fellow teenagers had watches. We lived very modestly. And it wasn't even acceptable for a school kid to be sporting a watch. I got my first watch as a present from my father right after high school, when I started medical school. Not naval academy, but medical school. Yet, the sea didn't want to release me even then. In medical school, we had military officers' training on submarines. But that's a subject for a different story. Back to the day when Shvarts appeared in our yard and struck up a conversation with Natasha and me, and then gave me his champion bicycle, on which I rode around for at least an hour. I raced along the arrow of Novosiltsevskaya Street from my house toward the Kushelevka station, then dashed back in order to traverse Engels Prospect and speed along Lanskoy Road all the way to Chernaya Rechka, the Black River, where Pushkin was mortally wounded. Mortally wounded in a duel, all because he was jealous of his wife. Natalia, Nathálie, Natasha. . . .

When I returned, Shvarts was still standing by the window and talking with Natasha. The residents of our house were occupied with their Sunday chores: slowly strolling about the yard, playing dominos, bringing out the gramophone for a dance party. All of these maneuvers didn't affect Shvarts and Natasha, as if they were standing on an island in the middle of the river. Of course, everyone noticed everything. It would have been impossible to be positioned outside the window of the building's most beautiful girl and remain unnoticed. Besides, Shvarts's fame was so great, and his appearance in our yard was such an exceptional event, that none of the residents would have doubted the suitability and propriety of Shvarts's prolonged stop at Natasha's window. Instead, they would have all been proud of this, as if the champion had paid a single visit to all of us. Something like this swelled up in my heart. Not unlike a collective pride for one of my fellows in the beehive, who had been visited by such an exceptional bee. Even my love for Natasha had been temporarily displaced by feeling this collective admiration of Shvarts and pride that he had paid our courtyard his champion visit. That is, in this moment of a collectivized experience of Shvarts, even Natasha seemed to me (and certainly to others) to be a part of the universal courtyard, an aspect and function of our collective beauty. Certainly Shvarts could have been tempted by other attractions: a game of chess, let's say, with our unsurpassed master Yurka

Dmitriev. Or by the opportunity to talk about pomology with the guard Yodko. Yes, there were many things Shvarts could do or talk about with many people. But he chose beauty. Fantastic! Indeed, it was precisely this thought process which resulted in our distinctive sense of joint responsibility: no one from our yard so much as uttered a word to Natasha's mother about the champion's visit and their prolonged chat at the open window. And as always, the old Circassian lady returned from her "Beer-Water" stall late in the evening, cooked her infidel food on the kerosene stove, and locked herself up in her room, without ever saying a word to anyone. "The darkie is counting stolen money," the residents inferred, and kept silent about Natasha and Shvarts.

But there was definitely something to keep quiet about. And on this account, I found myself in a psychological trap that I myself had helped Shvarts set up. I was in love with Natasha, and this love dictated that I would follow the chivalrous code of honor, that is, to carry out the wishes of the Beautiful Lady. And Natasha's main wish was to spend time with Shvarts. But that same love was making me suffer precisely because my Lady was spending time with him, and not with me. Meanwhile, the cycle races continued, and Shvarts always won. Every time, this was our victory, a victory for our entire yard community.

Most often Shvarts appeared in our yard on his bike in the afternoon hours, when we all hung out in the yard: smoking, playing cards, pitching coins against the wall, kicking a soccer ball, and so forth. Natasha was in tenth grade and would get home around three in the afternoon. Then came June, school was over, and our daily existence was permanently relocated from indoors onto the street. Shvarts would let me use his bike, and I would go riding around for a whole hour, sometimes longer. He didn't entrust his racing machine to anyone else. Sometimes I secretly let my friend Bor'ka Smorodin have a turn on the champion bike. Shvarts would no longer just stand at Natasha's window, but after handing me his bike, he would go inside. He was supposed to be helping Natasha prepare for her math final. Shvarts would leave me his bike and I would ride all around my native Vyborg Side of town, returning in an hour or an hour and a half to knock at Natasha's window. Shvarts would then come out into the yard and ride off on his bicycle. But sometime he arrived on the tram. And on a few occasions, Shvarts came in a cab. He would collect Natasha and they would catch a movie at Giant Theater over by the Finland Station, or go for ice cream at Smiles Café, which was two tram stops from our house, near the Svetlanovsky farmer's market. But more often than not, Shvarts came by bicycle. He was employed as a coach at some sports club. I was jealous of Shvarts and Natasha, but couldn't help continuing to adore Shvarts. This state of adoration, despite all my jealousy, forced me to look forward to his arrivals, to taking the bicycle, which he let me have as a token of our special friendship (and also so that he wouldn't have to leave this treasure on the street unattended), forced me to look forward to taking the treasured bike and riding around the neighborhood, enjoying the pleasure of speed and all the while feeling the torments of self-betrayal.

This continued for a month or a month and a half. It was now the middle of July, the most magnificent time in Leningrad. We loafed about the yard all day. Or we would go swimming in the ponds at Ozerki. Or rove around the grounds of the Forestry Technical University campus. Of course, in the intervals between roving around, playing games, or swimming in the ponds, some of us read books, went to the library, walked to the grocery store, or visited relatives. But these were secondary activities. Most important was our yard's collective existence. And for me, the climax of this existence was the mad romance of Shvarts and Natasha. It now seems to me that at a certain point I even cooled down toward both of them. My love for Natasha was gone, like water poured into the sand. And along with it went my adoration of Shvarts. I was even tired of riding on his champion bike.

And all the same, I continued to meet Shvarts at the appointed time in the yard, to take his bicycle and circle around the neighboring streets and roads, of which I had suddenly become sick to death. Most likely, everything had gone away along with my waned infatuation and adoration. One day I was waiting for Shvarts under Natasha's window at the previously appointed time. Either I looked grim, or I greeted him without the usual enthusiasm, or a premonition of something was reflected in my look and reluctant hello. Seeming to notice my coolness, Shvarts asked: "Danya, have you changed your mind about becoming a racing cyclist?"

"No," I answered. "I haven't changed my mind."

"Then take the bicycle and practice. In the fall I'll arrange for you to train with the teenage group at our sports club!"

"Great!" I answered. "Fabulous!"

"Come back in about an hour and half. Natasha and I need to review Newton's binomial theorem. One needs to know the binomial theorem back and forth to pass the entrance exams to the College of Economics."

I rode around without enthusiasm. Lazily I circled the alleys of the Forestry Technical University. From time to time I returned to the huge hanging electric clock outside Lanskaya railroad station: Was it time to return? I couldn't take it any longer and went back earlier than I was expected. It's important to believe in premonitions. I set the bicycle under Natasha's window and joined up with our boys who were playing cards on the stoop of the communal laundry. We were playing poker for chump change, but if one was very, very lucky, one could raise enough through the winnings to buy a pack of the cheapest *papirosy*, Little Star, or even a movie ticket. We all smoked then and were fanatical moviegoers. I got lucky in cards. In my hand I had the Joker, and also the ace of diamonds. I could swap one more card and then bluff. I was about to ask the dealer for a third card, when Bor'ka Smorodin yelled:

"Natasha's mother on the horizon!"

Indeed, from the crook of Novosiltsevskaya Street, waddling from side to side, came the old Circassian lady. In both hands she carried heavy grocery bags, which enhanced her pendulum-like swaying. Why was she returning home at such an unusual hour? No one had any idea, but everyone, of course, thought of Shvarts. What would happen to him and Natasha when her mother entered the room!? I dashed to the window and knocked. No one answered. The old lady had already turned off the street and was walking toward the house on a path between the firewood sheds and the lawn surrounding the ancient oaks. I dashed to the door of the communal apartment, where Natasha lived in one of the rooms with her mother, and where Shvarts was visiting her, he with whom she was now reviewing Newton's binomial theorem. I ran across the hallway, which also served as a communal kitchen with the shared stove, sink, and lavatory. I navigated between the kitchen tables, placed near the partitions between the rooms of the apartment's residents. There was Natasha's room. I knew this because one day in early spring, when she was sick for a long time with bronchitis, I brought her an apple. Yes, this was her room. I listened closer. I couldn't hear the voices of Natasha and Shvarts. I knocked at the door. No one answered. Some internal instrument for measuring the speed of the old Circassian lady's steps was tapping out the expiring minutes. I shoved the door. It opened. Shvarts and Natasha were in bed. Shvarts's swarthy back covered Natasha. I saw only her face with half-closed eyes and a half-opened mouth, and her mouth issued some mournful and blissful noises, which were unfamiliar to me at the time. I heard the bang of the apartment door. By effort of will and mind, borne out of an unknown something (Was it empathy? Contempt? Chivalry in the spirit of Schiller's ballad "The Glove"? Male solidarity? The love I had once felt?) I hauled the dining room table to the door and pressed my body against it. The old woman pushed the door. She knocked. "Natasha, open up!" she screamed. Then she started rummaging in her bags, looking for the key.

"Out the window," I cried to Shvarts and Natasha.

But they already knew what to do. To the sounds of the old lady's knocking and screaming, they pulled on their clothes, lowered down a chair, opened the window, and jumped out. Then it was my turn to escape. I was crawling over the windowsill when the old woman managed to push away the table and burst into the room. She hustled to the window and caught sight of me, as I ran across the yard in the direction of the park. This was our salvation, the vast grounds of the Forestry Technical University.

A wild scandal broke out. The old Circassian was sure that I was committing debauchery with Natasha. Indeed, all the evidence was against me. But no one so much as squeaked a thing. Natasha returned home the next morning after spending the night God knows where. Her mother beat her black and blue, and forbade her to leave the house. Of course, it was unavoidable that the old lady demanded from my mother that she punish me in the harshest way. My mother asked me:

"Is it true, Danya, that you were in bed with Natasha?"

"No mama, it's not true."

"So then, who was?"

"A different guy," I answered.

"Why then did you get mixed up in this, Danya!" said my mother. "It would suffice if you could answer for your own transgressions."

Soon Natasha developed an acute form of TB with endless bouts of coughing, fever, and pulmonary hemorrhages. She was put in the TB clinic next door to our house. The bicycle races continued all through the rest of the summer, but Shvarts no longer participated in the competitions. Among the crowd of fans it was rumored that he had moved to Moscow and had taken a job as coach for the Wings of Soviets racing team. I don't know how long Natasha spent in the TB clinic. She didn't return to our building. The old Circassian lady couldn't bear the disgrace, and exchanged her room for something else on the opposite end of Leningrad. Natasha must have forgotten about me. And really, for me everything had broken off much earlier, even before she and Shvarts ran out the window and I covered up their escape from Natasha's old mother.

I got married and moved to Moscow. One time, Mira and I were vacationing in the Crimea. We were staying in Yalta. There we quickly rented an old shanty, dropped off our suitcases, and went to catch some evening sea air at the embankment, there where Chekhov's young lady with a white Pomeranian used to take her strolls. That same Anna Sergeevna, whom Gurov met in Yalta and fell in love with. In short, one day, about fifty to seventy years later—that is, already in our time and, quite possibly, on the first evening when Mira and I set out for a stroll on the Yalta embankment—at one of the tables of an open-air café, there sat Shvarts and Natasha. They were sipping wine and kissing.

2004
Translated from the Russian by Margaret Godwin-Jones

Notes and Commentary on the Stories

About the Translators

Notes and Commentary
on the Stories

MAXIM D. SHRAYER

Behind the Zoo Fence

David Shrayer–Petrov wrote the short story "Behind the Zoo Fence" ("Za ogradoi zooparka") in Providence, Rhode Island, his home in 1987–2007, and dedicated the story to his wife, Emilia (Mila) Shrayer. It appeared in the Los Angeles Russian weekly *Panorama*, in two consecutive issues (June 18–24, 1997, and June 25–July 1, 1997). The story was reprinted in the Philadelphia–based annual *The Coast* (*Poberezh'e*; 1998), and the Moscow–based annual *World of Paustovsky* (*Mir Paustovskogo*; No. 19, 2002), and subsequently included in Shrayer–Petrov's collection of short stories *Carp for the Gefilte Fish* (*Karp dlia farshirovannoi ryby*; Moscow, 2005). A brief, documentary version of the events informing this work of fiction is told in Shrayer-Petrov's memoir *The Hunt for the Red Devil: A Novel with Microbiologists* (*Okhota na ryzhego d'iavola*, Moscow, 2010), in Chapter 8, also titled "Behind the Zoo Fence."

the Garden Ring (*Sadovoe kol'tso*): a beltway-like succession of multi-lane avenues encircling the center of Moscow and serving as one of the city's principal thoroughfares.

Moscow Zoo: one of the oldest in the world, the Moscow Zoo is comprised of the so-called Old Territory (old campus) and New Territory (new campus), which are divided by Bolshaya Gruzinskaya Street and connected by an overpass. The Filatov Children's Hospital, where Dr. Garin works, is located on Sadovaya-Kudrinskaya, a section of the Garden Ring, and abuts the New Territory of the Moscow Zoo.

Dr. Garin: even though telltale signs indicate that the protagonist, Dr. Boris Erastovich Garin, is Jewish, Shrayer-Petrov has given him a name loaded with rich Russian cultural baggage. The writer Nikolai Garin-Mikhailovsky (1852–1906) is remembered for his popular autobiographical tetralogy, *Tyoma's Childhood*, *School Boys*, *University Students*, and *Engineers*. Erast Garin (1902–1980) was a well-known Soviet stage and screen actor, director, and screenwriter. As a literary character, Garin appears in Aleksey Tolstoy's science-fiction novel *The Hyperboloid of Engineer Garin* (1927). Additionally, the aura of the writer Aleksandr Grin (1880–1932), who is said to be Dr. Garin's favorite writer and whose name is loosely anagrammatized in Garin's, also colors the story, expanding the limits of commonsensical verisimilitude and allowing for flights of romantic fantasy. Last but not least, the spirit of Anton Chekhov hovers over the story, and Shrayer-Petrov tips his hat to the great doctor-author in a number of ways. To name just two: the last name of Dr. Garin is a perfect anagram of Dr. Ragin, the protagonist of "Ward 6" (1892), arguably Chekhov's most famous short story on the subject of medicine, madness, and society; and Natasha Altman is placed in Ward 7 at the Filatov Hospital, the lucky number hinting at her miraculous recovery. Furthermore, the last name of the Garins' friends, the Gurovs, is the same as that of Gurov, the protagonist of "Lady with a Lapdog" (1901). For a discussion of Chekhovian traces in Shrayer-Petrov's short fiction, see the afterword in his collection *Autumn in Yalta: A Novel and Three Stories*, edited by Maxim D. Shrayer (Syracuse University Press, 2006).

papirosa: Russian hand-rolled style cigarette with a blank "air" filter.

Filatov Children's Hospital: Founded in 1842, the Filatov Children's Hospital is Moscow's first—and Russia's second oldest—hospital for children. In 1965, after relocating from his native Leningrad to Moscow, his wife's hometown, Shrayer-Petrov worked at the Filatov Hospital as chief of clinical laboratories.

Anapa . . . Krasnodar: a resort located on the northern part of Russia's Black Sea coast close to the Sea of Azov, Anapa is administratively a town in the Krasnodar Region of the Russian Federation.

Natasha was going into her senior year of high school. . . . : the original has "*into her tenth grade*"; in the old Soviet system, one normally entered elementary school (first grade) at the age of seven and graduated from high school (tenth grade) at the age of seventeen or eighteen.

dacha: Russian country and/or vacation house (and the property on which it stands), often in a suburb or in a Soviet-era countryside vacation housing development (*dachnyi posëlok*), the latter traditionally comprised of summer cottages on small plots of land.

"*Delo shvakh . . . Pretty damn hopeless.*": This idiomatic expression combines the native Russian noun *delo* (business, matter) and the Germanic adjective *schwach* (weak; lacking), which is also used in Yiddish. This bicultural expression enjoyed popularity among Russian Jews, probably because of its Yiddish-like quality, even though an expression like that does not exist in Yiddish.

Snegiri (literally, "bullfinches," from *snegir'*, bullfinch): a railroad station and small town located about thirty-one miles northwest of Moscow, traditionally a settlement where Muscovites had dachas.

Vosstaniya Square (literally, "Uprising Square"): a major square in Moscow's center on the Garden Ring; in 1992 the original pre-Soviet name, Kudrinskaya Square, was restored.

the Highrise (*vysotnoe zdanie*): here refers to the highrise tower in Vosstaniya Square, one of the "seven sisters" monumentalist towers ("*stalinkie vysotki*") erected in Moscow in the late 1940s and early 1950s and embodying the so-called Stalinist Empire style.

Chekhov Street (Ulitsa Chekhova): the name, from 1944 to 1993, of Malaya Dmitrovka Street in the center of Moscow, running from the Pushkin Square to the Garden Ring; another instance of Shrayer-Petrov's Chekhovian "signs and symbols" in the story.

Old Circus: in post-World War II Moscow, there were two circuses, the Old Circus on Tsvetnoy Boulevard, founded in the 1880s, and the so-called "new circus," the Big Moscow State Circus on Vernadsky Prospect, founded in 1971. The Old Circus has since been renamed Nikulin Circus on Tsvetnoy Boulevard, after the famous actor and clown Yuri Nikulin. Tsvetnoy Boulevard (literally: Flower Boulevard) is a section of the so-called Boulevard Ring (Bul'varnoe kol'tso), a series of boulevards girding central Moscow.

A Russian Liar in Paris

Written in April 2009 in Boston, Shrayer-Petrov's home since 2007, "A Russian Liar in Paris" ("Lgun'ia Ivanovna v Parizhe" [literally, "The liar Ivanovna in Paris"]) was published in the weekly *Jewish World* (*Evreiskii mir*; 12 May 2009), and reprinted in the New York-based bilingual magazine *Slovo-Word* (68, Fall 2010)

Hôtel Les Muguets: partially fictitious name; a Hôtel Muguet is located in a different arrondissement of Paris.

Rue Cardinal Lemoine: street in the 5th arrondissement of Paris. For the Russian literary imagination transplanted onto American soil, the street is especially significant as Ernest Hemingway's first Parisian address in 1921–1922, memorably described in *A Moveable Feast* (1964), one of Shrayer-Petrov's favorite books since its publication in Russian translation.

Otradnoe: village in the Krasnogorsk district of the Moscow Province, northwest of the city of Moscow; this common name of Russian villages is used here with fictional license.

Volokolamsk: town and district center in the northwest corner of the Moscow Province, off the Moscow–Riga Highway.

Vologda School: a loosely identified group of Russian-language writers of the post-Stalin years, who cultivated the cultural and stylistic traditions of peasant, folkloristic poetry and usually set their works of fiction in provincial Russian rural areas, allegedly less corrupted by the Soviet environment. The name "Vologda School" comes from the ancient Russian city of Vologda in Russia's northwest. A number of well-known writers came from Vologda or called Vologda their home in the 1960s–1980s, among them poets Nikolai Rubtsov and Olga Fokina and prosaists Aleksandr Yashin, Vasily Belov, and Viktor Astafiev. Some of the prose writers associated with the Vologda School are better known in criticism as members of the Russian Village (or Country) Prose movement (Russian *derevenshchiki*).

Koltsov, Klyuev, Radimov: Aleksey Koltsov (1809–1842), Pavel Radimov (1887–1967), and Nikolai Klyuev (1884–1937), Russian poets who worked in the peasant vein and variously incorporated elements of Russian rural folklore into their verse.

Kazakov: Yuri Kazakov (1927–1982), one of the most celebrated Russian short-story writers of the 1960s–1970s.

Belov: Vasily Belov (1932–2012), along with Valentin Rasputin (b. 1937) and Viktor Astafiev (1924–2001), constituted the leading triumvirate of Russian Village prose writers.

Nagibin: Yuri Nagibin (1920–1994), very well-known Russian prose writer and screenwriter, one of the dominant figures of Soviet literature in the 1950s–1980s.

The French Cottage: title of the novel by David Shrayer-Petrov, started in the Soviet Union in the 1970s and completed in the United States in the 1990s. Published in 1999, the novel features the author's alter ego, the science writer Daniil Geyer, and his investigation of the life and legacy of the great French-Canadian microbiologist Félix d'Herelle (1873–1949).

Bunin: Ivan Bunin (1870–1953): major Russian poet and prose writer, one of the greatest masters of the short story, the first Russian writer to receive, in 1933, the Nobel Prize for Literature. An émigré, Bunin lived in France from 1921 until his death, spending long periods of time in Paris and in Grasse, in the Maritime Alps.

Yves Montand (1921–1991): famous French actor and singer of Jewish–Italian and French origin.

La Pénsee Russe: the French name of *Russkaia mysl'*, a Russian-language newspaper appearing in Paris from 1947 to 2006, once a pillar of the Russian émigré community in France. Since 2006 a publication under this title has been appearing in London.

Stethoscope (*Stetoskop*): Paris-based international Russian-language magazine of avant-garde and experimental literature and arts.

White Sheep on a Green Mountain Slope

Composed in August–September 2003 in Providence, "White Sheep on a Green Mountain Slope" ("Belye ovtsy na zelenom sklone gory") appeared in the Moscow-based Jewish monthly *L'chayim* (*Lekhaim*), January 2004, and was included in Shrayer-Petrov's *Carp for the Gefilte Fish* (2005).

Knowledge Publishing House . . . Knowledge Association: renditions of the Russian "Izdatel'stvo Znanie" and "Obshchestvo Znanie." Originally founded in 1947 on the initiative of a group of scholars as the All-Soviet Association for the Dissemination of Political and Scientific Knowledge, in 1963 the association was renamed the All-Soviet Knowledge Association.

sovkhoz: abbreviation of *sovetskoe khoziastvo*, literally "Soviet farm," a Soviet state-owned farm or agricultural estate, distinct from the structure of a collective farm (*kolkhoz*).

shashlyk (*shashlik*): marinated pieces of meat grilled on skewers over coals; a staple of cuisine in the Caucasus that is also very popular all over Russia and the former Soviet Union; compare "shish kebab."

Circassians . . . in Israel: the Circassians (Cherkesses) is a common name for the members of the Adyghe nation (Adygs), a North-Caucasus ethnic group; the majority of the Circassians left North Caucasus in the course of its conquest by the Russian Empire in the nineteenth century and formed a diaspora in the Ottoman Empire. Outside the modern-day autonomous regions and republics of the Russian Federation, descendants of the Circassians reside in Turkey and the Middle East. About four thousand Circassians presently live in Israel; they are Sunni Muslims. The Israeli Circassians have been well integrated into Israeli society, and, since 1958, have been serving in the Israeli Defense Force.

Brezhnev came to power: Leonid Brezhnev (1906–1982) became First Secretary of the Central Committee of the Communist Party of the Soviet Union by ousting Nikita Khrushchev (1894–1971) from power in a bloodless coup.

Khrushchev's debacle at the Manezh public exhibition of 1962: Khrushchev's public outburst on December 1, 1962, while he was attending an art exhibit at the Manezh Hall (Manezhnyi zal) near Red Square in Moscow, is usually considered the beginning of the downward spiral of the Thaw. Some of the works exhibited at the Manezh were by avant-garde and nonconformist Soviet artists such as Ernst Neizvestny and Eli Beliutin. Lacking the critical vocabulary and cultural wherewithal to appreciate what he was seeing, the Soviet leader made quite the dunce of himself by comparing the exhibited avant-garde art to "dog shit" and calling the artists themselves "faggots."

Ibragimbekov brothers, Rustam and Magsud: Rustam Ibragimbekov (b. 1939), famous Azerbaijan-born Soviet and post-Soviet screenwriter, whose credits include *White Sun of the Desert* (1970) and *Burnt by the Sun* (1994); Magsud Ibragimbekov (b. 1935), Azerbaijani Russian-language writer, older brother of the screenwriter. In the 1970s, Moscow's Malaya Bronnaya Theater commissioned Shrayer-Petrov to compose several song lyrics for its production of Rustam Ibragimbekov's play *Their Own Path* (1973).

Rashid Behbudov (1915–1989): Azerbaijani singer and actor, well-known in the Soviet Union for performing songs in over half a dozen languages; a Theater of Song in Baku is named after Behbudov.

family-and-school: "Family and School" ("Sem'ia i shkola") is the name of the Soviet Russian–language monthly magazine for parents, devoted to problems of family, child-rearing, and education; also a popular expression, which Soviet people employed with a measure of irony or skepticism, just as Shrayer-Petrov's narrator does in the story.

Vladimir Lugovsky's poem "The Cadet's Hungarian Dance": Vladimir Lugovskoy (1901–1957), prominent Russian Soviet poet, in the 1920s one of the principal members of the Literary Center for Constructivism; "The Cadet's Hungarian Dance" ("Kursantskaia vengerka," 1940) is one of his best-known post-1920s poems.

Ilizarov: Gavrill Ilizarov (1921–1992), visionary Soviet orthopedic surgeon and researcher of Mountain-Jewish origin; inventor of the Ilizarov apparatus for lengthening limb bones, founder of the All-Union Kurgan Center for Restorative Traumatology and Orthopedics.

"We are Azeri, and that Ilizarov is a Tat, a Mountain Jew": Mountain Jews (Kavkazi Jews; Juhuri) are Jews who had originally migrated from Persia to the Caucasus, forming communities mainly in present-day Azerbaijan and Dagestan, and also, to a much lesser extent, in Northwest Caucasus (e.g., Chechnya). They speak Tat, a southwestern Iranian language, and in the former Soviet Union the name of this language sometimes mistakenly served as an ethnic category, referring both to the Mountain Jews and to the Tats, an Iranian ethnic group of Moslems residing in the Caucasus; some scholars regard the Moslem Tats as descendants of Islamized Mountain Jews. In the story, Shrayer-Petrov highlights a scenario of crypto-Mountain Jews in Northern Azerbaijan, who had been

compelled to convert to Islam but continued to practice their ancestors' faith clandestinely, akin to Marranos on the Iberian peninsula.

burka: here a cape-like coat made from felt or karakul and traditionally worn by men in the Caucasus and also used by some imperial Russian cavalry troops; despite a shared etymology, not to be confused with *burqa*, a garb that is traditionally worn by some Moslem women.

Asaf Zeynally (1909–1932): renowned Azerbaijani composer who sought to synthesize Azeri music traditions with Russian and Western classical music; Zeynally died prematurely at the age of twenty-three.

Round-the-Globe Happiness

Shrayer-Petrov wrote "Round-the-Globe Happiness" ("Krugosvet-noe schast'e") in October–December 2003 in Providence. It appeared in the Philadelphia-based annual *The Coast* (*Poberezh'e*), in 2006, and was reprinted in the Italian-based online magazine *Drugie berega* (*Other Shores*) (8[40], August 2007). It was also included in Shrayer-Petrov's collection of short stories *Carp for the Gefilte Fish* (2005). A keen reader of Saul Bellow might hear, in the episode of the narrator's illness resulting from a trip to the Caribbean, echoes of Bellow's last novel *Ravelstein* (2000), which Shrayer-Petrov read upon its publication and admired.

St. Isaac's: St. Isaac's Cathedral (Isaakievskii sobor) is St. Petersburg's largest Russian Orthodox church and arguably its most famous cathedral. Built in the first half of the nineteenth century in neoclassical style, it features a famous gold-plated main dome. A landmark of St. Petersburg, St. Isaac's is visible from afar throughout much of the city.

Ladispoli: town and resort located about thirty-five miles northwest of Rome on Italy's Tyrrhenian coast in the Lazio region. Incorporated only in the 1880s, Ladispoli shares a train station with its neighbor Cervetori, well-known for its Etruscan sites. In the 1970s–1990s, Ladispoli, along with Ostia and other nearby towns, served as a transit holding place for Jewish refugees from the former Soviet Union and other countries such as Iran, who were waiting for refugee visas, mainly to the United States and Canada. Shrayer-Petrov has described Ladispoli in several works of fiction, including the story "Blind Twig in the Stream" ("Slepaia khvorostinka") and the novel *Third Life* (2010), the latter a sequel to his refusenik novel *Herbert and Nelly* (written in 1979; first complete edition 1992). In his memoir *Waiting for America: A Story of Emigration* (2007), Maxim D. Shrayer described the experiences of Jewish refugees spending a summer in Ladispoli.

Theatre by W. Somerset Maugham: a Russian translation of this 1937 novel about Julia Lambert, an English actress having an affair with a much younger, self-serving man who is unworthy of her, enjoyed much popularity in the Soviet Union.

Shishkin: Ivan Shishkin (1832–1898), Russian landscape painter, member of the Itinerant movement (*peredvizhniki*). Shishkin gained national fame for his depictions of Russian pastures and forests.

David: Jacques-Louis David (1748–1825), French painter in the neo-classical vein, especially recognized for his depiction of the death of his friend Marat after his assassination by Charlotte Corday, and subsequently for his paintings featuring Napoleon.

Repin: Ilya Repin (1844–1930), a preeminent Russian painter, equally celebrated for his scenes of provincial Russian life (e.g., "Barge Haulers on the Volga"), his paintings treating historical subjects (e.g., "Ivan the Terrible and His Son Ivan"), his portrayals of contemporaries (e.g., portraits of Lev Tolstoy and Modest Mussorgsky), and the impressionist-style paintings of Repin's latter years.

Kandinsky: Wassily Kandinsky (1866–1944), a Russian-born painter who left Russia for Germany in 1921 and subsequently moved to France, where he died; one of the principal modernist visionaries of the twentieth century.

Chemiakin: Mihail Chemiakin (b. 1943), Russian-born painter, sculptor, and graphic artist known for his richly grotesque imagination. He emigrated to the United States in 1971.

Tselkov: Oleg Tselkov (b. 1934), Russian painter who, in the 1960s and 1970s, was among the Soviet Union's leading nonconformist artists. Since 1977, he has resided in Paris.

Adik: Shrayer-Petrov gives this central European, most likely German or Austrian, tourist a name that perhaps suggests a Russian diminutive of Adolf while also signaling *ad* (derived from the Greek "Hades" and meaning "hell" or "inferno").

Pushkin's Zemfira: Zemfira is the female protagonist of Aleksandr Pushkin's narrative poem *The Gypsies* (*Tsygane*, 1824), the last of Pushkin's "southern" romantic long poems. In *The Gypsies*, one Aleko, a restless young nobleman, follows Zemfira to a Roma (Gypsy) encampment but is unable to adjust to their ideas of freedom and law and is banished after he kills both Zemfira and her lover.

A Storefront Window of Miracles

Shrayer-Petrov wrote "A Storefront Window of Miracles" ("Vitrina chudes") in March 2009 in Boston, modeling the topography of the story's fictional New England town on the East Side of Providence, Rhode Island, where he had spent almost twenty years. Dedicated to the writer's son, the story appeared in the New York based bilingual magazine *Slovo-Word* (No. 73, 2012).

Trediakovsky, Derzhavin, Pushkin, Nekrasov, Blok, or Brodsky: Vasily Trediakovsky (1703–1768), one of the principal literary figures of Russian neoclassicism; Gavrila Derzhavin (1743–1816), major Russian poet linking neoclassicism and romanticism; Nikolai Nekrasov (1821–1877), a dominant and very influential mid-century Russian poet; Aleksandr Blok (1880–1921), great Russian Symbolist poet; Joseph (Iosif) Brodsky (1940–1996), Russian-born bilingual American poet and 1987 Nobel Prize laureate.

Mimicry

The story "Mimicry" ("Mimikriia") was composed in 1996 in Providence, Rhode Island. The New York-based *Interesting Gazette* (*Interesnaiaa gazeta*) published it in the 11–17 April 1998 issue. It was reprinted in the now-extinct, New York-based Russian edition of the *Jewish Daily Forward* (*Forverts*; June 2–8, 2000), and included in Shrayer-Petrov's collection of short stories *Carp for the Gefilte Fish* (2005). The story invites a comparison with Shrayer-Petrov's earlier "The Love of Akira Watanabe," also set in Rhode Island and featuring cross-cultural encounters between a Russian émigré intellectual and other immigrant academics affiliated with a local university. The later story appears in English in the collection *Autumn in Yalta*.

The Russian original features an epigraph from Vladimir Nabokov's English-language short story "Conversation Piece, 1945." Originally published in *The New Yorker* as "Double Talk," this was one of the earliest works of American literature to decry denial of the Shoah.

Little Compton: town in southeastern Rhode Island, a popular area for summer homes.

Nymphs (*Nymphalidae*): while the name inescapably evokes associations with minor Graeco-Roman female deities, Turkin's passion is the *Nymphalidae*, a family of butterflies. Vladimir Nabokov, to whom the story alludes in a number of ways, described several butterfly species from the *Nymphalidae* family, among them *Cyllopsis pyracmon nabokovi*, known as Nabokov's Brown or Nabokov's Satyr; *Clossiana freija nabokovi*, known as Nabokov's Fritillary; and *Cyllopsis pertepida dorothea*, known as Nabokov's Wood Nymph.

Cipollino . . . Sholem Aleichem's Motl . . . An-sky's Dibbuk: Cipollino (Italian literally "little onion") is the protagonist of Gianni Rodari's *The Adventures of Cipollino* (1957), a political children's tale that was very popular in translation in the Soviet Union; Motl (Motel) is the main character of Sholem Aleichem's novel *Motl the Cantor's Son*, its second volume left unfinished at the time of the writer's death in 1916; *The Dibbuk* is the name of S. An-sky's world-famous play, originally composed in 1911 in Russian, subsequently recreated in Yiddish as *Between Two Worlds*, then translated into Hebrew by Hayim Nachman Bialik, and finally restored in Yiddish by An-sky himself in 1920.

Haidamak: member of an armed band in eighteenth century Ukraine; the Haidamaks (Ukrainian plural Haidamaky) rebelled against Polish nobility but inflicted violence not only on Poles and Catholics but on the area's Jewish population; in the Polish language and culture, derivatives of the term Haidamak pejoratively refer to Ukrainians.

Caucasian Chalk Circle *(as in Brecht)*: *The Caucasian Chalk Circle* (1944) is one of Bertold Brecht's best known plays. Structured as a play within a play, it was set in Georgia, transparently disguised as "Grusinia" (*Gruzinia* being a variant Russian name for Georgia).

Jews migrated to Armenia during the rule of Tigranes the Great: historians hold that under Armenia's great ruler, Emperor Tigranes the Great

(140–55 BCE), a sizeable Jewish community was founded in Armenia. The Jews of Armenia were completely assimilated and lost their identity.

Shakespeare and the Jews: title of a book by James Shapiro. Published by Columbia University Press in 1997, it reignited critical discussion of *The Merchant of Venice* and Shakespeare's other Jewish connections.

The Mannerheim Line: named so after the Finnish Field Marshal Carl Gustaf Emil Mannerheim (1867–1951), this was a fortification line built along the Finnish-Russian border to defend Finland from attacks across the Karelian Isthmus. Following the Soviet-Finnish war and under the terms of a peace treaty signed on 12 March 1940, Finland ceded to the Soviet Union the Karelian Isthmus and Eastern Karelia, both of which still (2014) remain parts of the Russian Federation.

[a]merikanka (literally Russian feminine "an American female"; here "American [bet]"): usually a type of a betting arrangement whereby after winning, the winner gets to ask for a wish or favor; the loser(s) cannot turn it down and must carry it out. In the story, Astrid proposes a somewhat modified version of *amerikanka*, offering to carry out any wish of the man who wins the swimming competition.

Vyborg Side (Russian Vyborgskaya storona, named so after the city of Vyborg on the Karelian Isthmus): constitutes one of the principal geographical sections ("sides") of the city of St. Petersburg (Leningrad). The Neva divides St. Petersburg into three main areas: northern, southern, and eastern. The Vyborg Side, traditionally a working-class and industrial area and a Bolshevik stronghold during both 1917 revolutions, makes up the eastern portion of the northern main area of the city, along with Vasilievsky Island and the Petrograd Side, from which the Vyborg Side is separated by the Bol'shaya ("Big") Nevka.

Pyotr jan: in Armenian the word *jan* is added to the first name as a form of endearment, to mean "dear" or "darling"; Astrid and the narrator speak Russian with each other, and she adds *jan* to the narrator's first name, Pyotr.

"*. . . the more fortuitous, the more genuine . . .*" (original Russian, "*i chem sluchainei, tem vernee . . .*"): a famous line from Boris Pasternak's poem "February, to take out the ink and to weep! . . ." (1912).

Utyosov: Leonid Utyosov (1895–1982), famous Soviet pop and jazz singer and actor of Jewish-Odessan origin.

Where Are You, Zoya?

Shrayer-Petrov started "Where Are You, Zoya? ("Gde ty, Zoia?")" on Cape Cod and completed the story in Providence, in 1996. The story appeared in the New York-based weekly *Jewish World* (*Evreiskii mir*; 11 October 1996) and was collected in Shrayer-Petrov's book *Carp for the Gefilte Fish* (2005). The dedicatees, Charlie and Natalie Plotklin, friends of the author and his family since 1991, have a house on Upper Cape Cod.

Fordik: Russian affectionate diminutive of the car make Ford; while living in Providence, Shrayer-Petrov drove a Ford Escort for over a decade.

Berta Yakovlevna. . . . ; . . . the widow of the celebrated Jewish poet Gankin, who wrote in Yiddish: the first name and patronymic of Shrayer-Petrov's character coincide with those of Berta Yakovlevna Selvinskaya, wife of the major Jewish-Russian poet Ilya Selvinsky (1899–1968), whom the author admired and personally met in Moscow in the 1960s. In January 1942 Selvinsky, a frontline journalist and political officer, witnessed the immediate aftermath of the execution, by the hand of Nazis and their accomplices, of thousands of Jews just outside the city of Kerch in Crimea. Selvinsky composed and published "I Saw It," the first poem of bearing witness to the Shoah in the occupied Soviet territories, which became nationally famous in 1942. For details, see Maxim D. Shrayer, *I SAW IT: Ilya Selvinsky and the Legacy of Bearing Witness to the Shoah* (Boston, 2013).

At the same time, the fictional last name of Berta Yakovlevna's late husband, the Yiddish poet Gankin, echoes the name of Shmuel Halkin (1897–1960; Samuil Galkin in the Russianized spelling), a prominent Yiddish Soviet poet who was arrested in 1949 but was not executed like the majority of those arrested in connection with the Jewish Anti-Fascist Committee because he suffered a heart attack, and then ended up in a prison camp, which he survived.

Slavik: diminutive of the name Slava, itself commonly derived from a number of Russian names such as Vyacheslav, Svyatoslav, etc.

translators . . . transporters: the English translation cannot do full justice to the original, in which Shrayer-Petrov employs a Russian pun based on the close verbal affinity of the Russian words *perevodchik* ("translator"; plural *perevodchiki*) and *perevozchik* ("mover," "transporter"; plural *perevozchiki*). Among the Moscow chapters of Shrayer-Petrov's literary memoir *Vodka and Cakes* (*Vodka s pirozhnymi*, 2007), there is a chapter titled "In Charon's Boat" and devoted to the Russian (Soviet) school of literary translation. In it, Shrayer-Petrov quotes another author punning that Soviet literary translators into Russian are actually *transporters*, since they *transport* the verses originally composed in various languages of the Soviet nations across the river Styx and into the Russian-language Soviet mainstream.

Nizhneangarsk: town at the northern point of Lake Baikal in Siberia, originally planned to be developed as the center of the western end of the Baikal–Amur Mainline (BAM) railway. For a detailed account of Shrayer-Petrov's travels in East Siberia and the Baikal Lake regions, see his memoir *The Hunt for the Red Devil* (2010).

Alfredick

The story "Alfredick" ("Al'fredik") was written in 1987–2003 in Providence. It appeared in the New York-based bilingual magazine *Slovo-Word* (64, Fall 2009), and was reprinted in 2010, in an online issue of the St. Petersburg-based magazine of literature and arts *Aesthetoscope*. The story was collected in Shrayer-Petrov's book *Carp for the Gefilte Fish* (2005).

Alfredick: when used in Russian, the non-Slavic name Alfred follows the conventional native pattern of diminution: Alfred-Fred-Fredik; Alfred-Alfredik. The form Dik is a less common derivation from the diminutive forms Fredik or Alfredik. Even though elsewhere the story mentions a play about "the old King of the Goths," to a cultural Russian the name Alfred evokes associations with Western monarchs (e.g., Alfred the Great, king of the Anglo-Saxons, and his cultural lore) to a much lesser degree than one might assume. For a Russian audience, the name suggests a linkage of Shrayer-Petrov's fictional character to the story and atmosphere of Verdi's *La Traviata*, in which the principal male character and Violetta's lover is called Alfred(o) Germont. At the same time, to a Russian ear the diminutive form Alfredik (here Anglicized, tongue–in–cheek, to Alfre*dick*) tends to evoke uncomplimentary associations, suggesting that its bearer is both a sensualist and a morally slippery type.

Jokes about the bushy-browed Lyonka (Brezhnev): jokes about the Soviet leader Leonid Brezhnev were a staple of Soviet popular humor in the 1970s and early 1980s. An example: Brezhnev is riding to the airport, his feet clad in one black and one brown shoe. His assistant tells him: "Comrade Brezhnev, we must turn around and go back to change." Brezhnev replies: "You see, hmm . . . I have the exact same pair at home."

Birobidzhan: city in East Siberia, capital of the Jewish Autonomous Province of the Russian Federation. Originally designed to forge a politically advantageous alternative to Zionism, the Soviet plan for the creation of a Jewish enclave in the Far East, in the Amur River basin near the Soviet–Manchurian border, was put forth in 1927. The population grew slowly, many Jewish settlers returning home after temporary stays in Birobidzhan. In 1930, a Jewish national district was incorporated with 2,672 Jews out of the Birobidzhan area's total population of 38,000. By 1934, the Jewish population of the Birobidzhan area was a little over 8,000, instead of the projected 50,000. Yet the Soviet leadership pushed on with its plan, making the area a Jewish Autonomous Province in 1934. While the Birobidzhan project initially stirred enthusiasm among Soviet Jews, it existed primarily as an ideological tool of the Soviet leadership, attracting support and even enlisting settlers among Jewish Communists abroad. According to Soviet data for 1959, 14,289 Jews, or about nine percent of the total population, were living in the Birobidzhan area, and fewer than 2,000 of these called Yiddish their native language. The Jewish Autonomous Province, the only such unit in the Russian Federation, has weathered the collapse of the Soviet Union and has a Jewish population of about 2500 Jews (about one percent of the province's total population).

Chapayev, Pet'ka, and Anka: this highly popular series of Soviet jokes about the Civil War hero Vasily Chapayev (1887–1919), his adjutant Pet'ka (Pyotr), and the machine-gunner Anka (Anna) had its origins in the 1934 screen adaptation, by the Vasiliev Brothers, of Dmitri Furmanov's novel *Chapayev* (1923).

Chernyakhovsky Street: street in the northwest of Moscow named after the Soviet general, World War II hero Ivan Chernyakhovsky (1906–1945); located outside the Metro station "Aeroport," the street was best known for its prestigious apartment buildings erected after the war to house writers and filmmakers.

Krotov . . . Romantic Theater: the names of both the author and the theater are fictional. At the same time, in light of the alleged membership of the writer Krotov in the literary group The Serapion Brothers (see commentary below) and of whatever else the reader learns about him, it is conceivable that the fictional writer might have had some of his sources in the early career of the writer Veniamin Kaverin (1902–1989).

Academia: based originally in Petrograd (Leningrad) and later in Moscow and active in 1921–1937, the publishing house ACADEMIA distinguished itself above all with its beautifully illustrated and elaborately printed editions of Russian translations of classical literature.

The Serapion Brothers: Russian literary group, whose guiding spirit, in 1920–21, was the Jewish-Russian writer Lev Lunts (1901–1924). Active until 1929, the group included the prose writers Konstantin Fedin (1892–1977), Vsevolod Ivanov (1895–1963), Mikhail Zoshchenko (1895–1958), Nikolay Nikitin (1895–1963), Mikhail Slonimsky (1897–1972), and Veniamin Kaverin (1902–1989); the poets Elizaveta Polonskaya (1890–1969) and Nikolay Tikhonov (1896–1979); and the critic Ilya Gruzdev (1892–1960). The poet Vladimir Posner (1905–1992) and the writer and theorist Viktor Shklovsky (1893–1984) were initially close to the group, as was the playwright Evgeny Shvarts (1896–1958). Lunts proposed the group's name after E.T.A. Hoffman's collection *The Serapion Brethren* (1819–21). Hoffman's hermit Serapion and his brethren became an allegorical model of literary salvation. The Serapions used coded names: Lunts's was "Brother Buffoon"; Kaverin's, "Brother Alchemist"; and so forth. In addition to camaraderie, humanistic values, and a penchant for fantasy, the Serapions shared a commitment to narrative fiction and a Westernizing cultural orientation.

Ticket from Moscow to Vienna: Vienna served as the entry point to the West for Jews emigrating from the Soviet Union; from Vienna one either traveled directly to Israel or waited in temporary transit, usually to continue to Italy, where most Jewish refugees would stay longer, expecting to receive visas to the United States, Canada, and other destinations.

Dinner with Stalin

Shrayer-Petrov wrote "Dinner with Stalin" ("Obed s vozhdem") in 2008 in Boston. It was published in the New York-based international Jewish online magazine *We Are Here* (*My zdes'*) in October 2008, and reprinted in the Philadelphia-based annual *The Coast* (*Poberezh'e*) in 2009 and also in a 2010 print chapbook of the St. Petersburg-based multimedia magazine *Aesthetoscope*.

The Russian original bears an epigraph from Ray Bradbury's short story "Darling Adolf" (from the collection *Long After Midnight*, 1976), a political fantasy in which an actor playing Hitler, in a movie featuring a re-enactment of the 1934 Nuremberg Rally, temporarily takes on Hitler's life and legacy. Bradbury's story is referenced directly in the text of "Dinner with Stalin," not just in the epigraph. Bradbury's fiction was immensely popular in the Soviet Union, and Shrayer-Petrov originally read the story in Olga Akimova's Russian translation (titled "Dushka Adol'f"). Ray Bradbury, whom Shrayer-Petrov met during Bradbury's reading at Brown University in the 1990s, subsequently endorsed Shrayer-Petrov's collection of stories *Jonah and Sarah: Jewish Stories of Russia and America*, edited by Maxim D. Shrayer (Syracuse University Press, 2003): "We have been waiting a long time for a new collection of Jewish tales to arrive and finally they are here . . . And an excellent collection. . . . Highly recommended."

Pushkin's son Aleksandr: the great Russian writer Aleksandr Pushkin (1799–1837) was mortally wounded in a duel and died from the wounds. Pushkin had four children with his wife Natalya Pushkina (née Goncharova): two girls and two boys. Their second child, Aleksandr A. Pushkin (1833–1914), had a long career in the military and in public service, and retired as a general.

Shereshevsky: Lazar Shereshevky (1926–2008), poet and literary translator, especially from the Lithuanian and the languages of North Caucasus; Shrayer-Petrov's colleague and acquaintance in the 1970s.

Moscow writers' local union: in the Soviet Union, the official status of literary professionals was validated by membership in writers' professional organizations, from the elite Union of Soviet Writers down to writers' local unions, such as the one described in the story. There were several such writers' local unions in Moscow alone. After expulsion from the Union of Soviet Writers for deciding to emigrate, Shrayer-Petrov found temporary refuge at the local writers' union affiliated with the Soviet Writer (Sovetskii pisatel') publishing house.

OVIR: abbreviation for Otdel viz i razreshenii (literally Department of Visas and Permissions), an institution which, in Soviet times, handled both exit visas for Soviet citizens and entry visas for foreigners. A Jew who wanted to emigrate from the Soviet Union would start the process by "applying" (submitting his or her papers) to the local branch of OVIR. Refuseniks who were reapplying for exit visas or petitioning that their case be reconsidered usually went to a local city or regional OVIR office, or even to the central OVIR office in Moscow.

Mitasov: Egor Mitasov is the pen name of Grigory Mitasov (b. 1933), a professional billiards player and coach and also a poet.

Shklyarevsky: Igor Shklyarevsky (b. 1938), well-known contemporary Russian poet, translator, and critic.

Uncle Styopa . . . Sergei Mikhalkov: Uncle Styopa (Russian *diadia Stepa*) is the name of a celebrated character of four narrative poems for children by Sergei Mikhalkov (1913–2009). Mikhalkov was best known as the author of the Uncle Styopa cycle and a cycle of fables, and as the coauthor of the lyrics of the Soviet national anthem, which he subsequently revised as the national anthem of the post-Soviet Russian Federation. Uncle Styopa, a law enforcement officer and a cardboard embodiment of the idea of Soviet goodness, is distinguished for his height, love of children, and absence of negative character traits.

Karabakh: Nagorno-Karabakh, during the Soviet period an autonomous region, mostly populated by ethnic Armenians, within the boundaries of the Azerbaijani Soviet Republic. Through political and military conflict in the late 1980s and early 1990s, escalating into a war following the collapse of the Soviet Union in 1991, the Armenian majority in the landlocked Nagorno-Karabakh sought reunification with the Republic of Armenia. The conflict created a refugee problem in the region. Presently

(2014), Nagorno-Karabakh is an unrecognized republic, its status awaiting resolution.

the Marjanishvili Drama Theater in Tbilisi: theater in the capital of Georgia named after the great Georgian stage director Kote (Konstatin) Marjanishvili (1872–1933).

. . . the operatic abduction of Pushkin's Ludmila by the grey-bearded dwarf, the sorcerer Chernomor: in Pushkin's epic poem *Ruslan and Ludmila* (1820), based on Russian folklore, the evil wizard Chernomor (derived from *Chernoe more*, the Russian for "Black Sea") abducts Princess Ludmila, who is rescued by the noble knight Ruslan. Mikhail Glinka based his well-known eponymous opera of 1842 on Pushkin's epic poem.

Alazani Valley: the name of a geographic area in Georgia and Azerbaijan, formed by the valleys of the Alazani and the Agrichay rivers and extending along the southern foothills of the Greater Caucasus range. Alazani Valley, often referred to as Kakhetian Valley, is an ancient center of viticulture and a home to Georgia'a wines, once famous all across the Soviet Union, among them the semi-sweet white "Alazani Valley."

fah-tah-grah-fik: Stalin spoke Russian very fluently, but with a thick Georgian accent, which is rendered in Russian through phonetic transcription and which the English translation also seeks to render, albeit playfully.

tamada: this Georgian term for the toastmaster at a feast has firmly entered the Russian language and spread across the former Soviet Union.

Borzhomi: name of the mineral water bottled in the spa town of Borzhomi in south-central Georgia. During the Soviet period, this mineral water was considered the finest in the country, and it still enjoys popularity among ex-Soviets.

. . . lyrical poem "Morning," written by Comrade Stalin in his youth: as a young seminarian, Joseph Stalin composed lyrical poetry in his native Georgian. The poems even impressed the distinguished Georgian poet Ilya Chavhavadze, who published a selection of Stalin's poems in the periodical he edited, under a pseudonym; the poems were subsequently anthologized in Georgia. In the story, the visiting Georgian actor recites a Russian-language adaptation of a poem by the young Stalin, titled "Morning."

"March of the Artillerymen" (Russian "Marsh artilleristov," 1943): a widely performed wartime Soviet song, lyrics by Viktor Gusev, music by Tikhon Khrennikov. After Stalin's death the lyrics were revised and Stalin's name was removed.

The Valley of Hinnom

Shrayer-Petrov wrote "The Valley of Hinnom" ("Ushchel'e Geenny") in January 2004 in Providence. Originally published in the Moscow-based Jewish monthly *L'chayim* (*Lekhaim*; August 2004), the story was collected in Shrayer-Petrov's *Carp for the Gefilte Fish* (2005).

Sasha, D'Anthès, Natasha: the reference is to Aleksandr (diminutive Sasha) Pushkin, his wife Natalya (diminutive Natasha), and the French nobleman Georges-Charles de Heeckeren d'Anthès. Indignant of D'Anthès's inappropriate courtship of his wife Natalya, Pushkin challenged him to a duel, at which D'Anthès mortally wounded the great writer.

Osya, Marina, Dima: the reference is to the poet and essayist Joseph (Russian Iosif, diminutive Osya) Brodsky, the artist Marina Basmanova, who was Brodsky's great love and mother of his son, and the Russian-American poet Dmitri Bobyshev (diminutive Dima), who had an amorous relationship with Basmanova in 1963.

Sid: in Russian one cannot differentiate between the conventional Anglo-Saxon spelling Syd(ney)/Sid(ney) and the spelling Cid, which points to the Castilian aristocrat and warrior Rodrigo Díaz de Vivar (1043–1099), known as El Cid (El Campeador). It is therefore challenging to render in Russian the rich aura of El Cid's cultural legacy without being overexplicit. Both Pierre Corneille's tragic comedy *Le Cid* (1638) and Jules Massenet's opera of the same title (1885) were based on the life and cultural mythology of the Spanish hero and lurk in the background of Сид, the Russian spelling of both (El) Cid and Syd/Sid. An abbreviation of the variant English spelling, Sid, has been used here in translation, so as not to over-inflate the connection between the story's contemporary Jewish-Russian boy and the historical and cultural aura of El Cid/Le Cid.

underground Jewish Theater: to reconstruct the historical background for this story, one should consider that throughout the 1960s–1980s, two principal forces shaped the intellectual life of the Jewish underground in the Soviet Union. The *politiki* ("politicians") firmly stood on the rock bed of Zionism and aliya (repatriation of Jews to Israel). The *tarbutniki* or *kul'turniki* ("culturists," from the Hebrew *tarbut* or the Russian *kul'tura*) fantasized about legal cultural autonomy while seeking to revive Jewish life in Russia. The underground Jewish theater groups in the Soviet Union celebrated the joy of the Jewish holiday of Purim by mounting annual Purimshpiln: Purim plays based on the kernel story about the beautiful Esther, the villainous Haman, and the wise and enterprising Mordecai. These plays were performed at private apartments and other unsanctioned venues. For Soviet Jews of the postwar years, associations with ancient Babylonia rang close to home. Sometime in late 1986 or early 1987, an underground troupe consisting mainly of refuseniks approached Shrayer-Petrov with the idea of writing a Purimshpil. Roman Spektor, the troupe's charismatic leader, appeared in minor parts and referred to himself as the "acting director." The author's experience of writing a Purimshpil, in which myth, memory, and contemporary Soviet history mingled and lived on, forms a personal backdrop for the events of this fictional story. In March–April of 1987, the troupe performed Shrayer-Petrov's Purimshil about two dozen times in private apartments across Moscow; performances by several other underground Jewish troupes also took place in Moscow during the 1987 Purim season. For information about the history of official Jewish theaters in the Soviet Union, see notes below and also Chapter 9 in Maxim D. Shrayer, *Leaving Russia: A Jewish Story* (Syracuse, 2013).

. . . *Mikhail Lermontov's* The Spaniards: as a young man, Mikhail Lermontov (1814–1841) composed the unfinished tragedy *The Spaniards* (*Ispantsy*) in 1830; its entire surviving text was first published in 1880. Set in Spain some time between the fifteenth and seventeenth centuries, the play depicts the persecution of *Marranos* and *conversos* by the Spanish Inquisition and focuses on a young Romantic hero's realization of his own Jewish ancestry. The play's sympathetic portrayal of Jewish victimhood made it an attractive candidate for translation into Yiddish (by Aron Kushnirov) and staging by GOSET, the Moscow State Jewish Theater, in 1941. The great Jewish actor and director Solomon (Shloyme) Mikhoels, who directed the theater from 1928 until his assassination by the Soviet secret police in 1948, took a special interest in the letter and spirit of Lermontov's tragedy. The theater was shut down in 1949, during the darkest years for Soviet Jewry.

David and Goliath, *a play by the contemporary Greek playwright Petropoulos*: this is a doubly encoded self-reference. "David and Goliath" ("David i Goliaf," 1987) is the title of one of Shrayer-Petrov's best known short stories (the English translation is included in his volume *Jonah and Sarah: Jewish Stories of Russia and America*). The Greek last name "Petropoulus" suggests the same etymology as the writer's patronymic, Petrovich, and his Soviet-era pen name, Petrov. Consider also the Greek author and intellectual Elias Petropoulos (1928–1993), who was persecuted in Greece during the junta years and went into political exile in France.

the Birobidzhan Theater: a number of Jewish theaters operated in the Soviet Union in the 1920s–1940s. In 1933, a State Jewish Theater was founded in Birobidzhan, the capital of the Jewish Autonomous Region; the theater was closed in 1949 along with the other Jewish theater companies across the country. In 1977, the Jewish Chamber Musical Theater (KEMT) was established; although formally incorporated in the Jewish Autonomous Province and assigned to Birobidzhan, the theater operated out of Moscow. In 1981 another Jewish troupe, the Show Group Freilechs, was founded in Birobidzhan. The story most likely refers to the Jewish Chamber Musical Theater.

the *Jewish shepherd David prevails over the Palestinian giant Goliath*: this political pun does not quite come off in a contemporary Anglo-American translation, as it lacks the Soviet ideological context of the 1970s and 1980s. Following the Six-Day War and the overwhelming Israeli victory, the Soviet Union broke off diplomatic relations with Israel and pursued an openly and unabashedly anti-Israeli campaign. The daily fabric of Soviet life was saturated with pro-Palestinian propaganda. While to the native Russian ear in the Soviet 1980s, the adjective *palestinskii* (Palestinian) may evoke *filistimlianskii* (Philistine) to a slightly greater degree than it does to a native Anglo-American ear, what makes the comment more poignant in Russian is the baggage of political history. The point Shrayer-Petrov's narrator makes is that in the late 1970s and early 1980s, a contemporary retelling of the biblical story of David and Goliath might have flown in the face of the Soviet anti-Israeli rhetoric.

Cavafy: this is in fact the opening stanza of Shrayer-Petrov's poem "More from Cavafy" from his collection *Dve knigi* (*Two Books*, 2009). In "In the Direction of the Sea" ("Po napravleniiu k moriu"), one of the book's two principal cycles, two poems were inspired by Shrayer-Petrov's reading of Cavafy's poetry in English translation.

Elokhov Church: one of Moscow's most beautiful Russian Orthodox churches, built in 1835–1845.

"the time of Ochakov and the conquest of the Crimea": a famous line from Act 2, Scene 5 of *Woe of Wit* (1824), Aleksandr Griboedov's play in verse; this line, referring to the subjugation of the Crimea and conquest of parts of the Black Sea coast by the Russian Empire in the late eighteenth century, is commonly used in Russian to indicate that something is ancient history or old hat.

"Gop-and-smyk": one of the best known Russian gangster songs dating to the early twentieth century and also known in its more colorful, Odessan version, with an admixture of Yiddish and Ukrainian, and of Odessan dialectal expressions. The famous Soviet performer Leonid Utyosov (1895–1982) popularized the song in the cultural mainstream by recording and performing it widely in the 1920s and 1930s. Possibly referring to the nickname of a historical Odessan gangster, the term gop-and-smyk (Russian *gop-so-smykom*) apparently means either a swift attack (e.g., robbery) followed by an equally swift escape, or the actual robber (*gopnik*, in the criminal lingo) with his special tools (*smyk*).

Zhiguli 6: Soviet car model. In 1970 the Volga Automobile Plant (VAZ) started manufacturing Zhiguli, compact automobiles based on the Italian Fiat. Introduced in 1976, Zhiguli 6 (*shesterka*; model VAZ 2106) was an upscale sedan developed on the basis of the original Zhiguli, known as "Model 1" (VAZ 2101).

the Kutuzovsky Prospect: named after the great Russian military leader Mikhail Kutuzov (1745–1813) and developed as a major Moscow artery running to the south-west from the center of Moscow and eventually becoming the Mozhaisk Highway. A section of the Kutuzovsky Prospect originally built in the 1930s in Stalinist monumentalist style served as a residential area for the Soviet elite, including the top party officials. It is there that a housing complex serving some of the diplomats and foreigners stationed in Moscow was located.

Pelevin or the brothers Strugatsky: Viktor Pelevin (b. 1962), contemporary Russian trend-setting fiction writer of the post-Soviet 1990s; Arkady Strugatsky (1925–1991) and Boris Strugatsky (1933–2012), brothers who published under the collective nom de plume Strugatsky Brothers (Brat'ia Strugatskie), were the dominant Soviet science fiction writers of the Soviet 1960s–1980s.

Mimosa Flowers for Grandmother's Grave

Written in Moscow in 1984, during the worst years of the refuseniks' limbo, "Mimosa Flowers for Grandmother's Grave" ("Mimozy na mogilu babushki") is one of Shrayer-Petrov's earliest short stories. He lightly revised it in the 1990s, and it was first published in the New York-based Jewish weekly *Jewish World* (*Evreiskii mir*; 21 March 1997), and subsequently collected in his book *Carp for the Gefilte Fish* (2005). A shorter account of the passing and funeral of Shrayer-Petrov's paternal grandmother Feyga (Fanya) Shrayer (1878–1963) is found in the writer's memoir *The Hunt for the Red Devil: A Novel with Microbiologists* (Moscow, 2010), in Chapter 7, titled "Mixed Infections."

Solomon: the first name of Shrayer-Petrov's semiautobiographical protagonist, the young microbiologist Solomon, is not only a logical metonymic substitution for the author's own first name (David-Solomon), but also a name that has its roots in the writer's early attempts to write in the autobiographical vein. On 28 July 2011, Shrayer-Petrov commented in an email to the editor of this volume: " . . . some time in the [. . .] 1960s I started writing a novel in verse [titled *Solomon Novoseltsev*], being then under the influence of the richness of sound and the wide span of the personal-civic intonation in [Anna] Akhmatova's [epic] *Poem without a Hero*. For some reason, I gave up writing the novel after a dozen pages. The manuscript ended up in my archive. I recently perused it. Preserved to this day is the spirit of those years, of studenthood, first loves, and so forth." The last name of the hero of the abandoned novel in verse, Novoseltsev, indirectly points to Novosiltsevskaya Street (renamed Novorossiiskaya in 1952); near the intersection of this street with Engels Prospect stood Shrayer-Petrov's childhood home in the Lesnoe neighborhood of Leningrad (St. Petersburg). Presently, only a small lane in Lesnoe bears the name Novosiltsevsky Lane. The Novosiltsevs were a Russian noble family, its most famous representatives including Nikolai Novosiltsev (1761–1838), one of the closest associates of Emperor Alexander I, and Vladimir Novosiltsev, an officer killed in a famous duel in 1825 just steps from the site of Shrayer-Petrov's childhood home. Thus, there is double irony in the choice of the hero's name: unlike the Russian aristocrats the Novosiltsevs, the Russian Jew Solomon Novoseltsev, whose ancestors hailed from the former Pale of Settlement, can never claim to be fully at home in Russia. Solomon's last name differs from that of the aristocratic Novosiltsevs by one letter only, but this difference augments its origin in the Russian noun *novosel'e* (literally new residence or new home) and subtly underscores that Solomon's family were still strangers in their Leningrad abode.

Aunt Betya . . . Isaac . . . Kamenets-Podolsk: the story alters the names, yet references Shrayer-Petrov's family background. Shrayer-Petrov's family hails from the area of Kamenets-Podolsk (Kamianets-Podilsk in Ukrainian), once the provincial capital of Podolia, presently reduced to a district center in the Khmelnytskyi Province of Ukraine. Kamenets-Podolsk, or simply "Kamenets," as the natives and locals still refer to it with fondness, has many Jewish claims to fame, including Mendele Moykher-Sforim's service as a teacher in a local Jewish crown school in the 1850s. In Kamenets-Podolsk and its environs, the Shrayers worked in the flour milling business. Judaic traditions were respected in the family, but in the 1910s the lifestyle and educational ambitions were increasingly those of the urbanized Jewish bourgeoisie. Born in 1910, Shrayer-Petrov's paternal grandfather Peysakh (Pyotr) Shrayer had four siblings who survived into adulthood, including an older brother, Yakov, an older sister, Berta (whose fictionalized self appears in the story as Aunt Betya), and two brothers who were close to him in age: the younger Abram and the older Moisei. Moisei, known in the family as Munia, is the historical antecedent of the story's Isaac (Izya), Solomon's uncle who sailed from Odessa to Jaffa in 1924. Following the derailment of the New Economic Plan, the rest of the Shrayer family left—practically fled from—Kamenets and settled in Leningrad, where David would be born in 1936. In the British Mandate of Palestine, Moisei Shrayer changed his last name to Sharir and became a land-surveyor; he remained loyal to the socialist ideals of his youth. He would never again see his parents and three of his four siblings, and died in Tel Aviv in 2004. Shrayer-Petrov met his uncle for the first time in 1987 in Italy, after having already composed "Mimosa Flowers for Gradmother's Grave," and subsequently saw him in Israel.

Leningrad's Institute of Tuberculosis: founded in 1923 as a research institution, in 1983 the Institute of Tuberculosis (Leningrad) was merged with the Institute of Surgical Tuberculosis (founded in 1930), to form the Research Institute of Pthisipulmonology. In the autumn of 1961, following his return to Leningrad from Belarus, where he had served as a military physician, Dr. Shrayer-Petrov entered graduate school at the Leningrad Institute of Tuberculosis; in 1964 he completed the experimental part of his dissertation work, and in 1966 defended his candidate's dissertation (PhD equivalent), which dealt with mixed TB infections.

Ligovsky Prospect . . . Zelenina Street . . . Chkalovsky Prospect: the Institute of Tuberculosis (and its present-day successor institution) is located on Ligovsky Prospect, a major artery running from the northwest to the southeast through the center of St. Petersburg and intersecting with the Nevsky Prospect at Vosstaniya (Uprising) Square, site of the Moskovsky train station. Solomon's grandmother (and Shrayer-Petrov's historical paternal grandmother) lived at the corner of Bolshaya Zelenina Street and Chkalovsky Prospect on Leningrad's Petrograd Side.

Vyborg Side: one of Leningrad's principal parts; see above, Notes on "Mimicry."

bazar: in the Russian game of dominos, the bank of chips to which players go in the absence of needed chips is known as *bazar* (bazaar), the Persian-derived, common Russian term for an open-air market.

brichka (in English also spelled *britchka*): a light four-wheel carriage, usually partly covered with a leather top.

the Jewish cemetery: the Probrazhenskoe Jewish Cemetery on the outskirts St. Petersburg, founded in 1875.

balalaika: a three-stringed, triangular-shaped native Russian instrument, standardized in the 1880s as a family of variously voiced (sized) stringed instruments.

Mozart. His Symphony No. 40 in G minor. . . ."I will never forget you, darling. . . . Please remember me, my love. . . .": Mozart's Symphony No. 40 in G minor (1788) was and remains one of Shrayer-Petrov's favorite works of music, and he claimed to hear, in the main theme of the symphony's part 1, the Russian lyrics *"Ia tebia nigodga ne zabudu,/ ty menia ne zabyvai"* (two lines of truncated anapestic trimeter). In translation, these lines are rendered with metrical exactitude at the expense of minor alterations and additions of words.

The House of Edgar Allan Poe

The story "The House of Edgar Allan Poe" ("Dom Edgara Po") was written in March 2009 in Boston and published in the *2011 Prose* issue of the St. Petersburg-based multimedia magazine of literature and arts *Aesthetoscope*, and was reprinted in the Russian magazine *Mlechnyi put'/ Milky Way* (2, 2011). Edgar Allen Poe (1809–1849), especially his story "Gold-Bug" (published 1843) and his poem "The Raven" (published in 1845 and subsequently known in a number of Russian translations), enjoyed something of a cult status during the Russian fin de siècle. What is particularly intriguing in the case of Shrayer-Petrov and his story "The House of Edgar Allan Poe" is that the writer spent two decades in Providence, Rhode Island and took a personal interest in the legacy of Poe's visits to this historic New England city.

The House of Edgar Allan Poe: the title of the story, and the "house" itself, were inspired by the house of Sarah Helen Whitman on Benefit Street in Providence, Rhode Island. According to Poe's biographers, the writer visited Providence several times in the 1840s. In Providence he courted Whitman, one of his life's main love interests. See notes below for further details.

a Russian émigré of the "third wave" . . . : this refers to the division of the twentieth-century outflux of émigrés from Russia and the former Soviet Union into three principal waves. The "first wave" refers to the émigrés who left in the wake of the 1917 Russian revolutions and the ensuing civil war; the "second wave" refers to the émigrés, many of the them of so-called displaced persons (DPs), who left during World War 2 and the occupation of the USSR by the Nazis and their allies; the "third wave," to which Polyakov belongs, mainly refers to those émigrés who left in the course of the Exodus of Jews from the former USSR in the 1970s–1980s.

Rockefeller Library of Brown University toward Benefit Street . . . : the Rockefeller Library is the main library of Brown University. The Brown campus is located on the so-called College Hill overlooking downtown Providence. Several streets, including Angell Street, Waterman Street, and College Street, descend from the Brown campus down the hill, first intersecting the historic Benefit Street and North and South Main Street, which run parallel to the Providence River, then going over the river into the downtown area.

Valery Bryusov (1873–1924): one of the key literary figures of Russian symbolism and a pivot of the Russian fin de siècle. While the earliest Russian translations of Poe's "The Raven" date to the 1870s, Brysov, who translated "The Raven" into Russian in 1905 and refined it subsequently, walked in the footsteps of another major symbolist literary figure, Dmitri Merezhkovsky (1865–1941), who had translated "The Raven" in 1894. Other Russian translations followed suit, including a notable one by the Zionist leader and Jewish-Russian writer Vladimir (Ze'ev) Zhabotinsky, completed in 1931.

Sashenka Tverskaya: Sashenka is an affectionate diminutive of both the Russian female name Aleksandra and its male version, Aleksandr. While Sashenka's origin is deliberately obscured in the story, the last name "Tverskaya" probably points to the Russian noble origins of her paternal ancestors and evokes the name of Princess Betsy Tverskaya, an important secondary character in Tolstoy's novel *Anna Karenina* and a close witness to Anna and Vronsky's romance.

the Providence Athenaeum . . . number "88" . . . Sarah Helen Whitman: The Providence Athenaeum is a private membership library that was opened at 251 Benefit Street in Providence in 1838 and was built on the site of an earlier one, The Providence Library Company. 88 Benefit Street is the location of the house where the poet Sarah Helen Power Whitman (1801–1878), a Providence native, was living when she met Poe in 1845. During their courtship and Poe's visits to Providence, Whitman and Poe had some of their rendezvous in the Providence Atheneum. The engagement was broken in late December 1848.

Helen/Lena/Lenochka Whitman: Helen is the Anglicized version of the originally Greek first name, which enjoys great popularity in Russia, Elena being the full name, Lena a common diminutive, and Lenochka a common affectionate diminutive.

zhuzhelitsa . . . ground beetle . . . Beata . . . : *zhuk* is the most generic Russian word for beetle or bug. *Zhuzhelitsa*, a feminine noun, is a word commonly used in Russian to refer to the ground beetle, regardless of the beetle's gender. The latter, however, forms a gendered aura in the mind of the Russian speaker; hence, in the original, Polyakov gives the magic beetle the euphonic female name Zhuzha, derived from *zhuzhelitsa*. Considering both the importance of preserving the beetle's feminine aura and the creature's anthropomorphic qualities and stated beauty, the name Beata was chosen to replace Zhuzha in translation and also to compensate for the original's play of sound and meaning: compare "beetle Beata" and "*zhuzhelitsa* Zhuzha."

Karl the dwarf: here translation cannot do full justice to the alliteration and word play of the Russian original. *Karlik*, the modern Russian word for "dwarf," which had most likely come into the Russian language, perhaps by way of Polish, from the German *Kerl* (chap; guy; fellow), sounds exactly the same as a standard Russian diminutive of the first name Karl. Thus *karlik Karl* ("Karl the dwarf") in Russian is both poetically redundant and colorful.

Tula . . . Yasnaya Polyana: the ancient Russian city of Tula is the capital of the Tula Province south of Moscow. Lev Tolstoy's estate of Yasnaya Polyana, now a national museum, is located in the Tula Province.

" . . . so tight that even a mosquito wouldn't be able to get its nose in": in light of Lena Whitman's own Russian origins, this literal translation of the Russian idiom *"chtoby i komar nosu ne podtochil"* captures the letter and spirit of her instructions to Beata.

Trubetskoy, Raevsky, Masha Malevich, and the Death of Mayakovsky ·

Shrayer-Petrov wrote "Trubetskoy, Raevsky, Masha Malevich, and the Death of Mayakovsky" (*"Trubetskoi, Raevskii, Masha Malevich i smert' Maiakovskogo"*) in 2004 in Providence. The story was published in the Philadelphia-based annual *The Coast* (*Poberezh'e*), 2008. The author included it in his memoir *The Hunt for the Red Devil: A Novel with Micro-biologists* (Moscow, 2010), where it appears as an embedded authorial digression-story in Chapter 19, "The Refusenik Doctor." Multiple ironies emanate from names of the students taking the microbiology course. For more information, see notes and commentary below.

the bronze monument to the first Cheka leader Dzherzhinsky . . . the headquarters of the central committee of the Bolshevik party . . . the standing remnants of Moscow's medieval walls . . . the Choral Synagogue . . . Solyanka Street: The narrator is driving through the historic center of Moscow from the northwest to the southeast. Felix Dzherzhinsky (1877–1926) was the original boss of the Cheka, the first incarnation of the Soviet secret police, eventually known as the KGB. A large monument to Dzher-zhinsky used to stand in Dzerzhinsky Square facing the headquarters of the KGB; in the post-Soviet times the original name of the square, Luby-anka, was restored and the monument to Dzherzhinsky was removed, while the present-day heir to the KGB, the FSB, remains in the original location. On his way, the narrator passes (on his right) the building in Staraya (Old) Square which formerly housed the Central Committee of the Communist Party and (on his left) the area of Moscow known as Kitay-gorod, where remains of Moscow's medieval walls are still visible today. Then he turns into Arkhipova Street (now known by its historical name, Bolshoy Spasoglinishchevsky Lane), a short hilly street where the Moscow Choral Synagogue is located. Solyanka Street, one of the oldest streets of Moscow, begins just a block from the location of the Moscow Choral Synagogue and runs down in the direction of the Yauza River, where it ends at Yauza (Yauzzskie) Gate.

Zhiguli: Soviet compact car make; see Notes on "The Valley of Hinnom."

medical college: a wide network of specialized junior colleges existed in the former Soviet Union. The so-called medical college (*meditsinskoe uchilishche*), not to be confused with medical school (*meditsinskii institut*), trained nurses and laboratory assistants.

Pokrovsky Boulevard: this picturesque boulevard in the center of Moscow forms the eastern section of the Boulevard Ring (see also Notes on "Behind the Zoo Fence"). It runs north to south and connects with Chistoprudny Boulevard at the Pokrovsky Gate and with Yauzsky Boulevard at Vorontsovo Pole (Field).

. . . the writers' local union: see Notes on "Dinner with Stalin."

Yelena Bonner (1923–2011): trained as a pediatrician, Bonner was a well-known Soviet human rights activist and second wife of the famous Soviet physicist turned prominent dissident, Andrey Sakharov (1921–1989).

rather extraordinary, downright famous last names: Misha Trubetskoy, Sasha Raevsky, and Masha Malevich: the name and conduct of Misha Trubetskoy alludes to Prince Sergey Trubetskoy (1790–1860), one of the leaders of the secret Northern Society, who was elected "dictator" in advance of the Decembrist uprising (15 December 1825) but failed to appear on the Senate Square. Trubetskoy was, nonetheless, sentenced to death for his participation in the conspiracy, but his sentence was commuted to life at hard labor. In the Russian historical context of a conspiracy or secret protest, the name Trubetskoy signals failure to carry out an agreed-upon conspiratorial plan. In the context of Russian history, the name of Sasha Raevsky hints at General Nikolay Raevsky (1771–1829), one of Russia's most celebrated military leaders during the Napoleonic Wars; in 1815, Raevsky entered Paris at the side of Emperor Alexander I. Raevsky was connected, through familial ties and those of camaraderie, to members of the Decembrist movement, and was devastated by the punishment of his relatives and friends by Emperor Nicholas I following the Decembrist uprising. Kazimir Malevich (1879–1935), one of the key figures of the Russian avant-garde, founded the suprematist artistic movement and attributed deep philosophical significance to the purity of geometrical forms.

Félix d'Herelle . . . Georgi Eliava . . . Beria: the great French-Canadian microbiologist Félix d'Herelle (1873–1949) was the discoverer (or, as is still a matter of debate, co-discoverer) of bacteriophages and founding father of phage therapy. In 1934–1935, d'Herelle worked in Tbilisi, capital of Soviet Georgia, where unique opportunities were initially created for him, due in part to the agency of his friend and junior colleague, the French-trained Georgian microbiologist Georgi Eliava (1892–1937), who had founded a research institute in Tbilisi. D'Herelle returned to Paris, apparently hoping to return to Tbilisi; in 1937, Eliava was arrested and purged on the order of Lavrenty Beria (1899–1953); then the party boss of the Transcaucasian region, Beria, enjoyed Stalin's growing favor and subsequently became head of the People's Commissariat of Internal Security (NKVD) and one of Stalin's principal henchmen. In the 1970s, Shrayer-Petrov, who was conducting research on phage therapy, became fascinated with d'Herelle and researched the then–untold story of d'Herelle's "Georgian" period by going to Tbilisi and interviewing the surviving associates of Eliava and d'Herelle and gathering documentary materials on what was then a hushed-up topic. He had by that time completed the first version of *The French Cottage* (*Frantsuzskii kottedzh*), a novel in which a young Jewish-Russian scientific journalist investigates the truth about d'Herelle's work in the Soviet Union while also seeking to know the mystery of his own father's past. Shrayer-Petrov negotiated the publication of the novel but those plans were undercut by his becoming a refusenik and being isolated from academic and literary public life in the Soviet Union. Eventually, after immigrating to the United States, Shrayer-Petrov contributed the essay "Fèlix d'Herelle in Russia" to the Paris-based *Bulletin de l'Institute Pasteur* in 1996, and also expanded and revised the text of *The French Cottage*, which appeared in Russia, in 1999.

Kazbek: popular brand of Soviet *papirosy* ("air" filter cigarettes), named after Mount Kazbek, the seventh highest peak in the Caucasus Mountains.

Geyer: the Jewish-Russian science writer Daniil Geyer is Shrayer-Petrov's fictional alter ego and the main character of his novel *The French Cottage* and of several short stories (in his collection *Jonah and Sarah*: see the story "Hurricane Bob"). Note also that a semiautobiographical first-person narrator by the name of Daniil (diminutive Danya) appears in several other stories in this collection, including "White Sheep on a

Green Mountain Slope," "Round-the-Globe Happiness," and "The Bicycle Race"; on the name Daniil (Danya) in Shrayer-Petrov's fiction, see also Notes on "The Bicycle Race."

Pobeda (literally Russian "victory"): large Soviet passenger car make produced in 1946–1958 at Gorky Auto Works (GAZ).

chernukha: derived from the Russian adjective *chernyi* (black), this late Soviet-era, Russian-language idiomatic term has entered the cultural mainstream to describe a mode or point of view in literary, musical, or visual arts, most commonly in jokes, ditties, songs, narrative fiction, and cinema, which focuses on the dark, gruesome, and ugly aspects of Soviet living and thereby seeks to break the public silence and subvert the official status quo.

Ordzhonikidzhe: the prominent Bolshevik leader Sergo Ordzhonikidzhe (1886–1937) was a member of the Politburo, People's Commissar (Minister) of the Heavy Industry, and Stalin's close associate. Varying accounts of his disapproval or tacit approval of the show trials and purges have been proposed. His death was officially deemed a result of a heart attack, although it has also been argued that he committed suicide or was murdered on Stalin's order.

Anna Antonovskaya's . . . The Great Mouravi . . . Giorgi Saakadze: the Russian-language historical page-turner *The Great Mouravi* (*Velikii Mouravi*, 1942) by Anna Antonovskaya (1885–1967) reconstructed the life and times of Giorgi Saakadze, the legendary seventeenth-century Georgian politician and warrior known as the Great Mouravi.

Bogolyubov: the last name of this young man is derived from the Russian noun *Bog* (God) and the Russian verb *liubit'* (to love), and therefore clearly signals his connection to religion and faith.

Chistoprudny Boulevard: a very pretty section of Moscow's boulevard ring, Chistoprudny Boulevard encompasses a series of small ponds known as Chistye Prudy (Clear Ponds) and runs southwest from Sretensky Boulevard to Pokrovsky Boulevard.

Baptist Church . . . Evangelical Christian Baptists: Moscow's central Church of the Evangelical Christian Baptists is located in Malyi Trekhsvyatitelsky Lane off Pokrovsky Boulevard, just three blocks south of Pokrovskie Gate, where Chistoprudny Boulevard meets Pokrovsky Boulevard (see notes above). The church and movement known as Evangelical Christian Baptists (Evangel'skie khristiane-baptisty) was formed in 1944 from a merger of Baptist and Evangelical Christian church communities in the Soviet Union. Evangelical Christian Baptists were disenfranchised and persecuted during the Soviet period.

Mayakovsky: Vladimir Mayakovsky (1893–1930) was one of the most talented and influential Russian modernist (futurist) poets, and is credited with transforming the landscape of modern Russian poetry. Mayakovsky's death was officially deemed a suicide, although the exact circumstances remain uncertain. In the middle 1930s, Mayakovsky was deemed a canonical Soviet poet, his legacy warped to serve the Stalinist regime.

The Bicycle Race

"I've been writing this story my whole life," states Shrayer-Petrov in the opening sentence of "The Bicycle Race" ("Velogonki"). He finally committed it to paper in November 2004 in Providence. The Copenhagen-based Russian-language magazine *New Shore* (*Novyi bereg*) published it in 2007. Set in postwar Leningrad and featuring the autobiographical protagonist Daniil (Danya), this story is a satellite on one of the orbits of Shrayer-Petrov's novel *Strange Danya Rayev* (2001). Published in English in 2006 as part of the volume *Autumn in Yalta: A Novel and Three Stories* (Syracuse University Press), *Strange Danya Rayev* depicts the prewar childhood of a Jewish boy in Leningrad, his evacuation to a remote Uralian village in 1941, following the Nazi invasion of the Soviet Union, and his return to the destroyed Leningrad in 1944. Consider also Shrayer-Petrov's memoiristic story "Lanskoy Road," set in the 1940s in the author's childhood neighborhood and published in English in the collection *Jonah and Sarah*. Finally, the story dialogues poignantly with one of Shrayer-Petrov's best known works of short fiction, "Autumn in Yalta" (1992), in which the main character, a physician and TB researcher, is fatally in love with the actress Polechka, who suffers from tuberculosis. A section of the earlier story and the ending of the later one both take place in the Crimean coastal resort of Yalta.

Novosiltsevskaya Street and Engels Prospect: site of Shrayer-Petrov's childhood home in the Lesnoe neighborhood of the Vyborg Side of

Leningrad (St. Petersburg). Novosiltsevskaya Street, presently called Novorossiskaya Street, becomes Lanskoe Highway past the intersection with Engels Prospect. About the Vyborg Side, see the Notes on the stories "Mimicry" and "Mimosa Flowers for Grandmother's Grave"; for further details of the area's history, see the Notes on Shrayer-Petrov's novel *Strange Danya Rayev* in the volume *Autumn in Yalta: A Novel and Three Stories.*

Forestry Technical University: Lesotekhnicheskaia akademiia, formerly Forestry Institute, founded in 1803 and renamed S. M. Kirov Leningrad Forestry Technical Academy in 1929; located in the Vyborg District of Leningrad (St. Petersburg) and surrounded by a sprawling old park. Shrayer-Petrov grew up across the street from the Academy and its park and campus.

Shvarts . . . Cherny: the historical antecedent of Shrayer-Petrov's fictional character was Eduard Chernoshvarts, a distinguished Soviet cyclist and champion of the Soviet Union. The last name "Chernoshvarts" is derived from a fusion of the Russian adjective *chernyi* (black) and the Germanic *shvarts* (*schwartz*=black). Eduard Chernoshvarts and the soccer forward Boris Levin-Kogan, both of them Leningrad-based Jews, were famous Soviet athletes of the 1940s.

Kushelevka railway station: this railway station serving suburban trains takes its name from Kushelevka, a historical area and neighborhood of St. Petersburg located east of Shrayer-Petrov's (and Daniil's) native Lesnoe neighborhood.

Circassian (Russian *cherkeshenka*): see the Notes on "White Sheep on a Mountain Slope."

Giant Theater: Gigant (Giant) movie theater was built in 1934–1936 and was Leningrad's biggest film venue at that time.

Ozerki: a historical area in the north of St. Petersburg; still a suburb in the 1940s, when the story was set, Ozerki was incorporated into the administrative Vyborg District of Leningrad in 1963. Ozerki (literally "little lakes") originally took its name from a series of lakes, and was developed into a popular recreational area in the nineteenth century.

Schiller's ballad "The Glove": in this famous ballad by Richard Schiller, composed in 1797 and titled "Der Handschuh" in the original German, a noble knight rescues a glove dropped by a beautiful lady into the midst of a pit where wild beasts—a lion, a tiger, and two leopards—threaten to maul any intruder, and then throws the glove in the lady's face, presumably as a sign of contempt and not desiring her favor.

Yalta. . . . Chekhov's young lady with a white Pomeranian: located on the southeastern tip of the Crimean peninsula (administratively, part of Ukraine), Yalta is the largest resort in the Crimea and was the site of the Yalta Conference (February 1945). For many Russian readers, Yalta is above all Chekhov's Yalta. Chekhov, who suffered from TB, first visited Yalta in 1888. Chekhov kept returning to Yalta, also spending time in other coastal resorts in its environs. A deterioration of Chekhov's health in 1897 led to the writer's permanent move to Yalta, where he was based during the last five years of his life. In Yalta in 1899–1904, Chekhov wrote the plays The *Three Sisters* and *The Cherry Orchard*, and a number of his greatest stories, among them "Lady with a Lapdog" (1899), in which the main characters are called Anna and Gurov. Known for their mild and dry Mediterranean-like climate, Yalta and its environs (Simeiz, Alupka, Gurzuf) have been a traditional destination for those suffering from respiratory and lung ailments. The area used to house many sanatoria.

About the Translators

Arna B. Bronstein and Aleksandra Fleszar (translators of "Dinner with Stalin") are both professors of Russian and Slavic studies at the University of New Hampshire. Long-time collaborators and seasoned translators, they have co-authored *Making Progress in Russian* and other textbooks widely used across the Anglophone world. Their previous translations of Shrayer-Petrov's works include the novel *Strange Danya Rayev* in the volume *Autumn in Yalta: A Novel and Three Stories*. They are completing a translation of Shrayer-Petrov's novel-dilogy *Herbert and Nelly*.

Margaret Godwin-Jones (translator of "Behind the Zoo Fence"; "A Storefront Window of Miracles"; "Where Are You, Zoya?"; "The Bicycle Race") received an MA in Russian from Boston College in 2010 and an MA in translation studies from American University in 2012. A graduate of Maxim D. Shrayer's seminar on literary translation at Boston College, she has previously translated avant-garde and Silver Age Russian poetry.

Leon Kogan (translator of "The Valley of Hinnom") grew up in Yaroslavl, Russia, and subsequently spent almost a decade in Israel. He received an MA in Russian literature from Boston College and is presently a doctoral candidate at Brown University. His research interests focus on creative connections between Jewish-Russian visual and literary artists. A graduate of Maxim D. Shrayer's seminar on literary translation at Boston College, Kogan has published Russian-language fiction and nonfiction and has previously translated the prose of Yuri Olesha.

Margarit Tadevosyan Ordukhanyan (translator of "White Sheep on a Green Mountain Slope"; "Round-the-Globe Happiness"; "Mimicry";

261

"The House of Edgar Allan Poe") was born in Yerevan, Armenia, and holds a PhD in English from Boston College. She teaches at Hunter College. Her academic publications include articles on exile and literary bilingualism. A graduate of Maxim D. Shrayer's seminar on literary translation, Ordukhanyan has translated from Russian and Armenian. Her current translation projects include Vache Sarkissyan's trilogy *Akeldama*. She contributed translations to Shrayer-Petrov's collections *Jonah and Sarah* and *Autumn in Yalta*.

Emilia Shrayer (translator of "A Russian Liar in Paris"; "Alfredick"), David Shrayer-Petrov's wife, is a native of Moscow and a graduate of the Moscow Linguistic University. A former refusenik, Emilia Shrayer immigrated to the United States in 1987 and retired in 2008 from the Rockefeller Library, Brown University. She is an English–Russian/Russian–English translator and interpreter. Her translations into Russian, with David Shrayer-Petrov, include works by Erskine Coldwell and Australian poets. She has translated into English a number of works by Shrayer-Petrov, including a scientific monograph and several stories featured in *Jonah and Sarah* and *Autumn in Yalta*.

Maxim D. Shrayer (translator of "Trubetskoy, Raevsky, Masha Malevich, and the Death of Mayakovsky"; "Mimosas for Grandmother's Grave"): see the editor's biography on pp. vii–viii.